NEVER
GO
HOME

NEVER GO HOME

A NOVEL

CHRISTOPHER SWANN

CROOKED
LANE

NEW YORK

Published in the United States by Crooked Lane Books, an imprint of The Quick Brown Fox & Company LLC.

Crooked Lane Books and its logo are trademarks of The Quick Brown Fox & Company LLC.

Library of Congress Catalog-in-Publication data available upon request.

ISBN (hardcover): 978-1-63910-082-8
ISBN (ebook): 978-1-63910-083-5

Cover design by Melanie Sun

Printed in the United States.

www.crookedlanebooks.com

Crooked Lane Books
34 West 27th St., 10th Floor
New York, NY 10001

First Edition: August 2022

10 9 8 7 6 5 4 3 2 1

To Kathy, as always.

There is nothing more terrifying than a broken human being.

—*Bill Coffin*

CHAPTER ONE

PEOPLE CROSS ME AT THEIR PERIL. I DON'T HAVE THE LUXURY OF ignoring open cruelty, because it makes me angry. I don't turn into a green monster and start throwing pickup trucks around, but when I'm truly angry the amygdala buried in the folds of my brain starts whooping like twin howler monkeys, overwhelming the inner Vulcan, if you will, of my frontal cortex, and then I tend to do rash, inappropriate things.

Like now.

BOBBY BONAROO IS just starting to wake up. His breathing has quickened, and his jaw shifts as if he is about to open his mouth. Instead, he opens his eyes and looks straight up at me, standing over him. "Wha?" he manages. "Wha the fuh?"

"Morning," I say brightly. I've clamped a utility work light to a nearby railing and turned it to face downward so it doesn't shine directly into Bobby's face, but it casts enough light so we can see each other. "Was last night good for you? 'Cause I had a lot of fun."

He frowns slightly, like we've run into each other at Kroger and he can't quite remember my name. I'm wearing a black tactical jumpsuit, very different from the tight skirt and low-cut top I was wearing last

1

night, so his confusion is understandable. Then he takes in my long red hair and his eyes widen. "You," he says.

"Me," I say.

He glances around, disoriented but recovering nicely. I can almost read his mind, not that Bobby Bonaroo is a hard nut to crack: *what happened, why does my head hurt, why am I lying on my back, why is the redhead from last night smiling at me?* My guess is the women Bobby dates don't tend to smile much the morning after.

"It was Xanax in your scotch," I say. "The dizziness, headache, memory loss? Xanax."

"What the fuck?" Bobby Bonaroo says, and his voice echoes in the vast space around us. He tries to sit up, then tries to move his arms, but he can only lift his hands an inch or so. The chain binding him rattles and clinks, and his eyes widen further. He manages to lift his head enough to look down at his hands and see the manacles on his wrists. The chain that connects his wrists runs beneath him, under the small of his back. There is a rope around his chest, snug beneath his armpits. Bobby looks further down to see his legs are wrapped with duct tape. He starts jerking back and forth, trying to get loose. "Get me the fuck out of this!" he shouts.

I crouch down so he can see my face more clearly. "Do you like Tom Hanks movies?" I ask politely.

Bobby Bonaroo stares at me like I just suggested we should eat a baby.

"*Catch Me If You Can* is sort of an underrated performance of his," I continue. "The one where he's the FBI agent chasing Leo DiCaprio? Sure, Leo's young and hot and charming, but Tom Hanks just won't quit chasing him. He never stops. I mean, he gets the French police to work on Christmas Eve."

Bobby Bonaroo is not dumb. He has assessed his situation and found himself tied up in an unknown location, at the mercy of a woman he thought would be an easy lay and who has instead drugged him and is clearly crazy. With a visible effort, he takes a deep breath, then another. "I never saw that one," he says.

I smile, appreciating the gesture. "It's not a great work of cinematic art," I admit. "But it's fun to watch. And it illustrates a point."

The conversation is already taking a toll on Bobby. When I don't continue, he says between clenched teeth, "What point?"

"The bad guy always gets caught in the end," I say. "It's a movie, granted, and the point's not always true. Not by a long shot. But it's true in this case."

Bobby narrows his eyes. Playing along is clearly not his forte, so he opts for threatening. "Lady, I don't know who you think you are, but you're fucking with the wrong guy."

"Oh, I'm pretty sure I've got the right guy," I say. "You're a private contractor with American First Defense. You ran an immigration detention facility called Casa Madre, which, I mean, the name alone is laughably obscene."

Bobby glares at me, which is less impressive than he wants it to be, considering he's trussed up like a damsel in distress on a railroad track. "You drug me and tie me up—no, *chain* me up," he says, "and you want to talk to me about Tom fucking Hanks and my job?"

"How many girls did you have in Casa Madre, Bobby? Four hundred?" I lean forward, my eyes on his. "All between the ages of ten and seventeen. All separated from their parents."

Bobby Bonaroo shakes his head in disgust and looks away, his gaze directed up into the dark.

"Maria Flores," I say.

That gets his attention. He looks back at me, and for a moment I see a flicker in his eyes. Guilt, maybe, but that might just be optimism on my part.

"She died in your prison because one of your people gave her the wrong meds," I say.

"Wait," Bobby says. "Is *that* what this is about?"

"Other girls reported being abused or raped by guards."

"I had nothing to do with that," Bobby says, his voice rising. "The guards who gave that girl the wrong medicine were punished. I told the government lawyer—"

"After Maria Flores died, you tried to get Casa Madre labeled a 'childcare center' so you could house more kids." I hear the edge in my own voice. "How much did you get paid per kid?"

"What is this?" Bobby Bonaroo asks. "Some sort of revenge or something? I closed that place months ago!"

"There are still kids missing," I say. "They haven't all been reunited with their families."

He stares at me, incredulous. "That's on Health and Human Services. I just ran the facility."

"Where a child died and others were raped," I say. "And you tried to erase all your records of everything having to do with Casa Madre so you could cover up all the shit that went down in there."

We stare at each other for a long moment, Bobby weighing his options. Then he shakes his head again. "You stupid bitch. I *know* people. People you don't want to fuck with."

"Tough talk from a guy who profits from little girls." I lean away and shift so now I'm kneeling by his side.

I'll give him this, Bobby Bonaroo has balls. He sneers up at me. "Tough talk from a woman who has me tied up on the floor."

I place one hand on his hip and the other on his shoulder, bracing myself. "You're not on a floor."

I shove him, hard. He rolls off the side of the catwalk, the chain rattling against the metal mesh, and drops. His scream echoes through the darkness as he falls. Then his scream is cut off as the rope connecting him to the catwalk snaps taut and pulls tight, jerking him to a stop some eight feet above the concrete floor. The catwalk shudders, but I tested it earlier this week and know it will hold. Bobby Bonaroo now hangs by a rope looped like a noose beneath his arms. He's crying and cursing in a steady flood; the fall may have dislocated a shoulder. I walk over to a winch bolted to the catwalk and start cranking, bringing Bobby back up a foot at a time. It's hard work and I'm starting to sweat by the time the top of Bobby's head is level with the catwalk. My legs are already burning from having to fireman-carry his ass up here earlier.

"You're a lot of work, Bobby," I say.

"Fuck you," he bawls. "You fucking cunt."

"I'm looking for someone who was in Casa Madre."

"Go to hell."

I hit the release clamp on the winch and Bobby plummets toward the floor again. He screams even louder than before. This time, when the rope yanks him up short, he bellows like a bull being gelded. Definitely dislocated a shoulder this time. Slowly I winch him back up, panting by the time he is back up level with the catwalk. I lean over the railing to get a closer look at him. With his hands chained together behind his back, he already looks a little like a carved figurehead on the bow of a ship, with his chest thrust out, but now his left shoulder is cocked at an awkward angle, his left arm hanging nerveless and unmoving. Fat beads of sweat run down his face, and his eyes are closed and he's moaning.

"Bobby," I say, snapping my fingers, and his eyes open, bright with pain. Slowly, he focuses on me. "I'm looking for someone. Don't make me drop you again."

"Okay," he gasps, the word wrenched out of him. "Okay, okay. Oh, God."

"She's fourteen," I say. "A real stunner. She likes Coca-Cola and her daddy's *pepián*. It's a stew they make in Guatemala."

Bobby is starting to go into shock, his eyes rolling back. I sigh and reach out and grab his left shoulder, and he snaps his head back and screams from the pain. The echoes take a while to subside.

"We're all alone here, Bobby," I say when he quiets to a reasonable whimper. "No one can hear you no matter how loud you yell. I don't want to hurt you. Well, maybe that's a little bit of a lie. But I won't drop you anymore if you give me what I want."

"Yes," he manages between sobs. "Yes, okay, yes. I—I don't know . . . you said a—girl?"

"I'm not giving you her name," I say, wagging a finger at him—*naughty*. "Then you could find her yourself, punish her and her family for what I did to you. Plus I know you don't know them by name. There were too many of them. Probably weren't even people to you."

Despite the pain Bobby is in, his frustration is obvious in his voice. "How can I help you find someone if you don't tell me their name?" he cries out.

"I need the password to your laptop," I say. "The one that was locked in the trunk of your Lexus."

Bobby pauses, his mind darting around like a bat in a cave trying to find an exit. I take a step toward the winch and its release clamp, and Bobby sings out a twelve-digit alphanumeric code, which I commit to memory.

"Okay, you got it," Bobby says. Tears stream from his eyes, snot from his nose. "Now get me out of this thing. Please."

"Give me a second," I say, bending over so Bobby doesn't see the syringe in my hand. I pluck the cap off the syringe and stick it into the back of his left arm. Bobby yelps and tries to turn his head around toward me. "What the hell!"

"Ketamine," I say, capping the now-empty syringe and replacing it in the cargo pocket of my pants. "Great pain management and excellent safety record." I hesitate. "Unless you have a history of schizophrenia. You don't, do you?"

"Get me out of this fucking thing!"

"It'll take five or ten minutes and then your shoulder ought to feel better," I say. "If you're lucky, you'll pass out and take a nap. Some people puke after they wake up from a dose, but you're upright so you probably won't choke to death."

"You are *not* leaving me here!"

"Actually," I say, scanning the catwalk to make sure I haven't left anything behind, "I am. I'll call the cops and let them know where you are once I'm gone. And Bobby? Don't come looking for me."

The string of curses he shouts after me as I take a set of stairs to the floor is inventive. I make a note of a couple of them, filing them away for future use.

OUTSIDE, IT'S EARLY Sunday morning and already hot, the sun a hard white star in a clear sky. By noon, the empty parking lot will be baking. Finding this shuttered Sam's Club outside of San Antonio was an extra bonus. I could have just driven Bobby Bonaroo a couple of hours outside the city and interrogated him on some back road in the hill country, but there are always people driving by or wandering up, curious and eager to help. People are annoying that way. And you might think Texas is full of vast, empty tracts of land outside the big cities, but the state is peppered with towns and hamlets and tourists and truckers and farms, on and on and on. It's too damn big and I feel too exposed here. I need to get back to the East Coast, where states are a more manageable size.

Bobby Bonaroo's Lexus, which I drove here with the unconscious Bobby, is parked in a loading bay at the back of the building, hidden from the nearby street. It's a beautiful car, and I swear it purred when I drove it last night. But I can't risk driving off in Bobby's car and getting pulled over. I could drive it to the center of the parking lot and set it on fire—that would be a nice touch, and then I wouldn't have to bother with calling the cops to cut Bobby down as the smoke would be a giant LOOK HERE sign. But I don't have any kerosene or anything to start a fire. Maybe I could siphon the gas tank. Suddenly I'm bone weary—I didn't sleep at all last night, what with picking up Bobby Bonaroo in a dance club, spiking his drink, walking him out to his car, driving him here, carrying him up to the catwalk, et cetera—and all I want is to crash at my motel room for an hour or so and then hit the road. I have things to do before that, though, and the clock is ticking. Bobby might be knocked out by now, so I should be safe and clear for a few hours, but better safe than sorry, and setting fire to Bobby's Lexus is a luxury I can't afford. So I leave the Lexus behind.

My pickup truck, dented and dusty and bought with cash at a used lot in Brownsville, is parked behind a dumpster across from the loading bay. Inside the truck, I remove the red wig I've been wearing for hours and start the engine so the A/C can crank on. Then I retrieve Bobby Bonaroo's laptop from underneath the passenger seat. I open the laptop, wait for it to power up, and enter the password he gave me. I'm almost surprised when it works. Bobby's desktop is a mess of separate docs and files, and I spend fifteen minutes searching through his data. I see all sorts of interesting things, including what looks like money skimmed off from government contracts and diverted into private accounts—I don't have time to dive into it but it looks shady as shit. Finally I find what I'm looking for: the single remaining copy of all the records from Casa Madre.

Buried in the Casa Madre file is a manifest of prisoners, and after a few seconds I find Yoselin Asturias and her location—foster care in North Dakota. Jesus, these people. Still, I breathe a sigh of relief. Yoselin could have vanished into the ether, but here was proof of where she had been sent just a few weeks ago, according to the dates in the file. Using a throwaway cell phone, I set up a personal hotspot, then email a copy of the file to the Asturias family using a Gmail account I promptly delete afterward.

What I did to Bobby Bonaroo was outright bonkers and involved breaking at least half a dozen federal laws. And it worked. I've found lots of things are a matter of willpower—if you want to do something badly enough, and you have the time and the capability to do it, then all that's left is your resolve. Most people balk at certain predictable limits. I tend to vault straight over them, and so some people call me crazy. I'm a mess, don't get me wrong, but I'm not a psychopath. Psychopaths don't have to worry about bothersome things like a conscience or guilt. I'll admit there have been times in my life when I've wondered whether it would be easier to be one of those lost souls who don't share a sense of empathy with the rest of the human race. But while I may be crazy—have even been hospitalized—I'm smart enough to realize that I'm better off having emotional connections, however stunted or odd, with other people. So I'm more of a high-functioning sociopath. I've just decided to put that part of me to good use. I'm good at finding people—a skill I honed by looking for, and finding, the man who killed my parents, although he very nearly killed me first—and I'm often willing to do things most people won't do, or just can't. I've chosen to side with the better angel of my nature, to join Gryffindor over Slytherin, to be a white hat in a dark world. Or whatever other stupid metaphor you want to use.

But now, sitting in this parking lot on a bright Sunday morning, having just found one immigrant family's missing daughter and putting the hurt on a scumbag like Bobby Bonaroo, I don't feel like patting myself on the back, or like I just won one for the good guys. I don't even really register a sense of accomplishment. Mostly I just feel tired. Is this what's waiting for me down the road? Another empty parking lot, secretive emails, short bursts of violence followed by long, tedious hours of waiting and watching, mostly alone? My brother lives alone, but he has neighbors and friends, and our uncle. Our parents were both killed by a bad man with a gun, and for months beforehand my father had been struggling—and my mother, too, to be fair—but they had at least died together. What about me? Somehow I don't see myself dying at age ninety in a bed surrounded by my loving family. More likely I'll die in a back alley or a stairwell, chasing someone who ought to be caught and punished, only to be shot or stabbed or thrown from a great height, or otherwise killed in some spectacularly violent fashion.

"Fuck it," I say aloud, and I put the truck in gear and drive out of the parking lot, leaving Bobby Bonaroo and those nagging doubts behind me. Time to get to the motel and call the cops before I leave town. I need to figure out the best way to get to North Dakota.

THE LONE STAR Inn is about as original as its name. Picture any generic roadside motel from the 1970s, with the same paint and decor as it had on opening day, and that's where I've been staying while visiting the greater San Antonio metro area. Even the people who run the place look like they stepped out of a sitcom about a motel: they're an older couple, husband and wife, named Bert and Shirley. Bert favors a comb-over and wears cardigans against the chill of the air conditioning. Shirley is plump, with blue hair and a tired cheerfulness, like a cruise director who woke up one day to find herself managing a motel off I-10 but makes the best of it. Bert is on duty when I pull into the Lone Star's parking lot, and through the plate-glass windows of the lobby I can see Bert sitting behind the front desk, taking a nap. I roll past and down to the end unit and park. I need a nap myself, and a shower, and then I'll call the cops before hopping on the highway. Maybe I've got some protein bars left to eat. A Clif bar and gas station coffee: breakfast of champions.

I step out of the truck, and my brain, fuzzy around the edges, lurches into alert mode. I crouch slightly before I realize I'm doing it, using the truck door as cover. Part of me wonders when this became a thing, my initial instinct to treat every situation like I'm walking around in Syria or Yemen or some other place where the citizens are happily killing one another. I don't even know what triggered this until I see the door to my motel room. The window next to it has the curtain drawn, like all the other rooms, but there's a bright seam of lamplight at the very edge of the curtain. I turned all the lights off yesterday when I left, just before I hung the *Do Not Disturb* sign on the door handle. The sign is still hanging from the door. No maid turned on the light, then.

I scan the motel parking lot, then the closed doors of the rooms. Seeing nobody, I reach back into the truck and from underneath the driver's seat pull out a CZ 75 9mm. Holding the pistol low, I dash across the parking lot toward my room. Nobody shouts or steps out from another doorway, and when I reach the building I flatten myself against the wall to one side of the door to my room. With my left hand I take my room's key card out of another pocket—my jumpsuit has all sorts of pockets, holding all sorts of things—and slide the card into the slot above the door handle. The tiny light next to the slot blinks green, and I push the handle down and open the door, going in crouched, my pistol up to cover the room.

The bedside lamp is on and I can see a man—Black, bald—standing next to my bed about ten feet away. His back is to me and his hands are already raised to shoulder height. "Don't move," I say, reaching for the zip tie cuffs I have in yet another pocket, my pistol aimed dead-center at his back. "Get down on your knees."

"On *this* carpet?" the man says in a familiar deep voice.

Relief floods me and I lower the pistol. "Caesar!"

Caesar turns his head to look at me, lowers his hands, and raises an eyebrow. "Nice jumpsuit."

I put the pistol down on the nearby dresser and kick the door closed behind me before crossing the room to hug him. He smells like eucalyptus and burnt cinnamon. "How did you find me?" I ask, my face still pressed against his chest.

He *hmm*s in response, and I can feel it vibrate from deep inside him. "Twitter."

"Twitter?" I lift my head and look up at him, still wrapped in a hug. "Are you kidding? My Twitter handle is generic as hell!"

"Yeah, @lady10456 does seem like a Russian bot." He gives me a smile this time, a brief flash of teeth.

I release Caesar and take a step back, fully taking him in for the first time. He's wearing a black T-shirt and chinos, like he's an engineer at Google. "How'd you know that was me?"

He shrugs. "Someone starts arguing on Twitter about how *Voyager* was a horrible *Star Trek* show except for the half-Klingon chief engineer, it's probably you."

"It's true! Torres was the *only* decent character—wait, you found me because of a *tweet*?"

"Couple dozen of them. Went through the metadata, narrowed your location down to San Antonio . . ." He shrugs again, as if he had found a book on a library shelf instead of locating a single person in a nation of three hundred and thirty million people—a single person who didn't particularly want to be found.

I drop into the one chair next to the dresser, my initial relief now withdrawing in the face of exhaustion, an exhaustion that is not entirely due to the fact that I've been awake for over twenty-four hours. "Why are you here, Caesar?"

He sits on the bed, even that simple movement an exercise in grace and balance, like most everything Caesar does. Watching him walk across a room is a lesson in the physics of movement. "That's my girl. Right to the point."

I roll my eyes. "Keep calling me your girl and Frankie'll get jealous. Is he all right?"

Caesar nods. "He's fine."

My mouth is dry and tastes foul. "My uncle?" I hope my voice sounds more neutral than I feel. To say my relationship with my uncle is complicated would be a gigantic understatement.

"Mr. Lester has some . . . challenges," Caesar says. "But nothing he can't handle." His eyes are on mine, dark and deep and sober.

"So it's Ethan." Something shifts in my gut, a lazy rotation, like a whale coming to the surface and then, with a roll of its fins, disappearing again. I lean my head back and close my eyes, fatigue settling on me like summer smog in Atlanta. "I told him not to look for me."

"Your brother needs your help," Caesar says.

"I tried to help him last year. And *that* turned out well."

Caesar says nothing, but I keep my eyes closed. Last year a woman tried to hurt my brother and used me to get to him. I reacted poorly and people died. Caesar very nearly died himself while trying to protect me. When it was all over, I left Atlanta. It was the right call then and it's the right call now. Ethan's better off without me fucking up his life.

"He says it's about your father," Caesar says.

I open my eyes and stare at Caesar, who sits on my bed and looks placidly back at me, legs crossed at the ankle, hands clasped on his lap, a counselor awaiting his client's decision.

CAESAR DRIVES US to the airport in his rental, a new Mercedes that is white as pearl, I having sold my pickup to Bert and Shirley for a ridiculously low price. Before we left, Caesar copied Bobby Bonaroo's hard drive onto his own portable laptop, encrypting the copied data before erasing the original files on Bobby's machine. Then he produced a hammer and we took turns smashing the laptop into bits before sweeping the pieces up into a trash bag. As an afterthought I put my red wig into the bag as well. Besides taking a five-minute shower and changing into jeans and a T-shirt, the only other thing I did was disassemble my CZ pistol and fling the separate components in different directions into the weeds and scrub behind the motel. I have a permit for the pistol under a false name, but I don't need to give anyone a reason to flag me because I have a firearm in my checked luggage. I also didn't want to just toss the CZ into a dumpster where someone might find it and use it to hold up a liquor store or shoot somebody.

As Caesar refills the rental car at a gas station near the airport, I shove the bag with Bobby Bonaroo's smashed laptop and my red wig into a trash can, then take out my cell to make two calls. The first is to Ellie Mangum, the immigration lawyer who introduced me to the Asturias family. I get her voice mail as I had hoped and leave her a message saying something has come up and I can't head to North Dakota right now after all, but she has all the information she needs to find her lost cat and I'll be in touch when I can. The second call I make is to the San Antonio police department, and I tell the bored operator that there is a man tied up in an abandoned Sam's Club and give her the address, then hang up. When I was taking a shower, Caesar made additional copies of the files detailing the money Bobby had skimmed off contracts, then emailed those to both the San Antonio police and the local DA. Bobby Bonaroo is going to have his hands full.

When we are back on the highway, I roll down the window and toss my cell phone out. I watch it bounce on the asphalt and then disappear underneath the wheels of a Peterbilt semi behind us. Then I turn back around and face forward, not seeing the traffic or the airport or anything—it's as if it has all been blotted out, the entire world, and all that is left is a blank, an emptiness. I know that blank space will be filled in soon, colored and peopled by reality. The idea frightens me. Sometimes that blank space is safer.

CHAPTER TWO

ON THE FLIGHT FROM SAN ANTONIO I SLEEP HARD, DREAMING ABOUT things I don't remember, which is probably for the best. The only image that lingers is of dead flowers in a garden. By the time we land in Atlanta, I almost feel human.

When the plane is on the ground and taxiing to its gate, Caesar turns his phone on, and almost immediately it starts blowing up with alerts. He frowns at the screen.

"Frankie?" I ask.

Caesar shakes his head. "Your uncle. Wants me to meet him at the airport."

I stare at him. "Did you tell him I was coming to Atlanta?"

"No. He sent this almost an hour ago." He taps the screen and holds the phone to his ear for a few seconds, then lowers it and taps the screen again. "No answer."

"Why would he want you to meet him at the airport?"

Caesar shrugs. "The man doesn't always explain himself."

"It's me." Ridiculously I feel myself sinking into my airplane seat, like a toddler refusing to get out of the car. "He knows I'm coming home and wants to talk to me, or get me to do something for him. Or lock me up for my own safety or some paternalistic bullshit."

"Avuncular," Caesar says, sliding his phone back into his pocket. "You mean avuncular bullshit. Means uncle-like."

"I know what avuncular means. Where is he?"

"Probably at baggage claim, waiting for us."

"Fantastic," I mutter.

Hartsfield-Jackson International Airport in Atlanta is a series of long terminals connected by a train with a pleasant, female robotic voice announcing concourses. It's what the near future must have looked like to folks back in the 1980s. Today that train feels like that old ride at Disney World, the Carousel of Progress—people like the idea of it, but the reality is a little embarrassing. It's a shame, really. People get into winged metal tubes and are hurled into the stratosphere at around five hundred miles an hour and then land safely in another part of the world. For that fact alone, airports ought to be temples of wonder to the miracle of flight. Instead, they're mazes to be navigated as quickly as possible so people can get to their cars and then sit in traffic jams on the interstate.

Caesar and I deplane at Concourse E with our carry-ons and move like cattle through the corridor to pack into the train, which lurches along and finally releases us into the main terminal. Caesar hates parking at the airport, so the plan was to get a taxi and drop Caesar off at his place before I went on to Ethan's house in the suburbs. Of course, that was before Uncle Gavin decided to swoop in and surprise us.

"I didn't tell him, Suzie," Caesar says.

"I know," I say, tucking a loose strand of hair behind my ear. "I believe you. It's fine. You're probably right and he's not here because of me. We'll see him and then I'll go to Ethan's."

"You're doing that thing with your hair again."

"What thing?"

"Pushing it behind your ear. You do that when you're nervous."

"Bitch, please. First of all, you don't even *have* any hair—"

Caesar stops in the middle of the flow of people streaming past baggage claim. An elderly woman stops just short of colliding with Caesar and gives him the evil eye. I smile back at her, showing all my teeth, and she scurries on. Caesar pays no attention, his eyes fixed on a small crowd on the other side of the belt barriers separating us from baggage claim. "Dude, what—" I say.

He grips my upper arm, gently but with intention, and I follow his gaze. Two cops are backing people up from a knot of EMTs huddled around someone they have just lifted onto a stretcher. Something dark and oval-shaped lies on the tile floor beside the stretcher. A tweed flat cap. The same kind of hat my uncle wears. I register this at the same time that I realize the man on the stretcher, an oxygen mask clamped to his face, is Uncle Gavin.

I pass through the crowd like a fish through water, arrowing toward my uncle. A cop steps in my path, palms up. "Please, ma'am, keep back."

"But—" I gesture at the stretcher. My face crumples into a precursor to an ugly cry. "That's my uncle. I need to see, please."

The cop hesitates, then steps back so I can pass. I grab Caesar by the hand. "Come on, honey." I drag him past the cop before either of them can say anything.

Up close, Uncle Gavin doesn't look good. His face is gray as cement, his eyes closed. One of the EMTs is saying something about his blood pressure dropping. I stand there, staring at my uncle, unable to move because I'm ten years old and sitting on the floor of my house, blood on my hands and in my lap, staring at my father who is bleeding out on the living room floor, my mother dead on the couch, my brother shot like I am and screaming for Dad.

Uncle Gavin opens his eyes. They are black as tar and they are aimed directly at me.

"We have to move," an EMT says.

"Wait," I say, stepping forward, eyes still on Uncle Gavin. "I'm his niece. What—"

"Ma'am, you'll need to step back—"

"I'm not going anywhere. What happened?"

Uncle Gavin moves his hand—slowly, too slowly—up to the oxygen mask and pulls it down from his nose and mouth.

"Sir! Please don't—"

Uncle Gavin is mouthing words, his dark eyes fixed on mine. I step forward. "What?" I say, bending low. "I can't hear—"

"Peaches," my uncle says.

"Ma'am." An EMT faces me from the other side of the stretcher. "We have to go *right now*." He puts the oxygen mask back onto my uncle's face, and then they are rolling him away to the glass door exit, beyond which is an ambulance with red lights flashing. Uncle Gavin's eyes remain fixed on mine until the EMTs turn the stretcher so he no longer faces me. I bend down and pick up the flat cap, holding it in both hands as I watch them load Uncle Gavin into the ambulance and drive off in a squawk of sirens.

GOD INVENTED CIGARETTES for moments like this, pacing around a hospital waiting room. There are *No Smoking* signs posted every twenty feet, and I don't smoke, but I want to light up anyway as a big fat finger to the universe.

"Suzie," Caesar says from his chair where he's been sitting.

"Don't tell me it's going to be okay." I march past him and then turn to retrace the same path I've been walking for twenty minutes.

"I'm not," Caesar says.

"Heart attacks aren't okay."

"No."

An hour earlier when we arrived at Grady Memorial, an exhausted-looking doctor in scrubs told us that my uncle had experienced a myocardial infarction and they needed to run more tests.

"Why the hell was he at the airport?" I'm kneading Uncle Gavin's flat cap in my hands, worrying at it like a crazed milliner. "Did you know he would be there?"

"No," Caesar says, answering that question for the third time. Maybe fourth.

"And what the fuck did he mean by *peaches*?" I turn about sharply and my leg hits a side table, nearly spilling its glossy magazines to the floor. I ignore it and march on. "Does he have some kind of special peaches at the bar? A peach grove? I don't—"

"Suzie."

"*What?*"

"Your brother is here," Caesar says. "Just texted me."

The nearest elevator door rumbles open, and I turn to see Ethan and Frankie step out into the hallway.

As usual, Frankie is dressed like it's date night, in a wine-colored dress shirt and dark skinny jeans and black Chelsea boots. He embraces Caesar and they hold each other tightly. "We came as soon as we could," Frankie says into Caesar's shoulder, then steps back, hands on Caesar's shoulders. "You okay?" He glances at me with a heartbreak smile. "Hey, Susannah."

I smile, not trusting myself to say anything—my throat swells with grief and my eyes sting. I don't want to cry. Frankie is Ethan's best friend and works for my uncle, just like his father Ruben did before he died. Of a heart attack, I remember. I shove that thought away and turn my attention to my brother. "Hey," I manage.

Ethan stops just outside of hugging distance and my heart throbs painfully. This wasn't the reunion I'd imagined. My plan had been to wait until I was sure Ethan wasn't at home, then pick the lock on his back door—wouldn't be the first time—and go inside to play with his dog Wilson until Ethan got home and I could surprise him. Stupid, maybe, but that was my plan. Now we are in a hospital and we stand apart, staring at each other. My brother is wearing athletic shorts and a faded green homecoming T-shirt from the Archer School, where he teaches. Usually I'd crack a joke, point out how Frankie is dressed for the club while

Ethan looks like he's been eating Doritos on the couch, but even I realize the moment isn't right for jokes.

"Any word on Uncle Gavin?" Ethan asks. His red hair is mussed, like he's just been woken up, and his eyes are haunted by some strong emotion—grief, or fear.

"Heart attack," I say, and then the tears spill down my face and I reach up to angrily brush them away. That's when Ethan steps forward and grabs me in a bear hug. I'm so startled I raise my foot reflexively, prepared to stomp on his instep and twist away. But I lower my foot and lean against my brother with a ragged sigh, allowing him to hold me up for a few moments.

"Is he . . . ?" Ethan murmurs against my ear.

I shake my head. "They're running tests."

"The Lester family?" someone says, and I look up from Ethan's shoulder to see the same exhausted doctor from earlier. There's no blood on his scrubs. I'm not sure if that's good or bad.

Ethan disengages from our hug. "I'm Gavin Lester's nephew," he says.

"Me too," I say. "I mean, he's my uncle. I'm his niece."

The doctor nods as if I'm making perfect sense. "I'm Doctor Lewis. Your uncle has pulmonary valve stenosis. The valve in his heart that allows blood to flow into the pulmonary artery and then the lungs is not working. We inserted a balloon through a catheter to keep the valve open for now, but the valve needs to be replaced. Your uncle needs surgery."

"Okay," I say.

"Wait a minute," Ethan says at the same time.

I turn to Ethan. "What?"

"What's this surgery mean?" Ethan asks Dr. Lewis. "Did something happen to the valve? Was it damaged?"

"It's congenital," Dr. Lewis says. He sways on his feet, as if sheer willpower is the only thing keeping him from curling up in a nearby chair for a nap. But his eyes are alert and trained on us. "The pulmonary valve opens and shuts to regulate blood flowing out of the heart to the lungs. Today it just shut and wouldn't reopen."

"So he needs it replaced," I say. "Problem solved. Right?"

Dr. Lewis looks from Ethan to me and back to Ethan. "You would need to decide what kind of valve your uncle wants," he says. "There's a mechanical one or a tissue valve, usually taken from a pig. We can go over the pros and cons of each."

"But then he'd be fine, right?" I say.

The doctor tilts his head slightly, a man looking at an unbalanced scale. "It's open-heart surgery, which is serious for anyone, and your uncle is in his sixties. But otherwise he's in good health, and he's stable right now. With a little luck and some rehab, your uncle should be fine."

"Can we see him?" Ethan asks.

Dr. Lewis nods, his head wobbling on his neck. "It will have to be brief, though. You can come back tomorrow to talk with him about his options." He looks at a chart in his hand. "Do either of you have authorization to make medical decisions for your uncle?"

"I do," Ethan says.

"You do?" I hate the surprise and the squeaky resentment in my own voice.

Ethan shrugs. "I'm the one who lives here."

I know he doesn't mean anything by it and is just stating a fact, but his words hit me like a gut punch. I'm still thinking of a reply when he reaches for his back pocket and pulls out an envelope that's creased like he's sat on it. He tries to straighten out the crease and then holds it out to Dr. Lewis. "I've got medical power of attorney for my uncle. It's notarized if you need to see it."

"That's not necessary right now," Dr. Lewis says. "If you'll follow me." He turns and heads down the hallway, the four of us trailing him.

We pass a nurses' station and turn a corner, and the doctor stops outside a closed door. "Only family members allowed," he says, glancing at Frankie and Caesar.

"We're all family," I say before anyone else can speak. Ethan nods in agreement, and I can feel Frankie and Caesar standing behind me in the hallway. Dr. Lewis just returns Ethan's nod and opens the door.

Inside lies Uncle Gavin, an oxygen tube taped to his face, an IV line snaking from the back of one hand to a drip bag. His eyes are closed and he looks even grayer in the fluorescent light than he did on the stretcher at the airport.

Dr. Lewis checks a monitor that quietly beeps, announcing that my uncle's heart is still beating. "Five minutes," he murmurs, then leaves. Strangely, I miss the doctor once he's gone, and we all stand silently in the room as if we're in a church waiting for the priest to show up and begin the service.

I stare at Uncle Gavin lying in his bed. He's not supposed to be here. He should be sitting behind his massive, messy desk in his office above Ronan's, the bar he owns in Midtown. Many times I've stood in front of that desk as he's torn me a new one or, more rarely, said something gruffly approving. He took us in, me and Ethan, after our parents were killed. Our mom had cut him off years ago because "he made bad choices." Later Ethan and I learned that Uncle Gavin is a sort of jack-of-all-trades for the Atlanta underworld. Need to unload some stolen jewelry? Get a fake passport? Learn which city council member or judge would be receptive to bribery? Uncle Gavin is your guy. Frankie's father Ruben was my uncle's right-hand man, and now Frankie works for him, following in his father's footsteps. Caesar does too, using his technological wizardry to bring Uncle Gavin's business into the twenty-first century. For a short time Ethan worked for our uncle, too, until he went to college and left that life behind.

And me? Uncle Gavin took a long, hard look at me, like a sculptor examining a block of marble, and then he helped chisel and shape me into the person I am today—a hunter. It wasn't easy. I was an ungrateful bitch to Uncle Gavin when Ethan and I moved in with him. He repaid me by teaching me how to survive and giving me a purpose. And now he's lying unconscious in a hospital bed.

The *beep* of the heart monitor, the buzzing recessed light above Uncle Gavin's head, the soft tread of the nurses in their sneakers as they hurry down the hall, all of it sets me on edge. My jaw hurts, and I realize it's because I'm clenching my teeth hard enough to crack a walnut. I don't want to look at my uncle lying there, so I find myself staring at a picture hung on the wall across from him. It's a shitty mauve watercolor that will probably be the first thing Uncle Gavin sees when he opens his eyes. Why can't they get some decent art on the walls, or a photo of the ocean or something? Jesus.

I flinch when Ethan takes my hand, and when I stare at him he gives me an exhausted smile. "I hate hospitals too," he says.

I drop his hand and pace to the door, then back again. It's a short trip, but I need to move or I'll start screaming. "He said something to me about peaches," I say. "Uncle Gavin."

Ethan frowns. "Peaches?"

"Before the EMTs loaded him up in the ambulance. He whispered it to me."

"What does it mean?"

"How the hell should *I* know?" I'm stalking now, three steps to the door, whirl, stalk back to the bed, repeat. Pretty soon I'll start waving my hands around like a lunatic. The nurse will have to call the orderlies, big meaty guys who don't talk, just immobilize the patients, waiting for restraints or for a doctor or nurse with an injection. I've faced their kind before. "Maybe he was picking up a delivery at the airport."

"We're in Georgia," Ethan says in his didactic high-school-teacher voice, like I'm one of his students. "Who would send peaches—"

"Yeah, we're the Peach State, I get it, I was born here too. So maybe he was sending some."

"Sending peaches. From the airport."

"You're right, Ethan, I'm just a fucking nutjob babbling out of my ass over here."

"Susannah—"

"*What?*"

"*Mierda*," Frankie mutters, and we all stop and look at him. He's leaning against a wall with his hands in his pockets, looking at the floor. He raises his eyes to mine.

"He didn't mean the fruit," he says. "Peaches is a man."

"What man?" I say. "Who is he?"

Frankie sighs. "His real name is Antoine Daniels, but he goes by Peaches. He bankrolled Li'l Whizz back when he was getting started."

I look blankly at Frankie. "Who's Li'l Whizz?" I ask.

Frankie blinks. "Um, the hip-hop star? Won a bunch of Grammys? He's, like, a midget?"

Caesar clears his throat. "I think the appropriate term is 'little person,'" he says.

Frankie shrugs. "My bad. Anyway, when Li'l Whizz hit it big, Peaches got a percentage. Turned around and reinvested a lot of that in his neighborhood, made him a local hero."

"What neighborhood?" I ask.

Frankie hesitates and glances at Caesar, then Ethan.

"What?" I say.

Frankie opens his mouth, hesitates. "The Bluff," he finally says.

The words bring a stillness to the room. Caesar watches me. Frankie seems embarrassed. Ethan looks stricken. I say nothing. That simple phrase, *the Bluff*, is like a knife slicing through the meat of my heart. But I keep my face impassive.

"So he's, what, a developer?" I ask, my voice steady.

Frankie shakes his head. "He's a gangbanger. Real protective of his turf. Sureños 13 tried to move in. That's a prison gang—"

"I know who the Sureños are," I say. "This Peaches guy stood up to them?"

"Put down half a dozen of them this spring," Frankie says.

This didn't make sense. Uncle Gavin was a criminal, but he didn't deal drugs or get involved in gang wars. "So what kind of business would Uncle Gavin have with this Peaches?" I ask.

Frankie shrugs again. "No clue."

"Come on," I say, my voice sharper than I want it to be. "You're like his right-hand man. You don't know anything?"

"I told you, I don't *know*," Frankie says, his voice rising to match mine. "You think if I did I wouldn't tell you?"

Frankie and I are facing each other, anger and frustration radiating off both of us like heat off asphalt in August. I clench my fists. Frankie glares at me, his jaw set.

In a low voice, Caesar says, "Mister Lester doesn't tell us everything, Suzie."

I take a deep breath, trying to ignore the jackhammering of my heart, and unclench my fists. "Sorry, Frankie," I say. "I know you'd tell me."

Frankie sighs, and his eyes turn sad. "Hey, it's okay. I'm sorry too. Your uncle's lying here in the hospital—"

Ethan, who has been standing by our uncle's bed this entire time, interrupts. "Okay," he says like a coach about to tell his squabbling players to knock it off. "We need to let Uncle Gavin get some rest. Susannah, we're gonna have to talk about this heart valve replacement, figure out the next step."

"What's to talk about?" I say. "He needs the surgery. The doc can tell us about the choices tomorrow, like he said. And we'll see what Uncle Gavin wants."

Ethan gets the same stubborn look he had when he was a teenager butting heads with Uncle Gavin. "I want to talk to Doctor Lewis some more. It's not that simple."

I fold my arms across my chest. "It's exactly that simple."

"Really?" Ethan says. "So you can sign off on the insurance forms? You know whether or not he should get a pig valve or a mechanical one? Do you know what medications Uncle Gavin is taking?"

A small voice in my head is saying *He's got a point.* I ignore it. "How would I know what pills Uncle Gavin takes? Don't *you* know that?"

Ethan throws up his hands in exasperation. "Yes, because *I'm* the responsible one, *I'm* in charge, *I* know everything."

"Man, it must be exhausting, carrying that cross everywhere."

His face grows hard. "Fuck off, Susannah."

"Gladly." My fingers are itching to do something—fix a motor, make a fist—and I can't stay in this room anymore, arguing with my brother and trying not to look at my uncle in the hospital bed. "I need to pee," I say, and before Ethan can respond, I open the door and stomp into the hall.

I get all the way to the elevator before I hear Caesar say behind me, "The ladies' room is the other way."

"I'm good," I say, watching the elevator floor numbers count down.

"Suzie," Caesar says, and I sigh and turn around to face him. He's got my duffel bag over his shoulder—I'd left it in Uncle Gavin's hospital room. "What are you doing?" he says.

"Doing what I do," I say. "I'm going to find Peaches."

He frowns. "Find Peaches? Why?"

"Because I have to *do something.*" I gesture down the hall toward my uncle's room. "I can't fix anything here. I can't sit in that room and see my uncle . . ." I take a breath. "My uncle was having a heart attack, and when he saw me, he had time to tell me one thing. And he chose to give me a name. So I'm going to go find Peaches." I pause. "Plus Ethan's being a dick."

Caesar considers responding to that. Instead, he says, "I'll come with you."

"No." I shake my head. "Thank you, but you go home with Frankie. This is something I need to do. But if you could tell me where Peaches lives or hangs out, that would help."

He hesitates. "Are you sure?"

"Yep. I mean, I could do it myself, but I'd need access to a laptop and it'd take longer—"

"I meant are you sure about me not coming with you."

"Oh," I say. "Um, yeah. I'm sure."

He narrows his eyes slightly. "Don't do anything stupid."

I hold my hand to my chest. "Me?"

He shakes his head, exasperated, then hands me my duffel bag. "I'll find you an address."

"Tell me your cell number," I say. "I'll get a phone and text you in an hour."

He recites his number and I commit it to memory just as the elevator dings and the doors slide open. I step into the elevator and wave goodbye as the doors close.

CHAPTER THREE

Outside the sun is going down, although it's leaving the day's heat behind like a shroud dropped over the city. My hair is damp against my neck in the short time I wait for a cab. Uber is more convenient, but it also leaves an electronic trail. Old habits die hard.

The cabbie's name is Fitzroy and he has a wide smile and a Jamaican accent. "Where to, miss?" he asks once I climb in the backseat.

"The Store-N-Go on Tenth Street," I say, and Fitzroy nods and pulls away from the curb.

Fitzroy doesn't chatter at me or sing along to the radio or carry on a conversation on his phone, just drives calmly through downtown Atlanta. It's a minor blessing because I need to get myself together, focus on the task at hand and not on the anxiety spiking in my brain. And then I realize with all the drama about my uncle I forgot to ask Ethan why he sent Caesar to track me down in Texas, what he needs my help for. I reach for my phone, intending to call Ethan and ask, only to remember that my old cell is now a bunch of aluminum and glass on a San Antonio highway. "Son of a bitch," I mutter. Fitzroy glances in the rearview at me, but he says nothing. I sit back in my seat and look at the city sliding past. I'll touch base with Ethan tomorrow. For now, I need to work on finding Peaches.

I close my eyes and breathe slowly in through my mouth, taking the breath from my belly, then into my ribs, then my chest, then up to the crown of my head. I hold my breath for a count of five and then exhale slowly. I do it again, drawing air into my lungs, holding it, then releasing it. I don't try to empty my mind or think of nothing, which is pretty impossible for me; I just let my thoughts swim past like fish in a tank without focusing on them. Instead, I focus on my breathing. A calm descends, muting the sounds of traffic. I'm making myself be still, gathering my strength. Settling into hunter mode.

By the time I open my eyes, the sun has fully dropped below the horizon and the streetlights are glowing. Fitzroy brings the cab to a stop outside the Store-N-Go. It's a large three-story cube dropped onto an Atlanta city block between a Midas auto service center and a Subway. Fitzroy calls out the fare and I add an extra ten dollars. His smile broadens, and it's a nice smile that reaches his eyes. "Thank you, miss," he says. "You need me to stay here?"

"Why would I need you to stay here?"

He shrugs, still smiling but a bit more serious. "Lots of cabs outside Grady Hospital, not so much here." He gestures at the general vicinity. "And a nice girl like you, walking alone in this place . . ." He trails off and shrugs again.

I look him in the eye. "I'm not a girl," I say. "I'm not nice, either."

His eyes widen. "No offense, miss."

I grin, hoping it doesn't come across as threatening. "None taken. Thanks, but I'll be fine." I grab my duffel and get out of the cab, then lean back in the open rear door. "You got a card?"

Fitzroy passes me a card with his name and number. I pocket it and close the door, and he gives me a casual salute as he drives off into the evening.

This Store-N-Go has everything I want in a self-storage facility: privacy, good security, and 24/7 access for customers. I type in the entrance code on a pad at the side door, and the door unlocks with a click. It leads directly into the storage units—no need to bother with anyone in the front office. I step into a well-lit hallway and walk past several storage bays, all with orange pull-down doors. My footsteps echo off the concrete floor. I stop at Unit 127 and unlock the combination padlock, then pull the orange door up, the loud ratcheting of it echoing through the empty building.

The storage unit is five feet wide and fifteen deep, essentially a large walk-in closet. No ball gowns or dress shoes in here, though, just some plastic storage bins and duffel bags. I make sure no one is in the hallway before I step inside the unit. I have similar storage units in half a dozen cities, all paid for on a monthly basis by a dummy corporation Uncle Gavin set up. It's a lot more convenient than hauling a bunch of gear around with me.

From one storage bin I take a tactical jumpsuit, a pair of leather-reinforced high tops that are lighter than they look, and a leather jacket. I strip right there in the unit and put on the jumpsuit. Pretty sure that's against Store-N-Go's company policy, but oh well.

From a large duffel bag I pull out a boot knife, a collapsible baton, a canister of red pepper spray, an S&W Model 60 five-shot revolver, and a CZ 75 pistol, along with spare magazines for the CZ and a pair of speedloaders for the five-shot and holsters for both. The CZ goes in a cross-draw holster on my left hip; the S&W sits in a pancake holster at the small of my back. The rest of the gear goes on my belt or various other places. I put on the leather jacket, which effectively covers all of this. Although Georgia is an open-carry state, I'd rather not advertise I'm packing. There are other goodies in the duffel bag, but I zip it shut.

If I were a man, all this hardware would be weaponized testosterone, a threatening expression of power. Some men carry guns to project fear-lessness in a kind of commando cosplay—*mine's bigger, don't fuck with me.* I don't pretend I'm not afraid. The world is a terrifying place, with some awful people in it. I don't carry all this gear to project anything. I carry it to keep myself safe, and I'm good at using it when I have to. But tonight, when I'm wired six ways to Sunday on adrenaline and anxiety, part of me wants an excuse to draw down on someone.

Only part of me, though.

From one more storage bin I retrieve a motorcycle helmet with a dark smoke face shield and a set of keys. I leave my street clothes and duffel in the storage unit, close and lock it up, and then walk down the hall toward the back of the building, the weapons a comfortable weight beneath my jacket.

I exit through another door into a parking lot at the back of the Store-N-Go. It's no cooler outside than it was a few minutes ago, and I begin to sweat underneath the leather jacket as I walk through the lot. The lot doesn't have a roof but is surrounded by a ten-foot-high chain-link fence topped with razor wire. Underneath a waterproof cover is my motorcycle, a Triumph Thruxton 1200. I'd prefer a car—bigger, more storage, easier to take passengers—but for moving around a city quickly and getting in and out of tight spots, a motorcycle is hard to beat. I remove and fold up the cover and put it in the bike's storage compartment. Helmet on, I start the motorcycle and back it out of its space, then pull forward to the gate, tripping the photoelectric sensor so it opens. The bike rumbles beneath me—it wants to be unleashed. I know how it feels. I roll out of the lot and down an alley between the Store-N-Go and the Subway. When I hit the street, I open up the throttle and shoot off into the night, heading west.

Toward the Bluff.

The air is hot and the breeze does little to cool me off underneath my leather jacket, but the heat isn't the only reason I'm sweating.

AT A CIRCLE K on Northside, I buy a Diet Coke and a burner phone and text Caesar from the parking lot. I'm halfway done with my Diet Coke when he sends me back an address on Aaron Street. *All I could find*, he texts.

Insert kissy-face emoji here, I text back, then slide the phone into my jacket pocket and mount my bike.

Atlanta is constantly rebuilding itself. During the Civil War, whatever parts of Atlanta the retreating Confederates didn't destroy, General Sherman put to the torch. Ever since, contractors have made a good living in this city, whose Latin motto, "Resurgens," means "rising again." And now that ceaseless cycle of rebuilding has reached the Bluff. For every ugly or abandoned house, there is an empty lot or brand-new construction. Same thing happened in my uncle's neighborhood, Grant Park, east of the city. Urban renewal with a vengeance.

Lipstick on a pig, as Uncle Gavin would say.

When I was a teenager, in an early iteration of Self-Destructive Suzie, I pissed off a would-be thug named Luco and basically dared him to do something about it, in front of his posse. He responded by dragging my ass to the Bluff and doing bad things to me. I don't dwell on it. But to me the Bluff is cursed, a place of nightmares. The very soil is rotten. The city has poured millions of dollars into the Bluff and surrounding neighborhoods in an effort to revitalize the area. But I'd be perfectly fucking fine if the entire place was bulldozed and buried under asphalt and concrete.

Aaron Street is a microcosm of Atlanta—out of a dozen lots, three are empty, three have houses so new they look like freshly painted toys, one has an empty shell only a crack dealer would find inviting, and the rest have small but intact houses, their yards neat and clean of trash. The Baptist church at one end of the street and the heavily fortified liquor store at the other are the final, ironic touch.

The address Caesar sent me is a bungalow with white siding and a screened-in porch on one side like a box. There's a light on over the front door, moths droning around it in circles. I park my bike on the street and stuff my helmet into the cargo compartment, then take a deep breath to settle myself before I walk up the concrete path to the front door. I imagine men behind the windows of the white house, crouched in the shadows, waiting. My heart is beating at a fast clip, more in anticipation than fear. But I know that at least some of the men who are now watching me are not inside the house.

I ring the doorbell and then step back and stand with my hands clasped in front of me, like a pastor making a house call. My head is buzzing now, the way a performer must feel just before the lights dim and she takes the stage. I'm acutely aware of the two holstered pistols beneath my jacket, the yellowed light from the bulb over the front porch, the distant sounds of traffic, the scuffed red paint on the front door. I'm ready for whatever is behind that door.

It opens. A woman stands there, Black and older, with gray hair and glasses, a woman who might have been called big-boned when she was younger and has now shrunk some but without losing much if any of her dignity. "Yes?" she says.

I have some options here. One, demand to see Peaches. Two, take the old woman hostage. Three, play dumb. Four, make up a story about who I am and why I need to see Peaches.

Instead, I smile. "Good evening, ma'am," I say. "My name is Susannah Faulkner. Are you Mrs. Daniels?"

"I am." Her expression does not change.

"I was hoping to talk with your son, Antoine."

"Are you the police?" the woman asks.

I suppress a laugh. "No, ma'am, I am most definitely not."

"Do you sell drugs?" she asks.

I shake my head. "No."

She considers me with the same implacable expression. "Why do you want to speak to my son?"

While my voice remains pleasant, I can hear the strain underneath. I wonder if she can hear it too. "It's about my uncle," I say. "Gavin Lester."

Mrs. Daniels stares back at me for a beat. Somewhere a few blocks over, a dog begins to bark. Mrs. Daniels sighs. "I suppose you should come on in, then," she says, and she turns and walks into the house, leaving the door open for me.

IF ANYONE TRIED to swing a cat in Mrs. Daniels's living room, they would damage a lot of ferns and plastic-covered furniture. Mrs. Daniels brings out a tray of iced tea and places it on a glass coffee table before settling into a white leather BarcaLounger. The chair is situated under a windowsill that's teeming with ferns, which give her a leafy green corona. I sit across from her on a floral-print couch, the plastic squeaking beneath me, and keep an eye on the front door.

"Antoine doesn't live here," Mrs. Daniels says. "Hasn't for years."

"But I bet he stops by often to check in on you," I say. "Just like I bet someone in the neighborhood has already told him you've got a visitor. Probably one of the men hiding in the empty lot across from your house. Right now your son is probably wondering who this White girl is that's bothering his mama."

Mrs. Daniels doesn't correct me—*oh, you aren't bothering me*—but she doesn't kick me out, either. She picks up her glass of iced tea, sips it, and puts it back down on the coffee table with a *click*. I have the feeling that she and I are conducting some kind of elaborate stage play. My head is still buzzing and I'm itching for a confrontation, but for the moment I can deal with whatever game Mrs. Daniels and I are playing. I pick up my own glass of tea and sip it, tasting mint and lemon and sugar.

"You have a nice house, Mrs. Daniels," I say. "Very trim, as my mother would say."

She gives a *hmmph*. "Are you surprised, Miss Faulkner?" she says. "To find such a house in this neighborhood?"

Her question surprises me. I've only been in one house in the Bluff before, and it was nothing like this one. "I'm just giving you an honest compliment, ma'am," I say.

"Flattery," she says, as if the word were a disappointment in her mouth. "But I shall receive it in a spirit of love. I keep my house straight because the Bible tells us to keep to the straight path. The righteous keep their ways straight, while the wicked fall by their own wickedness."

Now she's throwing Bible quotes at me. I throttle the urge to pull out my boot knife and clean my fingernails with it. "Do you see me as one of the wicked, ma'am?" I ask.

Mrs. Daniels *hmmph*s again. "I don't see you wearing a halo," she says. "You are bringing your own wickedness with you."

"That's certainly true," I say, looking her in the eye. "But I'm not the only one."

We stop speaking for a short time, sipping our tea and looking everywhere except at each other. The minutes drip away, one at a time, each more agonizing than the last. I think of Uncle Gavin lying in the hospital, his room probably dark now. I wonder if he's sleeping, and if he knows he's sleeping. I wonder what business he has with Peaches.

"Ah," Mrs. Daniels says, sitting a bit straighter in her BarcaLounger, just before I hear someone outside walking up the path to the front door.

"I wouldn't make any quick movements," she says, just as if she were saying *I think I'll have another glass of tea*. "Just sit still."

Before I can come up with a smart-ass response, the front door opens. The first man through wears dreadlocks, a red tank top, and mirrored sunglasses. Behind him is a big man in an oversized blue Braves jersey, his head shaved, tattoos circling his muscled arms. Both men come into the room and stand on either side of the front door, staring at me. Underneath his tank top, the dreadlocked man has something tucked into his waistband.

I display my teeth in a grin. "Hi, fellas," I say. Neither responds, although the one with dreadlocks has to suppress a twitch in the corner of his mouth.

A third man enters wearing an Atlanta Hawks cap, its bill stiff and cocked at an angle toward the ceiling, and a short-sleeve button-down so white it practically glows. He has a round face and a wide, expressive mouth that looks like it could hold a broad smile. Right now he isn't smiling. He pays no attention to me but walks straight over to Mrs. Daniels. "Hey, Mama," he says, bending to kiss her on the cheek. "How you doin'?"

"I'm fine," Mrs. Daniels says. "This is Miss Faulkner. Says she wants to talk to you about her uncle."

The man looks at me for the first time since entering the room. His expression is flat as a wall and just as welcoming. I nod at him from my seat on the couch, making sure my hands are on top of my knees, in plain sight.

"I don't know you," Peaches says. "Why you botherin' my mama?"

I look at Mrs. Daniels, my eyebrows raised, then back to Peaches. "I'm not bothering her," I say. "We're just visiting. I'm having iced tea."

The dreadlocked man unfolds his arms, bringing his hands closer to his waist. The larger man in the Braves jersey shifts on his feet.

Peaches speaks like he's throwing down a challenge. "You ride into my hood and come to my mama's house?"

I keep my breathing even, my hands still on my knees. *Bring it*, a voice like a lover's whispers in my head. But I need to play this out, learn what I can from Peaches. "I had to find you," I say, keeping my voice steady. "This was the quickest way I knew how."

We all eyeball each other. It's hard to tell because of his mirrored sunglasses, but I'm pretty sure Dreadlocks is checking out my breasts. Part of me wants to unzip the front of my jumpsuit just to fuck with him, but Mrs. Daniels would probably stroke out in her BarcaLounger. Instead, I raise my hands from my knees and then let them drop back down to my thighs with a soft clap. "Well," I say, and I stand up, ignoring Dreadlocks's alarm. "Mrs. Daniels, thank you very much for the tea."

Everyone else stops moving, and for a second I think Dreadlocks is going to pull out that something stuck in his waistband. Then Peaches leans over to kiss his mother on the cheek again. "We goin' out on the porch, Mama," he says. "Let you go to bed."

"All right," Mrs. Daniels says. "I'll see you tomorrow at the rec center." She turns her gaze on me. "Miss Faulkner," she says by way of goodbye.

Peaches looks at me, then at Dreadlocks, and jerks his chin toward the back of the house.

CHAPTER FOUR

DREADLOCKS LEADS US THROUGH MRS. DANIELS'S WORN BUT CLEAN kitchen to the screened-in porch. His bald partner in the Braves jersey ambles along behind us. A shotgun has somehow materialized in his hand, the barrel so short that the whole thing is no longer than his thigh. He smiles when he sees me glance back at him, and I turn away, hiding a smile of my own. It's almost like they're flirting with me.

The porch holds a set of battered wicker furniture with a light dusting of pollen. I stand by a cushioned chair but don't sit. Dreadlocks and the man with the shotgun each take a position in a far corner of the porch, flanking me while also being able to see out into the yard and the street.

The screen door opens and Peaches steps onto the porch, letting the door swing shut behind him with a *bang*. "You got some adamantium balls comin' here," he says, standing by the door and looking at me. "Either that or you crazy. White girl drivin' up on a goddamn motorcycle." He looks disgusted, like I've failed some sort of test and he's taking it personally.

"I just have a couple of questions and then I'm out of your hair," I say.

"I look like Google to you?"

"It's about my uncle, Gavin Lester."

39

That gets a reaction, a flash of understanding in his eyes, and then it's gone, replaced by a thin smile just shy of a smirk. "Your uncle, huh? Why, you doing a genealogy report for school?"

He's pushing my buttons deliberately, and knowing that makes it easier to resist responding. But the buzzing in my head from earlier is increasing, like a swarming of bees, and I want answers, and in Peaches's smile I see the same kind of dismissive sexist bullshit I saw on Bobby Bonaroo's face, and on the faces of a hundred men who have run their eyes over me and written me off as unworthy of respect. It's the same sneer I saw on Luco's face when he pinned me to the ground and reached for the waistband of my jeans.

"Just tell me what I want to know and I'm gone," I say. I manage to keep my voice steady.

Peaches cocks his head like a bird considering a fat worm. "Girl, I don't have to tell you a goddamned thing."

I grit my teeth, the twin howler monkeys in my brain starting up. "I am not a girl."

Peaches rolls his eyes and looks at his two goons. "Get this bitch off my mama's porch," he says.

The big man approaches first, the sawed-off dangling from one hand, a slow smile on his face. He's used to intimidating people. The top of my head barely reaches his shoulder, and he's probably got seventy pounds of muscle on me. He could snap me in half. In other words, he's a distinct threat.

Finally.

I extend my left arm and spray a canister of red pepper gel directly into the big man's face. Gel's better than aerosol spray—easier to aim and far less likely to drift back into my own eyes. It's also nonlethal, although it makes your eyes and mouth feel like they're on fire. The big man screams and falls to his knees, wiping at his face, the sawed-off clattering to the porch floor. Dreadlocks runs at me, his footsteps thundering on the wooden boards, but I've already drawn my baton and extend it with a flick of the wrist. I spin and swing the steel rod, striking his chest and sending him crashing into a wicker sofa. A cloud of yellow pollen erupts from the cushions, dusting his mirrored sunglasses. When Dreadlocks tries to stand up, I hit him in the head with the baton. It's just a tap, not hard enough to crack his skull. He drops back onto the couch like he's suddenly decided he needs a nap.

I turn and put the end of the baton against Peaches's chest, pinning him against the wall of the house. Peaches hasn't moved except for his mouth dropping open. With the Hawks cap on his head, he looks a little like a kid who just got his ass handed to him on the playground. My head is humming now like I'm on my third or fourth beer, except I'm completely stone sober and grinning like a maniac.

"I don't like being called 'girl,'" I say.

Peaches flicks his eyes toward the big man moaning on the porch, then back to me. Without looking, I sweep my foot across the floor to the right, connecting with the sawed-off I know is there and sending it sliding across the porch and well out of reach of anyone. I risk a glance at the big man, who is still on his knees, wiping at his eyes and bawling. Dreadlocks is still sprawled unconscious on the couch. Satisfied, I turn my attention back to Peaches. "All you had to do was let me ask my question," I say.

Wariness and anger wrestle in Peaches's face. "That's not how your uncle said we would do this," he spits.

So I wasn't imagining his reaction earlier. "He's in the hospital," I say. "Didn't exactly have time to give me the down-low on whatever kind of secret handshake you all have."

Peaches frowns. "Hospital?" He's not so much concerned as wary.

For some reason my throat feels like it's squeezing shut, or maybe clogged with glue, and I clear it. It takes me a second to realize it because I'm sad for my uncle . . . and afraid. "Heart attack," I manage to get out. "He should be okay." I lower the baton but keep it extended. "The last thing he said to me before they put him in an ambulance was your name. Why?"

"He asked me to do something for him." Peaches glances again at the big man moaning on the porch. "Lemme help Billy wipe that shit out of his eyes."

I consider this for a second, then shrug. I've shown all three what I can do and don't need to be a badass right now. "Okay. Get a pitcher of water and a clean hand towel."

Peaches goes back inside and I retract the baton and put it back in its holster on my belt, then move across the porch, away from the door and both of Peaches's men. Dreadlocks is still dreaming on the wicker couch. I draw my CZ and just hold it, the barrel pointing down. "It'll be okay," I tell Billy, the big man moaning. "We'll wash out your eyes."

Billy is on all fours now, rapidly blinking and shaking his head like a dog that's bitten into something nasty. "Fuck you," he manages. I sigh. So much for peacemaking.

PEACHES RETURNS WITH a blue pitcher and a dishcloth and without a glance in my direction takes care of Billy, talking to him in a low voice as he pours water over his face and wipes it away with the dishcloth. It's oddly comforting, like watching a nurse take care of a child. But the thought of nurses makes me think of Uncle Gavin in the hospital, and I take deep breaths to try to keep relaxed. My nerves are all jittery in the aftermath of our scuffle. I've already picked up the sawed-off shotgun and put it on the porch by my feet, and I'm still holding the CZ, although I don't think I'm going to need either of them.

When Billy is sitting in a chair, still blinking furiously and glaring at me, Peaches goes over to peer at Dreadlocks on the couch. "Man's gonna have a hella headache when he wakes up," he says, still not looking at me.

I reach into a pocket on my jumpsuit and pull out a foil packet. "Here," I say, and when Peaches turns to me I toss him the packet. He catches it and reads the label.

"Acetaminophen?" he says.

"Give him that over the next twenty-four hours," I say. "No ibuprofen, no aspirin. After that, he can switch to whatever makes him feel better."

"Now you a doctor?" Peaches shakes his head. "You a strange girl. *Woman*," he adds, correcting himself. He gives a little eyeroll when he says it, but I ignore it. Baby steps.

Peaches continues to look at me, like he's evaluating something. "I know who you are," he says.

"And who's that?"

"You the girl Luco Stevens grabbed."

It's like Peaches just tore a hole in my brain and hauled out my memory of that night, black and wriggling. Luco dragging me kicking and screaming into an abandoned house two blocks from where I'm standing right now. Luco backhanding me across the face when I refused to settle down. Luco raping me in that house, in front of his goons, just before sticking a needle full of heroin into my arm.

I realize I'm squeezing the CZ and force myself to relax so I don't accidentally fire a round into the porch. "Is that a problem?" I ask, hearing the rough waver in my voice and hating myself for displaying weakness.

Peaches keeps looking at me. "I watched Luco grow up here," he says finally. "He was no good. Got what he deserved in the end, probably."

"Goddamn right," I say.

We say nothing for a few seconds, the silence sitting heavily on the porch. Through a curtained window I see the kitchen light go out. Mrs. Daniels is going to bed.

"My uncle and you," I say. "What's the deal?"

Peaches takes a breath, exhales out his nose. "Like I said, he asked me to do somethin' for him. Find somethin'."

"Find what?"

"You'll see," Peaches says. "I made a call." He glances out at the street, and I follow his glance. Two cars are pulling up to the curb behind my bike, an old Town Car and an older Malibu that looks like it was rolled here end-over-end from Alaska. A black Mercedes SUV is already parked in front of my bike. The Mercedes must be Peaches's ride.

I gesture to the porch door. "After you."

Billy lumbers to his feet, eyes still weeping from the pepper gel, and stomps past me out the door and down the porch steps into the yard. Peaches follows, and I bring up the rear, holstering the CZ. I leave the sawed-off on the porch. Dreadlocks is still in naptime.

By the time we get to the street, four men have gotten out of the Malibu and stand in a semicircle in the street, on the far side of both vehicles. A tall man in a Five Stripes jersey gets out of the Town Car, holding an Uzi. He opens the rear passenger door and steps back.

A man stumbles out of the back of the Town Car like he was shoved out. He's a gawky guy with a mop of curly brown hair, muddy freckles spackled across his face. In a green T-shirt and khaki shorts, he looks like he should be manning a register at REI, not riding around in a Town Car in the Bluff. He brushes his hair out of his face and peers at us. "Are you a cop?" he says to me.

I turn to Peaches. "What is this?"

"That's who your uncle asked me to find," Peaches says. "Tane Kamaka. He's all yours."

"What?" I look at the curly-haired dude, then back to Peaches. "What do you mean, he's all mine?"

"Because if you're a cop," Tane Kamaka says, "I've been kidnapped."

Peaches gives me a broad smile. "Tell your uncle I delivered his package." He nods at the tall guy with the Uzi, who gets back in the Town Car. Then Peaches turns and heads back up the yard to the porch, Billy following him. The other men start getting back in their cars.

"What the fuck is this?" I say, loudly. "Who is this guy? What am I supposed to do with him?"

"You're welcome, Doctor Woman," Peaches says without turning around. Billy points at me with a murderous glare, then stumps after his boss. The Town Car and the Malibu drive off into the night, leaving me standing in Mrs. Daniels's front yard with a stranger my uncle supposedly wanted Peaches to find.

"So you're not a cop," Tane Kamaka says.

"No," I say, stalking to my bike. My earlier buzz has vanished, replaced by the beginnings of a headache unfolding behind my eyes. I glance up at the porch, which remains dark. Fucking Peaches. I should have tapped *him* on the head with my baton.

Tane Kamaka half-runs to keep up with me. "Hey, I'm kinda hungry," he says. "Not that anybody gives a shit, but those guys kept trying to feed me rice and Chinese fast food, which is kinda racist, but whatever. I'm not even Asian. I'd kill for a burger or fried chicken or something. Whoa, is that your bike?"

I turn abruptly to face Tane Kamaka so that he almost collides with me. "Who are you?" I demand.

Tane blinks. "I'm Tane Kamaka," he says. "Kamakawiwo'ole, actually, but Kamaka's easier to say. Although then everyone assumes I'm Japanese or—"

"Who are you when you're not at home, Tane?"

"I—what?"

"What do you do?"

Tane's eyes flick down the front of my jumpsuit and a smile gathers in his face. I can read what he's about to say as if it's displayed on his forehead. With both hands I grab his green T-shirt and pull him to me so our noses are almost touching.

"If you make a joke about 'doing' me, or say *anything* sexual," I say, "I will rip your tongue out of your mouth and beat you to death with it. Now what do you do?"

He rolls his eyes to try to take in my expression, but he's so close all he can see is my own dark eyes burning into his. I can smell fried pork and scallions on his breath. He's got blackheads on his nose.

"Numbers," he manages. "I'm a numbers guy."

I narrow my eyes. "Math or accounting?"

"Yes. I mean, both."

I let go of him and he staggers back a step. Before he can get his balance, I jab him with questions. "You work for Peaches?"

"Who's Peaches?"

"The nice man with the Hawks cap who gave you to me."

"No, I don't know him."

"You know Gavin Lester?"

"No. That your uncle?"

"How do you know he's my uncle?"

"The nice man with the Hawks cap said he was supposed to deliver me to your uncle. Like I'm a UPS package. You don't look like the kind of person who calls her uncle Peaches, so when you asked me about Gavin Lester, I guessed that's your uncle."

"Who you don't know."

"Lady, I don't know who *you* are."

"I'm Gavin Lester's niece."

"Thanks, that's very helpful."

I'd like to continue this talk, maybe with the help of a knife to scare Tane Kamakawiwo'ole so he'll stop dancing and just tell me what I want to know. But suddenly I'm aware that we are standing alone in the middle of a street at night, in a part of town where no one who doesn't live here should be. There are no other lights on in Mrs. Daniels's house, but I'm pretty sure Billy is glaring at me from behind a curtain, begging for a chance to come at me again. And there's no telling who is hiding in the abandoned house across the street. But I can feel their eyes on me.

"We're leaving," I say. "You get on behind me and hold me by my waist. Move your hands around or try and touch me anywhere else and you'll lose an eye, you got it?"

Tane nods, jerkily. Still, he says, "Do all your threats have to do with maiming?"

Annoying, but gutsy. I'm reluctantly impressed. "I just like being clear. Maiming tends to make an impression." I take my helmet out from the storage compartment and put it on, then throw one leg over the seat and mount the bike. "Climb on, Tane Kamakawiwo'ole."

He does, exactly the way someone who has never been on a motorcycle would. "So," he says against the back of my head, his voice vibrating through my helmet, "what about a burger?"

I close my eyes and count to ten. It doesn't help.

CHAPTER FIVE

I DRIVE SLOWLY BECAUSE THE THRUXTON ISN'T BUILT FOR TWO people and it's illegal for me to have a passenger. I don't need one of Atlanta's finest to pull me over so Tane Kamaka can start bitching about being kidnapped and how he wants a hamburger. Thankfully the Thruxton's engine is loud enough that conversation is impossible as long as we are moving. Tane's hands are firmly on my hips—no splaying of his fingers, no squeezing, nothing. He's practically a gentleman until our first stop sign. My helmet is very insulated, but when I roll to a stop I can hear his muffled voice over the idling motor. "What about that burger?"

I rev the throttle, drowning him out, then shoot across the intersection so he nearly falls off the rear of the bike.

The burner phone I bought at Circle K is crappy but still has Bluetooth, and my helmet has an integrated headset so I can make and answer phone calls while riding. Using voice activation, I tell the crappy burner phone to call the one number in its memory.

Caesar answers on the second ring. "Suzie?"

"I found Peaches, who had a package for Uncle Gavin. And by 'package' I mean a number cruncher named Tane Kamaka. That name ring a bell?"

"Tane Kamaka? No. What did you do with him?"

"Put him on the back of my bike. He's hanging on to me for dear life right now."

Behind me, Tane Kamaka shouts, "Who are you talking to?"

I ignore him and pass a slow-moving pickup truck, then weave back into my lane. "I'm heading your way," I say to Caesar. He and Frankie live in a loft west of Midtown, about a mile and a half away from where I am now. "Hoping you and Frankie could keep this guy at your place for a day or two while I figure out what to do with him."

"Can't do it," Caesar says. "We're renovating. The kitchen got torn out today, and now the water isn't working. Frankie's on his phone arguing with the contractor. We're probably going to a hotel tonight. Sorry."

"Shit. Okay, change of plan. Any news about Uncle Gavin?"

"No. What are you going to do?"

"I'll figure it out."

"Be careful."

"Love you, too," I say, and end the call.

"Hamburger?" Tane shouts.

I turn north onto Lowery and gun it. Hamburgers will have to wait.

"WHAT ARE WE doing here?" Tane asks as I roll into the parking lot at the back of the Store-N-Go.

I park the bike in my spot and cut the engine, then get off the bike and remove my helmet. "You talk a lot."

"I do that when I'm nervous." Shakily, Tane climbs off the bike, stumbling a bit. "This doesn't look like a hamburger place."

"Shut up about food. I need to make this stop first." I pull the motorcycle cover out of the bike's storage compartment. "Help me with this. Then we'll go inside and I'll call a cab so we can go where we're going, and then I'll buy you a hamburger."

"I can buy my own hamburger," Tane says sullenly, but he grabs one end of the bike cover and helps me put it over the Thruxton. Then he follows me to the back entrance to the Store-N-Go, and I punch in the code and open the door, gesturing for him to enter first.

Again, the corridors inside are empty. Motorcycle helmet under one arm, I usher Tane to my storage locker. I put the helmet on the floor, open the combination lock, and pull up the door with a ratcheting crash. "Step inside my parlor," I say. Tane says nothing but slouches into the locker. I pick up my helmet and step in after him. It's cramped inside with both of us and the storage bins, but it'll have to do.

"Turn around and face the wall," I say.

"Why?"

"Because I need to—"

Tane spins to face me and holds his hand out, pointing something at my face. "Don't move!" he shouts. "Or I'll spray you with it, I swear to God."

I stare at him. The sonofabitch has my pepper spray in his hand.

"What the fuck are you doing?" I say.

"Get down on your knees and put your hands behind your back."

"I'm not getting on my knees."

"Do it. No, actually, keep your hands where I can see them."

"Which is it, Tane? Hands behind my back or where you can see them?"

"Where—where I can see them." His eyes are wide and he's sweating, but he holds the pepper spray steady enough. "Do it."

"You're pointing it the wrong way, dumbass."

When Tane glances at the canister in his hand, I swing the motorcycle helmet I'm still holding so it cracks across his arm. The canister flies out of his hand and bounces off the locker wall. Tane cries out in pain but tries to kick me. I sidestep the kick, drop my helmet, and grab his arm, pinning it behind his back. He yelps and stands on his tiptoes. I kick his feet out from under him and send him to the floor, landing on top of him so all the air whooshes out of his lungs.

"You asshole," I hiss in his ear. I'm furious that he stole my pepper spray off my belt—he must have done it when we were getting off the bike. Maybe earlier. "What did you do that for?"

He coughs, trying to catch his breath. "You're gonna shoot me in the head," he says finally. "What the hell else am I supposed to do?"

"I'm not going to *shoot* you."

"You told me to turn and face the wall."

"I told you to face the wall because I need to change my clothes and you're not going to watch me while I do it."

Tane pauses, considering. "Oh," he says.

I haul him up and push him against a wall, then pull out a pair of zip tie cuffs and put one around his wrists. Part of me is impressed, reluctantly. Another part of me wants to punch him in the face. Instead, I take a deep breath and sit Tane down and put another zip tie around his ankles. He doesn't resist, as if all his energy has drained away. While I take off my gear and strip off my high-tops and jumpsuit and put on my street clothes, Tane sits docilely in the corner, facing the wall, not saying a word.

"You should have waited for me to start getting undressed," I say.

Tane raises his head, listening, but he says nothing and continues facing the wall.

"I would have been more vulnerable that way," I continue. "Harder for me to react if I'm half out of my clothes."

Tane clears his throat. "I'll remember that next time I try to mug you in a storage locker."

A FEW MINUTES later we are on the street in front of the Store-N-Go, waiting for a cab. I've got the duffel bag with most of my gear over one shoulder, although I've kept the boot knife strapped to my leg and the revolver is holstered at the small of my back under the leather jacket. Tane has remained quiet, looking anywhere but at me. While he's not a big guy, he's taller than I am, so it must sting that I took him down so easily.

"What's up, buttercup?" I say. "You haven't bitched about getting a hamburger for a whole five minutes."

Tane clears his throat, looking down the street. "The pepper spray wasn't pointed the wrong way, was it?"

"Nope," I say cheerfully.

He nods, his face glum.

Soon a cab pulls up to the curb, and Fitzroy leans across the front seat to look through the open passenger-door window. "Hey there, miss," he calls out. "Got your call. You got company, I see."

I steer Tane into the back seat and get in next to him. "Hi, Fitzroy," I say. "Thanks for picking us up."

Fitzroy smiles in the rearview. "Long as you pay me, miss, I'll pick you up anytime. Where we goin'?"

"Chastain Park. Can we go through a drive-thru on the way?" I look at Tane. "You like Steak 'n Shake? Good hamburgers."

Tane tries hard not to smile, but I still see the corners of his mouth shift. "Uh, yeah, sure," he says.

Fitzroy nods. "There's one off Northside at West Paces."

I grin, feeling ridiculously pleased for some reason. "*Vámonos, muchachos.*"

IT'S LATE BY the time Fitzroy drops us off in Chastain Park. The neighborhood is sleeping and we are the only ones on the street—all the residents are tucked inside their nice homes, feeling secure and safe. They don't know how thin that illusion of safety is. Still, I don't want to ruin that illusion for them, like it was ruined for me and Ethan. No one should have to go through that.

I pay Fitzroy, who takes my cash and holds his hand to his heart in a gesture of thanks, then drives slowly off into the night. I'm hot and sweaty and tired. My duffel bag hangs heavy off my shoulder. Tane is holding a pair of grease-stained paper sacks, now mostly empty, and a milkshake.

"You get enough to eat?" I ask. In the cab he inhaled two double cheeseburgers and an order of fries.

Tane sips on his milkshake, and only when there's a loud gurgle does he stop. "Probably," he says. He looks tired but content, full of carbs and meat and milkshake. "Where are we?"

"Your new home for the next couple of days."

We walk up the driveway, which is long and humped from tree roots. Ethan's house, which he rents from his neighbors Gene and Tony, could fit in some of the living rooms around here, but aside from my uncle's place in Grant Park, Ethan's house is the closest thing to a home that I know. Not that I've ever stayed here for more than a few weeks at a time, but that's longer than anywhere else I've lived as an adult. It's sentimental as hell, but no matter where I've been over the past few years, I've taken comfort in the idea that my brother is here in his 1940s bungalow, grading papers and living a productive, boring life.

"What's wrong?" Tane asks.

"What?"

"You looked kind of sad for a sec."

"I'm fine."

A light is on over the front door, and as we approach the steps, barking erupts from inside the house. Tane freezes.

"What's the matter?" I ask.

Tane actually takes a step back from the house. "There's a dog."

"Yeah. You don't like dogs?"

The barking continues, loud and insistent. Tane turns a white face to me. "You know this dog?"

"Oh, yeah. Fucking vicious, man."

The front door opens and Wilson, Ethan's mini dachshund, bolts out and down the stairs. Tane actually gives a high-pitched yelp and raises his hands, palms out, in defense. Wilson makes a beeline for Tane, snout down, sniffing furiously, and then he begins capering around Tane's feet, yipping excitedly and leaping against his shins.

"What the fuck?" Tane cries.

"He wants you to rub his belly." I crouch and spread my arms wide. "Wilson! What's up, pup? You forget your Aunt Suzie?"

Wilson barrels over to me, jumps up against my chest, and licks my nose. Then he flops onto his back and paddles his front paws. I oblige and scratch his belly. "You're just a big belly slut, aren't you? Yes you are," I say. Wilson's eyes are half closed, his tongue drooping out of his mouth.

Tane slowly uncringes and stares at me. "'Fucking vicious,'" he says in disgust.

"Susannah," someone says, and I look up to see Ethan on the front porch, arms folded across his chest.

"Hey," I say. "Any news about Uncle Gavin?"

Ethan shakes his head. "Doctor wants to meet with us at one o'clock tomorrow at the hospital, talk with Uncle Gavin about his . . . options." He glances at Tane, then back at me.

To me Tane says, "That's your brother?"

"Yep," I say. To Ethan, I shrug apologetically. "Sorry to stop by so late. I figured it's summer, you aren't teaching, so maybe you could put up with a couple of house guests for a night or two?"

"I'm teaching summer school," Ethan says. "Got class at eight AM tomorrow."

Of course he does. Nice planning, Suzie. "I'm sorry, Ethan," I say. "I didn't know where else to go."

Ethan sighs. "I know. Caesar already called me." He turns back to the front door. "It's not like I'm gonna sleep anyway. Come on in."

CHAPTER SIX

I FILL ETHAN IN AS WE SIT IN HIS LIVING ROOM, HIM IN AN ARMCHAIR, me on the floor playing with Wilson. Tane is taking a shower in the one bathroom.

"So Uncle Gavin was at the airport to pick up Tane," Ethan says. "Did this Peaches guy tell you why Uncle Gavin wanted him?"

"Wasn't really in a position to ask," I say. I throw Wilson's rope bone and he scrabbles across the hardwood floor to chase it. "Peaches dumped Tane on me and left with his posse. But I intend to find out as soon as Tane gets out of the shower."

We fall silent, watching Wilson bring his rope bone back to me so I can throw it for him to chase again. Neither of us has brought up last year, how I upended Ethan's life and how he saved me from jumping off a bridge, then later from being killed by our parents' murderer. We don't tend to talk about that kind of stuff. We lived through a dark, dark time, and we survived. That should be good enough. Still, there's always an underlying tension between us, a dark thread that ties us together. It's more than sibling rivalry. If I had a gun to my head, I'd say it's because of how we reacted so differently to being orphaned. Ethan became a teacher, like our mother, and I became a hunter seeking vengeance. And we resent each other—Ethan for having to look out for me because that's the last thing our father told him to do before he died, and me for feeling guilty about that.

And if our parents hadn't died? Would I resent my brother? Would I have gone to college and then chosen a career, gotten married, raised children of my own? Would I not be the person I am now, prowling through the dark underside of the world, trying to do something good?

I think about all this in the time it takes me to retrieve Wilson's rope bone and toss it and watch the dog scramble to retrieve it. I think about all this pretty often, actually.

I glance at Ethan and see that he looks exhausted, dark circles like soot smudged beneath his eyes. He stares at the television screen, which is blank and dark, as if he is watching a show only he can see. Wilson trots back with his rope bone in his mouth, then drops to the floor and starts to gnaw on it.

"I still can't believe Alex Trebek died," Ethan says, still staring at the television screen. "I turned on the television the other day and saw an ad for *Jeopardy!* and I thought, how will Suzie and I play *Jeopardy!* again?"

"Ethan," I say.

"I heard they were thinking about LeVar Burton to host, and I knew you'd love that, being a *Star Trek* geek, but—"

"Ethan, why did Caesar fly halfway across the country to find me and bring me home?"

Ethan only grunts and continues staring at the television.

I forge ahead. "Caesar said it has something to do with Dad."

At this Ethan shoots me a look that is so bleak and despairing something inside of me cries out even as it shrivels like an orchid in blazing sunlight. Then he raises a hand and rubs his eyes. "This guy came to the house last week," he says. "Tall, crew-cut, looked like he stepped out of *Soldier of Fortune*. Says his name's Finn."

"Finn? That his first name or his last?"

Ethan shrugs absently. "I didn't ask. He said he wanted to talk to me about Dad."

My jaw and shoulders tighten. "Why?"

"He said he served with Dad in Iraq."

No one that our father served with in Iraq ever came by our house, or our uncle's house, as far as I know. Dad never introduced us to any of his fellow soldiers. When his National Guard unit was deployed to Iraq, it was as if he had gone to another world, a different planet with no tangible connection to this one.

"You think he was lying?" I ask. "This Finn guy?"

"No . . ." Ethan is staring at the TV again, but now he's focusing, scanning his memory. "I don't know how to explain it. I believe him that he was a soldier, and I'm pretty sure he's telling the truth about serving with Dad. But it's like he's on stage and trying hard to impress you. And at the same time you can't ignore him. He was very . . . charismatic, I guess is the word. When he walked in here, it was like someone had turned on the lights and they were all shining on him."

"What did he say about Dad?"

Ethan shakes his head. "He was talking about money that some U.S. soldiers stole in Iraq. Finn was part of it." He gives me that same bleak look of despair. "And he says Dad was part of it too."

"He says *Dad* was part of it?" I stand up quickly. Wilson lifts his head, startled, and gives a single *woof* that sounds like a question. I ignore Wilson and pace around the living room. "That's bullshit," I say. "Dad was a lot of things, but he wasn't a thief."

"Finn seemed pretty convinced," Ethan says.

"Some stranger shows up at your door and spins a story about Dad being a thief and you just believe him?" I'm working myself into a nice little fury, pacing around the living room. If there were a punching bag here, I'd be whaling away at it. Instead, I just flex and straighten my fingers, trying not to form fists. "He was a *banker*, Ethan. Dad worked with money all the time. He wouldn't steal it."

"What, that's just Uncle Gavin?"

I stop pacing and glare at him. "What the hell does *that* mean? Uncle Gavin isn't Dad. Stay focused."

"Think about it, Suze." Ethan leans forward, elbows on his knees. "When Dad came back from Iraq, he was different. Angry, sad, both all mixed up. Something was eating at him. Maybe it was guilt."

"Or maybe it was PTSD."

"Yeah, but from what? Dad never told us anything about trauma or stuff on the battlefield. Maybe we just made that up to explain—"

"Oh, come *on*. We made that *up*? He was an emotional whipsaw! Yelling one minute, crying the next, then he'd go all stoic for days—"

"I know, I was there too."

I can feel my anger coiling up, waiting for a chance to be unleashed. It's part of the old pattern of behavior I fall into with Ethan. But that's not why I'm here. "Hold on," I say, hand raised and palm out, as if telling my emotions to stop. "What does this Finn guy want? He didn't show up out of the blue to talk about Dad for no reason. What does he want?"

Ethan leans back, deflated. "He thinks Dad moved all the money they stole. And Finn doesn't know where it is."

My heart sinks. "And he wants his share," I say. Ethan nods. "What kind of money is he talking about?"

Someone says, "Big pallets of cash."

Ethan and I turn to stare at Tane, who's standing at the other end of the living room, drying his curly reddish-brown hair with a towel. He's wearing gym shorts and a faded Archer School football T-shirt of Ethan's.

"How long have you been standing there?" I ask. I'm annoyed that I didn't hear him turn off the shower or come down the hall.

Tane shrugs. "Long enough, I guess."

Wilson scampers over to Tane and drops his rope bone at Tane's feet, then looks up, tail wagging. Tane kicks the rope bone across the floor and Wilson chases it under a side table next to where Ethan sits.

"What big pallets of cash?" Ethan asks.

Tane drapes his towel around his neck. "The U.S. government flew in big pallets of cash to try and stabilize things after they invaded Iraq," he says. "Largest transfer of cash in history."

An uneasy feeling builds inside me, like someone just struck a tiny tuning fork in my chest. "How much cash?"

Tane shrugs again. "Billions. Maybe forty billion."

Nobody says anything for a moment. Even Wilson stops gnawing on his rope bone.

I clear my throat. "Forty *billion* dollars?"

"Maybe," Tane says. "Nobody knows for certain."

"What do you mean nobody knows for certain?"

Ethan reaches down to scratch behind Wilson's ears. "I read about this," he says. "It was Iraqi money, right?"

Tane nods. "Financial assets of Saddam Hussein's that the U.S. froze. It was supposed to be used to rebuild the country. All carefully counted and accounted for on our end. And then they flew all that cash to Baghdad and a bunch of it just disappeared."

"And nobody cared?" I ask. I'm still trying to imagine losing track of billions of dollars.

Tane shrugs again, a goofy lifting and dropping of his shoulders. It's both adorable and annoying. "It wasn't American taxpayer money, so the CPA didn't really care as long as people got paid and projects got funded."

I knew what the CPA was—the Coalition Provisional Authority, the American-run transitional government of Iraq put in place right after the invasion. Dad had bitched about how much they'd fucked things up. I look hard at Tane. "You seem to know an awful lot about it."

Tane tugs on the ends of the towel around his neck. "Call it professional curiosity," he says. "It's a first-class fuck-up in accounting. Careless."

I'm all about interrogating Tane to better understand his professional curiosity—and what exactly his profession is—when a thought hits me. "Ethan, why did Finn get in touch with you now? Dad's been dead for years."

Ethan shakes his head. "I don't know. I just told him I didn't know what he was talking about, and he told me . . ." Ethan hesitates again.

"*What?*"

"He told me to talk to my sister," he says.

That tuning fork in my chest is now thrumming. "He told you to talk to *me*? Why?"

Ethan lifts his hands. "I don't know. He said he'd be in touch."

"Shit." I go to the window and try to see outside. It's all black.

"What?" Ethan says.

I cup my hands around my eyes and peer out the window at the front yard. Other than the footlights that illuminate the front walk, I see nothing. "You haven't seen him since?" I ask.

"No."

"When was this?"

"I don't know. Tuesday, maybe. Yeah, last Tuesday night."

"Hey," Tane says. "Is something wrong?"

Down at the end of the driveway I see movement, but it's a car driving by. "You notice any new cars in the neighborhood the past couple of days? Cars you've never seen before, parked on the street, maybe following you to school?"

Tane looks like a definition of confusion. "Who are you people?"

Ethan shakes his head. "I'm not in the habit of checking out every car that's parked on the street."

"I am," I say. I step away from the window and unzip my leather jacket, although I refrain from checking the revolver at the small of my back. My brother hates guns, and I don't want to freak him out any more than I have to.

Tane, of course, opens his mouth. "You've got a gun, right?"

Ethan stares at Tane, then me. "A gun?"

"It's a revolver, not a machine gun. Don't get your panties all twisted." I move to the kitchen. "Gonna take a look around. Just stay inside." Before Ethan can respond, I slip out the back door, closing it softly behind me.

Outside the night is still humid, the air close. Sweat beads at my hairline. Next door, Gene and Tony's yard is bathed in spotlights, their house lit up like the spaceship in *Close Encounters of the Third Kind*. Dad loved that movie, the mystery and the sense of wonder at the heart of it. When we watched it with Dad, Ethan talked about camera angles and movement, the physics of filmmaking, but I just snuggled next to our father and watched, wide-eyed and swept up in the story.

And now Dad is dead and my brother and I now have to deal with a different story in which Dad is a thief. I don't know if the story is true or not, but I intend to find out. Starting with finding out who this Finn guy is.

I make my way into the thin strip of woods behind the houses on this street. The woods are in shadow, but the lights from Gene and Tony's house allow me to see the drainage ditch that runs through the trees. I step over the ditch and walk a few yards through the woods until I reach the backyard of the house behind my brother's, on the other side of the block. This house is dark, no exterior lights, and I hurry through the yard to the driveway and then to the street. No lights come on, no one shouts or calls out a warning—all the good citizens are asleep. I turn left and walk down the street, sticking to the sidewalk for now. Most of the houses here are dark as well, an occasional light glowing over a front door.

The road curves to the left and dead-ends into Ethan's street. His house is to the left, a few lots up. Thankfully the nearest streetlight is maybe forty yards away, and at this street corner someone planted a row of hedges that's now overgrown and gives me a place where I can crouch and surveil the area. I wish I had my night vision binoculars, but after a minute my eyes adjust. Ethan's street runs arrow-straight about a quarter of a mile until it hits Roswell Road, and I have a straight line of sight down virtually the entire length of it. There isn't a single car parked on the street, although several are sitting in driveways. A stranger wouldn't park in someone's driveway to surreptitiously watch Ethan's house, not without risking a 9-1-1 call from a homeowner or a neighborhood-watch-type citizen, eager to report an imagined crime. So if someone is keeping eyes on Ethan's house, they'd be doing it from somewhere hidden, behind heavy undergrowth, or maybe from a garage or storage shed.

Slowly I walk up the street, swiveling my head from left to right. A fuzzy blue light shines through the front window of one house—someone is up late watching TV. Up ahead, Gene and Tony's house blazes in the night, and from this angle I can't see Ethan's house. The other houses are dark. Across the street looms a monstrous pile of wooden framing wrapped in Tyvek, a new mansion that's far too big for its narrow lot. From at least a block away I hear the distant bark of a dog, along with the muted sounds of traffic on Roswell. Otherwise, the street is as silent as a tomb.

I'm two lots down from Ethan's driveway when the back of my neck prickles and I casually step off the street and into someone's front yard where I'm at least partially hidden by a squat Japanese maple. It's a sensation I tend to trust—I'm being watched. No cars are passing; I see no one on the street in either direction. Maybe a nosy neighbor is peeking out a window and moved a blind to see better.

Then the house under construction draws my eye again. It's catty-corner across from Ethan's house, and the upstairs windows would have a perfect view of Ethan's driveway, maybe even his front yard. I squint and peer into the darkness. Nothing is moving in the windows. But that prickling doesn't go away.

I cross the street and slowly make my way up to the construction site, trying to keep hidden as much as possible behind garbage cans and trees. My eyes are glued to the front of the house. No movement, nothing. The driveway to the house, a trail of concrete gleaming in the night, leads around the back. I hurry down it, hoping no lights flash on and pin me to the wall like a prison searchlight.

The backyard is muddy and strewn with debris, and there is what looks like the beginnings of a back porch that's framed and roofed but has no walls, only clear plastic sheeting. I slip between two of the sheets onto the porch. The air is still and hot and cloying. Before me is a framed open doorway in the back wall of the house where the builder clearly intends to put in a set of double doors. I step through the gaping hole into the house, all senses tingling now. The light, already dim, grows dimmer. Inside the air is dusty and dry as an oven, and I breathe slowly through my open mouth to minimize the chance that I'll sneeze. Almost as an afterthought I unholster my five-shot revolver and hold it low in a two-handed grip.

Slowly I creep through a massive space that will probably be a great room at the back of the house. I'm aiming for what I think is the front hallway, where there should be a set of stairs. The darkness and the skeletal frames of the walls, some of which are covered in Sheetrock, turn the inside of the house into a maze. I nearly run into frames twice, once blundering into what I suspect is a bathroom—two pipes sticking up from the concrete floor like PVC stubs—and once almost stumbling through an open doorway. Around me the house is silent but watchful, as if waiting to see what I will do next. I hold my revolver low but ready to bring to bear on any target. I hear nothing, but that prickling sense doesn't go away. Somebody is in here, or has been recently.

My shins hit a short stack of lumber lying in shadow halfway across a hallway, hard enough to make me bite my lip to keep from crying out, but otherwise making hardly any noise. I step around the lumber and into the front hall, a set of stairs leading up. Light from Gene and Tony's house shines through the front windows, turning the inside of this house into streaks of light and shadow. The two front rooms off the foyer are empty, so I creep up the stairs into the dark, crouched and holding my revolver in front of me like an unlit flashlight.

At the upstairs landing I look both ways down a long corridor that runs the length of the house. I'm interested in the front of the house, particularly the first room on my left, which would have the best view of Ethan's driveway and house across the street. I step to the outside of the framed doorway, then crouch and pivot, the revolver pointing into the room. It's empty. Smoothly I stand and step through the doorway, scanning the room. Nothing moves. There are two windows in the front wall. I walk toward them, careful not to expose myself to anyone watching outside. Near the closest window I stop and crouch. It's hard to tell, but it looks like the Sheetrock dust on the floor has been disturbed, as if someone had been standing or sitting here. And then I see a Coke can sitting on the windowsill. There are still beads of condensation on the outside of the can.

I don't even hear him. One second I'm staring at the Coke can, and the next an arm snakes around my neck. Reflexively I raise my hands, trying to point the revolver back and behind me at my attacker. The man jams his hip into the small of my back, angling me away from him. The revolver is torn from my hand and thumps to the floor. My hands scrabble at the man's elbow, now jammed underneath my chin. A vise starts squeezing my neck, a forearm on one side, bicep on the other. Classic sleeper hold. He's not trying to crush my windpipe—he's trying to restrict blood flow to my brain. I kick wildly, trying to find purchase, but he's leaning back and lifting me up on my toes. Everything starts swimming in my vision. It usually takes ten seconds for a victim of a sleeper hold to pass out. That's my last conscious thought before everything goes black.

I SLOWLY SWIM up to consciousness and open my eyes to darkness. My throat aches like one big swollen bruise. I cough and spit, making sure my airway is clear. It is. I sit up, taking my time. I'm in the same room where I passed out, everything dark except for the light from the street leaching in through the window. The room is spinning like I just stepped off a carnival ride, one of those swirling octopus-arm things bolted together by a sullen, resentful guy with a beer gut and a general antipathy toward human beings, women specifically. On the plus side, I'm not tied up or dead.

I lean forward and place both palms on the floor, bracing myself as I will the room to stop moving. As soon as it does, I get to my feet. Whoever attacked me—and I'm willing to bet a thousand bucks his name is Finn—is long gone. I find my S&W on the floor. It feels light so I check the cylinder. Empty. A black, oily anger rises in me. The son of a bitch unloaded my revolver and took my bullets.

I go the window to glance outside. That's when I notice that the Coke can is gone, but in its place are four bullets, standing neatly in a row. He left me four bullets and took one, a final *fuck you*. My hands tremble ever so slightly as I pick up the bullets and reload my revolver. But beneath my mounting rage runs a smaller but brighter thread, like a seam of precious ore in rock. It takes me a moment to realize that it's fear.

WHEN I WALK back into Ethan's house, Wilson yips and then dances around my feet. "Good boy," I say, rubbing behind his ears.

Ethan lurches up off the couch in the den. "What time is it," he says, rubbing his face. "Where were you?"

"Getting choked out in the house across the street." My voice is tight with anger even as I scratch Wilson's belly.

Ethan sinks back down onto the couch as I tell him what happened. When I finish, he says, "I need to call Frankie."

"No," I say. "Not yet."

"Why not? This guy attacked you."

I stand and stretch my neck one way, then the other. It's sore, but I'll live. "He didn't shoot me, or even really hurt me." It costs me something to say that, but it's the truth.

"No, he just squeezed your neck until you passed out. And if he got the drop on you, then he's dangerous."

"Thanks for the backhanded compliment," I say. "Seriously, he could have done anything to me, and he didn't. He just wanted to send a message that he's for real, but he also doesn't want us dead. He just doesn't want to talk at gunpoint." And then I sit up suddenly, my nerves frazzled but pinging away. "Where's Tane?"

"Passed out on my bed. Guy was falling asleep on his feet. You take the couch. I'll go back to my room. It's a king-sized bed, he won't even know I'm there."

I want to argue for form's sake, but a wave of fatigue rolls over me, dragging me in its wake. "'Kay," I manage. "We'll go see Uncle Gavin tomorrow, yeah?"

Ethan nods, then surprises me by giving me a hug, and I surprise myself by hugging him back. He holds onto me for a few seconds, then releases me and goes back to his bedroom. Wilson looks after him, looks at me, then announces his decision by walking over to his corner bed in the den. He yawns, pads around in a circle on his bed, and flops down.

I'm too tired to even change out of my clothes, but I put my S&W in its pancake holster on the coffee table within arm's reach. Then I lie down on the couch and pull a throw blanket over me, sinking like a stone into a black pool of sleep.

CHAPTER SEVEN

My dreams are hard and fragmented, like images or scenes flashed up on a screen: a bicycle, a long hallway, a forest covered in kudzu. The clearest image I have is of kneeling in a garden, pulling dead flowers out of the dirt.

I wake to sunlight streaming through the windows, the throw blanket snarled around my feet. I sit up and free my feet from the blanket. My neck is a little stiff and bruised, but nothing some yoga and coffee can't cure. Maybe I'll go for a run today. The morning is bright with possibility. My dream of pulling the dead flowers out of a garden has left me feeling oddly comforted. Dad used to garden—it was one of the few things we did together. Ethan always had his nose in a book, and Mom was usually busy grading papers or running errands, so I'd help Dad weed or spread mulch, as much as a seven-year-old could help.

Wilson, curled in his bed, opens a single eye to gaze at me, then sighs. "Who's a sleepyhead?" I say, grinning. Wilson's ears twitch, but then his eye drifts to a close.

There's a Post-it note from Ethan stuck on the TV, saying he's gone to work and to please take care of Wilson. It's signed: BE CAREFUL—ETHAN. I'm both touched by my brother's concern and annoyed that I didn't wake up when he came out of his room. Usually a single footstep brings me wide awake. I must have really needed the sleep.

Somebody knocks on the front door, four hard raps. Wilson, startled, barks and shoots out of his bed, making a beeline for the door. I glance around—no one else is in the den or the kitchen. Is Tane still asleep in my brother's room?

Whoever is outside knocks again, and Wilson gives off a fresh volley of barks. "Just a minute," I call out, then grab my revolver from the coffee table. Holding the revolver behind my leg, I crack open the front door just enough so I can block the doorway and keep Wilson from running outside.

Two people crowd the tiny front porch. One is a Black woman in a gray pantsuit and purple blouse, her hair a halo of highlighted brown curls. The other is White, a bald fireplug of a guy in a blue suit and red tie. The woman's face is calm, professional, a neutral mask. The man is all scowls and eyebrows—resentment wafts off him like a bad cologne. I know exactly what they are before they say a word.

"Ms. Faulkner?" the woman says.

"That's me," I say.

She holds up an ID. "I'm Special Agent Rondeau with the FBI. This is Agent Scott. We'd like to ask you a few questions."

I make a show of examining Special Agent Rondeau's ID, giving me time to scope the situation—what my old Krav Maga instructor, Jakob, a retired Israeli soldier, called a threat assessment. I learn a few things:

Agent Scott's jacket doesn't quite hide the bulge of a holster on his left hip. My guess is that's intentional—he wants everyone to know he's carrying.

If Special Agent Rondeau is carrying, it's probably in a pancake holster at her back. It makes me like her a little.

Their car, a silver Ford Fusion, sits in the driveway, the front grille a wide oval like the open mouth of a whale shark.

I don't see any other feds or anyone else in the front yard.

According to her ID, Special Agent Rondeau's first name is Alisha.

This all takes a good ten seconds, long enough for Agent Scott to scratch his neck irritably. Rondeau doesn't move a muscle. Meanwhile Wilson continues to whine and bark, jumping against my leg and trying to get outside so somebody new can scratch his belly.

"Okay, Special Agent Rondeau," I say. "How can I help you?"

She gives me a professional smile that could mean anything from *thank you* to *go to hell.* "May we come inside?"

I smile back. "You may not."

Agent Scott actually snorts like an annoyed bull.

"This is my brother's house," I say. "He's at work and isn't much of a housekeeper. Plus his dog is going bananas. Give me one second and I'll come outside." Before either of them can speak, I close the door and turn the deadbolt. "Hush," I say to Wilson, reaching down to pet him. He licks my hand, then whines at the front door. I put my revolver back in its holster on the coffee table, then place a *New Yorker* magazine over it. I slide my feet into my sneakers, and that's when Tane peeks out from the short hallway to my brother's room. He's in a T-shirt and boxers and looks decidedly uncaffeinated—his mop of hair is a tangled mess and his eyes are puffy with sleep. Before he can say a word, I cross the room and put my hand over his mouth. His eyes widen slightly, then go even wider when I lean in close to whisper in his ear. "FBI at the door," I say, barely above a breath.

Tane rears back, my hand still over his mouth, and shakes his head emphatically. I nod, remove my hand from his mouth, and point back to the bedroom. He vanishes. My palm is moist from Tane's mouth and I wipe it on my leg. Then I go through the kitchen and out the back door, leaving Wilson inside.

I walk down the driveway to the front yard, whistling a Dirt Plow song so I don't startle the Feebies. I also take the chance to look around and confirm that the house isn't surrounded by a SWAT team. It's already warm, the sky a summer blue that promises heat and afternoon rain.

Both Feebies are still on the front porch and turn toward me as I walk, still whistling, around the corner of the house. Agent Scott's hands are on his hips like he's the angry assistant principal in a bad sitcom and I'm the wayward student. I smile and wave. "Sorry. Had to take care of the dog and put some shoes on."

The Feebies come down the steps, Special Agent Rondeau first and Agent Scott following, and we meet on the front walk. Without preamble, Rondeau reaches into a jacket pocket and produces a photograph. "Have you seen this man, Ms. Faulkner?" she says, handing me the photo.

I take the photo and look at it and see Tane Kamaka standing on a stage in front of a curtain, a plastic ID on a lanyard around his neck. It's not a bad picture of Tane, actually. He's wearing chinos and a navy button-down and smiling like he doesn't have a care in the world.

"Nope," I say. "Don't know him."

Rondeau doesn't blink. "Please look carefully, Ms. Faulkner."

"I did. Never seen him before. What'd he do, rob a bank?"

Agent Scott apparently cannot contain himself any longer. "We know you know Kamaka."

"Not in this time line," I say.

Scott tilts his head slightly. "Come again?"

"Never mind. I do not know anyone named Tane Kamaka."

Scott smiles, a smug curling of the lips. "Then how do you know his first name is Tane?" he says. "We didn't mention it."

I blink slowly and look down at the picture in my hand. It's all I can do not to gape open-mouthed like a kid busted for lying. Agent Scott falls for it. Just as his smile widens, I hold the picture out to him. "Because the guy in this picture is wearing an ID that says Tane Kamaka." I shrug. "Kind of figured it out from that."

Scott scowls, which does little to improve his appearance. Rondeau's face remains calm and neutral, but I swear for a second something passes across her eyes, like the beginning of a smile. I'm suddenly aware of how attractive Alisha Rondeau is, of her smooth skin and athletic build, her curly highlighted hair. Something flutters in my chest like champagne bubbles rising. Jesus, now I'm getting hot and bothered by a Feebie.

Agent Scott is hot and bothered in a different kind of way. He snatches the photo out of my hand. "You'd better be sure, *Miz* Faulkner," he says.

"Thanks for the *miz*," I say. "That's practically feminist of you. And I'm sure."

Scott isn't ready to let it go. "Lying to a federal agent is a crime. Not that your family would be all that worried about it. Especially your uncle."

Everything pinballing around in my head slows and then goes still. "Excuse me?"

He eyeballs me. "I heard he was in the hospital. That's a shame."

The icy calm in my head evaporates and anger churns in me like lava. That smug curl of Agent Scott's lips reappears—he knows he's scored a point. I'm not surprised the feds have an eye on Uncle Gavin. But Scott's contempt is more than a public display of general assholery. It runs deeper than that. It almost seems personal.

Slowly I smile, although it doesn't reach my eyes. "Agent Scott, right?" I say. "So Scott's your last name? I hope so. It'd be kind of silly if it were your first name. Like Agent Tommy. That wouldn't exactly strike fear into the hearts of criminals. It'd be sort of embarrassing."

I know at least half a dozen ways to incapacitate an attacker, some more painful and damaging than others. I review all of them as Agent Scott's face turns blotchy with anger. Ethan has accused me of pushing people too far. Looks like I've done it again. Scott actually shifts his stance as if preparing to reach out and grab me.

Rondeau steps to his side. "Agent Scott," she says, and there is steel beneath her calm. She takes the photo from his hand.

Scott glares at her, then straightens, his shoulders relaxing a fraction. But he's not happy about it. He doesn't like his partner, that's clear, but whether it's because she's a woman or she's Black or for some other reason, I don't know. Something to file away for possible future use.

Special Agent Rondeau turns to me with that calm, professional gaze. "If you do happen to see this man," she says, "please call me. Any time, day or night." She hands me a business card, and as I take it I can smell her faint perfume, eucalyptus and oranges and cedar.

"You didn't answer my question about him," I say. "What did this guy do?"

"He's a person of interest," Rondeau says. "Have a good day, Ms. Faulkner."

"Susannah," I say. "Or Suzie, if you like."

Rondeau gives me a courteous smile, then walks past me so I get another whiff of her perfume. Agent Scott stalks after her, nearly brushing against me on the front walk. He smells like he's been dipped in pine tar. Need to change deodorants, my guy. I stand in the front yard, holding Rondeau's card and gazing after them as they get into their silver Ford. Scott is in the driver's seat. He cranks the engine and reverses down the driveway, the bumps and dips not doing the car's suspension any favors. He backs into the street and then peels off.

I continue standing in the front yard, thinking. Why is the FBI looking for Tane? How did they know I know him, or that I was at my brother's house? Did they guess I'd be here and got lucky? Again I look around the yard but see no one. And why did Agent Scott seem so pissed off about Uncle Gavin?

After a few moments I walk back up the driveway and go through the back door into the kitchen, where Wilson greets me, tail wagging happily. I let him out into the backyard, where he runs into the small patch of grass and pees, then runs back into the house and looks at me like I should be proud. "Good boy," I say, closing the door. "Tane!" I call out. "They're gone." I walk into the den, Wilson trotting at my heels. "Tane!" Nothing. I imagine him hiding under Ethan's bed and go down the hall to the bedroom. "Tane?"

He's not under the bed, or anywhere in the bedroom or the bathroom or the spare bedroom, which is really Ethan's storage room. There's nowhere for him to hide in the den. "*Shit*," I say, causing Wilson to look at me in alarm. Tane has clearly skedaddled. He must have gone out the back while I was talking to the Feebies. And then I see my duffel bag on the floor where I left it, but now it's unzipped. I rummage through it. Son of a bitch took some of my cash. None of my other gear is missing from the bag. Then I look at the coffee table and see the *New Yorker* that I'd placed over my revolver is now in a different place on the table. The revolver, of course, is gone. I burst out the kitchen door and look around the backyard, then into the trees I went through last night. There's no sign of him.

I spend half an hour looking for him, circling the block and jogging up and down Roswell Road. I talk to the people manning the cash registers at the three nearby gas stations, then question the staff at the Waffle House. I ask the Korean woman running the dry cleaners on the corner, the cashiers at the Kroger, even the two people on the sidewalk waiting for a MARTA bus. Nothing. Tane has vanished. By the time I walk back to Ethan's house, I'm good and pissed—at Tane, at the FBI, and at myself. I sit on the couch and think while Wilson watches me with worried eyes.

I'm good at finding people. But usually I have a few leads—place of business, last known residence, a credit card, a utility bill, ATM receipts, something. With Tane, I have two leads. One of them I'll see in the hospital with Ethan this afternoon. God knows if my uncle will be in any condition to talk, or if he'll be willing to say anything. Then again, he's the one who sent me to find Tane.

Which leaves me with my second lead—Peaches. And he almost definitely won't want to talk to me, especially if I try to crash his mother's house again.

His mother . . . I close my eyes and concentrate, shutting out any distractions. Mrs. Daniels said something last night, just before Peaches and his two goons shepherded me out onto her back porch . . . I open my eyes, remembering. Quickly I do a Google search on my phone and confirm what I thought. Then I call Caesar.

He picks up on the second ring. "Please save me from contractors."

"You clean?" I ask.

"I assume you're referring to my phone. And yes."

"Tane's gone. FBI showed up this morning looking for him, and he bailed while I was talking to the agents in the front yard."

Caesar is silent for a moment. "What do you want to do?"

"Can you come pick me up? I need a ride and want some backup."

"Give me an hour. Where are we going?"

I start digging through my duffel bag, looking for clean clothes. "To a ribbon-cutting ceremony," I say.

FIFTY MINUTES LATER Caesar rolls up the driveway in Frankie's car, a cobalt blue '71 Trans Am with a white racing stripe. Frankie and his father rebuilt it when Frankie was in high school, and since then Frankie has constantly tinkered with it, adding upgrades while maintaining its old-school, muscle-car charm. Ethan calls it the Frankenstein, a name that's both dumb and a little clever. Even though Ethan says a pool of oil forms underneath the Frankenstein every time it's parked, there is something viscerally pleasing about the rumble of the engine, the sense of power under the hood.

I leave Wilson inside the house with some extra kibble and lock the back door with a spare key Ethan keeps in his detached garage under a paint can. Then I get in the passenger seat of the Frankenstein, closing the door with a solid thunk. "Frankie must *really* like you if he lets you drive his car," I say.

Caesar grunts. "Had to put in a Bluetooth sound system for him. Only way he'd give me the keys. Where to?"

"A new rec center in Vine City. It opens today. There'll be speeches, probably some kids in their Sunday best standing for pictures, local press. Google says Li'l Whizz will be there."

Caesar reverses down the driveway. "And Peaches?"

"Last night his mother said she'd see him at the rec center today. Figure it's worth a shot."

Caesar backs out of the driveway, and I glance at the house under construction and see workers in jeans and hard hats. Finn won't be there anymore, but I still scan the windows. Then Caesar shifts into first and we drive down the street, leaving the construction site behind. The Frankenstein's V-8 lets us know it could go much faster than it is right now.

"You and Frankie said Li'l Whizz is a hip-hop singer?" I ask.

Caesar nods, then says, "Hey, Siri, play 'Alabaster' by Li'l Whizz."

There's a *bing* and then through the car speakers a familiar and unmistakable male voice says, "Playing 'Alabaster' by Li'l Whizz."

I stare at Caesar. "That was Samuel L. Jackson's voice."

Caesar keeps his eyes on the road as a hip-hop song starts playing, heavy beats and auto-tuned rapping.

"Caesar," I say, "why is Siri talking in Sam Jackson's voice?"

Caesar is quiet for a moment. "Frankie thought it would be cool," he finally says.

"Sure, if you want Nick Fury playing your music and telling you when to take a left."

"I hate it," Caesar mutters.

"This song? Or the fact that Mace Windu is the car's DJ?"

"I'm reprogramming it today."

"'Say "what" again, motherfucker!'"

Caesar glares at me. "If you quote another line from *Pulp Fiction* or anything else, you can get out and walk."

I hold my hands up in a sign of peace and we drive another mile, listening to Li'l Whizz sing about how his lady is pure like alabaster.

"This is more like trap music," I say. "All the snare drums and hi-hats."

"Thanks for whitesplaining trap for me," Caesar says. "Why do you care about finding this Tane so much?"

"Because my uncle wanted me to find him. And now I've lost him."

Caesar shrugs. "He skipped out on you. That's different."

"Still need to find him. He's involved with something big. The feds want him, and I'm hoping Peaches can tell me why."

Caesar is quiet for a few moments. "I just don't want to see you get hurt."

"You know I hunt down people for a living, right?"

His tone is flat and hard. "Not in the Bluff."

We drive in silence past Chastain Park. Sunlight filters through the trees. On the golf course, a guy in an aqua polo shirt whacks a ball down the fairway and watches it sail into the morning sky. Another beautiful day in suburbia.

I settle into my seat and look straight ahead. "A couple of weeks after Frankie went to prison," I say, "I found a newspaper article in Ethan's trash can. Had a mugshot of one of the men who came into my house the night my parents died, the one who fought with my dad. Sam Bridges. The article said Bridges had been arrested on a drug bust. The police were looking for his partner."

"Ponytail," Caesar says. He knows Ponytail, or Donny Wharton, and has the scars to prove it.

"I didn't know at the time why Ethan had that article, or why he threw it away. I kept it. And I decided I would find Ponytail."

"You were, what, fifteen?"

"Old enough to know I didn't know anything about how to track down somebody like him. So I waited. Kept that article under my pillow like a love letter. Took self-defense classes and learned how to shoot a pistol. Ran cross-country to get in shape. Even shadowed a PI for a day the summer before my senior year, learned about surveillance and skip tracing. The day I graduated from high school, I went to Uncle Gavin and showed him that article. He said he'd told Ethan he knew where both Bridges and Ponytail were, asked what he wanted him to do."

Caesar stops at an intersection and lets an old couple walk across in front of the Frankenstein. "You mean he was asking if Ethan wanted them killed," he says.

I stare at the old couple, both wearing enormous walking shoes like life rafts for their feet. The woman holds onto the man's arm. The man raises a hand in thanks to Caesar. "Ethan said no," I say. "Which he should have. If Uncle Gavin had had them killed on Ethan's word, Ethan wouldn't have been able to live with it." I took a breath, let it out. "But I could."

The old couple finally makes it across the street and Caesar drives through the intersection. "So you told your uncle you'd do it," he says.

"Uncle Gavin had Bridges arrested, but Ponytail got away from the cops. I said I'd find him. I was pretty clear what I wanted to do to him. Told my uncle I wanted his help but I'd do it without him if I had to."

Caesar takes a long curve smoothly, palming the steering wheel. "What'd he say?"

"He took me for a drive in his big old Lincoln Navigator. It was dark, after nine o'clock. I thought he wanted to talk alone in the car while he drove around, but he didn't say anything except tell me to put my phone and my wallet on the dash. I did." I wait a beat. "He drove me to the Bluff. Parked right outside the house where Luco Stevens raped me, where Frankie shot him on the front steps. I was pissed. Why take me there, of all places? He looked at me, wearing that stupid flat cap of his, and said, 'This is where the second worst thing in your life happened. And now you want to run off and track down the man responsible for the very worst thing that happened to you?'"

I pause. We roll past a series of mansions set back from the road, front lawns the size of soccer fields.

Caesar says, "What did you do?"

"Got out of the car and slammed the door and told him to fuck off."

Caesar smiles. "Bet he didn't like that."

"He rolled down the window and said, 'I'll be waiting for you at the bar.' And he drove away."

Caesar brings the Frankenstein to a stop at another intersection and turns to stare at me, his smile gone.

"Took me two hours to walk to Ronan's," I say. "I had to hide a few times, fight off one dude who tried to grab me. My uncle left me alone in the Bluff, at night, with no phone and no money, as a test. To see if I could make it out on my own. And I did. So going to a rec center in the Bluff in broad daylight is not going to hurt me."

Caesar's hands tighten around the steering wheel, but he says nothing, just drives.

CHAPTER EIGHT

T HE VINE CITY REC CENTER IS A LOW, WHITEWASHED STUCCO building with yellow and green trim behind a cinder-block wall topped with ornamental spikes. Balloons tied to the open front gates bob in the breeze. A banner that reads WELCOME TO YOUR NEW REC CENTER! hangs above the double front doors, which are closed. Caesar pulls into one of the last open spaces in the parking lot to the right of the main building. I see local news vans from 11Alive and Fox 5. At the back of the lot, a tent provides shade to a crowd gathered before a stage, where a man in a gray suit and bright pink tie is emphatically waving his arms as he speaks. Next to the tent are foldout tables loaded down with lidded foil pans and stacks of paper plates and sweating pitchers of iced tea and water covered in plastic wrap to keep the flies off.

Caesar and I get out of the Frankenstein and make our way to the back of the crowd. There are easily a couple hundred people here. Aside from a handful of TV reporters, I'm the only white face under the tent. That will make it easier for Peaches to see me, which I'm fine with. And just as I think of him, I spot Peaches on one side of the stage. In his pin-stripe suit, Peaches looks like a respectable gangster. He is standing with a handful of other people, including what I think at first is a child in a red suit, a white flat cap, and sunglasses. Then I realize it must be Li'l Whizz.

He's all of four feet tall. Behind him, two enormous men dressed all in black stand with their feet planted and hands clasped before them, like ushers waiting for their collection plates.

The man in the gray suit and pink tie is working up a sweat as he talks, praising the work of various people in getting the new rec center off the ground. "And I would be remiss," he says, his voice carrying easily without a microphone, "if I did not thank Mr. Antoine Daniels for his persistent patronage of this facility."

"Nice alliteration," I say to Caesar as the crowd applauds, Peaches nodding and smiling in acknowledgment.

"That's Reverend Darby," Caesar says, indicating the man in the gray suit and pink tie. "He preaches at Mount Zion Baptist over on Griffin."

"How do you know him?"

"I went to church there when I was a kid."

"I thought your family lived down in East Point."

"They do. We moved out of Vine City when I was a teenager."

He answers easily enough, but there's something in his voice, a troubled undercurrent. He continues to watch Reverend Darby onstage, his face a placid mask. He glances at me, then returns his attention to the reverend. "The church wasn't so welcoming when I got older."

"Because you're gay?"

"That and the fact I went to prison for attempted murder."

"You were protecting your sister," I say. "Her husband was beating the shit out of her, he deserved to get chucked out a window. And I thought churches were all into the whole forgiveness-of-sins thing."

Caesar shrugs, his eyes still on the reverend. "To err is human, to forgive divine," he says. "Let's just say Mt. Zion is all too human."

Before I can say anything else, Li'l Whizz takes the mic. The crowd whistles and cheers. His voice is both high-pitched and gravelly, like Bugs Bunny with a two-pack-a-day habit. "Let's give it up for Reverend Darby," the hip-hop star says. The crowd applauds and Reverend Darby closes his eyes and smiles, shaking his head. Off to the side, Peaches is ushering some teens onto the stage. They form two ragged clumps, the boys trying not to look nervous and the girls bumping into each other and giggling.

"When I was growing up on these streets," Li'l Whizz says in his high gravelly voice, "I got into all kinds of trouble. And it wasn't no good trouble, either." Laughter from the crowd. "I didn't have a place like this rec center to keep me on the straight and narrow. I got lucky with my music, found me a good place in life. But too many kids don't have that chance." He throws out his open hand toward the teens. "A place like this, it can change lives," he says. More applause, the teen girls joining in, the boys all solemn and unmoved, although I catch one of them hiding a smirk.

Li'l Whizz starts singing "Amazing Grace." In song his voice is transformed, smoothed out and powerful. The crowd joins in like a makeshift backup choir. I'm surprised when all the teens on stage join in. I catch Caesar's eye and nod my head to indicate the stage, then start making my way through the crowd, Caesar following. We head toward a set of steps at the left side of the stage. I spot Peaches's mother near the front row in a sleeveless green dress and a wide-brimmed white hat with enough flowers and bows to stock a gift shop. By the time Li'l Whizz finishes the song and the crowd erupts in applause and shouts of *Amen* and *Sing it brother*, I have made it to within ten feet of the steps.

"Let's eat, y'all," Li'l Whizz says, and the crowd shifts and turns its attention to the tables of food. Meanwhile, Li'l Whizz and his bodyguards come down the steps, followed by the teenagers, another man in dress pants and a yellow button-down, and then, finally, Peaches. The man in the yellow shirt is Billy. He's as huge as he was last night. Billy walks down the steps in front of Peaches, starts to scan the crowd, then sees me and comes to a dead stop on the bottom step. "Aw, hell no," he says.

Peaches, still coming down the steps, almost collides with Billy. "Man, what the—" Peaches says, then looks up and sees me. His face hardens.

I wave. "Hey, y'all," I say. "Your eyes better today, Billy?"

Billy snarls and takes a step toward me. Caesar moves between us. Billy stops, looks Caesar up and down, and sneers. "Nigga, get outta my face."

Billy is half a head taller than Caesar, but Caesar looks up at him calmly. "You get out of mine," he says.

"I wasn't trying to make fun of you," I say to Billy. "I was asking nicely. Pepper gel stings."

Peaches puts a hand on Billy's arm, and after a moment Billy takes a step back, his eyes angry and locked on Caesar. Peaches looks almost as angry as he takes me in. "What you doin' here?" he says.

"I need your help."

Peaches smiles, unpleasantly. "Ain't that a bitch. I'm all outta help. Especially for you."

"It's about Tane Kamaka."

"He's your problem now."

"Looks like the feds have a problem too. You want to talk to me, or to them?"

Mrs. Daniels shuffles up, another older lady holding her arm. Luckily her friend is short enough to duck underneath Mrs. Daniels's hat. "Antoine, we're going to get some food," Mrs. Daniels announces. Then she notices me and raises her head, her hat tilting precariously. "Miss Faulkner."

"Mrs. Daniels," I say. "Good to see you again."

She raises an eyebrow. "It's surprising to see you again."

Peaches's smile doesn't change, but he glances at his mother, then at the nearby teenagers, who are surrounding Li'l Whizz, and at the news reporters with cameramen behind them. "Mama, you go on, I'll be there in a little bit." To me he nods toward a side entrance to the rec center. "Inside."

THE INSIDE OF the rec center is new and clean and smells of fresh paint. It's also deserted. We sit in a windowless office off the main lobby. The office has a glass door and a desk and three chairs and nothing else.

Peaches sits behind the desk and puts his feet up on it. I take one of the chairs in front of the desk. Billy and Caesar stand in opposite corners of the room and eye-dagger each other.

"I don't like being threatened," Peaches says.

I raise my hands in a shrug. "I'm not threatening." I look at Caesar. "Was I threatening?"

"You did mention the feds," Caesar says, keeping his eyes on Billy.

"That's not a threat," I say to Peaches. "I'm not sending them your way. But they're looking for Tane. They came to my brother's house this morning and showed me a picture of him, asked me if I knew him."

"What you tell them?"

"I lied and said I never met the man. And while I was talking with them, Tane bolted. He's gone. So now I have to find him."

Peaches shakes his head. "Sounds like you in a world of trouble."

"I'm touched by your concern."

"Ain't no concern. Like I said, it's your problem. What you gonna do, call the feds and say, 'Officers, go talk to the big bad Black man, I don't know nothin''? Please."

I stifle a sigh. If there was a way to bottle all the energy men used to posture and puff out their chests, I could run the entire planet with it. "Antoine, I know your mama is smart, so maybe you got dropped on your head when you were a child. It's *our* problem, yours and mine. How did the feds know I had Tane in the first place? Who knew he was with me? Who saw him with me?"

I sit back in my chair and watch Peaches figure it out. His eyes narrow.

"You think one of mine told them," he says.

"Unless you did."

"The fuck would I do that for?"

"Then you have a mole, Peaches. Somebody told the feds they saw Tane Kamaka ride off on a motorcycle with me."

Peaches looks up at the ceiling, thinking. "Who were the feds came to your brother's house?"

"Special Agent Alisha Rondeau and Agent Scott. Rondeau is a Black woman. Scott's a bald White guy who seemed extremely pissed about everything."

Peaches brings his gaze back down from the ceiling. "I know Scott," he says.

"How do you know him?"

Peaches smiles. This one isn't unpleasant; it's the smile of someone who's pulled off an impressive magic trick. "Who you think I took Tane away from?"

"You . . . *stole* Tane from the FBI?"

From his corner, Billy says, "Peaches don't play."

"Start from the beginning," I say. "Start with my uncle."

Peaches takes a long breath, then lets it out slowly. "Your uncle and me, we do business from time to time. I provide services for him, and sometimes he lets me know things so I can avoid future problems. But this time, he wanted something big."

"Tane Kamaka," I say.

Peaches nods. "And he was willing to pay. Had to pay a lot. Wanted me to bust him out of federal custody."

"You had to break him out of *prison*?"

"He wasn't in no prison. Federal custody, I said. Like witness protection. Scott had him in a motel down in College Park."

"Why was Tane in witness protection?"

"Your uncle said he saw something."

"Saw something?"

"Something *los Sureños* didn't want him to see. A group of them, anyway."

Sureños 13 again. They keep coming up. Why would my uncle be involved with a prison gang run by the Mexican Mafia? I look at Caesar, who gives me a tiny shrug. He doesn't know, either. "What do you mean, a group of them?" I ask.

"A new one trying to move into Atlanta. Run by a man goes by Bala. They ain't welcome."

Like lots of gangs, the Sureños have been in Georgia for years now. But also like lots of gangs, they're not a tightly knit group organized on a national level. They operate in loosely affiliated cells spread out all over the country. Sometimes those cells even fight each other, except in prison, or if the *jefes* in Mexico put a stop to it.

"I heard you took out a few Sureños this spring," I say. "They work for this Bala?"

"They did."

"They retaliate yet?"

Peaches cracks his neck. "Not yet. But we ready for them." In his corner, Billy grunts in agreement.

"So Tane saw something illegal and the feds were protecting him?" I ask. "Was he going to testify against the Sureños? Why would my uncle want you to grab him?"

Peaches shrugs. "He didn't tell me."

"My uncle wanted you to kidnap somebody from under the nose of the FBI, and you didn't ask why?"

"I asked. He wouldn't say, just paid me a lot of cash."

"And you trust my uncle?"

Peaches laughs. "I don't trust no one that much. But your uncle always has reasons. Plays a long game, know what I'm saying? He don't want the Sureños here any more than I do."

I shake my head. This doesn't make sense. Why kidnap Tane? What had Tane seen? And if Tane was going to testify against the Sureños, and my uncle didn't want the Sureños to establish a bigger foothold in Atlanta, why keep Tane from testifying against them in court? Unless Tane knew something else my uncle didn't want to come out in court. Or he couldn't wait for a trial that could take a long time. Or he needed Tane to tell him something before he told the feds. Or a bunch of other possible reasons.

"You said Tane was under witness protection," I say. "That's the U.S. Marshals, not the FBI."

Peaches shrugs again. "I said it was *like* witness protection. Buncha feds with guns hiding a dude in a motel room. What's the difference?"

Another thought teases me from behind a wall of fog. I can't see it clearly, just the blurred outlines. *The FBI, not the U.S. Marshals.* It matters, but why? I feel like a child trying to grab a balloon floating just beyond reach.

"How'd you do it?" I ask. "Snatch Tane?"

Peaches grins. "It was D's idea."

"D?"

"Guy you hit over the head with your fancy baton. Gave him a concussion."

He means Dreadlocks. "Is he okay?"

"He be a'ight. So the feds have two motel rooms next to each other. Both rooms got old-ass A/C units. Now D's momma used to work as a motel maid, he grew up helping her clean rooms and shit. He knows how easy it is to fuck up the A/C, just cut a line in a hose or coil or whatever. He does that outside one room with a pair of pliers, takes five seconds. The A/C dies. A motel room in Atlanta in June with no A/C? Pretty soon the feds inside are sweating, call the front desk for a repairman. D already at the front desk, pays the manager to tell the feds he's sending someone up right now. D goes up there in a old jumpsuit carrying a box of tools, looks like a repairman. The two feds let him in the room, D pulls out a piece from his toolbox and covers them while Billy and the rest of the crew come in. They knock out the feds, go through the connecting door into the next room where Tane is, and surprise the other two. They tie them all up and drive off with Tane." His grin widens. "Whole thing took like two minutes. Didn't even have to pull a trigger."

"Let me guess who the agent in charge was."

"One bald-headed asshole named Kevin Scott." Peaches takes his feet off the desk and plants them on the floor. "Billy said the dude was *pissed* when they tied him up. He lucky they didn't put a pillow over his face and shoot him in the back of the head. We took Tane to the airport right then to hand him off to your uncle. When he didn't show, we came back here. Then you rode up on your motorcycle like the girl-with-the-dragon-whatever, and you know the rest."

I don't know the rest, not by a long fucking shot, but I know more than I did earlier. No wonder Agent Scott was pissed, having his prisoner snatched right out of his hands. But none of this tells me where to find Tane. "And you have no idea where Tane might be now?" I ask.

"Nope. I'm more interested in who told the feds about your ass." Peaches stands. "And I intend to find the fuck out."

I stand, not to measure up to Peaches but because it looks like our meeting is over. "Did my uncle tell you where Tane lives?"

"Nope," Peaches says again. "But with his last name, I'm guessing a Pacific island." He nods at Billy, who glares once more at Caesar and then follows his boss out of the room. I listen to their footsteps recede, followed by the side door to the outside opening and then closing.

"Now what?" Caesar asks.

I slowly clench and unclench my fists. I don't feel especially like punching anything; the physical action calms me. And I need to be calm to figure out what's next. I look at my cheap burner phone and see it's a few minutes before noon. I have to be at the hospital at one o'clock.

"Can you drop me off at Ronan's?" I ask.

CHAPTER NINE

Caesar drops me by the service door to Ronan's and then drives off to meet with a bunch of contractors at his and Frankie's loft.

Uncle Gavin named his bar after Cill Rónáin, the village where he and my mother were born. Cill Rónáin is on Inis Mór, one of the Aran Islands off the west coast of Ireland. Today the town and island are called by their anglicized names, Kilronan and Inishmore, but growing up in Uncle Gavin's house, Ethan and I learned the original Irish names. When it came to naming his bar, though, Uncle Gavin went with Ronan's because he wanted his customers to be able to pronounce it.

Ronan's is on West Peachtree in Midtown and looks pretty much like a bar that also serves food—plate-glass windows, dark green trim, the daily specials etched on a chalkboard, a long bar with a brass footrail and high-back bar stools, a scattering of tables, booths along two walls, a dart board in a corner. Ethan worked here after school for a few years, washing dishes and running errands for Uncle Gavin, which is how he met Frankie. As a teenager I spent less time here than my brother did, occasionally picking up a shift for someone, but mostly I sat in a back booth, drinking an endless supply of lemonade or Coke and ostensibly doing homework.

Most importantly, I learned how to watch and listen, fading into the background, and I figured out early on that the business that went on at Ronan's wasn't all about selling beer and burgers.

The service door is off the tiny lot to the side of the bar, a lot that holds a dumpster and two parking spots, one for Uncle Gavin and one for Frankie. Usually Uncle Gavin's Navigator is parked here, but Frankie retrieved it from the airport yesterday and left it at Uncle Gavin's house in Grant Park. The parking space is empty now except for an oil stain and a couple of weeds growing out of a crack in the asphalt. It's wrong that my uncle's SUV isn't parked there. I turn my back on the empty space and face the service door. The door is an ugly, scarred thing that looks like it's been beaten and kicked more than a few times. But it feels solid enough when I bang on it with my open palm.

The door swings inward to reveal a huge man with no neck and a shaved head, wearing an ill-fitting suit. He looks me up and down. "If you don't got a delivery, fuck off."

"My name's Susannah Faulkner," I say. "My uncle owns this bar."

The man blinks, then smiles crookedly. "Sorry 'bout that, Miss Faulkner. Didn't recognize you. I'm Gus. I work for Mr. Shaw."

Johnny Shaw is Uncle Gavin's lawyer, who wears seersucker suits and likes it when people mistake him for an old coot, right before he cuts them off at the knees. Gus is his driver-slash-bodyguard, has been forever. Ethan once said Gus reminded him of Luca Brasi in *The Godfather*, big and a little slow but loyal. I've only seen Gus two or three times in my life, and always sitting behind the wheel of a car.

"You moonlighting for Uncle Gavin now?" I say.

"Mr. Gutierrez needed some help," Gus says. He means Frankie. I doubt Frankie hired Gus to wait tables, unless he wants to scare off the customers. If his size alone wouldn't intimidate you, his too-tight jacket shows the bulge of a shoulder holster.

"Come in, come in." Gus steps back out of the doorway, holding the door open with a hand the size of a dinner plate. He's so big I have to squeeze past him into the hallway. But I notice how his eyes rake the lot outside before he shuts the door and throws a dead bolt.

The hallway is the same as always—wood floor worn smooth, the smell of beer and fried onion rings and some kind of orange-scented industrial cleaner. Gus lumbers down the hall behind me as I pass the bathrooms and a couple of doors that lead to private rooms. Then I'm through a swinging door and past the stairwell that leads up to my uncle's office, and I walk into the kitchen. It's the lunch hour so the kitchen is humming. Two waitresses are shuttling in and out with service trays of sandwiches and hamburgers. A kid is spraying dirty plates and shoving them into a dishwasher. A woman wearing a hairnet stands in front of the stovetop, brandishing a spatula and cooking something in a sizzling pan.

"Mr. Gutierrez is out front," Gus says, meaning the dining room. "You can go upstairs and wait in the office, Miss Faulkner. I'll go tell him you're here."

I nod and turn toward the stairs, but then Gus clears his throat and I turn to look back at him.

"I just wanted to say I'm sorry," he says. "About your uncle. Mr. Lester's a tough old bird, though. He'll be okay."

I stare at Gus. He could probably take a chair to the head like it was a throw pillow. Except for a hint of sadness in his eyes, he looks about as comforting as a stone floor. He barely knows me. And yet his simple words thaw something in my chest. Maybe it's lack of sleep, or stress, or just the way Gus stands there looking earnest and slightly uncomfortable, but I step forward and put my arms around his very large body and lean my head against his chest in a hug. He goes very still, then awkwardly pats me on the back. It feels like being gently pawed by a gorilla. After a moment I let go and step back and smile at him. He returns the smile. Then I head upstairs to my uncle's office.

At the top of the stairs, off a short hallway with a faded carpet runner, is the door to the office. It's closed, and I put my hand on the doorknob.

Ethan and I never hung out in the office with our uncle. It was his workplace, off limits except by invitation, and those didn't come often.

I turn the knob and open the door. Inside, the office looks like it has always looked: a wall of bookshelves to the right, Oriental rug on the floor, a couple of upholstered chairs, and to the left a mammoth, claw-footed desk that even Gus would have trouble moving. The desk is littered with newspapers, file folders, loose sheets of paper, yellow legal pads, a tablet with a blank screen, a couple of ring-binder notebooks, and a mug half-filled with a brown liquid that is probably tea.

The first time I saw my uncle's desk, I was eleven, and I made fun of how messy it was. Uncle Gavin responded by telling me a story about Albert Einstein, whose own desk was famously messy. According to Uncle Gavin, someone once asked the famous scientist if a cluttered desk was a sign of a cluttered mind. Einstein replied by saying if that were true, then what was an empty desk a sign of? I learned later that quote was probably fictitious, and part of me wanted to say so to Uncle Gavin, but I realized it wouldn't matter. The facts might be wrong, but the point of the story itself, that the state of one's desk doesn't reflect his or her intelligence, was true. And I understood, even then, how important the stories we tell ourselves are, even when they aren't completely accurate.

Behind the desk is my uncle's chair, dark blue leather with wooden armrests. It always creaks when he sits in it. Seeing his empty chair is worse than seeing his empty parking space. I walk around the desk and lower myself into the chair. It tilts back beneath me. *Creak.*

Frankie comes through the open door, wearing a tomato-red shirt and black jeans. He stops when he sees me sitting behind my uncle's desk. I stand up quickly, the chair creaking and rolling back on its wheels. "Hey," I say.

"Hey," Frankie says. "You holding up okay?"

"Yeah, I'm okay." I step around the desk. "You?"

Frankie puffs his cheeks, lets out a breath. "I've got a bar tap that's broken, a dinner cook who just called in sick, and a cooler full of salmon

I have to sell this week before it starts to stink." He gives me a wan smile. "The usual."

"And the rest?" I ask. Meaning the other business.

Frankie runs a hand through his black hair. "That's more complicated."

"I saw Gus Cimino downstairs."

"Yeah, Johnny Shaw sent him over this morning."

"Why?"

"Because the sharks are circling." Frankie glances at Uncle Gavin's empty chair. "The people your uncle does business with are nervous. They want to know what happens next. And, forgive me for saying this, but some people are acting like he's already dead."

"What people?"

Frankie frowns, his nostrils flaring with disgust. "Brandon Cargill, for one. Wants to know why he should have to keep paying a percentage to Mr. Lester. The *pendejo* actually called me this morning and asked if the bar was for sale."

Cargill is a nasty piece of work who runs a garage on Northside. My uncle isn't an honorable man—hell, he's a criminal—but he generally operates in a moral gray zone rather than dealing with the darkest parts of the world he inhabits, like child trafficking or murder-for-hire. Cargill, by contrast, would kill a baby if he could make a profit from it. Mostly he deals with stolen cars, but he's always looking for the next big score and doesn't really care what he has to do in order to grab it. And he resents my uncle.

"I can pay a visit to Cargill," I say.

Frankie shakes his head. "Thanks, but I've got it. I have Gus here for security. Cargill's a problem, but he's also a coward. And Caesar told me you've got your own problems right now. That Tane kid you found, he ran off?"

I nod. "With the FBI looking for him. Frankie, I know Uncle Gavin didn't tell you anything about Tane or what he was doing. But is there anything else you can think of? Anything with the feds or Sureños 13, or anything Uncle Gavin might have said or done that's out of the ordinary?"

Frankie hesitates. "Only thing I can think of is something your uncle said maybe a week or two ago, about some guns. Somebody was looking to buy a lot of guns."

"What kind of guns?"

"AR-15s, AKs."

Most street criminals want a cheap handgun, maybe a shotgun or an Uzi if they want more firepower. But Frankie's talking about assault rifles. "Either somebody's prepping for the zombie apocalypse," I say, "or they want to start a war. This somebody have a name?"

Frankie shakes his head. "I don't know who the buyer was, but Brandon Cargill wanted to broker the deal. Your uncle told him no, paid him ten grand *not* to do it. Mr. Lester didn't make a big stink about it, just mentioned the payment and what it was for. I only remember it because you and I were just talking about Cargill. But that's the only unusual thing I can think of recently."

Unusual enough. Especially paying someone *not* to set up an illegal arms sale. I might have to pay a visit to Cargill after all. But I don't see how that has anything to do with Tane Kamaka or where he might be. And before I do anything else, I have to go to the hospital. Maybe Uncle Gavin will answer all my questions.

And maybe the Falcons will win the Super Bowl.

I DON'T WANT to deal with lunchtime traffic, so I walk a block south to the Midtown MARTA station to take a train to Five Points in the heart of downtown. Essentially MARTA is a two-track system, one north–south line crossed by another running east–west, and while it's nothing compared to the metro systems in New York or D.C. or Boston, it works, if only because everyone in this city drives a car, so traffic clogs the highways and streets like cholesterol clogs arteries. Sure, there's the occasional angry homeless guy on the train, shouting about space lasers or microchip implants while the other passengers pretend they can't see or hear him, and that's uncomfortable for most people. But the trains tend to run on time and are relatively clean, and if your destination lies on one of the two lines and you don't mind walking a bit, you could do a lot worse than MARTA. Plus it's easy to follow people through MARTA stations without being seen, or to ditch people trying to follow you. I've done both in the past, so I almost don't know what to do with myself when I pass through the turnstiles at Midtown and take the escalator down, just one more passenger.

The decor in the Midtown station, at least below ground, is brutalist, concrete walls and platforms, the only pops of color coming from the station signage. But on the southbound platform where I wait for my train, there's a poster advertising a Van Gogh exhibit, with a painting of two cut sunflowers that look a bit like flaming stars against a cobalt blue background. I stare at the picture, which opens a door in my memory. One weekend when we were kids, Mom took Ethan to a soccer game while I stayed home with Dad. As soon as Mom backed down the driveway, Dad jumped out of his chair at the breakfast table. "We're going to Pike's," he said, referring to a large garden and plant store. "Gonna get some sunflowers to plant for your mom." We hurried to Pike's and bought bags of soil and a bunch of black-eyed Susans, because one of the aproned gardeners at the store said they were related to sunflowers and low maintenance. By the time Mom and Ethan came home, Dad and I were sweaty and soil-streaked and we had most of the black-eyed Susans planted in the backyard where Mom could see them from the kitchen or den. It was really Dad who planted them—I just carried a few of the flowers across the yard and helped pat the soil around them. But I felt as if I'd designed the gardens at Versailles, and Dad called me his number-one helper. I carried a grin on my face for a solid week afterward.

That was the summer before Dad went to Iraq, before everything went wrong.

I board a train that sways and screeches through the tunnels beneath the city. Outside the train windows, light alternates with stretches of darkness. There's no angry homeless man in my car, just a man and a woman across the aisle in the middle of a whispered argument, a toddler strapped into a stroller next to them. The toddler looks hot and exhausted and is half-heartedly chewing on a pale yellow blanket. He gazes at me as I make faces and try to get him to smile. I'm rewarded with a drooling grin. Children fascinate me, how they're tiny little people who you can see literally learning how to walk or throw a ball or read. I can watch them play for hours. It's not some deep-seated maternal instinct; I have no interest in being a parent, although God forbid you say that out loud if you're a woman. I think children fascinate me because my own childhood was ruined by seeing my parents shot to death when I was ten. There's no continuous, forward-moving narrative of my life as a kid. Instead I have fragments of memories, the good side-by-side with the bad. In one, I'm helping Dad plant black-eyed Susans in a sunny spot in our backyard. In the next, I'm sitting in the hall outside my bedroom, my lap full of blood. This is my childhood. It's like having a precious vase that shattered and now all you have left are shards, but you still put those shards out on your hall table or whatever, this broken part of you on display. I look at the toddler gnawing on his blanket and hope he has a good life.

That's when the toddler's parents take their argument up a notch.

"—not the *point*," the man is insisting to the woman. "That's not the point at all. I'm working my *ass* off, for both of us, all *three* of us, and you want to complain about the laundry?"

The woman shakes her head, a weary denial. "That's not true," she says. "I'm not—"

"But you *are*," the man says. He has a banker's haircut and heavy eyebrows that make him look like he's scowling. It's like someone glued a pair of fuzzy caterpillars to his forehead. He'd be almost handsome if it weren't for those eyebrows. That and the fact that he's bitching at his wife. "You stay home all day with the baby," he continues, pointing at the toddler in the stroller without looking at him. "Is it really that hard to wash all the laundry? I'm not trying to be an asshole here, I'm just asking."

The woman looks exhausted. Even her dull brown hair looks exhausted. "Jay's not a baby anymore," she says. "He's running all over the house and he gets into everything and it's just, I'm trying but . . . I just need a little help—"

The man snorts and rolls his eyes. "Here we go."

"Just a little help," the woman continues, her words coming faster as if she can race her argument past him. "Maybe just twice a week, only two days. Marjorie has a full-time nanny and that's too much, I don't need a full-time—"

"Do not bring my sister into this," the man says, holding up a finger in his wife's face. "Do not."

"Hey," I say, putting just enough snap into my voice to interrupt them without shouting. They both stop talking and turn to stare at me. The toddler kicks his feet and grins at me. "Ba," he says. "Ba, ba, ba, ba."

"Yeah, ba," I say to him with a smile. I glance at the woman. "Cute kid," I say, and she blinks. Then I return my attention to the man. "Can you dial it down a little?"

"Excuse me?" he says, surprised but with an undercurrent of outrage.

"You're berating her in public," I say. "Thought maybe you should rein it in some."

Other passengers are watching us now with sidelong looks. I see the man realize we have an audience, and I know he's going to stand up a full second before he does.

"Baby, don't—" the woman says.

"Is there a problem here?" the man asks me, standing in the aisle. "I'm having a conversation with my *wife*."

I shrug. "A pretty public conversation. I'm just asking you to make it less public and less angry, that's all."

"Bankie!" the toddler shouts.

"Bankie," I say to him, agreeing. He shrieks happily and hurls his blankie in the air. It unfurls like a flag in a breeze and then collapses onto the floor in front of him.

"Don't talk to my son," the man says. He leans forward in a way that's intended to be domineering. "Don't talk to him. Don't listen in on other people's—"

"Honey," the woman says.

He pins her with a glare. "I've got this," he says. She closes her eyes. He swivels his head back to me. "I don't know what your problem is, but—"

"Bankie!" the toddler says, trying to lean forward to get the blanket on the floor of the train.

"Your son," I say, indicating the blanket. "He wants—"

"I told you to leave my son alone."

"Honey," the woman says, "she's just—"

"I said I've *got* this!"

"*Bankie!*" the toddler cries, now jerking forward against his seat belt and making the whole stroller move. He's going to pitch face-first onto the floor if he keeps this up. I lean forward and reach out for the blankie.

"What the fuck," the man says, and he swings his arm, knocking my hand away.

Everything goes white-hot. My hand shoots up between the man's legs and grabs his crotch. I stand up and squeeze. The man gives out a strangled, high-pitched cry and tries to fold in on himself. I reach out with my other hand and grip his shoulder, keeping him upright.

"Chad!" the woman says. She has her hand on the stroller, steadying it, but is staring round-eyed at us.

"I was reaching for your son's blankie," I say to Chad, his mouth an open O of shock. "He threw it on the floor of the train, and I was trying to pick it up and hand it to you to give to him. But you were too busy swinging your dick around. Wanted to make sure your wife knew who was in charge, yeah?" I punctuate my question with another squeeze and he yelps and rises up on his tiptoes, trying to escape the pain. "Wanted to make sure everybody knew who was in charge. Well, right now, Chad?

I'm in charge. Understand?" Chad nods, his face twisted in anguish. "Don't be an asshole, Chad. The world is full of assholes. You hear me?"

I let go of his crotch and push him away. He collapses back into his seat next to his wife, face red and wet with tears. He bends forward, moaning into his knees. His wife puts her arms around him and murmurs in his ear, then shoots me a hateful look. I realize the rest of the train car is staring at me. Even the toddler in his stroller is silent. Somehow I've become the crazy homeless guy on the train.

The train slows and the driver's garbled voice from the speaker announces Peachtree Center. It's the stop before Five Points, but I can't stay on this train any longer. I fight the urge to claw the doors open. Instead I bend down and pick up the toddler's blankie and hold it out to the wife. Don't want the kid to stuff it into his mouth after it's been on the floor of the train. The wife snatches the blankie from my hand as if I'm a rattlesnake that could strike.

Then the train comes to a halt and the doors open, and I'm out and onto the platform and I march past the crowd of passengers and the benches and the escalators to the far end of the platform, where I turn and march back, circling the platform, trying to outstrip the anger in my heart.

CHAPTER TEN

By the time I step out of the hospital elevator onto my uncle's floor—Jesus, my uncle's been here less than twenty-four hours and I already think of this as his floor—I'm late, but my heart is now limping along at its usual pace. Whatever anger I felt at the man on the train, I've left it behind to linger in the street like cigarette smoke. In its place is a brittle anxiety, both for my uncle and for what I almost did on the train. If I'd been carrying a pistol, I would've put it to that man's head. I wanted to scare him, even hurt him. And for what? For being an asshole? Take a number and get in line, brother, the world is full of them. An old therapist of mine, Dr. Ashan, would call what I did transference, redirecting my emotions about one person or situation to another, unrelated person or situation. I took all my grief and frustration and rage, and I unloaded it all on that asshole dad on the train.

But another part of me—the part that would shrug in the face of the devil himself, would say to him *what the fuck are you looking at*—has a different response: *Good.* That guy needed to be taken down a notch. And to be honest, Dr. Ashan was a pretty shitty therapist. For all the times I saw him in therapy, I would've gotten better results if I'd just watched a full day of *Sesame Street* episodes.

The logical side of me knows I'm avoiding hard truths, that my denials are bullshit. But this is my reality: my id, ego, and superego crammed into a car that's hurtling down the highway, all three of them fighting over the wheel.

Outside my uncle's room I pause and take a breath, then open the door. My brother and a nurse and Dr. Lewis are standing around my uncle's bed. They all look up at me.

"Suzie," Ethan says.

"Sorry I'm late," I say. "I rode MARTA and—" I stop talking when I see my uncle behind them. He's lying in the hospital bed as before, but now he has a breathing tube in his mouth. He looks even older and weaker than he did yesterday. And his eyes are open and gazing at me.

"He stopped breathing this morning," Ethan says. "They had to intubate him. They have to do the surgery now, Susannah."

"Your brother's right," Dr. Lewis says. "We would have intubated him anyway for the surgery, after administering general anesthesia, but we had to do it to keep his airway open. And now because he's already intubated, and we've already decided on a valve—" He looks at Ethan.

"Uncle Gavin wants the mechanical valve," Ethan says to me. "It's the best choice for him."

I nod. "Sure," I say. "Okay." I keep nodding, as if this will somehow make everything fine. I glance at Uncle Gavin and see that his eyes are still on me. Slowly he raises a hand that's attached to an IV drip and motions at me.

"Your uncle can't speak with the tube in," Dr. Lewis is saying. "And we need to get him to surgery, but you can have a minute with him." The doctor murmurs something to the nurse, but I'm not really paying attention because I'm walking toward the bed, looking at my uncle. I don't want to look at him. Not like this. He has tubes and wires running into his body and now has a stubby plastic tube sticking out of his mouth. It looks far too big to be there. His skin has the look of graying cheese. Maybe it's the fluorescent lights making it look worse than it is. I hope it's the lights.

"Hey," I say, taking Uncle Gavin's hand and gently squeezing it. "Uncle Gavin. You're gonna be okay." I hate hearing the lies come out of my mouth, but what else do I say? *Fuck which heart valve you want, you look half-dead, you won't even make it through the surgery.*

Uncle Gavin pulls his hand out of mine and reaches out toward something behind me. I turn and see the nurse holding out a small whiteboard with a marker. "He can't talk to y'all, but he can write on this," she says. "But please make it quick."

I put the whiteboard on Uncle Gavin's lap and place the uncapped marker in his hand. Uncle Gavin closes his eyes for a moment, then opens them. He gazes at me steadily, waiting.

I say nothing until the nurse leaves the room to give us a few moments, and then I glance at the curtain that cuts the room in half. "Is anybody . . . ?" I ask Ethan.

He shakes his head. "We're alone."

I look down at Uncle Gavin, who waits for me. Even with tubes running in and out of him and looking like death, his eyes are bright and focused on me. "I found Peaches," I say to him. "And Tane Kamaka."

Uncle Gavin makes a short movement with the marker on the whiteboard. He's drawn a checkmark.

"Why did you want Tane?" I ask.

Uncle Gavin writes so slowly, the letters shaky. *Stop gang war.*

"Gang war? Between Peaches and the Sureños? Bala's crew?"

Uncle Gavin nods.

"I don't understand," I say. "How could Tane stop a gang war?"

Uncle Gavin writes like he's submerged in a tank of water, the movements slow and exaggerated. He draws a $ on the whiteboard.

"Money?" I ask. "I don't understand. You . . . you had Peaches *take* him from the FBI. I thought he was a witness."

Carefully, Uncle Gavin shakes his head, the tube in his mouth moving back and forth. I have a sudden, irrational urge to yank the tube out of his mouth, then rip the IV lines and the monitors and everything out of his body. I can't do this. I can't look at Uncle Gavin like this. I watched my father die in our house, lying on his back and gargling blood. I can't watch Uncle Gavin die, too.

Uncle Gavin taps the whiteboard with his marker, trying to regain my attention. "Sorry," I say, and I take a deep breath through my nose, then exhale through my mouth. "I'm sorry," I say again.

My uncle keeps tapping the whiteboard. The dollar sign. He's tapping the dollar sign that he drew. Money. It's about the money, and Tane. Tane and the money. And then it hits me. I was so stupid, but now it's as fucking obvious as a horse in a bathroom.

"Tane was their money man," I say. "For the Sureños. He managed their money."

Uncle Gavin nods, once.

"So why did the FBI have him? And why did you want to take him away from them?"

Uncle Gavin holds up the marker, then pauses. He waves it at the whiteboard. I realize there's no space left for him to write. I take the whiteboard and wipe my hand across it, erasing it, and then I rub my palm on my leg. I hand the whiteboard back to him just as the door opens and the doctor and more medical staff enter the room.

"Give me a second," I say to them, then I lean closer to my uncle and drop my voice to a whisper. "I lost him," I say. "I lost Tane. He . . . the FBI came looking for him, and he ran away."

Uncle Gavin's dark eyes stay fixed on mine. I realize I'm crying and angrily brush the tears from my eyes.

"I'm sorry," I whisper, "but I'll find him. I'll find him."

"We have to go, Miss Faulkner, Mr. Faulkner," Dr. Lewis is saying.

"She's almost done," Ethan says.

Uncle Gavin finally takes his eyes off mine and looks at the whiteboard on his lap. He scrawls two lines on it. They both look like the signature of a drunk.

Dont trust FBI, the first line says.

The second line is: *BCS13.*

"Miss Faulkner?" The nice nurse is back. "We're gonna take good care of your uncle. Y'all need to let us do our jobs now. That's right, we've got him . . ." Somehow they have eased past me and have surrounded Uncle Gavin's bed. I step back, still wiping tears from my eyes. Uncle Gavin doesn't take his eyes off of mine, even when they start rolling his bed out of the room with him in it. Then he is out the door and down the hall, and I'm left in an empty hospital room with Ethan, holding a whiteboard and a dry-erase marker, staring at the open doorway like the answers to all the questions in my head are on the other side.

ETHAN AND I sit in the same waiting room we were in yesterday. Across from us sits an old woman in a faded blue dress, her gaze on the floor, while a younger, balding man next to her murmurs in her ear. She nods every once in a while but doesn't look at the man, who I'm guessing by the resemblance is her son. She just keeps staring at the floor, communing with her own grief and worry.

As much as I'm worried about Uncle Gavin's surgery, I don't want to think about it. If I can't do anything to affect the outcome, I have to focus my energies somewhere else. Right now, I'm thinking about the two messages Uncle Gavin wrote on the whiteboard. *Dont trust FBI* is at least straightforward, although the reasoning behind my uncle's warning isn't. Of course he wouldn't have a close relationship with the FBI—they'd like nothing more than to arrest him and throw him in prison. But he was very specific: he didn't trust the FBI with Tane. Or he doesn't want me to trust them. Agent Scott clearly dislikes my uncle. I wonder if Special Agent Rondeau might be more open to a conversation, although at this point I'm not sure how that would go, or what the point would be. *Hey, Alisha, wanna help me find the guy I lied to you about and said I didn't know?* Maybe if I could talk to her without her partner, I'd learn something. Meeting her for coffee in a public setting could work, although there would be a lot of variables I couldn't control—other customers, potential FBI agents pretending to be customers or passersby, traffic. Talking to her in private might be better, if I could surprise her without freaking her out or getting arrested. Figure out where she lives, tail her to her house or apartment or whatever.

And then what? I think. *She invites you in and you have a chat and maybe a glass of wine and see what happens?* I shake my head, dismissing the thoughts. Suzie's libido strikes again. Focus, girl.

The second message is more cryptic: *BCS13*. Is BCS a set of initials? A place? Maybe it's a five-digit password? If so, to what? The 13 could refer to Sureños 13, and if that's true then the S would probably be for Sureños. So what is BC? Peaches said the leader of the Sureños cell was called Bala, which is Spanish for *bullet*. Could that be B? And what's the C stand for, then? What starts with the letter C? Cryptic, for one—probably not it. Cola, castanets, computer, cell, cephalopod, ceiling, condition, cocaine, cap, capsule, capitulate, carbon, carburetor, car . . .

"Jesus," I say aloud.

"Suze?" Ethan says.

The balding man across from me stops talking to his mother and looks at me, startled. Even the old woman lifts her gaze to me.

"Sorry," I say to the old woman. To Ethan, I say in a lowered voice, "I have to go."

"What?"

"I have to go. Uncle Gavin gave me something to do and I just figured it out."

Ethan raises his hands and drops them in disgust. "So you're just going to bail. Again."

"I'm not—"

"Our uncle's in surgery, Susannah," he says, his voice low but threatening to grow louder. "Open-heart surgery. So whatever Uncle Gavin told you to do can wait."

I shake my head. "Listen, I have to find Tane. I lost him and I promised Uncle Gavin—"

"Tane isn't a puppy," Ethan says, louder. "He left. He's not your problem."

I so want to fight, to expend all of my anxiety and anger in another argument with my brother. I'm primed for it, have my lines all ready to go. And I can tell from Ethan's body language and tone that he's ready to throw down, too, and the hell with whoever overhears us.

Then I remember the guy from the train, how part of me was ready to shoot a stranger in the head because he was bitching at his wife. My heart sinks, a hollow stone. I've always had a dark, violent streak. But when did I become a walking time bomb, ready to explode at a moment's notice, and to hell with the consequences?

I stand. "Ethan, I'm sorry. I'm not going to fight with you. And I'll be back as soon as I can. But I think I know what Uncle Gavin wants me to do."

Ethan stays seated, looking up at me in disbelief. "Since when have you ever done what he wants you to do?"

"It's the last thing he asked of me before he got wheeled off to surgery. And I'm trying to clean up my mess."

Ethan shakes his head, clearly unhappy. "Go, then. I'll stay here. But what are you going to do?"

I walk down the hall to the elevator, and without looking back I answer him. "Pay a visit to Brandon Cargill."

CHAPTER ELEVEN

Cargill's place of business, ATL Body Shop, is a long, low garage on Northside Drive just west of downtown. Basically it's a series of five vehicle bays with an office at one end. The concrete-block exterior is painted white. Bad choice. A white house sitting in an acre of green grass might look good in Buckhead. But here, on this industrial strip of tire shops, gas stations, and welding supply stores, the garage's white walls have turned the color of an ashtray.

I ride past on my motorcycle, which, along with a few other items, I retrieved from the Store-N-Go after I left the hospital. There's a blue graffiti tag on the wall at one end of the garage. All the bay doors are open, but only two of the bays hold vehicles being serviced. I don't see Cargill, but he's probably in the office.

On the far side of the garage, I spot a black Ford F-150, chrome gleaming like metal teeth. That's got to be Cargill's ride. It's in a gravel lot sandwiched between the garage and a RaceTrac on the corner of North Avenue.

I turn left onto North Avenue and park my bike in a lot just across from the RaceTrac, paying the attendant ten bucks for a strip of asphalt. I now have a large top box mounted to the back of my bike—it's big but holds everything I need. I don't open it. Instead I walk back down to Northside and turn right, heading for the garage. Traffic rushes by with a stink of exhaust and oil. Across the six lanes of Northside, a low chain-link fence and a straggly line of trees border an empty field, beyond which is a business park, the outskirts of Georgia Tech, and the railroad tracks that originally put Atlanta on the map. And above it all looms the gray stone tower of Coca-Cola and, beyond that, the dark copper spire of the Bank of America building.

I cross North Avenue and walk past the RaceTrac, not hurrying, not ambling, but with a purpose. Projecting confidence is the first trick. If you hunch your shoulders or duck your face and keep looking around like you're making sure there isn't a cop nearby, people notice. Act like you belong and that you know what you're doing, and you can fool a lot of people a lot of the time. I walk up to the black pickup truck in the little gravel lot like it's mine. It's a Supercrew model with four doors and a huge interior. Through the windshield I see two-tone leather seats and a screen on the dash the size of a small flat-screen TV. The truck looks like your little cousin came to the big city wearing bling, trying to act grown up. It's backed in, facing the street, so I walk around to the tailgate. Behind the truck, I crouch and slap a small, magnetized box the size of a pack of cigarettes underneath the rear bumper. Then I stand back up and continue around the truck. I can see a door at the back of the building that probably goes into the office, but even if it's unlocked I want to eyeball the inside of the garage first, see what I'm up against.

At the front of the garage, I can see in the nearest open bay there's a red Mustang up on a lift, and a man in a gray coverall is standing underneath the car, looking up at the front axle. At the far end, to my left, another man is bent over the engine of an SUV. I see no one else in the garage bays. To my right is the office, basically a wall of Sheetrock across the width of the garage with a plate-glass window and a door in it. Through the window I see Cargill seated behind a desk, lazily spinning around in his office chair, talking into a cell phone. He's a tall, raw-boned man, skin pale as milk. His head is nearly shorn, with only a fuzzy remnant of blond hair on his scalp. As soon as I see him, my head starts humming like an electric razor. Time to dance. I walk into the garage.

"Help you?" calls the man working on the Mustang as I open the office door.

I ignore him and step into the office, pulling the door closed behind me. It's not much of an office—bad beige carpet, a crowded bulletin board, a couple of chairs, a wood-veneer desk, some file cabinets behind the desk. To the left is another door, which must lead out back. Cargill stops spinning in his chair and looks at me, phone still clamped to his ear. "Well, I'm not fixing it for free, Mr. Becks," Cargill says into the phone, a slight smile on his face, his eyes never leaving me. "I'm running a business. But once we identify the problem and can order the parts, I'm sure we can—"

"Hang up the phone," I say.

Cargill's smile remains fixed. "Hang on just one second, Mr. Becks," he says, then lowers the phone. His eyes wander over my body, his gaze eventually returning to my own. His smile widens, revealing teeth. "Lemme finish this call, sweetie, and then I'm all yours," he says. He raises the phone back to his ear. "Mr. Becks? Sorry about that—"

The humming in my head intensifies, a siren's call. The baton is in my hand and I flick my wrist and the baton extends with a *snick*. The smile drops off Cargill's face. I swing the baton, hitting the phone and sending it out of Cargill's hand to thump onto the carpet.

"Jesus *Christ*—" Cargill snatches his hand away like it's burned.

I use the baton to sweep some papers and a desk lamp to the floor. Cargill scrambles to stand up out of his chair, but before he gets to his feet I jab him in the chest with the baton. He loses his balance and falls back into his chair. I switch the baton to my left hand, freeing me to draw my CZ 75 just as the mechanic who was working on the Mustang rushes through the office door.

"Nope," I say, pointing the pistol at him. I glance at Cargill and push the baton into his chest, pinning him to his chair, then return my attention to the mechanic. "Close the door and have a seat," I say, waving the pistol to indicate a chair underneath the plate-glass window. The mechanic glances at Cargill, then shuts the door and takes a seat. Through the window I see the other man at the far end of the garage still has his head in the engine of that SUV.

"Girl, I don't know who the hell you are," Cargill says, "but you done fucked with the wrong man."

"You'd know if I fucked you," I say. "This is just foreplay." I remove the baton from his chest and cock it over one shoulder, my pistol covering both men. "Where's Tane Kamaka?"

"Who?"

I bring the baton straight down onto the desk. It makes a loud *crack* and leaves a dent. Both men jump. "Come on, Brandon," I say. Cargill's eyes flicker at the use of his first name—he hates it and insists that everyone call him Brad—but otherwise he doesn't move. "The guy the Sureños are looking for," I continue. "Curly hair, accountant. Ring a bell?"

Cargill spreads his hands and shrugs. "The Sureños?" He pronounces it *sir-rain-yos*. "What's that, some kinda mariachi band?"

I backhand him across the face with the baton. I was aiming for his nose, but instead I hit his cheek, opening an inch-long gash. He nearly falls out of his chair. Before the mechanic can even move I point the pistol at him and he raises his hands, the picture of cooperation.

"Oh, *fuck*," Cargill says, sitting up, hand to his face. Blood seeps out from behind his fingers.

I glance out the window and see the man at the far end of the garage is now in the driver's seat of the SUV, starting the engine. I move out of his line of sight and around the desk next to Cargill, who's cursing steadily, his hand still pressed to his face.

"Come here," I say to the mechanic in the chair. Reluctantly he stands, and I see him consider whether to do something—rush me, shout for help—but instead he walks toward me, still holding his hands up.

"Check out his face," I say, indicating Cargill, and step back, pistol trained on the mechanic. The man hesitates, then leans over Cargill, frowning. I hit him in the back of the head with the baton and he drops to the floor like a sack of wet sand.

Cargill uses his feet to push his chair away from the mechanic on the floor, but he comes to a stop when his chair runs into a file cabinet. He has one hand clapped to his face, covering half of it, and his uncovered eye glares at me through a sheen of tears and fury. "You fucking cut my *face!*" he says.

I push the end of the baton against the top of the desk to collapse it, then drop the baton into a pocket of my leather jacket. I holster my pistol and lean forward to grab Cargill by the front of his shirt, shoving my face close to his. "Tane Kamaka," I hiss. "You remember him now?"

"Okay, fuck, *yes,*" Cargill says, his one uncovered eye wide open. Blood runs between his fingers and down his jawline and chin, dripping to the floor. "I need a fucking doctor."

"You're going to need a team of doctors by the time I'm finished with you," I say. "Where's Tane?"

"I don't *know!*" he says. "The spics are looking for him. Ask them."

"I intend to." I pull Cargill forward in his rolling chair and push him face down onto the desk. He groans with pain but doesn't move. I keep my left hand on his back, planting him on the desk. With my right hand I reach into the pocket of my jeans and pull out a tiny round object, the size of a quarter, with a flexible wire sticking out of it. Being face down on the desk, Cargill can't see what I'm doing. I reach over and drop the object into the narrow space between the end of the desk and the wall. I make sure the wire isn't sticking out anywhere from behind the desk. Satisfied, I unholster my pistol and place the muzzle against the back of Cargill's head.

"Gavin Lester is in the hospital for one day and you think you can start calling the shots?" I put as much menace into my voice as I can. With the twin howler monkeys in my brain, it's not difficult. "You want to get in bed with the Sureños?" I lean closer. "You tell them they aren't welcome. I know what you're doing, Brandon. And it's not going to happen."

I leave him there, face-down and bleeding on his desk. Turns out the back door was locked from the inside, so I turn the bolt, holster my pistol, and step outside into a weedy lot behind the garage, letting the door swing shut behind me. I walk past the black truck and up Northside. Part of me wants to shoot out the windows and tires in Cargill's truck just for spite, but that would be indulgent.

It takes me less than three minutes to get to my bike, which has a good view of the garage just down the road. I open an app on my phone that receives the transmissions from the bug I planted in Cargill's office, then plug in a set of earbuds. I could listen on the helmet's headset, but I'm conspicuous enough and don't want to sit here for hours in my helmet. The specs on the bug say the range is a quarter of a mile, and I'm a little over half that and have direct line of sight to the garage. The signal is as clear as a cell phone call.

"—*on the floor,*" someone says.

"*Fuck the lamp,*" another voice says. Cargill. "*And fuck Jerry, too. Why didn't he jump her, or call your ass for help?*"

"*Just hold still, Brad, I gotta wipe off—*"

"*Ow! That hurts, motherfucker!*"

"*Sorry.*"

There are some indistinct sounds, and then the other man speaks again. "*Gonna prob'ly need stitches.*"

"*Just put the fucking butterfly bandages on. And then you and Jerry get out of here. Jerry? You paying attention? Christ, he's probably got a concussion. How many fingers am I holding up?*"

A third voice says, "*Gimme some fuckin' Advil or somethin'.*"

"Acetaminophen," I say aloud.

Another minute or so goes by of Cargill cursing and the other guy apparently trying to bandage the cut on his cheek. Any wound over half an inch ought to get real stitches. Cargill better hope his face doesn't get all infected and puffy. Not that I care terribly much. But Cargill is clearly in a hurry, which is what I was counting on.

My stomach rumbles, and I look longingly at the RaceTrac and its convenience store. Aside from a protein bar that I grabbed this morning before Caesar picked me up, I've eaten nothing today. But I don't know if I have time to grab any food. Good planning, Suzie. So I continue listening to Cargill mutter and bitch as the other man plays clumsy nursemaid.

Finally Cargill gets his two mechanics out of his office and I hear a door close. I keep my eyes trained on the garage down the street. No one steps in or out of the building. Then I hear Cargill speak.

"We got a problem." Pause. *"Yeah, I'm on a clean phone, I'm not an idiot. It's Gavin Lester's niece. She came in here and busted up the place, wanted to know where Tane Kamaka is."* Pause. *"I don't know. She knows you and your compadres want to set up shop here."* Pause. *"She didn't say shit about that."* Pause. *"Hell, yes, I still—"* Pause. *"Tonight? Shit. Yeah, okay, it's good. When?"* Pause. *"All right. Same place we talked about."* Pause. *"Fucking wetback motherfuckers. George!"* A thump like a drawer being closed, or someone bumping into the desk. Then footsteps. *"George!"* Cargill's voice sounds farther away. *"Call Lucas, we gotta move it up to tonight. No, I don't . . ."* Then his voice fades to background noise. He must have walked out of his office into the garage and out of range of the bug.

Rattling Brandon Cargill's cage seems to be working. I open another app on my phone and see the tracking device I put on Cargill's truck is blinking away. Now all I have to do is wait for him to lead me to wherever he's going—hopefully to Bala, or one of the Sureños. Then maybe I can find out more about Tane.

First things first. I call Ethan, who picks up on the second ring. Uncle Gavin is still in surgery—over three hours and counting. Then Ethan tells me to hang on and the phone goes silent. A minute later he comes back on. "He's out of surgery. Doc just told me. He's okay. He made it."

I let out a long, shuddering sigh. "God, I thought we might lose him. But he's okay?"

"He's okay. They want him to stay in the hospital for a couple of days and monitor him. How are you? Where are you?"

I look down the street at ATL Body Shop. Still no movement. "I'm fine. Making progress."

"Didn't answer my second question."

"Nope."

"Just be careful."

"Have you met me?"

Ethan laughs, quietly. "That's why I said that."

After I hang up I take a deep breath and slowly exhale, a smile making its way across my face. The sun dips a little lower in the sky, setting the trees across the street alight with golden-green fire. My heart is lightened the slightest bit.

I take a chance and duck into the RaceTrac for a sausage, egg, and cheese biscuit and a bottle of water, and as I'm waiting for the cashier I grab a can of double-shot espresso. I'd rather have a salad with some grilled chicken, but beggars can't be choosers, and I'm going to need the caffeine. When I walk back to my bike, Cargill's truck is still parked by the garage. I eat my biscuit and watch rush-hour traffic crawl by. Now it's a waiting game.

CHAPTER TWELVE

A PRIVATE INVESTIGATOR NAMED LEO NEVSKY GAVE ME MY FIRST
lessons in surveillance. He came to my high school for a job fair day. His
graying hair was a little too long and a little too greasy, and he looked
like he hadn't shaved for two days. But he was polite, almost courtly in
the way he treated me and a dozen other high school students when we
showed up in his assigned classroom to learn about the ins and outs of
being a PI. Most of the other kids were bored, but I was already planning to track down my parents' killer and I wanted to learn something. I
asked questions, took notes, and signed up to shadow him for one day in
the summer. That involved following a stay-at-home wife whose husband
was convinced she was having an affair. Mostly we sat in Leo's ten-year-
old Honda Civic down the street from the happy couple's house, a two-
story Colonial in Garden Hills.

After thirty minutes of sitting there with the windows down in the
muggy June heat, I was antsy. "How do you deal with watching someone
for hours?" I asked.

"You imagine scenarios, keep your brain occupied," he said.

I raised an eyebrow. "Like fantasies?"

If Leo was unsettled by a seventeen-year-old girl making sexually inappropriate comments, he didn't show it. He just smiled in a way that told me

he didn't smile too often. "Like gaming out possibilities in your head based on the situation you're in," he said. "Sitting in a car and watching someone for hours can be really boring. So you use your imagination and think about what could happen. We're supposed to be watching this woman. Let's say she gets in her Lexus and drives off down the street. What would you do?"

I shrugged. "Follow her."

"Sure, but how close? Do you let her get to the end of the street before you start the car? How about if she comes out of the house in workout clothes and goes for a run? Do we drive after her? Follow on foot? What if she climbs over the fence in the back? What if she walks out here and demands to know who we are?" He tilted his head and raised his eyebrows as if surprised by the endless possibilities that could unfold before us. "Your imagination is your greatest asset."

I imagined how I would react if Leo tried to make a move on me. Sure, he was old, but that didn't mean anything. So I imagined all of the ways I could render Leo Nevsky harmless—a palm strike to the nose, or a stab in the thigh with the pen I was holding, or an eye gouge with my hooked fingers. If we were on the street I'd deliver a short hard kick to the outside of his kneecap and drop him to the pavement.

"I think I get it," I said.

He smiled again, this one a bit less rusty. "The Navy SEALs have a saying: embrace the suck. Sitting in a car all day watching a woman who may or may not be cheating on her husband isn't anywhere near as tough as going through SEAL training. But the basic premise is the same— make the most of an unpleasant situation."

Nothing happened that day; the wife never left her house, and I have no idea what happened afterward. Leo shook my hand gravely at the end of the day when he dropped me off at my uncle's house and wished me good luck. I never saw him again. But I took that lesson to heart—make the most of an unpleasant situation.

While watching Cargill's garage I play mental games to occupy my brain without distracting me from my job. In a ten-minute period I count how many people walking into the RaceTrac are wearing blue, or have tattoos, or are women. I count how many cars I can see at one time on Northside when the light is red. I count how many cars have only a driver and no passengers, then how many have more than two people. Every thirty minutes or so I walk around my bike twice in both directions to keep the circulation going. I'd do jumping jacks, but that would be more likely to call attention to myself. Not that I think Cargill and company are worried about anybody watching. The only activity I see at the garage is when a white Toyota pickup with a Domino's decal delivers a couple of pizzas around six o'clock. I stretch my neck and ignore the rumbling in my stomach. I hear nothing of interest from the bug, just Cargill bitching about work and about how cold the pizza is. Luckily I charged my phone at the hospital so it's got plenty of juice left.

The sun slips over the horizon and the sky begins to darken, lights in the city towers shining through a thousand windows. Traffic starts to thin out. Most of the other cars in the lot are gone by now, and the parking lot attendant is eyeballing me, so I put on my helmet and ride out of the lot with a nod to the attendant and drive around the block until I'm on the street behind Cargill's garage. I park beneath an old oak tree. Now that it's getting darker, I can park my motorcycle on the street without being so conspicuous, and the tracking app is still beeping, so all I need to do is pay attention to it. Right now that beeping dot is where it's been for the past five hours, at Cargill's garage. I'm assuming that Cargill will take his own truck rather than get a ride from someone else, but I think that's a safe bet—his truck is so tricked out I doubt his pride would let him ride in anyone else's car if he had a choice.

Forty-eight hours ago I was getting ready to flirt with Bobby Bonaroo and slip Xanax into his scotch. Now I'm waiting to follow a scumbag like Brandon Cargill to a secret meeting with a Sureños gang leader named Bala. Life choices by Suzie. I'd much rather be at Ethan's house making him watch a Tom Hanks movie marathon with me. But Tane is in the wind, and if I had time and a credit card of Tane's I could find him soon enough, but the only lead I have is this Bala.

Why do you care about finding this Tane so much? Caesar asked me this morning. It's a good question. I think about Ethan's look of disappointment when I left the hospital to come here and spy on Cargill. Why *am* I doing this? A sense of obligation to my uncle, sure. Plus a sense of professional pride—I find people, so if someone I found goes missing, it's on me to fix that. And Tane seems like a nice guy, if a little goofy and clueless, so part of me is concerned about him. For him to be in bed with a bunch of hard-core prison gang members like Sureños 13 seems bizarre, although my guess is he stumbled into it and, once he was in deep, he was too afraid to leave. So he gets snatched by the FBI, only to get snatched again by Peaches and his crew. All while he just wanted a cheeseburger. D's plan to get into the hotel room by sabotaging the air conditioner was clever, an updated version of smoking someone out of a hidey-hole. Sitting on my bike on a June night wearing a leather jacket, I can appreciate air conditioning all too well. Still, something about the story bothered me when I first heard it, caught my attention like a snag in a muddy river—you can't see it, but you feel it. I do a slow scan of the street and try to remember what it was about Peaches's story that bothered me. The FBI guarding a witness instead of the U.S. Marshals is unusual, but not impossible. Maybe Agent Scott didn't fill out the proper interdepartmental paperwork to transfer Tane over to the Marshals. Maybe the Marshals were delayed in taking custody of Tane. Maybe—

The thought that's been bothering me cracks open like an egg and I curse at how my brain wanders around and figures things out in its own time. I call Caesar and stare up into the dark tree branches spread above me, listening to the phone ring in my helmet's headset.

"Suzie," Caesar says in my ears.

"I need a cell phone number for Peaches," I say. "Can you help me?"

There's a pause. "I'm eating dinner."

"You can't eat and use your laptop at the same time?"

"I'm eating dinner with Frankie," Caesar clarifies. "In a home that is empty of contractors."

"They finished for the day? Good. Hey, maybe Frankie can help, too. Does he know how to call—"

"I'm having a romantic dinner with my man and then I'm going to take him to bed," Caesar says.

"Fuck."

"Blunt, but accurate."

Either I'm blushing or the temperature just soared ten degrees in the last ten seconds. "I'm sorry, Caesar, I didn't mean to—I'm sorry to bother y'all, I . . . look, I'll just call tomorrow."

There's a fumbling sound on the phone and then Frankie says, "*Chica*, we gotta talk about your sense of timing."

"I'm sorry," I say. "Go have sexy time. I can—"

Frankie sighs dramatically. "Caesar already grabbed his laptop. What do you need, a number?"

"I need to call Peaches." My cheeks are still burning, but I press on. "One of his people is talking to the feds, and I think I know who. Just please find me a number and then you two go at it."

"Don't worry, we will."

"Seriously, I'm sorry."

"You sound cute when you apologize. You should do it more often."

"Admit mistakes? Like asking Caesar to program Samuel L. Jackson's voice into your car?"

"*Eres un pinche lata.*"

"Been called worse."

"We'll send you a number."

"Kisses," I say brightly, but he's already hung up.

The evening deepens. I can hear the traffic on Northside a block away, but on this side of the block are a vacant lot and a graffiti-tagged brick warehouse and some bungalows with overgrown yards. In the middle of the vacant lot across from me, a tiny light winks on, then off.

Another answers it. Lightning bugs. When I was a kid, seeing lightning bugs meant summer had truly started. I watch the lightning bugs wink on and off, floating in the gloom.

In the distance a dog barks, deep and gruff, a warning to passersby— *this is my yard.* I hope Wilson didn't pee inside Ethan's house. I wonder if Ethan is home or if he stayed at the hospital. I'm betting on the latter. My brother always seems to know the right thing to do in situations like that. I usually figure out what I should have done after the fact.

My phone dings and I look down at the screen. Caesar has texted me a phone number. I text him back an eggplant emoji, then add another one before I call the number. It picks up on the second ring.

"Who is this?" Peaches says.

"Acetaminophen," I answer.

Peaches barely pauses. "Doctor Woman. How you get this number?"

"D is your mole," I say. "Or he's lying about the A/C at the motel."

"Hold on," Peaches says. The phone goes silent but the call is still connected. I sit on my bike and watch the lightning bugs wink on and off in the darkness.

Peaches comes back on the line. "You got one minute."

"You said D told you he sabotaged the A/C in the motel room by cutting a wire or a hose outside the room, right?"

Pause. "Yeah."

"A/C units in motels are all inside the rooms. They're self-contained, you can't reach them from outside the room."

Longer pause. "The feds in that room called the manager to say the A/C was broken."

I nod encouragingly, even though Peaches can't see me. "Which means—"

"Somebody inside the room fucked up the A/C unit," Peaches finishes for me.

"And D knew," I say. "Which means he was talking with at least one of the Feebies."

Silence on the other end of the line. I say nothing and try to ignore the sweat at my hairline, my temples, under my bra.

"Why you tellin' me this?" Peaches asks.

"Because I'm looking for Tane and want to know what I'm walking into. I'm following a lead right now to Bala. And because I still feel bad about spraying Billy in the face."

"Bala?" Peaches says, a low growl.

Another ding on my phone. It's an alert from the tracking app. Cargill's on the move. "Gotta go," I say, and I hang up on Peaches before he can say anything and pull up the tracking app. There's the blinking dot, heading south on Northside. I put my phone into the stand on my bike so I can follow the dot while keeping my hands free, and then I see the dot turn west onto a side street. Uh-oh. If Cargill is circling the block, he will drive right past me in a matter of seconds.

I start my bike and head north, back toward North Avenue. I glance down at my phone and see the blinking dot has just turned onto my street. He's maybe fifty yards behind me. I look over my shoulder and see bright headlights, gaining. I face forward and gun it to the intersection, then lean hard into a right-hand turn back to the RaceTrac. Luckily traffic is light so no one plows into me. I pull into the RaceTrac and park my bike next to a dumpster, shielding me from view. The blinking dot has just reached North Avenue. After a few seconds, it turns my way—Cargill is coming right past me. I look around the dumpster and see his black-and-chrome truck stop at the light at Northside. The windows are tinted enough that it's impossible to tell at night how many people are in the vehicle, but I'm guessing Cargill isn't alone. When the light changes, he turns left onto Northside. I back out and follow him, just making it through the light. He's three cars ahead of me. Now it's a new game: follow the leader.

CHAPTER THIRTEEN

Cargill's truck turns onto Hollowell Parkway and I follow him, hanging back three, sometimes four cars. With the tracker I'm not afraid of losing him, although I don't want to get too far behind and have to keep looking at my phone when I need to pay attention to the road. He stays on Hollowell, heading west out of the city. We pass a closed Family Dollar store, a package store, and a Bank of America drive-thru ATM in the middle of a bombed-out shopping center, the parking lot full of enormous concrete cylinders and dumpsters and dirt. Just past that is a police precinct, a stone building that looks like a church minus a cross. Have to put your faith in something, I guess. Cargill flies past the station, and I follow.

About five minutes later we come up on a bridge that crosses over 285, the sixty-four-mile-long interstate that rings the city. People in Atlanta call it the Perimeter. In Atlanta, you're either ITP—you live inside the Perimeter—or OTP—outside the Perimeter. Right now Cargill is heading OTP. I'm not superstitious, generally, but crossing over the Perimeter tonight, I wouldn't be surprised to find some hooded skeletal being on the other side of the bridge, a gatekeeper welcoming us to the other side with an eternal, bony grin.

All that greets us are a Chevron and a BP flanking the road. Cargill's black truck passes both, and so do I. At Fulton Industrial, Cargill turns left, and before I can catch up the light turns red. While waiting for the light to change, I track Cargill's progress on my phone. The beeping dot moves slowly southwest toward Fulton County Airport, a small county airport better known as Charlie Brown. No commercial flights or big planes here, but lots of charter jets and prop planes. If Cargill is meeting Bala about guns, maybe someone is flying the guns into Atlanta via Charlie Brown. Security at such small fields is a joke.

The light goes green and I turn left, following Cargill's tracks. I glance down at my phone to see the beeping dot as it steadily passes the airport. So much for that theory. Soon enough the road rises slightly and I see rows of lights illuminating one of Charlie Brown's two runways. A jet screams overhead, a dark shadow winging its way into the night.

I catch up to the truck before we drive underneath the ugly green I-20 overpass. We are rolling through a flat, industrial area between the Perimeter and the Chattahoochee River, and soon I see Cargill's truck about a quarter mile ahead turn into a maze of warehouse buildings jumbled up against the eastern bank of the Chattahoochee.

I drive past the turn that Cargill took and then take the next one. The street I'm on winds its way into the heart of the industrial park. I pull into a parking lot of a U-Haul repair center to get my bearings. The blinking dot on my phone has slowed, then stops near the back of this cluster of buildings, about two hundred yards away from where I am. Most businesses in here are closed and dark, although streetlights illuminate the roadways. Google Maps says Cargill is parked by the loading dock of a warehouse that isn't identified on the map but is next to a concrete product supplier. I pull out of the U-Haul repair center lot and ride down the street, then I turn right one block before I reach Cargill's street. I pass a series of brick buildings all in shadow, then turn into a parking lot behind a contract flooring business and kill the engine. When I remove my helmet, traffic noise from Fulton Industrial washes over me, but other than that I hear nothing. The night is heavy and thick.

I stow my helmet under the seat and take off my leather jacket, then open the top box mounted on the back. I already have all my usual toys, but from the box I take a pair of night vision binoculars, which I clip to my belt, and then I lift out a Kel-Tech KSG bullpup shotgun. It basically looks like a large pistol mated with a rocket launcher, all just over two feet in length. I sling the KSG over my head and shoulder so it lies across my back, the muzzle pointing down. Frees my hands for other things. I screw a silencer onto my CZ. My hip holster accommodates the silencer, although the increased barrel length will make it harder to draw quickly. But this situation calls for stealth, not shotguns—not yet. I check the rest of the gear I'm carrying, put my leather jacket into the top box, and lock it. Then I walk out of the parking lot, cross the street, and head down the road that runs between a wedding store and the corporate office of a dessert company, making my way toward Cargill's truck.

Creeping down this street at night, I'm struck by how the whole place looks like a slightly nightmarish version of cookie-cutter suburbia, except with brick warehouses instead of two-story homes. Even the Bluff has a sense of life, of people living there. This empty tract of storage buildings and industries looks like something left after the apocalypse, a world devoid of human beings.

Behind the wedding store there's a narrow, empty parking lot backed by a thin scrim of pine trees. Beyond the trees sits the warehouse where Cargill's truck is located. I hurry across the parking lot and step into the trees, my feet crunching softly on dead pine needles.

Less than a hundred feet away is the loading dock of the warehouse. I drop to a crouch by a pine tree and unclip my night vision binoculars from my belt. Through them the night shades into green and black. There's Cargill's truck, parked to one side of the loading dock. And standing by the dock is Cargill along with three men. Facing them are half a dozen other men, most holding handguns or what look like machine pistols.

One of them, shorter but wide-shouldered with a closely shaved head, the only one without a gun, stands a step ahead of the others, talking to Cargill. I'd bet my motorcycle that he's Bala.

Although the traffic noise is practically nonexistent, I can't hear what Bala is saying, just a murmur of spoken words. In the past I've used a parabolic microphone that could capture outdoor conversations from a hundred yards away. A parabolic microphone would be nice right now, but I don't have a magic tote bag to carry all the gear I might want at any given moment. I'll simply have to get closer.

Before I can move, Bala and Cargill do. They turn and walk toward an open doorway in the back wall of the warehouse, their men following. They pass through the doorway, then close it behind them. Two men—Bala's, not Cargill's—remain outside on the loading dock. Sneaking in the back door is off the table.

I retreat back to the wedding store parking lot and jog down to the far end of the lot, maybe fifty yards, then turn back into the trees. Here the pines are a bit closer together and I carefully pick my way through the tree cover, not wanting to stumble over a stray root. I reach the edge of the tree line at the back of the concrete supplier warehouse, next to the building where Bala and Cargill are having a powwow. Through my binoculars I can just make out the two goons on the loading dock guarding the back door. My guess is that there are at least two more men watching the front. Let's hope there aren't any stationed on this side of the building.

There aren't any people here, but there is an unhitched semitrailer parked between the two warehouses. It's dark, but I can see weeds growing up around the wheels—the trailer has been here a while. I go around the trailer and scan the side of the warehouse. No doors or other entrances, just a brick wall with a single drainpipe running down from the roof. Not a single fire door? That's got to be some kind of OSHA violation. I cinch the shotgun sling tight, then approach the trailer. It's basically a big metal box with a pair of hinged doors at the back. As quietly as I can, I climb up the back, using the door hinges as steps. I skin one knuckle but I make it to the top. I glance toward the back of the warehouse, see no sign of a curious guard, and turn my attention to the warehouse. There's maybe three feet between the trailer and the warehouse wall. There's a rise in the ground here, so standing on top of the trailer, I'm not quite at eye level with the warehouse roof. Three feet horizontal distance, two feet vertical. Maybe two-and-a-half.

I hope the gutter holds.

I back up to the far end of the trailer, which now looks far too narrow, take a couple of deep breaths, and run toward the warehouse. On the second step, my foot strikes the top of the trailer too hard with a dull, echoing thud. On the third and last step I leap, arms outstretched, fingers extended like claws. My hands hit the gutter less than half a second before my legs swing forward from the momentum and my feet and one knee strike the brick wall. A sharp pain spikes through my leg, like someone kicked me in the kneecap, followed by a numbness. I ignore it and cling to the gutter, twenty or so feet off the ground. My arms and shoulders burn from the strain. No flashlight stabs through the darkness to sweep the wall, but I made too much noise. Someone will come check. Gritting my teeth, I try to swing my left leg up to the roof. On the third try I'm able to pull myself up enough to get the leg up onto the roof, and then I roll over the edge and lie on the flat rooftop, gasping for air. The stars above look down. I stare back, trying to slow my breathing. I'm lying on top of my shotgun, which presses painfully against my back, but I just need a minute.

After thirty seconds or so I get to my hands and knees, then ever so slowly move my head to peek over the roof's edge. I freeze. Even without the night vision binoculars, I can see the shape of a man at the back corner of the warehouse, cradling something in his hands. I'm pretty sure it's not a baby. I don't pull back, not wanting his peripheral vision to catch the movement. He takes a step forward, then another. He stops as if listening, his head slowly turning as he scans the trees, then the trailer. If he looks up, he might catch the outline of my head against the night sky.

Someone calls out from the back of the warehouse. The man down below turns to look behind him, and when he does I pull my head back and then slowly crawl away from the roof's edge. The roof is gritty and still radiates the day's heat. I hear the man below respond, then nothing. After I've crawled a few yards, I stand up, far enough away from the edge that no one on the ground would be able to see me. My right leg is pins and needles now as feeling returns, the knee a dull throb, but nothing is broken—it just hurts. I don't hear any more voices, only the distant hum of traffic on Fulton Industrial and, beyond that, I-20.

This isn't the first roof I've been on. It's not even the first warehouse roof I've been on. That realization makes me smile, although the smile feels sort of like a painting that hangs crooked on a wall. Most women my age have a regular job, are dating someone or already married, maybe even have a kid or two. Right now those other women are tucking their kids in bed, snuggling on the couch with their boyfriends or husbands, watching Netflix. Me, I'm two stories up, walking on an enormous flat surface over half the size of a football field, getting ready to spy on a meeting between two guys who should be in prison. If my parents could only see me now. But behind that thought is the warm pulse of a childhood memory: standing in a treehouse, pretending I was on a ship sailing through the branches of an oak tree, my father grinning up at me from the foot of the ladder. *What do you think, Suzie Q?* my father asked, and with joy rising like a sun in my chest I called back, *It's awesome, Daddy!*

I shake my head to clear it. This isn't the time for such memories. I pad across the roof toward a shack-like structure next to two enormous A/C units. It's a service door for access to the roof. And it's my access into the warehouse. Luckily it's not padlocked on the inside and just has an ordinary deadbolt and a pin and tumbler lock. Two minutes with my lock picks and I crack the door open very slowly. Darkness within. CZ in my hand, I ease into the darkness, pulling the door shut behind me.

CHAPTER FOURTEEN

I'm ON A SMALL LANDING WITH A LADDER LEADING DOWN INTO A LARGE open space. The warehouse. I can hear indistinguishable sounds, murmurs from below, like someone has left a radio on in a basement closet. I holster my pistol, then step back and down onto the ladder. I can only hope whoever is below doesn't happen to look up as I'm climbing down.

After two rungs I see the ladder leads to a catwalk that leads to the wall and then runs the perimeter of the warehouse. The catwalk hangs maybe seven feet from the ceiling. Below is the warehouse floor. A bad fall, though I'd more than likely hit one of the many stacks of crates or shipping containers below before pancaking onto the concrete. The front of the warehouse is dark and buttoned up tight. The murmuring comes from the back of the warehouse, where, near the back wall, two overhead lamps cast a dim yellow light on the proceedings there. But I can't see anything clearly from my vantage point. I need to get closer.

As quietly as possible I drop to the catwalk and crouch, scanning the floor below. No one moves down there, but the yellow light at the back draws me like a moth. I need to get closer and see what I can from up here, then get down onto the floor where I can hear conversations and stay hidden. Up here, I won't be able to understand anything they are saying. And if I'm spotted on this catwalk, I don't have a lot of options for where to go.

I stay low and walk toward the wall, then turn to follow the catwalk toward the back of the warehouse. Ten yards away there's a ladder that leads from the catwalk down the wall to the floor. The soles of my shoes don't make a sound, but I know if I move too quickly the catwalk might shimmy and groan. So I creep along, one step at a time.

When I reach the ladder, I stop and crouch even further down. I can see them—Cargill and Bala and some of their goons. They are standing around a large crate with the lid removed, but I'm too far away to see into the crate. I unclip the night vision binoculars from my belt and raise them to my eyes. The focus isn't perfect, and the lamps are like flares in the night vision lenses, but now I can see more clearly what's in the crate—long-barreled rifles, probably AR-15s. Then I move the binoculars slightly and Bala's face swings into view. He doesn't look happy. Neither do the two men next to him. Cargill is facing Bala, and while I can't see his expression, his body language suggests a salesman faced with an irritating customer. If I know Cargill, he's haggling over the price.

I lower the binoculars and put them back on my belt, then step onto the ladder and start to climb down. The ladder is bolted to the wall and doesn't creak, which is good. Still, I feel like a bug pinned to a display card—if anyone is close enough and looks up, I've got nowhere to hide.

Hand over hand, my face eight inches from the wall, I slowly make my way down. When I'm halfway down, below the tops of the highest stacks of crates, something stirs the hairs on the back of my neck. I turn my head to the left and I see an unshaven dude in jeans and a sleeveless T-shirt sitting on the floor, leaning back against a stack of crates. He's staring at me like a kid who's just walked in on his mom doing the mailman. He's ten yards away, too far for me to tackle or kick or even spit on. He also has a MAC-11 in his lap, a nasty little automatic weapon that could unzip my torso with one burst.

I don't have time to think. It's jump or swing. I hold onto the ladder with my left hand and swing away from the rungs like a door opening, my left hand and foot the hinges. With my right hand I reach for my CZ. It's a futile gesture. There is no way I can draw it in time before he raises his weapon and shreds me.

My hand grips the CZ and I actually have it halfway out of its holster when I realize the man isn't moving. His eyes are fixed on a spot just to one side of me, and they will be fixed on that spot forever because he also has a small, dark circle the size of a dime in his forehead. I slide the CZ into its holster and awkwardly swing back onto the ladder before climbing down the last few rungs to the floor. I step off the ladder, the CZ back in my hand, my eyes sweeping the shadows. Nothing except the murmur of conversation from the back. I run in a crouch over to the dead man. The crates on the warehouse floor are stacked so there are aisles between them, and the dead man is sitting just inside one of those aisles, like he's been tucked in there for a nap. His eyes are glassy, and he definitely has a bullet hole in his forehead, but his skin doesn't yet have that pallor that only dead men have.

I grab his left arm and lift it up, noting the 13 tattooed on the back of his hand, then lower the arm back down. Still loose, almost boneless— rigor mortis hasn't set in yet. He hasn't been dead long. I reach out with one hand and gently tip his head forward, bracing myself for a bloody exit wound and brains on the crate behind him. The crate is clean, the back of the man's head intact. I tilt his head back and the man resumes staring at the wall. The bullet must still be in his skull, which means it's small caliber. A .22 with a good silencer wouldn't make more noise than a bird fart, and a .22 subsonic round would ricochet inside a man's skull until his brain was like a block of Swiss cheese.

Based on the 13 tattooed on his hand, I'm guessing this is one of Bala's men. So who shot him in the face and then dragged him into this little alleyway in the crates? If Cargill or one of his boys did this, they'd likely be in twitching pieces on the floor right now. If Bala or his men did it, this dude would've already been wrapped up in a tarp and hauled out to a truck or van. Someone else did this, someone who may very well still be inside this warehouse. But is that someone an ally, or an even bigger threat than Bala or Cargill? I don't know and I don't have time to figure it out, but the fact that he left the man's MAC-11 behind says he's either careless or very confident. Holding my CZ low and ready, I head into the maze of crates, my ears and eyes wide open.

Heading down one aisle and then another, I feel like I'm playing a live version of those dungeon crawler computer games, the ones where you encounter goblins and skeletons on the first floor, then find the door to the next level down, where the monsters get harder and the treasures bigger. No skeletons or treasure here, but lots of goblins. I come out onto one of the main aisles, a regular highway through the center of the crate maze, and run into another one of Bala's boys. I almost step out right in front of him, but he's looking at his smartphone as he walks down the central aisle, all his attention riveted on the small window of glass in his hand, so he doesn't see me. I step back into the shadows and let him stroll past, still staring at his phone. Like the dead guy, he too is in T-shirt and jeans, like some working-class gangbanger, and he's also sporting a soul patch that's so last millennium. Once he walks past, I flit across the aisle behind him and into a gap between the crates on the other side, always angling toward the dimly lit back.

Soon I'm close enough to hear actual words in the conversation. The first is *chinga*, which doesn't bode well. Then Cargill's voice floats over the crates.

"Hey, amigo, don't get your panties in a wad," he says. "They're all yours, with more to come at the same price."

Bala's voice is low and about as friendly as a wolf's growl. "Which is not the original price."

"I told you, overhead costs," Cargill says. "Plus with that crazy bitch sneaking around, I need a little danger insurance, know what I'm saying?"

I turn down a narrow aisle that dead-ends into a stack of three crates. Bala sounds as if he is directly behind that stack. "I know exactly what you are saying," Bala says in his low growl. "Men like you always make excuses to take a little more for yourselves, and then a little more. You're like a remora swimming with sharks, nibbling at leftovers."

"Maybe," Cargill said. "But I'm the remora that's got the weapons you want. You wanna be a bigger shark, let's do business. *Comprende?*"

A pause. I lean forward against the stack, looking for gaps between the crates so maybe I can see the men. Then Bala says "*Vamos*" and the crate on top of the stack moves, scraping across the crate below it. I duck just as the top crate is removed by two of Cargill's men, nearly exposing me. I crab-walk back down the aisle as fast as I can before they pick up the other crates. I need to find another place to eavesdrop.

When I reach the end of the aisle, I stand and turn the corner, running right into Soul Patch and two other guys. He grins, showing me his teeth as well as the barrel of his own MAC-11. "Bala!" he shouts. "*Es la puta!*"

"Yeah, *la puta*," I say. "You guys are so fucking original."

Soul Patch plucks the CZ out of my hand and shoves it into his belt, then with his free hand grabs my shoulder and turns me around, pushing me face-first into a crate, the MAC-11 pressed against the back of my head. I stay calm, breathing through my open mouth, waiting for a moment. I hear footsteps running up, and more hands grab me, someone lifting the shotgun up and over my head. Then I'm dragged down the aisle and around the end of one wall of crates into an open space where Bala and Cargill are. I try to count Bala's men standing around the perimeter. Six or seven, including Soul Patch and the two goons holding my arms, plus the two outside. And whoever else might be wandering around the warehouse.

The men holding my arms let go of me, but Soul Patch pokes me in the back with the MAC-11 to let me know he's still paying attention.

Cargill's face is bruised and swollen around the butterfly bandages. He gawps at me. "The fuck are you doing here?"

"Shopping," I say, keeping my eyes on Bala.

Next to Cargill is the mechanic I knocked out earlier that afternoon. His name's Jerry, I remember. Jerry's eyes are wet with pain and anger. "You fucking bitch," he says. "You hit me over the goddamned head."

I shrug. "At least I didn't cut your cheek open. Brandon's gonna have a nice scar."

Bala tilts his shaved head as if to get a better angle on me. "This is the old man's niece?" he says.

"Yes, sir," Cargill says. "And he'll pay a pretty penny for her, too, even if he's all stove up in the hospital."

"Where's Tane?" I ask Bala.

Bala smiles, revealing yellowed teeth. "I heard you'd lost him. Don't worry, when we find him, I'll make sure to tell him that right before we killed you, you were asking about him."

"Wait, *what*?" Cargill says.

The howler monkeys in my head are hooting, but whether they're amused or scared I don't know. "*That's* a great idea," I say to Bala. "You shoot me in the head and my uncle will take you apart like a watch."

Bala's smile dims slightly, but not nearly enough. "Your *tío* is on death's door," he says. "I'm not worried about him."

"Let's think about this, Bala," Cargill says. "You know how much she's worth to a man like Gavin Lester? Or screw that, she *knows* things. About Lester's business. We could make a killing."

"Oh, Brad," I say, "I didn't know you cared."

"Ah, fuck you, you curly-headed cunt."

"Enough," Bala says, already bored. He holds out a silver-plated revolver, butt first, to Cargill. "Kill her."

Cargill recoils. "I'm not shooting anybody."

The howler monkeys are definitely scared. And also pissed. "You'll want my help finding Tane," I say to Bala.

"If you knew where he was," Bala says, "you wouldn't have asked this *cabrón*. Or me."

He's got a point, plus I'm just stalling. Soul Patch is a little too close to me, which could be good. But who has my shotgun, and is it pointing at me? There are too many men, any one of whom could put a large hole through me if I so much as sneeze.

Bala gestures at Cargill with the revolver. "Take this and shoot her."

"Why do you want me to—"

"Because you led her here," Bala says. "Because you couldn't handle her, and now I'm going to make you handle her. Take this and shoot her."

Cargill looks at Bala, looks at the revolver. He doesn't look at me. Slowly he reaches out and takes the revolver from Bala's hand. I can feel the men behind me moving off to the side, getting out of the line of fire.

"Brad," I say, "think about it." Cargill keeps looking at the revolver, not moving. "Think about my uncle," I say, my voice steady. "Gus Cimino is at the bar right now. You know what my uncle would have Gus do to you if you hurt me? You'd wake up in a basement tied to a radiator and a car battery, and Gus would be standing in front of you with a rusty knife."

Cargill raises his head to look at me. His expression is blank.

"Do it," Bala says.

"Shut the fuck up," Cargill says, but his eyes are on me. He raises the revolver and points it at my head.

"Brad," I say. My heart is trip-hammering and my brain is like a bird trapped in an attic, frantically trying to find a way out. I do *not* want to die because of Brandon fucking Cargill. "Don't do this."

Cargill's hand doesn't shake. The bore of the revolver's barrel looks big enough to drive a train through. "Get down on your knees," he says.

"I'm not getting on my knees."

Cargill thumbs the hammer back with a loud *snick*. "I said—"

There's a wet sound, like someone smacking a raw hamburger patty between their hands, and a clot of something dark and wet hits my arm. I look to see Bala, eyes wide and round, blood pouring down his shirt front.

"What—" Cargill says, the revolver now wavering.

Bala is able to raise one hand to his throat, which is torn open, and then he starts to fall. Before he hits the floor, I whip around, my left arm sweeping the MAC-11 away from me, my right hand rigid and aiming for Soul Patch's throat. I manage to club him in the ear instead. He fires, the sound of the MAC-11 like someone ripping a giant piece of corrugated tin in half. The long burst chews up the side of a crate and one of Bala's men, who jitters and flails for a second before he drops. He's holding my shotgun, which falls from his hands. I dive for the shotgun, six feet away on the floor.

Gunfire erupts all around me, both single shots and the brisk *rrrrpp* of machine pistols, but none of it seems to be aimed at me. When I pick up my shotgun and turn, Soul Patch is smiling as he points his machine pistol at me. He pulls the trigger. Nothing. The stunned look on his face is priceless. That's one problem with MAC-11s—they fire twelve hundred rounds a minute, so Soul Patch burned through an entire magazine in less than two seconds.

I raise my shotgun. *"Puta,"* I say, and I pull the trigger. The shotgun roars and Soul Patch flies back a yard or so as if he was kicked in the chest by a horse.

I crouch, shotgun at the ready, and take stock. Bala is down, as are a couple of his men and Cargill's mechanic buddy Jerry. I don't see Cargill. There's shouting at the back door, then more gunfire. Someone else is entertaining what's left of Bala's men. I step over to Soul Patch, who's lying in a bloody, broken heap, and retrieve my CZ.

Two men step out from behind a shipping container, one a slim dude holding an Uzi, the other an enormous man carrying a sawed-off shotgun. The one with the Uzi raises it, but the second man pushes the barrel down. "Not her, fool," he says.

"Hey, Billy," I say.

Billy nods. "Doctor Woman," he says.

There's a high-pitched whistle from the back. "Time to go," Billy says. He spits on Bala's corpse, then he and his Uzi-toting friend run toward the back. I follow them, because I have no desire to stay in a warehouse full of dead men.

We race through a few aisles and then out the back door onto the loading dock, where another of Bala's men is face down on the concrete in a pool of blood. Standing next to the body, his Hawks cap perched on his head, shirt crisp and white as a linen tablecloth, holding a silver-plated .45, is Peaches.

"Took you long enough," I say.

Peaches grins, teeth flashing in the night. "I ain't come to rescue your ass. You welcome, by the way."

"So why did you come?"

The grin slides off his face. "Turns out D wasn't just a snitch for the feds."

I look down at the corpse, then back at Peaches. "He was talking to the Sureños?"

"Motherfucker tryin' to play everybody. I'd be impressed if he wasn't suckin' Bala's dick. After you called, Billy got him to talk real quick. Told us about this little gun deal." Peaches looks at Billy. "We all good?"

Billy nods. "We gotta go, man."

The faint sound of approaching sirens punctuates Billy's remark.

"Hey," I say to Billy, "you take out any of Bala's men earlier tonight with a silencer?"

Billy frowns. "I look like James Bond to you? We came in right before you saw us, loud as fuck. Peaches, seriously, we gotta go."

"We out." Peaches trots down the loading dock stairs to the asphalt, Billy following. In the shadows at the back of the lot, a black Mercedes SUV rumbles to life, headlights off. Just before he gets into the SUV, Peaches calls out to me, "You find that Kamaka kid?"

I shake my head and start jogging toward the trees. The doors to Peaches's SUV slam shut, and the Mercedes rolls across the lot and around the front of the warehouse and out of sight.

By the time I run through the tree line and past the wedding store, then cross the street to the flooring business where I parked my bike, the sirens are getting louder. I shove the KSG into the top box and lock it shut, then throw on my leather jacket and helmet. I start the bike, the engine throaty and eager, and I keep the headlight off as I turn onto the street and head back toward the exit. Behind me I hear sirens and the squeal of tires as police turn into the first entrance to the industrial park. I didn't see Cargill leave, and I wonder if he got away. No time to track his jacked-up truck on my phone right now.

I see the reflection of blue lights off the trees before any police cars round the corner ahead of me. Damn it, now there are cops at both entrances. I lean and make a hard left, cutting across a narrow strip of grass and then behind a food distribution warehouse, where I stop between a dumpster and the warehouse. A few seconds later a police car flies down the street I was just on, siren blaring. I ride forward past the dumpster to the back of the warehouse, where an ancient pair of railroad tracks runs behind this building and the other ones backing up to it, trees lining both sides of the tracks. I turn right, onto the tracks, giving my Thruxton's shocks a real workout. By the time the trees fall away and the tracks cross the road I used to drive into the industrial park, the police have all congregated at the back of the park where the shooting happened and haven't yet sealed off all exits. I gun the bike down the road and out onto Fulton Industrial, speeding past more warehouses and gas stations until I hit Cascade and take a left, winding my way back through the dark wooded lots toward the city.

CHAPTER FIFTEEN

Wʜᴇɴ I ʜɪᴛ 285 I ᴛᴀᴋᴇ ɪᴛ ᴀɴᴅ ɢᴏ ɴᴏʀᴛʜʙᴏᴜɴᴅ, ᴍᴇʀɢɪɴɢ ᴡɪᴛʜ the traffic that even late on a Monday night flows around the city, a river of steel in a bed of stone. No police cars fly up behind me, no blue lights flash in my rearview. I've escaped the shitshow. But other than that, I didn't gain much, only that Bala didn't know where Tane was. At least the Sureños don't have him. So where is he? Has he bugged out of Atlanta? Maybe hopped a plane to Hawaii or the Solomons or some tiny atoll on the other side of the planet? Bala might have had some ideas about where Tane could be, but now I'll never know. I need to get back to Ethan's house and figure out my next move. Maybe tomorrow Uncle Gavin will be awake and coherent and can give me some direction. Not all of Bala's Sureños are dead, and if they can regroup after tonight, they'll want their money man back even more.

I take the Roswell Road exit, and as I ride up the off ramp, the King and Queen buildings rise above the tree line, just a couple of miles further down the interstate. The twin towers each have lattice crowns so the buildings resemble chess pieces: the Queen has a rounded arc, the King a squared-off top. Right now they are lit up with blue light, gleaming on the horizon. Last year I stood on this same bridge staring at the towers—they were green then—and working up the nerve to jump. Ethan found me and talked me off the bridge and into the hospital. He literally saved my life. Of course he did—that's his job, bestowed on him by our father as he lay bleeding to death in our house: *Watch your sister.* His last words. Watch your screwed-up disaster of a sister.

I drive down Roswell Road, passing the ice-skating rink and the adult entertainment shop and the gas stations where day laborers stand every morning waiting for contractors who need to hire workers cheap. Past them are apartments and a New Age bookstore and the red bull's-eye logo of Target, and at the top of the hill is the Church of Scientology and more apartment complexes and a Waffle House and a former strip joint-slash-gentlemen's club that has weeds thrusting up through cracks in the parking lot. And leading off of both sides of Roswell are side streets like tributary streams leading to residential neighborhoods, row upon row of houses, thousands of them rolling away into the night, only a few sputtering streetlights to hold off the darkness.

I turn onto Ethan's street, the motorcycle's throttled growl echoing in my wake. Across from Ethan's house, the construction site is dark and quiet. I give it the finger before going up Ethan's driveway, bouncing over the tree roots. The front windows of Ethan's house are soft yellow squares of lamplight in the dark. I'm home.

The kitchen door is open and I walk inside. "Ethan?" I call out. I grab a beer from the fridge. "You will not *believe* the evening I've had." I push the fridge door shut with my foot and pop the top off my bottle, draining half of it before I walk into the den.

I stop. Ethan has two chairs in his den, one on either side of his couch. Right now Ethan is sitting in the straight-backed chair that is really the fourth chair of the kitchen table set. He normally sits in the other, upholstered chair across the room, but now another man is sitting there. He's wearing a black T-shirt and pants and has ink-black hair with some silver at the temples framing a strong, craggy face.

"You must be Jimmy's daughter," the man in the upholstered chair says to me.

I'm not easily surprised, but I stand flat-footed and stare at the man for a good two or three seconds. *Jimmy's daughter* is not an identifier anybody uses to describe me. So it takes me a bit to realize the man is holding Wilson on his lap, both hands around the dog's small body.

I drop my beer and draw my CZ. The silencer is still attached and adds an extra half-second to my draw time, but the man doesn't move a muscle, except to smile. I aim my pistol at his forehead. "Let go of the dog," I say.

"Who, Wilson?" The man looks down at Wilson, the smile still on his face. "He's pretty happy where he is."

I realize the man isn't holding Wilson against his will; instead, he's petting him, one hand rubbing behind Wilson's ears, the other hand stroking his belly. Wilson thumps his tail when he sees me but otherwise lies prostrate on the man's lap, in a happy dog coma.

I take a step forward so I'm directly behind the couch, eight feet away from the seated man, pistol still aimed at him. "Put him down. Now."

The man mock-frowns, the smile still on his face. "If that's what you want." He gives Wilson a final pat and then with both hands lifts him off his lap. Wilson grunts in displeasure. The man sets Wilson down on the floor, then sits back in the chair, hands on the armrests, in clear view and empty.

"Come here, Wilson," I say.

Wilson wags his tail twice, then looks up at the man in the chair. A whine starts in his throat.

"Wilson!" I snap.

Head down, Wilson trots over to me, then hides his embarrassment by pretending to sniff around the couch.

The man in the chair displays his open hands. "I just want to talk. I'm unarmed."

Ethan jerks forward in his seat. *"Don't,"* he says.

The man and I both look at him.

Ethan winces apologetically. "Sorry, it's just . . . that quote. 'I'm unarmed.' From *Serenity*, the movie?"

The man shakes his head. "I must have missed that one."

"Sci-fi flick," I say. "The bad guy tells the good guy, Mal, he wants to solve their problems peacefully, like civilized men. Tells Mal he's unarmed. Mal says, 'Good,' then shoots the bad guy."

The man's smile widens. "I suppose I'm the bad guy in this scenario."

I shrug. "You're the one who said you're unarmed."

"Suzie," Ethan says, his voice strained. "You should listen to him."

"I don't want to," I say, my pistol still pointed at the man's head. "I've had to listen to a lot of assholes lately. And this one threatened you, then choked me out last night. I'm not too keen on listening to his sad tale of woe."

The man spreads his hands, slowly but calmly, not making a move, just a gesture of acceptance. "Is there any other kind?"

"And he's a philosopher too," I say. "Your name's Finn, right? Just the one name, like Madonna?"

Finn chuckles. His eyes crinkle and his mouth opens, revealing his tongue lying behind his bright white teeth. "Susannah, you are an adult portion. And I'm enjoying this back and forth we've got going on here. But I'm kind of on a timetable, and we have a lot to talk about."

"Busy evening?"

"Not as busy as you." Finn's eyes and smile are both pleasant. His eyes are hazel, shifting from green to blue depending on the light. "Following that truck from English Avenue all the way to the Chattahoochee? I thought we were going to Six Flags, maybe ride a roller-coaster. But then all those bad men in that warehouse . . . things got kinda dicey for a hot second."

I stand very still, staring at Finn. That pleasant smile is still on his face, but now he has a look in his eye, a dark, gleeful malevolence, the look of a devil toying with you. "You were tailing me," I say, making it a statement rather than a question.

"Lucky for you, too," he says. "When you got pinched, I distracted everyone by shooting that gangbanger in the throat. Gave you a chance, and you took it and *flew*, girl. That was fun to watch."

Dimly I register that Ethan is looking at me with serious questions on his mind. I have questions of my own. To stall for time so I can get a firmer grip on the situation, I ask, "What did you use, a silenced .22?"

He nods. "Good call. Yeah, I learned I was a pretty good shot in the Army. Among other things." He looks directly at the pistol in my hands for the first time, then back at me. "Susannah, I don't want to hurt you. I saved your life tonight. If I'd wanted to, I'd have let that milk-skinned redneck in his urban cowboy truck shoot you in the head. I could have done it myself when you found that *cholo* I tapped and then hid behind those crates. I wasn't twenty feet away, on top of a crate looking down at you, and you had no idea."

I shift on my feet, as if I need to steady myself in a strong crosswind. Finn is maneuvering me like he's moving a pawn on a chess board. My throat threatens to close up, and I take a deep breath, clench my jaw and unclench it. I'm not a pawn. I'm a motherfucking queen.

"Why?" I ask.

"I wanted to see what you were capable of," he says. "It's always a good idea to know your opponent. Or your partner, depending."

"Partner?" I glance at Ethan, who looks as confused as I am. "What the hell are you talking about?"

"I'll explain, but would you mind just putting the gun down? Fingers can get twitchy and slip, and I don't want to make a mess in your brother's house. Just hear me out."

I consider him down the barrel of my pistol. A few more ounces of pressure on the trigger is all it would take.

He holds his hands palms up, as if holding a tray he's about to serve me. "I can tell you what happened to your dad," he says.

Anger sweeps through me like a wave, threatening to pull me along with it. "My dad was murdered," I say, willing my hands to remain as steady as my voice.

"I know," Finn says, his eyes on mine, that earlier devilish look gone and replaced with what looks like sympathy. "I mean I can tell you what happened to him in Iraq."

This is not a man to be trusted. Any fool could tell that. But people like negotiating, exchanging and expending power. Gestures, even insincere ones, are appreciated. Conceding this small thing will increase Finn's confidence that he is in control of the situation, which is something I could exploit. And even if he's lying and has a weapon, I doubt he can draw faster than I can, with him seated and me standing.

And he says he can tell me about my father.

Without taking my eyes off Finn, I holster my pistol. Finn accepts my gesture with a nod, then settles back into his chair. As he opens his mouth to talk, though, I interrupt him, just to keep him on his toes. "Ethan told me you said our father was a thief. That's bullshit."

Finn shakes his head. "It's not. But it's complicated."

I lean against the couch and fold my arms, aware of how quickly I can draw my pistol. "So explain it."

"You can sit down if you like."

"I'm good."

Finn glances at my hip where my pistol is holstered underneath my jacket, then gives me a brief, knowing smile. "What did your dad tell you about Iraq?"

"He said it was hot."

"That's it?"

"He was a loan officer in a bank. Then his National Guard unit got called up for active duty and sent to Iraq. He did two tours and came home with PTSD. He didn't share a lot of stories. And he definitely didn't mention you."

Ethan shifts in his chair but I ignore him. Finn doesn't react to my barb except to sigh. "I'm not surprised he didn't mention me."

"Let's get back to the part about you calling our father a thief."

Finn pauses, considering, then draws in a deep breath through his nose. "I was regular Army and stationed in Baghdad, like your father," he says. "A lot of grunts didn't think too highly of the National Guard, thought they were a bunch of weekend warriors playing soldier. Me, I didn't care. We were all dropped into a country that didn't want us there. All of us knee-deep in the same chaos. So I didn't give a shit whether or not a guy was National Guard or regular Army or the Salvation Army— as long as he did his job and had my six, I'd have his.

"Now, your dad was a good guy. Cared about his men, knew how to be an officer without being a prick. He wasn't interested in sucking up to the CPA or setting himself up for a cushy career at the Pentagon. He just wanted to do his job and get back home." Finn scratches his jaw. "He talked about his family. Talked about the two of you. Said you were both whip-smart. Said Ethan read everything under the sun and that Susannah was going to be a hell-raiser." He levels his eyes at me. "He always smiled when he said that about you, though, so I don't think he meant it as a criticism. He loved you both. You and your mother."

Ethan's face is as flat and closed as a stone door. I hope mine looks the same way. When our father came home from Iraq, he was haunted and prone to mood swings, and that was what he was like for the last year of his life. That version of Dad, along with his murder, is the one that's burned into my memory. But Finn is reminding both of us about a different Dad, about the time before. I want to hear more, and at the same time I want Finn to stop because it's like someone scraping a knife against bone. I wonder if Ethan feels the same, then realize I don't need to wonder—of course he does. How else could you feel?

Ethan leans forward in his chair. "None of that explains why you called our father a thief," he says.

"I'm just trying to explain," Finn says. "Setting the scene."

"Pushing our buttons," I say. "Manipulating us so we'll be more likely to believe you."

Finn shrugs. "Everybody manipulates everyone else. A husband trying to get his wife in the mood, a guy trying to sell his neighbor a car, a kid wanting his parents to take him to the movies. You trying to get me to skip to the end of my story so you can dismiss it. That's just being human. It's how we're wired. But anyway." He pats his knees as if he's about to stand up and say goodbye. Instead, he's settling in.

CHAPTER SIXTEEN

"**Y**OUR FATHER'S PLATOON AND MINE GOT ASSIGNED TO A SECURITY detail," Finn continues. "A convoy of trucks, carrying cargo from the airport to the CPA headquarters in Saddam's old presidential palace. We had to drive seven miles through Baghdad. The most dangerous stretch of road in Iraq, maybe the world. We called it Route Irish. Bullets, rockets, mortars, you name it. Insurgents would plant IEDs, especially near the median. Or they'd put one in a vehicle near exits. Sometimes you'd have suicide bombers in vehicles ready to blow themselves to Allah as long as they took you with them. The road looked like a junkyard, bombed-out trucks and cars everywhere. And all those bombs would make craters in the asphalt, so the road was bumpy as hell. You ride in a Bradley for a security run on Route Irish, you learn pretty quick which god you believe in.

"That first convoy, your dad rode point in a Bradley. The trucks were driven by Iraqis. I rode in one of those trucks and kept my rifle pointed at the driver the whole time so he didn't do anything funny. He just kept sweating and muttering to himself, held onto the steering wheel like he was hanging on the edge of a cliff. Halfway to the Green Zone, we had to stop because there was a car blocking the road. This Iraqi family was standing around the car and looking at it, and so traffic stopped. A few Iraqis sped by in the breakdown lane, because nobody wanted to be stuck on Route Irish, but there wasn't enough room for our trucks to do that. Everyone was tense. Was the car stalled, or was it a trap so an insurgent could fire an RPG, or was it an IED?

"Your dad got out of his Bradley. No one liked riding in those things—they were armored boxes with no airflow and like a hundred and thirty degrees inside—but they could protect you from a bullet or shrapnel. Jimmy just walked toward the Iraqi family with a translator. I was watching from the first truck. Your dad talked to the father of the family, who started getting hysterical that an armed American soldier was approaching him. Somehow your dad calmed him down and decided the guy's car was really stalled, so he got a few of his grunts to push the car to the side of the road. Meanwhile the rest of us were gripping our rifles and trying to eyeball everything in every direction because we *knew* someone was gonna open fire or blow an IED. But no one did. We drove through Baghdad and got the trucks to the CPA, and the first thing I did after we got off duty was buy your dad a drink. Called him our good luck charm. Ethan, can I get some water, please? My throat's getting dry."

Without a word Ethan gets up and goes into the kitchen and gets a bottle of water for Finn, who twists off the cap and says "Cheers," then drinks. Ethan returns to his chair and sits, glancing once at me.

Finn lowers the bottle from his mouth and screws the cap back on. "Thank you," he says. "So. Turns out the cargo on those trucks was money flown in from the States. Over six hundred bricks of cash, each brick made up of a thousand bills. In that particular shipment, those were hundred-dollar bills." Finn pauses, allowing us to do the mental math.

In a low voice, Ethan says, "That's over sixty million dollars."

Finn nods, slowly. "All flown over in a single C-130 Hercules. And there were a lot more flights like that."

"Forty billion," I say.

"What?" Finn says.

"That's how much money I heard we flew into Iraq. Forty billion dollars."

Finn gives a lopsided smile. "That's what I heard too."

"So let me guess," Ethan says. His voice is harsh and it lights up my spine like a flare. Wilson, who has fallen asleep next to the couch, jerks awake, his ears raised in alarm. "You ran security for a few more convoys, and the thought of all that cash was too much temptation. Is that what you're going to tell us? A few million here or there, who would notice?"

Finn considers Ethan as if seeing him for the first time. The look in his eyes is cold, predatory, and I drop my hands to my hips so my fingers are closer to my pistol. Ethan glares back at him, as if daring Finn to say what we both fear—that our father stole money. That's why Ethan's angry, I realize. Because he's afraid it's true.

Then the predatory look in Finn's eyes vanishes and he sags back in his chair a bit, and I release a pent-up breath.

"Not exactly," Finn says. "I mean, everyone thought about it. You have to understand, Baghdad was flooded with cash. Money flowed in and out of the CPA's vault like it was a casino. Sometimes we ran convoys directly to the Central Bank of Iraq, pitched duffels full of cash into the bank lobby like they were bags of laundry. And no one was documenting anything. Once the cash was flown in and turned over to the CPA at the airport, keeping track of the money was an Iraqi problem. Someone might have to sign a half-assed receipt, but that was it. There was no accountability. It was corrupt as hell. How many contractors billed the CPA for shit that was four or five times what they actually spent? How many soldiers slipped a brick of cash into their rucksacks? It was like the fucking Wild West over there.

"Your dad, though, he just wanted to get home. Until Ahmed."

"Ahmed?" Ethan asks.

Finn's hand starts fidgeting, like he's twirling a cigarette between his fingers. "An Iraqi subcontractor in Baghdad. We had to deliver cash to him. He didn't want to come to the Green Zone to pick up his paycheck. Lots of Iraqis didn't, made them targets for militia groups or the Sunni insurgents or the fucking jihadists. So sometimes we'd have to get in a car and drive bags full of cash across Baghdad to deliver to some guy in the back of a pharmacy or a clothing store.

"This guy, though . . . Ahmed worked on the electrical grid, which was always having problems, so he was always busy. We were busy too. This was in March '04, and the CPA was handing over authority to the Iraqis at the end of June, so everybody was freaking out that the gravy train was going to be cut off. More flights carrying cash, more security details, more disbursements. Anyway, Ahmed insisted that we take the money to him in Sha'ab, a neighborhood on the north side of Baghdad. It wasn't far from Sadr City, which at that point was a time bomb. American patrols getting ambushed, police stations attacked. No way we were driving into Sadr City in a fucking Hyundai with five hundred grand in cash. We figured Sha'ab would be okay, though, so we went up there, me and your dad and an Iraqi translator and five other guys in two cars. Couldn't roll up in a Bradley or a Humvee without attracting attention.

"We got to the apartment building where we were supposed to meet Ahmed and left three men guarding the cars on the street. Ahmed's apartment was on the third floor, so we went up the stairs, one grunt and the Iraqi translator carrying the bags, the rest of us with our M4s ready.

"Ahmed was this short, balding guy who looked like he'd lost a lot of weight, skin hanging on his face, belt tight around his waist. Some Iraqis would serve Americans tea if you visited their homes. Ahmed, though, he was about as friendly as a cage. And it was clear this place wasn't Ahmed's home—there was a futon and some folding chairs and a table, nothing on the walls. It was a meeting spot. And there were three other guys there, all armed. That wasn't unusual in Baghdad, especially when there was money involved. But it felt wrong. Still, there were four of us and four of them, plus three more of ours outside. And we were just couriers, dropping off money.

"Ahmed made a show of looking in the bags of money and counting the bricks. He and our translator, Yousef, kept talking. I couldn't follow it too well, but it looked like Ahmed was concerned he'd been stiffed. The three thugs with him kept fingering their AKs and we all just stood on opposite sides of the room, facing each other while Ahmed and Yousef kept talking.

"I still don't know what the deal was—if Ahmed was being targeted, if one of the thugs in the room was with the jihadists, if someone told the insurgents a group of American soldiers was in Sha'ab, if someone just wanted to play with a new toy. Whatever the reason, I heard this loud, screeching *hiss* just before the window exploded. Someone from a nearby roof had fired an RPG at the apartment. But they hit the wall instead of the window—otherwise we'd all have been dead. It still knocked us on our asses. One second we're facing off against Ahmed and his thugs like half-assed gunslingers, and the next thing I know I'm on the floor, covered in glass, my ears ringing. I sat up, still holding my M4, and saw your dad getting to his feet. There was blood on his cheek, a cut from the glass, but otherwise he looked okay. Then he got this scared, angry look on his face and started shouting and raised his rifle. I couldn't hear him, but I understood enough to drop to the floor.

"One of the thugs with Ahmed, I don't know if he'd planned this all along or if the RPG made him lose his shit, but when he sat up he grabbed his AK and aimed it at me. Your dad shot him, a clean burst right in the chest. Then everyone started shooting. I saw Ahmed yank a pistol out of his belt, and then Yousef grabbed his arm and they both fell to the floor. Ahmed got up empty-handed and tried to make a run for the door, and I shot him in the legs and he dropped, screaming. I shot him again and he stopped screaming.

"It only lasted about ten seconds, but when it was over, Ahmed and his three guys were dead, and two of ours were down. One, a guy from my squad named Cortez, had been shot in the face. He was gone. The other was a Guardsman named Perkins, had a round in his shoulder. Screamed like a pig at a butcher's. I put a bandage on his shoulder and told Yousef to keep pressure on it. Your dad, he was just sitting on the floor, staring at the man he'd shot. Shock.

"Outside in the street there was gunfire. I looked out the giant hole in the wall and saw our three guys by the cars, exchanging fire with someone on a roof who was pinning them down. One of the cars was already trashed, tires blown, the windshield gone. I saw the muzzle flash from a roof maybe a hundred yards away. I raised my M4 and found the guy in my sights, but before I could fire a second guy stood up next to the one firing. The second guy had an RPG launcher and aimed it down the street. I got lucky and shot the guy just before he pulled the trigger. He bent forward, and then the roof blew up. He'd fired the RPG into the roof right in front of him. All gone in a big cloud of smoke.

"Nobody else seemed interested in shooting at us anymore, so I went back to check on your dad. He was on his hands and knees, throwing up. Yousef was talking to Perkins, telling him he would be okay. I walked around to secure the room, making sure Ahmed and his men were dead, and that's when I saw a door at the end of the kitchen. It was a bathroom, and there wasn't anyone hiding in it, but there were a lot of duffels in there, a dozen of them. I opened one up and found more bricks of cash, these ones wrapped in gold seals—hundred-dollar bills. Ahmed had been busy that day.

"So we took them."

It takes me a moment to realize Finn has stopped talking. "You took the money?" I say.

Finn nods. "We'd all been shot at, half blown up. I was pissed. And this fucker Ahmed had been raking it in, and when we tried to drop off another payment, he and his goons tried to kill us." He holds up a palm as if to ward off a protest. "I know he didn't fire that RPG, and he wasn't the martyr type. But I blamed Ahmed. I knew Cortez, the guy who'd been shot in the face. Had a baby girl at home he hadn't met yet. And Perkins, his shoulder was shot to shit. I knew he'd get patched up and honorably discharged, and then he'd probably end up addicted to painkillers. And your dad . . ." Finn slowly shakes his head, looking at the floor. "He told me later that was the first time he'd ever killed anybody.

It did a number on his head. He shot that man to save me, and it was as justified as anything could be. But he couldn't wrap his mind around it. So I saw all this cash sitting there, knowing that if we turned it in it would just flow right back out to another Ahmed, someone else who'd skim off the top, charge the CPA or the Iraqi government a million dollars for something that cost a third of that. The way I saw it, Ahmed had stolen this money from the CPA, maybe from other people, too. Why shouldn't we have it?"

"How'd you do it?" Ethan says. He leans forward in his chair, eyes fixed on Finn. "Get the money out? Did you hide it somewhere?"

"Not at first. Didn't have time. The grunts in the street had already radioed Camp Banzai just across the river. I knew we'd have soldiers on the scene in a few minutes. So Yousef and one of the two grunts guarding the cars carried Perkins down to the street, and your dad and I started hustling the bags down to the car that wasn't all shot up and tossed them in the trunk. Yousef and the other two saw what we were doing, but they didn't say a word. They were kinda busy trying to keep Perkins from bleeding out and taking care of their buddy who'd also been shot, plus keeping an eye out for anybody else with an itchy trigger finger.

"On the last trip down, I carried the duffel of money we'd brought to give Ahmed. It was torn up from the RPG and there was some blood on the bricks inside, but otherwise it was okay. The first Humvees and Bradleys were pulling up when I stepped out of the apartment building, troopers hopping out and establishing a perimeter. A medic checked out Perkins and the other guy and got them a casevac to Camp Banzai.

"Pretty soon a captain from 1st Brigade, 1st Armored showed up and asked what the hell happened. Your dad was still kind of a zombie at that point, but he told the captain how we'd taken the payment to Ahmed, how someone had fired an RPG, how Ahmed and his men started shooting and we fired back. Yousef piped up and told him I'd shot the guy with the RPG on the roof. That impressed the captain more than anything. He asked what happened to the money, and your dad looked at me. We hadn't talked about it really. I think Jimmy was probably still in shock when we were taking the bags down to the cars. I told the captain I'd put it all in the trunk and would take it back to the CPA. Showed him the trunk with the bag we'd brought, all shredded and bloody, on top of the others. He just nodded and I closed the trunk. And then your dad and I and Yousef drove off in the one car.

"It was your dad who came up with the idea of hiding the money in the water treatment plant. It was just outside the Green Zone, one of the construction projects sprouting up all over Iraq. And the contractor wasn't doing a damn thing. He'd built four walls and part of a roof and installed a few pipes, and then he abandoned it. Still billed the CPA for it. That half-assed building was the perfect symbol for post-invasion Iraq. Anyway, there were lots of hiding places in there, and it would be pretty easy to go off base to get there if we needed to. We hid the duffels inside of a sewer pipe that wasn't connected to anything.

"It was only meant to be temporary. The plan was that Jimmy would figure out how to get it all back to the States, and we'd split it five ways— a little over two million each for everyone in the room when the RPG hit. We'd take Cortez's share and set up a fund for his baby girl. Jimmy had saved up some leave time, so he was going to go home and figure out how to best move the cash, and the rest of us would stay down-range and keep an eye on the money.

"The best part? We returned the bag of cash we'd taken to Ahmed. All of it accounted for. Some POG at the CPA actually gave us shit for being Boy Scouts. No one suspected anything."

Finn pauses, then drinks from his bottle of water.

"And then?" I ask.

Finn slowly twists the cap back on his bottle. "And then the shit hit the fan," he says. "The next day, four Blackwater military contractors took a wrong turn in Fallujah and got ambushed. They were driving past some kebab shops when insurgents opened fire on their SUVs and threw grenades. Poor bastards didn't have a chance. A crowd showed up and torched their vehicles, then dragged their burned bodies out. It wasn't enough that they'd shot them and then turned them into charcoal. They had to beat them, mutilate their corpses. They tied one of the corpses to a car and dragged it through the streets. Two of the bodies were hung from a bridge. And the whole city cheered. And do you know why they were there, in Fallujah? They were escorting kitchen equipment. Some shitbird at Blackwater wanted to impress their client, so they rushed the job and sent four men who had never trained together, without armored vehicles, into Fallujah.

"A week later, Iraq was on fire. The Mahdi Army sprang up everywhere, attacking patrols and Iraqi police stations. We had to send tanks into Sadr City. Everything was fucked, and we couldn't unfuck it."

Finn puts his water bottle on the coffee table and clenches his fists, then slowly opens them. "I don't think I can explain it clearly," he says. "The whole country was at war, all these different factions united against the one thing they all hated more than each other—us. But in the Green Zone in Baghdad, some people kept acting like everything was fine. There was beer and barbecue and movie nights, fucking salsa dance lessons and shit. Meanwhile, a couple blocks away, if you went into an alley alone to take a leak, all anyone would find of you would be your dog tags in the gutter. And the money flights kept coming in. I know it was all Iraqi money in the first place, but it felt like we were just printing money and throwing it on a bonfire. It was obscene.

"When we first went into Iraq, with all that shock-and-awe bullshit, they said Iraqis would look at us as liberators. Tell that to the Marines in Fallujah. Tell that to the guys driving Route Irish. Tell that to the four Blackwater boys. I'd like to take those CPA cocksuckers and hand them over to whoever was running Fallujah. See them burnt to a crisp and hung up on a bridge, crucified with their own guts hanging out of them."

Finn is leaning forward in his chair as if he might spring out of it. His hands grip the armrests, and although he's grinning, his eyes are wide with hate. It hurts to look into his eyes. I do it anyway.

I'm not the most empathetic person. When I was a kid, I saw *The Lion King* at a sleepover at Fiona Gorchinsky's house. At the part when Mufasa dies and Simba tries to wake him up, every other eight-year-old was teary-eyed, and Fiona was straight-up sobbing. "He's dead," I said to Simba on the TV screen. "Get over it, kid." Fiona Gorchinsky never invited me back to her house again. The point is, I understand other people's emotions—most of the time other people are easy to figure out—but I don't always feel moved by what other people feel. So when other people emote, I don't always react appropriately.

Looking straight into Finn's gaze, though, almost knocks me to the floor. His anger and hatred blast out of him like heat from the sun. If someone more emotionally sensitive were taking the full brunt of this, they'd implode and melt like the Nazis at the end of *Raiders of the Lost Ark*. As it is, I'm astonished by the depth of Finn's hate. This must be what it feels like to stare into a black hole, a void that won't let even light escape.

Then Finn blinks slowly, like shuttering a window. His hands relax on the armrests and he leans back into his chair, his grin reduced to a half-smile, his eyes clear and a bit sad. But this time I see the mask for what it is.

"Sorry," he says. "I talk about Iraq too much, I get pissed off." He takes in a deep breath and blows it out, a cleansing.

After a moment Ethan speaks, his voice thick and slow—he must have felt it too. "What happened to the money?"

Finn nods encouragingly, a teacher pleased with a student. "That, Ethan, is *the* question. What happened to the money?" He picks up his water bottle and examines it as if seeing it for the first time, then takes the cap back off. "Your father's unit got reassigned to help with Vigilant Resolve. That's what they called the op to pacify Fallujah. A week later, we called a cease-fire. By the end of the month, we pulled out of Fallujah. Marines had to go back in by the end of the year. Anyway." He takes another sip, draining the bottle, then places it back on the coffee table.

"While Jimmy was in Fallujah, I scored more convoy security. One day the Bradley I was in hit an IED. Nobody died, but I got a nice gash in my head and shrapnel in my leg and got airlifted to the military hospital in Balad. By the time I got back to Baghdad, your dad had gone home on leave. The money was still in that empty sewer pipe, though. Jimmy hadn't taken it. But I didn't know how to sneak ten million in cash out of the country."

I remember Dad coming home on leave during his first tour. He'd been happy to see us, but he'd also been jumpy, preoccupied. I thought it was just because he'd been to war. "Did you hear from him?" I ask.

"He emailed me from the States," Finn says. "We'd set up a code. He asked if I still liked Bugs Bunny cartoons, which meant he'd found a way to move the cash. I emailed back and asked if he still liked Porky Pig, which meant the coast was clear and I was ready and waiting to help." Finn's mouth turns down and he looks grim. "And then it all went FUBAR because of Perkins."

Ethan frowns. "The guy who got shot in the shoulder?"

"He should've been shot in the head," Finn says, and that angry look flickers in his eyes before he reins it in. "I'd told him and Yousef both that Jimmy and I would take care of them. They each deserved a part of that money."

"Why only you four?" I ask. "Why not the three outside guarding the cars? They went with you and got shot at."

Finn shakes his head. "We talked about it. The men in that room suffered the most. Cortez died. Perkins got his shoulder wrecked. Your dad was shook up from killing a man. Yousef kept Ahmed from shooting one of us. Plus he was an Iraqi interpreter working for the U.S. Army—his life was fucked if he stayed there, and he knew it. He could help us with Iraqi officials if it came to that with trying to get the money out. I saved those three grunts from being killed by that RPG, so as far as I was concerned, we were even." Finn shakes his head again, this time like he's disgusted. "But Perkins . . . He was like me, too banged up to go in the field, so they stuck him on admin duty too. We both worked in the motor pool in the Green Zone, office work, boring as shit. Perkins kept talking about getting a medical discharge, trying to figure out how he could get one and keep his VA benefits. And he kept talking about the money we'd hidden. Say things like 'our retirement plan' and grin, like we were sharing a big secret, never mind the fact that other grunts in the office could hear him. Drove me crazy. All it would take was one guy with a stick up his ass to say something to an officer. I knew if someone questioned Perkins he'd fold like a napkin. I told him if he kept running his mouth I'd break his other shoulder and both his kneecaps. His reaction was to go to the water treatment plant and grab a brick and hide it in his Molly."

"Molly?" Ethan asks.

I speak before Finn can answer. "Modular Lightweight Load-Carrying Equipment. Army-speak for backpack." Ethan just looks at me. "What?" I say. "I read it in a military supply catalog." I turn to Finn. "How'd you know he stole a brick?"

"Because I knew he'd do one of two things when I confronted him," Finn says. "He'd either be scared and do what I said, or he'd be scared at first and later get mad and think he deserved some of that money himself. I bet that Perkins would do the second thing. I was right."

"What did you do?"

"I beat him to death with a tire iron."

No one says anything. Finn looks calmly at me. I don't see either guilt or pride in his face, just a blank look. I don't know if this is worse.

"A tire iron," I say.

"We were in a garage in the Green Zone at the time. I'd taken the brick out of his Molly and hid it in the garage while I was replacing batteries in Humvees. Perkins came storming in and got in my face. He knew I'd taken the money. I thought he wouldn't find out until later, when I could talk to him one-on-one about it. Instead he started shouting about the money. I punched him in the mouth just to shut him up—his left arm was all bandaged up and in a sling, so I felt bad about it. But Perkins was a big dude and he went nuts after I hit him. Ran at me and grabbed me with his right hand and plowed me into a workbench, knocked the wind out of me. Then he just started punching and kicking. He completely lost it, shouting and cussing at me. I grabbed the nearest thing I could find, which was a tire iron. Laid him out with one swing, pow, over his left eye. And I kept swinging. A pair of grunts pulled me off of him, but by that time I'd opened his head up like a rotten pumpkin.

"They put me in Leavenworth for twenty years on a manslaughter charge. Probably would have been less except for Perkins's arm being in a sling. They thought we fought over that brick, that I beat a crippled man to death over a hundred grand. They assumed one of us took the brick from the bag we were taking to Ahmed. I didn't say a word about the rest of the cash, not the entire time I sat in a cell. Just kept thinking about the money sitting in that pipe. I got out six years early for good behavior, even though I got a dishonorable discharge. I went looking for your dad. Found out what happened to him. The money, of course, was gone. I even went back to Iraq to be sure."

"You were in prison for fourteen years," Ethan says. "A lot could have happened. Somebody might have found the money and taken it, or told the Iraqi government."

Finn shakes his head. "It was your dad."

I look at Ethan, then back at Finn. "Why do you think our father took it?"

"It wasn't Perkins. And I doubt it was Yousef."

"Why?" Ethan asks.

"Because Yousef wouldn't know how to move that kind of money to the States," Finn says. "And it got moved. I went to visit Cortez's widow, Elena. She was living in a nice little house outside of Baltimore, where Cortez was from. Had a new husband, a dentist. Cortez's daughter Sofía was all grown up. Drove a BMW. At first I figured that was the dentist, but Elena told me it was from Hector. Said a year or so after Hector died, someone left a suitcase on her front porch. There were two million dollars in it, in cash, with a typed note that said, 'From Hector.' Your father must have sent it to her. She swore she didn't have any more, or know anything else about it."

"You didn't think maybe she was lying?"

"I was holding a gun to Sofía's head when she swore it," Finn says. "She was telling the truth."

"Okay," I say, and I draw my CZ and aim it at Finn, center mass. "Story time's over."

"Suzie," Ethan says.

Finn frowns quizzically. "Now you're going to shoot me?"

"Yes."

"Susannah," Ethan says, his voice louder.

My eyes on Finn, I say to Ethan, "I know how to clean up after shooting someone."

"And I'd love to hear how you learned to do that," Finn says. He plants his hands on the arms of the overstuffed chair in preparation to stand. "But I'm on the clock and have to get going."

I shift my aim so my pistol is pointing at his leg, and I'm beginning to pull the trigger when I realize Wilson is sniffing around Finn's feet. "Wilson!" I call. Wilson jerks his head up and looks at me. "Come!" Wilson puts his head down and slowly walks my way.

"You aren't going to shoot me," Finn says.

"The fuck I'm not."

"Suzie!" Ethan says.

"Shut up," I tell him. "We're not playing his game. I'm not helping him look for millions of dollars that he thinks Dad stole."

Calmly, Finn says, "He did steal the money."

"Even if he did, I don't know where it is," I say. "And I'm not going to help you find it. I don't need to. Of course you'll threaten us, and we'll tell you to fuck off, and then you'll come for me or my brother, or both of us, or maybe you're the kind of sick fuck who goes after dogs. But one way or another you'll try to force us to do what you want. So I'd rather just kill you now and hide your body and that'll be that."

Finn smiles. "Before you get all trigger happy, you'll want to see something. I'm going to reach into my pocket and pull out my phone. I'll do it slowly, no tricks." He looks me in the eye, and maintaining eye contact he slowly eases his hand around to his back pocket. I raise the pistol to aim directly at his forehead. He looks calmly back at me as he retrieves his phone from his back pocket. Then he swipes his phone open and taps it before holding it up to show me the screen.

I don't want to see whatever he wants to show me; I know I don't. I look anyway. In the small glass rectangle, I see a man seated in a straight-backed chair, facing me. He looks like he's secured to the chair by duct tape, his hands and forearms taped to the arms of the chair, his feet taped together. He's blindfolded and has a gag in his mouth, but I can see a mop of curly brown hair above the black blindfold. My heart drops like an elevator whose cable has just been cut.

"You recognize Tane, right?" Finn says. "Ran out the kitchen door right there while you were talking to the feds in the front yard. Practically ran right into me when he tried to cut through the trees. I had to choke him out and get him away from here before he did anything stupid like call for help. We had a nice chat. Funny kid. Likes hamburgers. Good with money. Which is fortunate, actually. Because whatever your dad did with that money, Tane can make it disappear and reappear clean as a nun's ass. But you'll need to find it first."

My mouth and throat are dry, but I force myself to swallow. "And if I don't?"

Slowly Finn leans forward, extending his phone toward me. I look again at the screen, at Tane tied to the chair. That's when I see the red digital clock on the floor next to the chair. It's counting down by seconds, and right now it's at forty-seven minutes and change. And then I see the wires leading from the clock to the bottom of the chair.

"Suze?" Ethan says.

"He's got Tane wired up to a countdown clock," I say. I don't bother to hide the tremor in my voice. To Finn I say, "What is it, C-4?"

"Semtex," Finn says, and he actually shrugs. "Just enough to blow him into lots of little pieces if I don't get back in time to disarm it." Unhurriedly, he stands up. "I'm gonna go, but I already gave Ethan my phone number. It's a burner number, so don't bother trying to trace it. Every day you'll give me a call at five PM, let me know what kind of progress you're making. I'm going to need something tangible in two days. Otherwise, I'll make your lives increasingly unpleasant, not to mention Tane's. And don't try to follow me, Susannah. I've already had you dead to rights twice now. If there's a third time, you won't be waking up from it. At least not in this life."

He turns and heads for the front door. I keep the CZ trained on the back of his head, even as he walks out the front door into the night, leaving the door open behind him. Wilson trots to the door but Ethan calls him back. I lower the CZ and head to the doorway, peering out at the dark. Of course, Finn is gone.

CHAPTER SEVENTEEN

An hour later, Frankie and Caesar are sitting with us in Ethan's living room. It's a war council, my attempt to regroup after hearing Finn's story and being burdened with the task of finding the missing cash from Iraq. Ethan has reclaimed his usual seat, although he seems uncomfortable—whether it's because Finn was sitting in that chair earlier, or because Ethan is sickened by Tane being held hostage, I'm not sure. Frankie is on the couch, looking like all he wants to do is lean his head back and take a nap. Next to him, Caesar sits quietly, impassive, listening to Ethan as he tells them what happened with Finn. I'm too agitated to sit and instead pace back and forth in front of the TV, occasionally providing commentary to Ethan's story.

When Ethan finishes, Frankie closes his eyes, exhausted. "So you have to find this money, otherwise this Finn guy blows up the Tane kid."

"Good summation," Ethan says. "You okay? You look awful."

"*Vete a la mierda.* I'm trying to run the bar and deal with your uncle's business and now help you and Suzie with Sergeant Psycho. I just need a minute."

Caesar is, as always, focused on the practicalities. "How far away do you think they are? Finn and Tane?"

"Somewhere in a ten-mile radius," I say. "If that countdown clock and the Semtex are legit—and I've got no reason to think Finn is lying about it—Finn only had forty-some minutes to get to Tane and disarm the . . . bomb." I'm reluctant to say the word aloud. "No way he's farther out than that, unless he's teleporting."

"So we're not going to find him by canvassing the neighborhood," Caesar says.

"There's over two hundred hotels within ten miles of here," I say. "That doesn't include rentals or VRBOs or abandoned buildings or whatever."

Caesar continues in his calm, steady voice. "Do you know what kind of car he's—"

"No, Caesar, I don't have the first fucking clue. He could be riding a unicycle or a flying unicorn for all I know."

His eyes still closed, Frankie says, "That would make him easier to find."

Ethan laughs, a hard, bright sound that makes me blink. We all look at him, even Frankie. "Sorry," Ethan says, displaying a sickly grin. "This is just . . . surreal. Guy shows up out of the blue, says our father helped steal millions in cash from a war zone, and if we don't help him get it back he's gonna blow up the accountant for a gang run by the Mexican Mafia. Did I miss anything?"

Nobody says anything for a minute. Wilson nudges my foot with his nose and I crouch down and rub behind his ears. "We're not going to find Finn by searching hotels," I say. "We need to flush him out, get him to show himself."

"How you gonna do that?" Frankie asks.

"The only connection I have with him is my cell phone," I say. "Have to call him every day at five PM, give him a progress report. Maybe we can use that. Right now, we've got a more immediate problem."

"Finding the missing millions," Caesar says.

I nod. "Or at least give Finn enough to show we're looking for it. And I want to find out everything there is to know about Finn. He was in the Army. And he was in Iraq the same time Dad was there."

"On it," Caesar says. "I'll use Garak."

Ethan frowns. "Garak?"

Frankie shakes his head. "He names his computers. Garak's the one he uses for especially shady shit."

"You named one of your computers after Garak from *Deep Space Nine*?" I say. "Caesar, I think I love you."

Caesar raises an eyebrow. "As flattering as that might be, I need to get Frankie home before he passes out on Ethan's couch."

"I'm fine," Frankie mutters. "Just a little tired."

"Home?" Ethan asks. "So the renovation's back on track?"

"Contractors got the water back on," Frankie says. He yawns. "I should go check on the bar first, make sure nobody's tried to burn it down."

"Gus is there," Caesar says, putting a hand on Frankie's back. "He'll handle it."

Frankie stifles another yawn. "*Vamos*," he says.

They leave by the front door, Caesar ushering Frankie as if afraid he'll tumble down the front steps. They look like a cute old married couple. Then Ethan closes the door and turns to look at me. "So this is bad."

"I'll take care of it," I say.

"Like last time?" Ethan rubs his face. "Sorry. That was . . ."

"It's okay," I say. "And if I have to, yeah. Like last time."

Ethan nods and we stand there in his den, saying nothing. Even Wilson is quiet, lying on the floor and looking from Ethan to me and back, waiting to see how we react.

"So what do we do?" Ethan says.

"I need to look through whatever papers and records we have from Mom and Dad's house," I say. "Do you have them? Or does Uncle Gavin?"

"I've got them. There's some bins in the storage room." Ethan pauses. "What are you looking for?"

"Something that might have to do with the money, or Dad's time in Iraq," I say. "There's probably nothing but it's a start. And tomorrow I'll go talk to Uncle Gavin, see if he knows anything."

Ethan rubs his face again. "Okay. Let me make some coffee and I'll help you go through all that stuff."

"No, you've got school tomorrow."

"It's summer school. I'll get someone to sub."

"You need to go to sleep is what you need to do."

"You think I'm going to be able to sleep after tonight?"

"Yeah, I do. You're half dead on your feet. You look almost as bad as Frankie."

"Now you're just being bitchy."

"You called me, remember? You asked for my help. I'm here. I'll take care of it."

"But—"

"I need you to go on having your normal life," I say.

We look at each other for a few moments. Then Ethan gives me a half smile. "Not sure I'd call my life normal."

"Compared to mine, your life is a Norman Rockwell painting. Show me those boxes and then go to bed. I'll let you know tomorrow if I find anything."

He hesitates, then walks down the short hall to the storage room. I crouch on the floor and rub Wilson's belly while I hear Ethan shifting things around in the spare bedroom. He comes back out carrying two large but shallow plastic bins, one on top of the other, and puts them on the floor. "Got a few more," he says and goes back down the hall. I look down at the clear plastic bins. They are full of envelopes and old bills and receipts and other papers, the kind of things Mom would file and store and then shred after seven years. Wilson rolls to his feet and trots over to sniff the bins, then looks up at me.

"I don't know," I tell him. "But I'm gonna look."

GOOD OLD LEO Nevsky also taught me about the importance of documentation, the paper trail we each leave behind us in the modern world, and how a good investigator could follow such a trail like a hunter following footprints and broken branches in a forest. A grocery list could indicate how many people were staying in a location, or how long the shopper planned to stay there, or if there were children or infants or someone with a special diet. A gas station receipt could be like a neon sign saying *He went this way*. And a phone bill was like manna from heaven.

"So you're like a trash detective," I said to Leo when he paused to take a breath during his presentation at our school's job fair. A few of my classmates snickered and Mrs. Shunnarah, our homeroom teacher, glared at me. But Leo just smiled and said that was pretty accurate.

Sitting in my brother's living room, I start going through the five plastic bins Ethan brought out from the storage room before going to bed. Each bin holds a year's worth of receipts and bills and bank statements, five consecutive years ending abruptly when my parents died. Ethan said these were all that was left—the rest had been thrown out or shredded or stored in the attic in cardboard boxes which had bloomed with mold. That's why Mom started using plastic bins with lids. I don't think I need to see anything dating from before Dad went to Iraq, anyway.

Five years of documentation is a lot. I start with the most recent year first, separating the papers from that bin into stacks on the dining room table—phone bills, gas bills, power bills, cable bills, credit card bills, bank statements, insurance claims and EOBs, medical records, sales receipts. I run out of room on the table and have to use the chairs. I'd spread it all out on the floor except Wilson would walk all over the papers or try to eat them or something.

This is the kind of work many new PIs find boring, but Leo said that this was a kind of logic puzzle, a game of inferences. What information was helpful? What could be ignored? How did you read a phone bill? A bank statement? What could you learn from an insurance claim or a credit card bill or a receipt from a plumber?

What I learn from looking through Mom and Dad's old receipts is that they spent a lot of money on our old house. They were killed in

September, but already that year they had replaced our dishwasher and our water heater. I remember the hot water running out while I was taking a shower and me screaming for Mom to fix it while I danced around in the tub under a stream of frigid water blasting from the shower head. The memory feels like someone just punched me in the breastbone, and I try to ignore it.

There's a bill from our old pediatrician, Dr. Fuller. She was a kind, patient woman with a broad face and broad smile who put up with all my medical questions as I showed off what I knew. I remember her raising her eyebrows at some of my questions—at my eight-year-old checkup I asked her about pubic hair and why we needed it—but she always answered my questions as best she could, if only to distract me while she looked in my ears or hit my patellar tendon with a reflex hammer to make sure my central nervous system was up to par. If only there had been a simple test like that to figure out how my brain was wired.

Enough, I think. This isn't a trip down memory lane. I need to be looking for anything that might have to do with my father and Iraq and missing money. Not that I'm expecting to find a bank statement showing a transfer of six million dollars into my parents' checking account. I'm not exactly sure what I'm looking for, which makes this exercise both potentially frustrating and intellectually challenging. Sherlock Holmes used to crave mental stimulation, which is why he would take cocaine when he had no crimes to solve. I don't snort lines when I'm bored, usually, but my brain likes to be used, so I put down the pediatrician's bill and apply myself to the task at hand.

An hour later, I've gone through the phone bills, banking statements, and credit card bills from three of the five bins. I've got various documents stacked on the kitchen counters, the couch, the two chairs in the den, and even the windowsills. Wilson was following me as I placed envelopes in various stacks around the room, but now he's collapsed on his bed and is snoring softly. Numbers and letters are starting to swim in my head, it's north of one o'clock, and whatever logic center exists in my brain is getting as mushy as an overripe avocado. It's time to throw in the towel, at least for tonight. It's the law of diminishing returns. The more time I put into this right now, the less efficient I'll be in terms of getting results. Or something like that. I'm not entirely fucking sure, because I'm exhausted and got shot at earlier this evening—or yesterday, whatever—and I just want to close my eyes and sleep.

I manage to put all the stacks on the couch into the appropriate bins and then lie down, sighing with relief. Wilson jumps up onto the couch with me and snuggles at the far end between my feet, and I'm worried my brain will decide this is the moment to kick on, a little burst of cortisol to wake me up, but instead I'm pulled under like a swimmer slipping underneath the surface of the water and drift down, down into the darkness.

I SPRING OFF the couch, grabbing the hand that is shaking me by the shoulder and bringing my other hand up to rake the man's eyes, when he shouts into my face, "Susannah! It's Ethan, Suzie. It's me."

Wide-eyed and panting, I stare at my brother who is gripping my wrist, my clawed hand inches from his face. "Suzie," Ethan says again. "It's me."

I wrench my hand out of his grip and press my hands to my eyes. "Sorry," I say. "Sorry, sorry."

I hear him shift on his feet but keep my hands over my eyes. Then he says, "Frankie called."

At his tone I drop my hands from my face. Outside the windows the sky isn't yet bright, but it's well past dawn. "What's wrong?" I ask.

My brother looks older in the morning light, dark shadows under his eyes. "Somebody trashed the bar last night."

"But Gus was there," I say. When Ethan hesitates, something cold forms in my gut. "Is he—?"

"He was hurt pretty bad," Ethan says. "He's in the hospital. But he's alive."

I pace across the den, back and forth, the movement allowing me to think, to remain relatively calm. "Tell me what happened."

"Frankie went in early this morning and found the front door kicked in. The whole place was wrecked, Suze. The bar stools, the chairs and tables, all smashed up. Smashed all the liquor too. They carved up the bar, and the kitchen . . . it was destroyed. The ovens, the grill, the dishwashing machine, all totaled. That's where they found Gus, on the kitchen floor. He was covered in blood. Not all of it was his. They beat him with baseball bats and stuck a knife in his chest, missed his heart by a centimeter. Found a broken bat on the floor next to him, along with some teeth. Not his."

In my mind I see Gus, about the size of a small grizzly, standing in my uncle's bar, telling me my uncle was a tough old bird, that he would be okay. There must have been a dozen of them to take Gus on. My head starts buzzing, but this time it's anger, a red pulse that's going to get louder and louder and will need some sort of release, soon. "It's the Sureños," I say. "Whoever's left after Bala."

"That's what Frankie thinks," Ethan says.

"Anybody tell Johnny Shaw yet?"

Ethan nods. "He's down at the bar with Frankie right now, talking to the insurance people." He's about to say something else when his cell rings. He answers. "Caesar? What's up?" Ethan listens for a few seconds, then picks up the TV remote and turns on the flat-screen. "Which station?" he says into the phone, flipping through channels. He stops on the local NBC channel. On the screen, a news anchor is talking with the words GANG VIOLENCE in the upper right-hand corner. Ethan turns up the volume.

". . . early morning hours in the English Avenue neighborhood, west of downtown," the anchor says. "The gunfire resulted in two men dead and at least five injured. At the same time, a fire broke out in a local garage, and fire department officials say the cause is likely arson. Reporter Charlie Flint has the story."

The screen cuts to video of Cargill's garage in flames the night before, firefighters manning hoses and spraying the building with water. A reporter says no deaths or injuries were reported, then adds that the police have not yet publicly made any connections between the shootout in English Avenue and this fire, although sources have told the reporter that the Atlanta PD believes the two incidents are linked.

I hold out my hand for Ethan's phone and he gives it to me. "This is retribution for yesterday," I say into the phone.

"That's what it looks like," Caesar says.

My head buzz is rising in volume, a song of the damned. "I need you to find the Sureños for me."

There's a pause. "We're not going to war with the Sureños," Caesar says.

"We're already at war. They trashed the bar and nearly killed Gus."

"Which is why Frankie called the police."

"The police?" My voice is sharp and Ethan stares at me, but I ignore him. "You think they give a shit about my uncle?"

Caesar's voice is remarkably, insufferably calm. "They care that a midtown business was vandalized and that there's a gang war threatening to explode in the city."

"It's already exploded."

"And you want to sweep in, guns blazing, and save the day?"

I can actually feel my jaw clenching, and I grip the phone to keep myself from throwing it across the room. "What the fuck, Caesar?"

"Let the police handle this, Susannah. They've got the manpower, and they like nothing more than putting armed gang members behind bars. Let them do their job. You have another job to do."

He means Finn and the missing millions, and keeping Tane alive. He has a point, but I'm not ready to concede it, not by a long shot. "I'm a good multitasker," I say.

There's a muffled exchange on the other end of the line, then Caesar says, "I've got to go. Please just stay away from the Sureños." And he's gone.

I toss Ethan his phone and pull my own out of my back pocket and find the number for Peaches that Caesar texted me yesterday. Yesterday? Feels more like weeks ago.

"What are you doing?" Ethan asks.

"Problem solving," I say, and I call the number. It rings once, then an automated voice comes on: "We're sorry, the number you are calling has been disconnected or is no longer in service."

"Son of a bitch." I end the call. Smart of Peaches to get rid of that number after I called it—if Caesar could find it, it's possible others could as well. And for all his efforts to save me from Bala last night, I'm pretty sure Peaches doesn't want to hear from me right now. Briefly I consider trying to find Billy, but I discard that idea—if he knew where the Sureños were, he would be there right now with a crew ready to burn them to the ground, and he wouldn't talk to me if Peaches was against it.

"What's going on, Susannah?" Ethan says.

"I need to find the Sureños and stop them before they do anything else."

"Look, I'm sure the cops are looking—"

"They could come here, Ethan," I say. I don't want to say the words out loud, as if that will make it come true, but I need to make Ethan understand. "They know that Uncle Gavin wanted to stop them from moving into Atlanta, which is why they trashed the bar. And they torched Cargill's garage because their deal with him went sideways last night. They're lashing out at everybody they think is an enemy, and I'm pretty sure I'm high up on their list right now. They could show up on your doorstep."

Ethan's face pales, but he has the same stubborn look our mother used to get whenever I was a pain in the ass to her, which was far more often than I care to remember. "The Atlanta PD will drop the hammer on them," he says.

I shake my head. Nobody is listening. "What'll they do, send a squad car to drive by a couple times a day? That won't stop the Sureños."

"And you want to do what? Go play vigilante? Get shot or—"

"I thought they'd be broken!" I shout, interrupting Ethan. "I thought after last night they'd be holing up somewhere, licking their wounds.

Instead they went all in. The bar, Cargill's garage, and Peaches's neighborhood. They hit three different targets the same night. There's more of them than we thought. And Bala's death only pissed them off. They won't stop until they're in prison or in the ground." I take a deep breath and pause for a moment. "I told you I need you to live your normal life. And I'll do whatever I need to do to keep you safe."

"Does that include dealing with Finn, too?" Ethan says. "Because there's a clock ticking when it comes to him. Him and Tane."

"I know. That's why I spent half the night looking at those boxes."

Ethan makes a point of looking around at the various stacks of paper on every flat surface in sight. "Find anything?"

"No. Not that I'm certain there's anything to find."

"You think Finn is just making this all up?"

"I think Finn thinks he's telling the truth."

Ethan looks at me strangely. "You don't think Dad did it, do you?"

"What, stole six million and made it vanish? No, I don't think he did. That wasn't Dad."

"*Dad* wasn't Dad, Suze. Not after he came back from Iraq."

"Jesus, this again."

"Yeah, this again. Come on, Suzie."

"Don't you have to go teach?"

Ethan looks at his phone for the time. "Fuck. Okay, can you watch Wilson, or take him to the vet—"

"I'm on it, Ethan. Go mold young minds or whatever."

He rolls his eyes and goes to grab his work bag. A few seconds later he bangs out the back door and is gone.

I let Wilson outside to pee and inspect the flower beds before he runs back inside for a bowl of kibble. Cute little doggo—his earnestness makes me smile. Then I look at all the paper stacks around Ethan's house and feel the smile slip off my face. Not enough coffee in the world to make me want to face this right now. Instead, I elect to go for a short run in the neighborhood. After I change into running clothes, I give Wilson a treat from a jar on the kitchen counter and leave him happily munching while I head out the back door and down the driveway. There's a crew of workmen at the construction site across the street, and I smile and wave as I run past, getting a wave and a whistle in reply.

I push hard, going eighty percent the whole two-mile run around a few blocks in the neighborhood. I hit Roswell Road and manage to weave around the few people on the sidewalk, still pushing hard and managing to suck in a lungful of exhaust. When I turn onto Ethan's street I kick into a flat-out sprint, legs pumping, arms slicing the air, sweat pouring down my face and chest. I run like I'm trying to escape time itself, like I can break through the barrier separating us from the past so I'll see Dad one more time and warn him what's ahead, tell him to take Mom and me and Ethan and go away somewhere so we aren't home when Donny Wharton shows up, a gun in his hand and a grin on his face.

I stumble into Ethan's driveway and nearly pitch onto my hands and knees but manage to stay upright. My lungs are sucking in as much air as possible, and I'm so sweaty I feel like I just stepped out of a pool. My palms flat against my kidneys, I walk up the driveway, trying to slow down my breathing and my heart rate. I might puke, but behind that I feel good, my body responding to the exercise by dumping endorphins into my nervous system. I'm lucky my nervous system still works relatively well. But I'm still a tiny bit disappointed when I reach Ethan's front yard and don't see a portal to the past anywhere, a shimmering doorway hanging in midair, waiting for me to walk through it. There's a doorway like that somewhere, one I'll have to walk through eventually, but that one leads to the same future that waits for all of us, and for the moment I prefer that door to stay shut and hidden.

Right now, the run has cleared my mind and given me an idea—another, different doorway to open. I head inside for a shower, and then to arrange a meeting.

CHAPTER EIGHTEEN

The outdoor seating for the Starbucks in Brookhaven is a handful of metal mesh tables and chairs and green umbrellas collected on a brick patio that's partially surrounded by some sort of faux split rail fence, like a corral for coffee drinkers. It's a bright, sunny day and I sit at a table in sunglasses and ballcap, sipping a venti iced latté and surveilling the shopping center parking lot in which this Starbucks is moored. Two skinny metrosexual dudes are sitting at a table on the far side of the patio, engaged in a hushed but earnest conversation. Otherwise I have the entire patio to myself.

Not for long. A silver Ford Fusion pulls into the parking lot from Peachtree Road and parks in one of the spaces across from me. The driver-side door opens and Agent Scott pops out of the car. Special Agent Rondeau exits more gracefully, says something to Scott, and starts walking toward me. Today her pantsuit is navy blue and she's wearing a white blouse underneath. Accents her skin and her highlighted brown curls. She looks impassive and all business. She looks sexy. Agent Scott is in a black suit but is wearing the same red tie he had on before. He looks like he sweats in his sleep. Rondeau takes long strides across the lot and Scott hurries after, his feet stabbing the pavement.

I lift my latté. "Special Agent Rondeau. Drinks are on me. You too, Agent Scott."

"No, thank you," Rondeau says. She walks around one end of the split rail fence and onto the patio, then stands behind a chair across the table from me. Two full seconds later Agent Scott is beside her.

I shake my plastic cup. "Coffee, Agent Scott?"

"I don't drink caffeine," he says, pulling a chair out so its legs squall against the bricks. He drops into the chair, glaring at me. Next to him, Rondeau pulls out her own chair and sits slowly, although I catch her side-eyeing her partner.

Scott cuts to the chase. "What's this about, Ms. Faulkner?"

"Friendly chat," I say. "Get to know each other. Share our favorite Tom Hanks movies."

The scowl on Scott's face deepens. "I'm not amused."

"For me it's a toss-up between *Apollo 13* and *Big*, but I've got a lot of honorable mentions."

"This is a waste of time." Scott shoves his chair back and stands. The two metrosexual dudes at the other end of the patio glance at us.

"Sit down, Agent Scott," I say, waving him back down. "I want to talk seriously. Pretty please."

Scott stares at me. I smile placidly up at him.

Special Agent Rondeau clears her throat. "What do you want to talk seriously about?" she says.

"Tane Kamaka," I say, still looking up at Agent Scott.

Scott's scowl twists into an ugly smile and he sits. "So you're ready to stop playing games."

"I'm not the one playing games."

He shakes his head, the ugly smile lingering. "How's your uncle doing? Getting used to hospital food yet?"

I start to chuckle, then laugh out loud. But I keep it in check, just as I keep my eyes trained on Scott. "That's your angle? Try to shake me up again by talking about my uncle? That played yesterday, which, to be honest, was a poor reflection on me. It was too early in the morning, I hadn't had coffee yet. But now you think you can just push that button and get me all upset? I'm not wired that way, Agent Scott." Still chuckling, I take a sip from my latté. "So," I say, putting my cup down, "when Tane got snatched right out of your hands at that motel, before that happened, how'd you sabotage the air conditioning unit?"

Scott's smile flickers and for a moment his eyes register shock, but he recovers quickly. "I don't know what—"

"I was thinking maybe you just snipped a wire so it died completely," I continue. "That'd be the easiest thing to do. But it would be kind of suspicious, especially if one of the other agents saw you messing with the unit right before it croaked. So I'm thinking you cut the coolant line when no one was looking. The fan would still keep running, but in a few minutes everyone would figure out it wasn't blowing cold air anymore. Hot summer day in a crappy motel room, and real quick someone would suggest calling the front desk."

The look on Scott's face could scorch paint off a wall. Special Agent Rondeau looks from me to Scott, then back to me. "What are you talking about?"

"She's just bullshitting," Scott says, practically spitting. "Trying to—"

"No wonder you were so pissed when D came in with his boys," I say. "You weren't expecting that. You thought it would be the Sureños."

Scott stands, his chair scraping the bricks.

"You and the standing," I say. "Sit down." I wave my hand beneath the mesh table so both agents can see I'm now holding the CZ. It's pointed at Scott. "And keep your hands very visible and away from your waist."

Rondeau stares at me. "This is a very bad idea, Ms. Faulkner."

"Call me Suzie, please." I wave the CZ again. "Agent Scott, sit down. Now."

For the third time, Scott sits. "Pulling a gun on a federal agent?" he says, his voice choked with fury. "You're fucked, *Suzie*."

"Not as much as you," I say. "D spilled. You were going to turn Tane over to Bala."

"Who is D?" Rondeau says.

"A gangbanger who works for Antoine Daniels, who you might know as Peaches. D was snitching for the feds *and* for the Sureños. Double the paycheck. Scott ever tell you he had a source with the Sureños? That was D. He either paid or threatened the motel manager to let him answer the phone that day, when he knew Agent Scott would call. He was supposed to let the Sureños into the motel room to grab Tane. Instead, Peaches's crew, with D, went to the motel before the Sureños got there. D couldn't warn Agent Scott ahead of time."

Rondeau is shaking her head. "I don't believe you."

"Really?" I nod toward Scott. "Look at him, Alisha."

She doesn't even react to my use of her first name. She just looks at Scott, whose face is a thundercloud as he stares at me. "Agent Scott," she says. Scott doesn't react. "Agent Scott," she says, something harder in her voice this time. He cuts his eyes toward her, then back at me.

"The Sureños have a lot of money," I say. "Crimes does pay, sometimes. I'm guessing Agent Scott has some debts, maybe a little gambling problem. And all that money is tempting . . ."

If Scott was angry earlier, now he's murderous. His eyes shine with tears and rage. "You—" he manages, and then he brings his fists down onto the table. He doesn't do it hard, but he hits the table loudly enough that the other two men on the patio beat a hasty retreat inside.

"I was beginning to think they might be feds, too," I say.

"Shut up," Rondeau says to me. To Agent Scott she says, "Is this true?"

Scott lowers his forehead until it rests on the table between his clenched fists.

Rondeau sits back, stricken. "Oh my God."

"Where are the Sureños, Agent Scott?" I ask. Scott keeps his head down on the table. "You communicated with them before, and I know they got money to you. You can get in touch with them. How?"

"No," he says. It comes out like a flat moan.

"I need the Sureños off the street," I say. "The Atlanta PD wants them bad. Let the cops have them. Just tell me."

He lifts his head. It's not pretty. Agent Scott looks wrecked, his eyes red-rimmed and haunted. "No cops," he says.

"Kevin," Rondeau says.

Scott looks at her and Rondeau visibly blanches at the desperation in his face. "They'll kill Timmy, Alisha," he says.

"The cops aren't your problem," I say.

He turns back to me, and I realize I'm looking at a man on the verge of coming unglued. "You think the Sureños don't have Atlanta cops on their payroll?" he asks.

I take my sunglasses off, still keeping the CZ covering both of them under the table, although I suspect Agent Scott has forgotten all about it. Scott needs reassurance before he falls apart. I give him a smile, hard-edged and deliberate and confident.

"Not the cops I know," I say.

IT TAKES A few more minutes, but over the protests of Rondeau, who keeps telling Scott to stop talking and get a lawyer, Scott tells me how to get in touch with the Sureños. Now he's sitting in the Ford Fusion, in the passenger seat, staring straight ahead through the windshield. I'm pretty sure he's not seeing anything. Rondeau and I are standing by the rear bumper of the car. The girl looks shaken. She is clearly not used to being . . . *surprised* isn't the right word. It's more like betrayed. Her partner has betrayed both the FBI and her, and Alisha isn't sure how to react to that.

"Who's Timmy?" I ask, to give her something she can respond to.

"Agent Scott's son," she says. She takes a breath, lets it out, visibly getting hold of herself. "Timmy has CP. He's in a wheelchair, severely disabled. Wife left them both. Agent Scott's been raising him alone, has a nanny to help when he's at work."

No wonder Scott was susceptible to bribes. I can only imagine what the health care costs are for his son. And now I feel a vague sense of guilt for thinking of Scott as just an asshole. But I don't have time for that right now. "Where does Agent Scott live?"

Rondeau stares at me. "Why?"

"Because after I call the cops, I need to get his son out of his home and somewhere safe."

She shakes her head. "Oh, no. You've done enough. I'll take care of it."

"Not a chance. Either tell me now or I'll find out anyway, but it'll waste time. And the sooner these guys get locked up, the better. Plus you've got to figure out what to do with him." I nod toward Agent Scott, sitting in the car.

Rondeau's eyes flare and she stares at me, her entire body language saying *Fuck off*. Most people would find this intimidating. *I* find it a little intimidating. But it's also hot as shit, and she has no idea.

I let her know with a look back, not breaking eye contact. It takes a little bit to register with her, but then I see confusion in her eyes, then understanding, then shock and embarrassment and . . . is that *excitement?* No—she's hesitant, awkward, a whole slew of emotions exploding in her like popcorn.

I grin. "Nice talking to you too," I say. "Now are you going to tell me where Agent Scott lives?"

To my astonishment, Rondeau gives me a grim little smile. "I am not," she says, and she actually quirks an eyebrow. "You think you're the first woman who's ever flirted with me?"

"Well, shit," I say. "And here I thought we had ourselves a special connection."

She waves me off with one hand, a dismissive gesture, but she's still got that grim smile. "I'll take care of Agent Scott," she says. "And his son. Timmy knows me and trusts me. You show up and the nanny will call 9-1-1 before you hop off your bike. I'll get them all somewhere safe."

"I know you have to follow some FBI rule and tell your boss everything that just happened. Just give me a few hours before you do that so I can set up the Sureños."

"You've got one hour."

I pout. "Alisha, after all we've been through?"

"Ninety minutes, starting now. And then I tell my boss. You just make sure you take care of your end."

THERE'S A WAFFLE House at nearly every interstate exit in Georgia, sometimes more than one. The Waffle House at Northside and I-285 is special, though. For one, Dad would sometimes take me here for breakfast. The hash browns were always good. For another, there is a gunmetal-gray Chrysler sedan parked at one end of the diner. No matter the time of day, according to Agent Scott, that Chrysler is in one of three spots by that end of the Waffle House.

A yellow cab comes up the off ramp from 285 and onto Northside, then turns into the Waffle House lot and parks next to the Chrysler. Fitzroy the cabbie gets out, his slacks and polo careworn but clean and ironed. Casually, neither fast nor slow, Fitzroy walks around his car to the driver's side of the Chrysler and folds the side mirror inward so it's flush against the door. Then he takes a piece of chalk from his pocket and, crouching by the front tire, draws a line across the top of the tire. Fitzroy puts the chalk in his pocket, walks back around the cab, gets in, and pulls out of the parking space before driving out of the lot, heading back onto 285.

Sitting on my bike at a BP station across the street, I watch all this through my binoculars. That was the easiest money Fitzroy ever made. If anyone had come out of the Waffle House, he could have just played the bored cabbie waiting on a fare. Scott said no one would come out, but I wanted to make sure. And I assume the Sureños know what I look like by now. But Fitzroy is nobody to them. Still, I wanted to be here when he moved the mirror and chalked the tire, in case one of the Sureños is around and trigger happy. And now Fitzroy is gone and two hundred dollars richer.

It's a smart kind of signal, the kind of thing spies did during the Cold War. Adjusting the blinds in a window just so, putting a piece of tape in a certain place on a particular telephone pole, moving a flower pot to a different spot on a porch—all subtle signals to a select few who know what they mean. Agent Scott told me the folded side mirror meant he wanted a meeting; the chalk mark indicated the meeting was urgent and should be that same night.

No one comes out of the Waffle House or saunters up to the Chrysler. Still keeping an eye on the car, I call Ethan. No answer—he's probably still teaching. When his voice mail beeps, I leave a message. "Hey, had to run some errands. Wilson's at home but should be fine. I'll take him on a walk this afternoon, get him some exercise." I think about what else I should say—*sorry we fought this morning, I'm tracking the Sureños, don't worry about Finn.* "See you later," I say, and hang up.

Next I call Frankie. He answers after five rings. "What?"

"Nice to hear you too," I say. "How's the bar?"

"How's the bar? It's a disaster, *chica*. If I'm not trying to get Gus's blood out of the grout in the kitchen, I'm looking at a hundred grand to replace the appliances."

"I'm sure my uncle had the bar insured."

"You ever had to deal with insurance agents on something like this?"

"Do you want to get the bastards who did it?"

"You have no idea. Wait. Tell me you aren't doing whatever it is Ethan says you do. Bird-hunting. Fuck, that's not it."

"You mean bird-dogging?"

"That one. Tell me you're not bird-dogging the Sureños."

"Not anymore. Who do you know on the Atlanta PD? One of Uncle Gavin's cops."

"Detective Panko. A few others. Why?"

I've been distracted during my phone call and didn't see the man come out of the Waffle House across the street, but suddenly I realize someone is standing next to the Chrysler. I lift my binoculars to my eyes and the man jumps into my vision. He's Latino, mid to late twenties, wearing a hairnet and a black apron with the Waffle House logo on it. Probably a cook, given the hairnet. He crouches to look at the front tire.

"Suzie?" Frankie says in my ear. "You there?"

I watch the man stand and pull a cell phone out of his pocket. He talks briefly to someone, then puts the phone back in his pocket. "Call Panko and tell him you know where the Sureños are," I say to Frankie, watching the Waffle House cook move the side mirror back to its normal position. "Or at least where they're gonna be by nine o'clock tonight."

CHAPTER NINETEEN

AFTER I WALK FRANKIE THROUGH THE WHOLE MEETING-WITH-THE-Sureños scenario, I text Special Agent Rondeau, just two words: *Message received.* I drop my cell on the ground and stomp on it with my boot heel until it's shattered, then toss it into a dumpster. Time to get another burner phone.

I GET BACK to Ethan's house just before two o'clock. Wilson dances around my feet and bolts outside to pee and chase chipmunks in the landscaping. I take him for a quick walk around the block before making a quick sandwich with some cold cuts from the fridge. Organic turkey, no preservatives. Ethan is turning into a total millennial.

I scarf down the sandwich and a vanilla yogurt from the back of the fridge—only one day past its sell-by date—and then turn back to the various stacks of paper waiting for me. I've got less than three hours before I have to call Finn with an update. The fact that I have to do this at all chafes me. I'm investigating my own father, and digging around in my parents' past feels . . . sordid, I guess, like I'm rifling through their bedroom. And it also brings up memories, and lots of my memories are potentially explosive. But then I think of Tane, sitting blindfolded and strapped to a chair wired to real explosives, and I start looking back through the paperwork all over again.

AFTER ANOTHER HOUR I have something.

I've been spending most of my time looking at my parents' financial records and any correspondence with Dad's old bank—again, not that I would expect to find a series of enormous deposits or anything, but I'd assumed there would be some sort of activity or notification of transfers or linked accounts or something. There isn't, and if there are any subtler clues, I'm not seeing them. Tracking people via their banking activity is one thing, but I'm not a forensic accountant, so if someone is working to hide some financial shenanigans, and they know what they're doing—like Dad would have known how to do, presumably—I probably won't discover whatever they've hidden.

So I put the banking stuff to the side and look again through the phone records.

When searching through data, I look for patterns. Human beings are pattern makers. We love the routine, the familiar, the tried and true. When I'm trying to find someone, I look for patterns in the chaos. And once I find those patterns, I look for breaks, changes, interruptions. Many times those changes will be random or meaningless, but more often than not that break in the pattern will be a thread I can pick at and loosen and unravel so it leads me right where I need to go.

And finally I find a loose thread. It's a phone number with a 703 area code, meaning northern Virginia. According to old phone bills, someone using our landline called that number six times in the year after my father returned from Iraq.

I go back through the phone records again, slowly, looking for any other patterns. The 703 number is hardly the only unknown number in the bills. It could be any number of things. An old friend. A repairman who had moved to Georgia and kept their old cell number. Or maybe a former client or colleague of Dad's—after he got fired from his first bank for screaming at a customer, Dad would regularly reach out to any contacts who hadn't already broken off with him, always searching for a better job.

One way to find out. I dial the number. After the first ring, it's picked up by a man, his voice crisp and tight as a snare drum. "OIG, this is Manning."

I have no idea what OIG means, so I improvise. "I'm looking for Steve Rogers," I say, using the first name that comes to mind. Then I wince. Real smooth there, Suzie—why not just say Tony Stark or Peter Parker?

"There's no Steve Rogers in this office," the man says. No hesitation, all business.

Wilson noses my ankle and looks up at me, tail wagging. I gently push him away with my foot. "Maybe I dialed the wrong office?" I say, letting my voice lilt upward at the end, trying to sound like a slightly helpless female.

"Are you looking for a particular service branch, ma'am?"

Service branch? "Army," I say automatically. "I'm sorry, which office is this again?"

"DoD inspector general," he says. "I can give you the number for the Army IG whenever you're ready."

He rattles off a number and I thank him and hang up. Then I jump onto the internet and look up the website for the Department of Defense. On the page for the DoD's inspector general, I find two contact numbers. One is a toll-free number, and the other starts with the same area code and prefix as the number I called, but the last four digits are different.

So years ago someone, probably Dad, called the office of the inspector general for the Department of Defense, and he used a number that isn't listed on their website. A private line, then, or at least a direct one—there was no operator or recorded greeting with a menu to navigate, just a good old-fashioned human. Why had Dad called the DoD? And why multiple times?

I get that old tingling of the nerves, the rush of discovery, an almost childlike excitement—*this is a clue. It means something.* I try to squash that feeling, or at least box it up so I can stay somewhat objective. When you are looking for something, it's all too easy to find something that might not actually be there—the mind tricking itself.

I text Caesar: *It's your favorite ST fan. Take my call, pls.* I wait two minutes, then call. Caesar picks up on the second ring. "New phone?" he asks.

"Yep. Learn anything from Garak?"

"Got the service record for one Gunnery Sergeant Edwin Roscoe Finnegan."

"I can see why he wants to go by Finn. Can you email me the record?"

"I didn't download the file. Didn't want to set off any alarms. Just went through a back door in an old DoD server—"

"Fine. What can you tell me?"

"He's from Missouri, got an Army ROTC scholarship to Mizzou and graduated near the top of his class before joining the Army in the late '90s. Stayed on after 9/11, deployed to Iraq in '03. Earned a Silver Star and a Purple Heart for trying to rescue a fuel convoy outside of Baghdad. That was before he beat that soldier to death and got twenty years in prison and a dishonorable discharge."

"So he was a hero right up until he wasn't," I say. "Something's missing. ROTC scholarship, excellent student, outstanding soldier . . . that doesn't seem like Finn. He's intelligent, sure, and he's a combat vet. And I know millions of dollars can make good people make bad decisions." *Like Dad*, a voice whispers in my head. I shove it away. "But Finn jumps from Boy Scout to murderer? That doesn't make sense."

Caesar's voice is almost like a purr. "That's because you don't have his sealed criminal record from when he was a teenager."

Despite the situation, I smile. "You are such a tease. Spill it."

"Property damage, assault, assault and battery, property damage with a motor vehicle."

"I like the last one. He drive over someone's mailbox?"

"He drove his pickup truck through the front door of a classmate's house. Sober."

"That's a special kind of crazy," I say. "What about the other charges?"

"Took a baseball bat to someone's car, a few dents and busted taillights. Threatened a girl. Got in a fight with the same guy whose house he plowed into with his truck."

"I'm surprised the Army took him. I know every soldier isn't a saint, but why wasn't he kicked out of ROTC at least?"

"Daddy was rich and made most of it go away."

"That makes sense. So Finn is entitled and has a temper." I think for a moment, watching Wilson sleeping in his dog bed. "But if his daddy is rich, why does he care so much about the Iraqi money?"

"Daddy cut him off once he went to prison. Cut him out of the will too. When his father died a few years later, all the money went to charities. Finn's mother died from cancer when Finn was eleven. No siblings."

"So the rich only child became a poor inmate with no inheritance." That could only have added to that deep well of hatred I saw in Finn's eyes. "Any chance you got his prison records?"

"He went back to being a Boy Scout when he was behind bars. That's how he got out early."

"I'm sure the thought of millions waiting for him outside was a strong motivator." Finn had been cast out of his family and its wealth, something he'd grown up with, something that had shielded him from the most serious consequences until his father had taken that shield away. And all this money from Iraq was his way back into that life.

"How about you?" Caesar asks. "You find anything you can pass on to him?"

"About the missing money? Maybe." I tell Caesar about the phone calls my father had made to the DoD. "What do you think it means?"

"Could your father have used some kind of financial conduit through the DoD to transfer the money from Iraq? A military bankroll program or something?"

"That's possible, but then why call the IG's office?"

Caesar's voice sound grim. "Maybe he was under investigation."

I think about it. "And then when he died, the investigation was dropped. Maybe. But wouldn't the DoD want to know what happened to millions of missing dollars?"

"I have no clue how the military would handle something like this. You'd have to ask them."

"Or talk to someone else who might know," I say. "Can you find the names of everyone involved in that shootout in Baghdad, and where they are now? Perkins is dead, and so is Cortez. But what about Yousef, the translator? And the three other guys with them, the ones guarding the cars? One of them might know something."

"You want anything else? Maybe some nuclear launch codes?"

"That's the Air Force, Caesar."

There's a pause. "What are you going to tell Finn?"

I glance at my phone and see I've got about forty-five minutes until I make the call. "I'll tell him what I've found in the phone records and that I'm going to track down whoever is left from his group. Maybe he knows something."

Another pause. "How is this going to end?" Caesar asks.

Unfortunately, I know the answer. "He'll probably kill Tane," I say. "And me and Ethan if he can. But not until he knows we've found the money or that there is no money to find."

ETHAN COMES HOME soon after I get off the phone with Caesar and finds me picking up the stacks of bills and other papers. "Already done?" he asks.

"Just with this part." I fill him in on the phone calls to the DoD's inspector general and what Caesar found out. Ethan crouches and rubs Wilson's belly while listening to me. When I finish, he shakes his head.

"This isn't going to end well, you know that, right?" Ethan says.

"You sound like you've been talking to Caesar."

"Seriously, Suzie. He's not going to let Tane go. He's got no reason to. You heard what he said about Tane basically laundering money for him."

"I know. And I don't want Tane to be punished for any of this. But no matter what Dad did or didn't do, we've inherited this mess, and I'm going to clean it up." I look at my phone. Ten minutes until I call Finn. "Shit, I forgot to check in on Uncle Gavin. Did you—"

"He's fine. Resting in the hospital. His body didn't reject the valve, so that's good. Doc says he might be able to go home in a couple of days."

We fall silent as I finish putting the last few stacks of bills into their plastic bin. Once I do that, I feel compelled to find a rag and wipe down every surface of Ethan's house, dust his blinds, clean his sinks. It's a compulsive urge to do something, engage in some sort of physical activity. I'd go for another run if I didn't have to call Finn.

At five o'clock on the dot, I dial the number Finn gave my brother. On the third ring Finn picks up. "Very punctual," he says. "I appreciate that."

He didn't ask who I was and I have a new phone, so he must only use this number for me. How special. "I've looked through all the bills and files we have from our parents," I say. "There's no record of any transactions that could point to the kind of money you're looking for. But I did find a phone number my father called several times over a couple of weeks, just before he died. The number goes to the inspector general's office at the DoD. Not the public line, a direct one."

"You didn't ask about your father, did you?"

"Oh, yeah. Right after I said I was looking for ten million dollars. No, I didn't mention my father."

"Don't be a smart-ass, Susannah. Anything else?"

"We think maybe he was being investigated by the DoD, but I don't know for sure. I'd like to confirm that. I need to track down the other men who were with you at Ahmed's apartment."

"I already told you. It was myself, your father, and Yousef."

"The three soldiers in the street saw you carry those duffel bags of cash," I say. "Maybe one of them knows something."

Silence. Ethan looks at me expectantly. I shrug. "Hello?"

"They won't know anything," Finn says. "They're dead. Two died in Iraq, one in the States. Drunk driver."

Another dead end. No pun intended. "You sure?"

"They were my men," Finn says quietly but with menace. "I know."

"Can you tell me Yousef's last name?" I ask.

"Hassan."

"Thanks. You're a big help."

I swear I can *hear* Finn grinning on the other end. "You're the one helping me."

"Let Tane go," I say. "He doesn't have anything to do with any of this." I agree with Ethan there's no chance he'll let Tane go, but I have to make an effort.

There's another pause. "I'm texting you a video," Finn says, and just then I hear the *bing* of an alert on my phone. "Go ahead and watch it while you're on the line with me."

I put Finn on speaker, then open the Messages app. There's one text with a short video attached. Ethan comes to stand next to me. We glance at each other, and then I open the video. It's Tane, tied to the same chair as before, a blindfold over his eyes and tape over his mouth. The camera is eye level with Tane and stable—if it's shot on a phone, my guess is the phone's on a stand. The light is bright and overhead. I can't make out any specific features of the location, just a blank gray wall in the background.

Finn steps into the camera frame and stands behind Tane's chair. With his left arm he encircles the top of Tane's head, immobilizing it. I can't see any expression on Tane's face because of the blindfold and the tape over his mouth, but his body stiffens.

Finn raises his right hand. In it is a pair of kitchen shears.

"Oh my God," Ethan breathes.

"The fuck are you doing?" I shout. "Stop it!"

"I've already filmed this," Finn's voice says over the speaker. On screen, Finn's mouth doesn't move. Still holding Tane's head still with one arm,

Finn raises the shears to Tane's ear, laying one blade along his earlobe. Tane tries to shout but the tape over his mouth muffles the sound, his cheeks bulging from the effort.

Finn looks up directly into the camera.

"Don't—" I say.

Finn closes the shears, slicing off Tane's earlobe. I can hear the slight crunch of the blades as they cut through the fatty tissue. Blood spurts onto Tane's shirt and flows down his neck. Tane screams, muffled by the tape, and tries to kick and flail his arms, but he's tied to the chair and Finn has him in a headlock.

Ethan makes a noise somewhere between a retch and a moan.

I stare at my phone. Finn keeps looking at the camera, no expression on his face. Tane is still screaming, sweat coating his face, blood from his ear now soaking the neck of his T-shirt.

The video ends.

Finn's voice issues from the phone. "Find my money, Susannah. Next time it won't be an earlobe. You call me tomorrow at five." He disconnects.

"Jesus," Ethan says. He's sitting on the couch, taking deep breaths.

"Put your head between your knees," I say, walking to the kitchen. I get a hand towel and run it under cold water in the sink, wring it out, then return to the den. Ethan is sitting with his head down between his knees. I lay the towel across the back of Ethan's neck. "Just breathe," I say, dialing Caesar. I put the phone on speaker as it rings.

Caesar answers immediately. "That was a short call."

"Finn cut off Tane's earlobe with kitchen shears," I say, tapping the phone screen. "I'm sending you the video he took of it."

"Mother of God," Caesar says.

"I need you to scan that video for any evidence about where they might be. I'll look, too, but you've got equipment I don't."

"On it."

I hang up and kneel down next to Ethan. His eyes are shut and he's breathing through his mouth. "You okay?"

He nods. "Just give me a sec," he says. His voice sounds mostly steady. I put my hand on his back and keep it there. Wilson comes over and nudges my other hand, then puts his front paws on Ethan's knee, tail wagging as he licks Ethan's face. "Okay, okay," Ethan says, lifting his head and rubbing Wilson behind the ears. Ethan looks at me, his face drawn and flushed. "What kind of person does that?" he asks.

"A broken one," I say.

Ethan takes a breath, lets it out. "You have to find that money," he says.

"I will," I say, and silently I add, *and I'm going to kill Finn, too.*

CHAPTER TWENTY

I SPEND THE BETTER PART OF AN HOUR PORING OVER THAT VIDEO. THE second time I watch it, I want to take a shower, one that will blast out the inside of my skull. After the fourth time, a numbness settles in, like I knew it would. The video is still horrifying, but I can now see the horrific part at a remove, as if it's behind layers of clear bubble wrap. That allows me to be more objective, analytical. And I see:

The chair Tane is strapped to has a wooden frame and dark red upholstery on the seat and on the back. Could be a hotel brand.

The wall behind Tane is a dove gray, unbroken by windows or doors or paintings, not even so much as a nailhead.

The floor is out of frame—I can only see Tane from the knees up.

The light from overhead is bright, too bright for a sixty-watt bulb—more like a fluorescent light.

The tape over Tane's mouth is a dull silver, standard duct tape, the same kind of tape that is wrapped around his arms and legs and keeps him in the chair.

The blindfold over Tane's eyes is a black rag, maybe a T-shirt, maybe not.

When Finn slices off Tane's earlobe, blood spurts and then starts running down Tane's neck, soaking the neckline and right shoulder of his

T-shirt. It's the same T-shirt I saw him wearing in the video Finn showed me last night. He must be filthy. God, I hope Finn cleaned and bandaged his ear.

Last night. Same shirt as he wore in the video last night . . . I watch today's video once more, this time with the sound off so I can focus on the visual. And there it is. Or rather, there it isn't.

I call Caesar. As soon as he answers I say, "Finn disarmed the plastic explosive for the video. There's no clock, no wires. So Tane's not on a hair trigger or anything."

"I missed that." Caesar sounds genuinely disappointed in himself. "Did you figure out the floor?"

"I can't see the floor. It's out of frame."

"I can't see the floor. I can't *hear* it, either."

"What?"

"Watch when Tane is flopping around after Finn cuts off his earlobe."

"Hang on." I put Caesar on speaker, then drag the playhead in the video back to just before the moment when Finn closes the shears around Tane's earlobe. Blood spurts and Tane screams and his body convulses as he tries to flail, but the tape keeps him anchored to the chair and Finn has him in a headlock so he cannot move much. But Tane does manage to buck the chair just a little. Another reason why Finn probably removed the wires to the C-4. I rewind and watch it again, see Tane strain against the tape binding him to the chair, hear him scream and watch him try to flail—

"Carpet," I say. "Tane manages to move the chair and it only makes a kind of thump."

"Not a hard floor," Caesar says. "That rules out concrete, tile, linoleum, wood."

"So we just need to find a room in Atlanta with carpet, or maybe a big rug," I say. "Should narrow down the possibilities to only a couple million."

"Susannah," Caesar says, "did you not see the kitchen shears?"

200

"Kind of hard not to see them, honestly. Why?"

"There's a brand logo on the head of the nut that joins the two blades, just above the handles. It's a brand that's sold mostly online, although you can also get it from Target."

"Great. There's only a dozen or so Targets in the metro area."

"Twenty, actually, in a twenty-five-mile radius. Narrow that down to ten miles from your house and you've got twelve, maybe thirteen."

I see where he's going with this. "You think Finn went out and bought a pair of kitchen shears?"

"If he did, he wouldn't have gone far from wherever he's holed up," Caesar says. "Not after he had Tane. He wouldn't order them online and have them delivered to his hotel room—either the delivery person might see Tane, or Finn would have to pick up mail at the front desk, which a clerk would remember. And I doubt he was carrying kitchen shears around with him beforehand."

"Maybe he broke into a house and found the shears in the kitchen."

"Too risky. He couldn't guarantee when the owners would come back. From what you've told me, Finn sounds like a planner. Unless he knew how long the owners would be gone, and he was certain there weren't any nosy neighbors, I don't think he'd break into an empty house and camp out there."

"So we locate Targets on the map and then look for hotels nearby," I say. "But not any hotel. He'd want some privacy, wouldn't want paper-thin walls so the neighbors could hear him talk to Tane." *Or interrogate him*, that voice in my head whispers. I shove the voice away again.

"That won't narrow it down a lot," Caesar says, "but it's a start."

"I still want to find Yousef," I say. "And the other three soldiers who were with them too. Finn said they were dead but I want to confirm that. He wouldn't tell me their names. According to him, two died in Iraq, one back home in the States from a drunk driver." Caesar doesn't reply. "Caesar?"

"Yes," Caesar says. "That's fine. I just . . ."

"What is it?"

Caesar sighs. "I'm just busy, Suzie. It's okay."

I close my eyes. Of course he's busy. He's helping to run my uncle's business, which is now under attack from the Sureños, and he and Frankie have to deal with the bar being trashed, and I'm not making things easier by telling him to scan a video of a torture session or to find soldiers who were in Iraq over fifteen years ago. "Call it a night, Caesar," I say. "You've already gone above and beyond."

"I do not mind helping you—"

"I know you don't," I say. "And I love you for it. But you've done enough today. I'll borrow Ethan's laptop and find these guys myself. I've got an idea for how to find Yousef. If I can't do it, you can use Garak or whatever you call your super dark web computer to track them down."

"I don't have a super dark web computer," Caesar says. "That's not a thing."

"Sure it is. Probably talks in Sam Jackson's voice, too."

"Good night, Susannah."

I smile. "Night, Caesar." I disconnect and look up to see Ethan watching me from his chair. "I can use your laptop, right? I'll delete the search history, don't worry."

He nods, wearily. "It's in my bedroom. I'll get it in a sec." He doesn't move from the chair.

"We need food," I say. "Pizza?"

Ethan shudders. "How can you eat after watching that video?"

"First order of business—survival."

"You are not quoting *The Wrath of Khan* at me."

"Too late. Get me your computer and then order some pizza. My treat."

Ethan goes and gets me his laptop, and as he calls to order delivery from Double Zero, I'm dialing a phone number from memory. It's three thirty PM in California, so she should answer.

She does. "Ellie Mangum."

"Did y'all find your lost cat yet?" I ask.

It only takes her a second. Ellie is wicked smart. "We did, thanks. And the family is excited. They're on their way to pick her up. Thank you."

The news warms my heart a little. The Asturias family looked for their daughter Yoselin for months, and I was happy to find her, even if she's in foster care in North Dakota. That's another hurdle for them to deal with, although with Ellie Mangum helping them they shouldn't have too terrible a time. The hardest part will be figuring out how to negotiate their lives once Yoselin is back, because things won't ever be exactly the same again. But no kid deserves to be taken from a loving family.

"Not to sound ungrateful, because I'm not," Ellie says, "but I'm surprised you called."

I've worked with Ellie twice now, and she knows the drill. Usually I keep a distance from my clients, giving them plausible deniability if anything I do in the course of my work for them goes sideways. So I understand her surprise.

"I need your help," I say. "I'm trying to find an Iraqi refugee who immigrated to the States sometime in the mid to late aughts. How would I do that?"

"Depends," Ellie says. "Was this person employed by or on behalf of the U.S. government?"

"He was a translator working with the Army in Iraq, so yes."

"Then he probably applied for a green card. If he got one, he'd be in the USCIS database. The IRS would have his info, too."

"Any chance you have access to the USCIS database?" I ask.

"How badly do you want to find this person?"

"Badly enough to send you to a spa of your choice for an entire weekend."

"Now, that is tempting. Even though the last weekend I took off was when Obama was president. What's the name?"

"Yousef Hassan. Y-O-U-S-E-F."

"Let me make a call, do a little digging."

"You're the best. I'll call you later—maybe from this number, maybe not."

"Gotcha. One more thing. About . . . that cat."

"Shoot."

"Whoever took her, what did you . . ." Ellie pauses. As a lawyer, she doesn't want to know about anything illegal I may have done. "Is that person okay?"

I think of Bobby Bonaroo sitting in a San Antonio cell. "No," I say. "He's definitely not okay."

There's a pause. "Good," Ellie says. "Gotta run. Call me later." And she's gone.

By the time the pizza arrives, I may have found one of the three soldiers. Stephen Chow, an Iraq War veteran, was killed in Miami when a drunk driver T-boned Chow's car. Chow's family sued the driver, who was the daughter-in-law of a wealthy family, so the whole incident got a write-up in the *Miami Herald*. Chow was Army, did two tours in Iraq, and—this is the clincher—served in the same company as Finn.

The three soldiers will have to wait. It's after seven o'clock—time to go watch the cops bust the Sureños.

ACCORDING TO AGENT Scott, he met the Sureños at a house in Doraville, northeast of the city just outside the Perimeter. The neighborhood is a wedge of homes sandwiched between two busy commercial roads, Buford Highway and Peachtree Industrial. The house is at the end of a cul-de-sac—one way in, one way out.

The cops have taken advantage of that.

From the roof of a Home Depot not quite a hundred yards away, I look through my binoculars and see the split-level brick house, some couple's dream home back in the 1960s. There are three cars parked in the driveway and a light on in an upstairs window, although I don't see any movement in or around the house. A short pan to the left with my binoculars and I see, outside the entrance to the cul-de-sac, a pair of Doraville police cars parked with their lights off. Beyond them is a large black van, behind which I can see a group of what looks like SWAT officers gearing up. I count at least a dozen, but the van may be blocking more. Normally for a bust on an armed gang like the Sureños, there would be over a hundred cops from a wide swath of local, state, and federal agencies. Whoever Frankie talked to must have kept this on the down-low, relatively speaking.

The sun is gone, leaving in its wake an angry red welt that even now is fading on the horizon. There's a single streetlight at the cul-de-sac entrance, but it's dead. I wonder if the cops cut it off, because it leaves the street draped in the kind of darkness that's perfect for people who don't want to be seen. As if cued by my thought, two four-man teams of SWAT officers start down either side of the short street, crouched and running in a standard two-by-two cover formation—two cops hold their positions and keep their weapons trained on the split-level house while the other two run forward until they reach cover and pause to allow the first pair to advance. Behind them, two more four-man teams form up. With my NV binoculars I can see more SWAT officers moving in the woods behind the houses. They're going to surround the split-level.

I lower the binoculars, and just then something to my right moves in my peripheral vision. If I had kept looking through the binoculars or lowered them a few seconds later, I wouldn't have noticed. I glance to my right, where I can see the entrance to the subdivision. A gray sedan has just pulled up to the curb there under a streetlight, maybe a hundred yards away from where I am on the Home Depot roof. The car is parked but the engine is still on—I see faint gray smoke from its exhaust pipe. Car must be burning oil.

I lift my binoculars to my eyes and the car leaps into magnified view. A gray Chrysler. The same one that was parked at the Waffle House. My stomach clenches like a fist. I can't see the driver clearly—there's glare off the windshield from the streetlight—but he has a clear view of the cul-de-sac like I do, although I'm higher up and can see more. If he has binoculars like I do, he'll see the SWAT teams. He'll warn the Sureños.

I pull my cell phone out and speed-dial Frankie. When he answers, I talk over him. "Call Panko and have him tell the SWAT guys to stop advancing on the house. The Sureños will know they're coming."

"What do you—"

"Just do it!" I hang up and look through my binoculars at the Chrysler. It is still sitting at the curb. I pan to the cul-de-sac. The SWAT teams have almost reached the house. They aren't stopping. Even if Frankie gets Panko, it'll take Panko time to call the cops, even more to convince them to stop. Shit.

I let the binoculars hang from a strap around my neck and draw my CZ, the silencer now off. I aim at a large oak tree at the edge of the Home Depot parking lot below me. Nobody is around the tree or in the section of the parking lot between me and the tree. I take a deep breath, then unload an entire clip, sixteen rounds, at the tree. The shots are loud, detonative, unmistakable for what they are. Even from this distance, I can see chips of bark flying off the tree trunk as if it's being attacked by invisible axes.

By the eighth shot, the cops at the entrance to the cul-de-sac, who are a good fifty yards farther away from the tree I'm using for target practice, are already responding. There are shouts and people running for cover. Spotlights stab out into the darkness, seeking the source of the gunshots. My hope is that the SWAT teams heard the shots, too. Surely someone has radioed them. Maybe they—

The split-level at the end of the cul-de-sac explodes, the flare of the fireball and the percussive sound hitting me simultaneously. The roof cracks like an egg and erupts. Bricks hurtle through the night like shrapnel. Bodies are blown back by the blast. The front door flies outward as if kicked by a giant, twisting through the air until it smashes onto the pavement of the cul-de-sac. Firelight turns the treetops golden. Fragments of the house rain down onto the street and other yards. Flames lick the night sky, thick dark smoke roiling above the roofs of nearby houses. A tiny figure, now illuminated as if by hellish stage lights, is crawling across the front lawn.

"Oh my God," I breathe.

I turn to look at the Chrysler just as it pulls away from the curb, moving fast and heading out of the subdivision toward Peachtree Industrial.

I stand and run across the roof, ejecting the empty clip from my CZ and loading a new one on the move. I manage to holster the CZ before reaching the edge of the roof and the built-in ladder I used to get up here. The Chrysler exits the subdivision and turns right. I slide down the ladder, the rails burning my palms as I drop to the parking lot. I'm going fast enough that when I hit the ground I stumble and fall, but I turn that into a roll and regain my feet, already running toward my bike. Sirens rise like a chorus of wails from the direction of the cul-de-sac and beyond. Ten seconds after the Chrysler has exited the subdivision, I'm on my bike, helmet on and the engine roaring beneath me. I shoot off into the night, crossing a corner of the Home Depot parking lot toward the exit that should put me on the same road as the Chrysler.

I fly out onto the road, nearly clipping an SUV which swerves to avoid me, the driver laying on the horn. I lean forward, bringing my face near the handlebars, and urge the motorcycle to go faster.

There's a bottleneck of cars up ahead at the Peachtree Industrial overpass. A tractor-trailer is half underneath the overpass and slowly turning left onto an access road, blocking the entire street. In that clog of cars, I see the gray Chrysler nosing its way to the right, trying to take the access road in the opposite direction. I lean right and hop the curb onto a sidewalk, passing cars as if they're parked. Just ahead, the Chrysler exits the bottleneck and takes the on ramp for the access road. I'm right behind it, maybe two car lengths between us.

Whoever is driving must notice, because he taps his brake lights. I brake hard, not wanting to slam into the back of the car, and just as I do he speeds up, increasing the distance between us as he heads up the access road. I gun the throttle, the bike lunging forward. Ahead, the Chrysler is accelerating, and at the last second jerks left across two lanes to get onto Peachtree Industrial. I fly around a slow-moving pickup and follow.

The highway is three lanes wide here. Traffic is steady, a few trucks in the slower right-hand lane. The Chrysler just pours on the speed, gray smoke issuing from the exhaust, but the driver handles the car like he's steering a barge, plowing left and right, cutting off other cars that honk indignantly in its wake. On my bike, I can easily weave in between vehicles, and I'm steadily making progress.

A wink of starlight from the Chrysler. Another wink and the windshield of a Jeep to my right spiderwebs. The Jeep runs off the road, hitting the grassy divider between the highway and the access road. I lower my head further and lean right, veering away. I look back and see the Chrysler's passenger side window lower, revealing the driver. He raises a pistol. I lean even harder to the right, lurching into the breakdown lane, putting a tractor-trailer between us. I speed up and reach for my CZ. When I pass the truck and veer back onto the highway, the Chrysler is in the far-left lane, and the driver notices me just as I raise my CZ. He crosses the empty lane between us, the car aimed directly at me. I get one shot off before I have to swerve back into the breakdown lane to avoid being run over.

The Chrysler tries to follow but a horn blasts and the tractor-trailer roars up behind us, forcing the car to swerve left. I brake and let the tractor-trailer pass, then slip into its wake, the bike wobbling in the slipstream. I shove the CZ into its holster so I can use my right hand to roll the throttle and accelerate. In the few seconds it takes me to do that, the Chrysler drops behind me and cuts across all three lanes of traffic to exit back onto the access road, an exit I have just passed.

I turn off the bike's headlight and turn hard right, nearly fishtailing as I cut back into the breakdown lane and then onto the grassy divider. I drive down the grassy incline toward the access road. Up ahead, the

Chrysler pulls off the access road onto a two-lane road that loops to the right around a copse of oaks, past a granite sign that says Millennial Park. A fancy corporate park. Perfect.

I hit the access road and then turn into the two-lane. Up ahead, the Chrysler's brake lights flash red as he navigates a long, looping turn to the left. I hug the inside curves of each turn, and then the road widens to four lanes and straightens, both sides walled in by trees pressing up to the road like dark sentries. The Chrysler is thirty yards ahead. With my headlight off, I hope the driver can't see me. I spend all of five seconds closing the gap between us, then realize this straight section of road is the best chance I'll have—up ahead, a series of streetlights, curved like the necks of swans, illuminates the road. Once we reach those, he'll definitely see me. I drop my hand off the throttle, causing the bike to slow, and I draw the CZ and lay my arm across the throttle to steady it and put three rounds into the rear windshield of the Chrysler. The glass starbursts and the car swerves left, then right. A rear tire blows, and the driver overcorrects to the left, the blown tire smoking, and the Chrysler drives off the road and slams into a kudzu-wrapped oak with an awful shearing crash of metal and glass.

I come up behind the wrecked car and brake hard to a stop, then jump off the bike, my CZ up and tracking. Steam hisses from the hood of the Chrysler, which is crumpled like a cardboard box, and there's an acrid scent of burnt rubber and scorched oil. The road is still deserted, although I suspect that won't last long. Something moves in the driver's side window. I fire a round into what's left of the front panel of the car. "Drop the gun out the window," I shout. There's a pause, and then a pistol is tossed out the window, landing with an ugly clatter on the street. I step forward and pick it up, flinging it into the nearby woods. "Get out of the car, slowly, both hands out in front of you."

The driver's door opens with a screech of metal and two hands appear, fingers splayed to show they're empty, followed by the driver. The last time I saw him, he wore a hairnet and a Waffle House uniform.

Now he's in jeans and a T-shirt with a Wu-Tang Clan logo, the kind of graphic tee you can buy at any Target, bougie cool at sweatshop prices. He's also bleeding from a cut on his forehead. He stares at me with dull brown eyes.

"Hi," I say. "Where are the rest of the Sureños?"

"*Chinga te, puta*," he says. His voice is a bit slurred but I figure that's from the head injury.

I shoot him in the foot. He drops to the ground with a cry, then starts screaming in Spanish. Blood begins to form a black pool beneath his foot.

"Tick tock." I wave my CZ. "*Los Sureños, por favor. Ahora.*"

He lifts his head and, gritting his teeth, smiles, then lifts his hand to give me the finger. "You're gonna die, bitch."

I shoot his hand and manage to take off his finger. He screams again, higher this time, and clutches his hand to his stomach.

"The next one is in your crotch," I say, aiming the CZ at said location. "*Comprende? Donde estan los Sureños?*"

He hesitates, eyes looking desperately for a way out. I fire again and he howls, then starts panting when he realizes I fired between his legs into the dirt. Before he can take comfort from that, I jam the now-warm muzzle of the CZ under his chin. His eyes roll as he tries to look at both the pistol and my face.

"*Los Sureños,*" I say, not taking my eyes off his. And just like that, I see his willpower snap.

"A house," he says. "There's a house. In Lawrenceville."

"I need more than a house in Lawrenceville."

"Sixteen thirty-four Racine! *Es la dirección!*"

"If they aren't there," I say, slowly twisting the barrel of the CZ into the soft flesh beneath his chin, "I will come back and chop off each of your toes and make you eat them."

"They're there! They're there! *Por favor, no mas, por favor—*"

I club him behind the ear with the pistol and he drops like a bag of mulch. From his back pocket I fish out his wallet and, with my phone, take a picture of his Georgia driver's license. It lists his name as José Rodríguez. I pull out a Visa credit card from the wallet, also in the name of José Rodríguez, and take a picture of the front and back of that as well.

In the distance, I hear approaching sirens. No doubt a concerned motorist called the police about a gun battle on the highway. I put José's Visa and ID back in his wallet and shove the wallet back in his pocket. It'll make it easier for the cops to identify him. According to the map on my phone, if I continue through this business park I'll hit Buford Highway, hopefully avoiding the police. I get back on my bike and ride off through the park, the streetlamps shedding cold light down onto the road. Through the Bluetooth connection in my helmet I call Special Agent Rondeau.

"Rondeau," she answers.

"Are Agent Scott and his son all right?" I ask.

"Where are you?"

"Are they safe?"

"You need to turn yourself in to the nearest police station, and I mean yesterday."

So she knows about the SWAT raid gone wrong. "I saw the house blow up," I say. "What the hell was it?"

"Someone left the gas on in the house and triggered some sort of explosive device remotely. That sparked a much bigger explosion."

"I tried to warn the cops. Did anyone die?"

Silence. I come out of a turn and the trees fall behind me as I ride into an empty parking lot the size of two football fields, a glass-and-concrete structure docked like a cruise ship in the center of the lot. I'm exposed and wish the night could swallow me. "Alisha. Did anyone die?"

"Two officers," she says. "Died almost immediately. Five more are in the hospital, one with severe burns."

I pull over, the engine idling, and close my eyes. I can feel the emptiness around me, the weird sense of space bathed in sodium light. "I tried to stop it," I say.

"You need to come in."

I open my eyes and stare at the office building gleaming in the dark. "Not a chance."

She lowers her voice. "If the police find out you're the source who gave them the Doraville house, they will think you set up the SWAT team."

"Which is bullshit, and also why I'm not coming in."

"Then every cop and federal agent in this city will be gunning for you."

"Listen," I say, actually waving my hand as if she could see it, as if that gesture could erase the problems I'm facing. "There was a gangbanger in a Chrysler watching the cul-de-sac. Name's José Rodríguez. I'll send you pictures of his ID and his Visa card. He took off as soon as the house blew. I followed him. The rest of the Sureños are at a house at 1634 Racine in Lawrenceville. If you find no trace of them there, I'll turn myself in anywhere you want. Call your boss and get the FBI and ATF involved. Call out the National Guard for all I care. We tried using a scalpel. Now you need a sledgehammer. Just make sure Agent Scott and Timmy are safe."

"They're here with me," Rondeau says.

"Then keep them safe. Go get the bad guys, and do it now."

"Suzie—"

I hang up, then text Rondeau the pictures of José's ID and Visa. Then I dial Ellie Mangum, and before the phone rings I'm already rolling across the parking lot. "Any luck yet with Yousef?" I ask when she answers.

"He's in Dearborn, Michigan. Big Muslim community there."

"That was fast. Thank you."

"You okay? You sound . . . tense, I guess. Are you driving?"

"Yeah, sorry. Can you give me his address?" She rattles off an address that I commit to memory. "Thanks, Ellie. I owe you that spa weekend."

I navigate around a lamppost, aiming for an exit through the trees up ahead. "I have to go. Keep me posted on that cat, okay?" I hang up before she can ask any more questions.

I make one more call, this one to Johnny Shaw, Uncle Gavin's lawyer. He's up all hours of the night, so he should be home and awake. Then I realize it's not even ten o'clock yet. This has been a hell of a day.

Shaw answers the phone, his voice worn—he's older than Uncle Gavin—but still blistering. "If you try to sell me an extended warranty on anything," he says, "I will shove a lawsuit up your ass and light it."

"It's Susannah Faulkner, Mr. Shaw."

"Susannah!" he says. "Haven't seen you for a spell. I'm so sorry about your uncle. How you holding up?"

I leave the parking lot behind and enter another curving drive. "I'm okay," I say. "Thank you. I heard about Gus. Is he all right?"

Shaw laughs, more like a seal bark than anything else. "Kid, it'll take a lot more than some punks with bats and knives to take out Gus Cimino. The man's tough as a rhino. What can I do for you?"

"Does Uncle Gavin still have that charter plane on call?"

"The Learjet? Sure. Where are you going?"

"Detroit. How soon could the plane be ready?"

"How soon do you need it? Are you in trouble?"

"No. Well, maybe. That's not why I need the plane. I just have to get to Detroit."

"Say no more. What name should I tell the pilots to be on the lookout for?"

"Alice James." I like Alice. She's a book collector, quiet but intense. Collects signed first editions of novels. I have a passport in her name, along with three others with their own aliases, but I haven't been Alice in months.

"The plane's at Peachtree DeKalb," Shaw says. "Ought to be ready in two hours. Just need to find a pilot. I'll text you his name and where to meet him."

"Don't do that until I call you again," I say. "I'm getting a new phone. Thanks, Mr. Shaw."

"Anytime, Susannah. I'll wait to hear from you."

I end the call, and as I come out of the trees and drive by a large retaining pond, I fling the phone into the water, then concentrate on the road, keeping an eye out for anything that might leap out of the dark.

CHAPTER TWENTY-ONE

I'M DRINKING A CUP OF COFFEE AT THE COUNTER OF A WAFFLE HOUSE at Peachtree Industrial and Clairmont, a mile up the street from Peachtree DeKalb Airport, when Ethan's Corolla pulls into the parking lot. I lay a five-dollar bill down on the counter and step outside as Ethan is taking my duffel bag out of his back seat.

"Thanks for bringing my stuff," I say.

He hands me my bag. "It's not a long flight," he says. "Maybe an hour and a half. There's a bunch of hotels by the Detroit airport."

I'm touched that he looked at flight times and hotels for me. "Thanks," I say again, slinging the bag over one shoulder. "You're not always a pain in the ass."

"You aren't leaving, are you?"

"What do you mean?"

We stand looking at each other in the parking lot. Overhead a plane comes in for a landing, a whine of engines and blinking red and green lights in the night sky. Ethan looks pointedly at the bag on my shoulder.

"It's a change of clothes and some ID," I say. "I'm just flying to Detroit. I'll be back by tomorrow night."

I realize some emotion is working itself out in his face. "You just left, last time."

I steel myself and then step forward and hug him. Caught off guard, he stiffens before hugging me back.

"I'm not leaving you," I say into his shoulder. I pull back and look him in the eyes. "I promise."

He nods, as if not trusting himself to speak, then clears his throat. "Be careful."

I assume a puzzled look. "Have you met me?"

He shakes his head, but he's smiling. I cinch the duffel bag's strap tight, then get on my bike and ride out of the parking lot, not looking back.

The plane is a Learjet 75 Liberty and belongs to a service owned by a former telecom exec who once needed my uncle's help. Part of my uncle's agreement with the man was access to a plane whenever he or his lawyer might need it. I called Johnny Shaw earlier from the Waffle House and he told me which hangar to go to and the names of the pilots. "Were you in Doraville earlier tonight?" Shaw asked me on the phone.

"No, why?"

"No reason, just a gas explosion that killed two cops and totaled a house."

"That's terrible."

There was a pause, and then Shaw *hmph*-ed. "Have a safe flight, Susannah," he said before hanging up.

The plane is outside the private hangar where Shaw said it would be. The two pilots, Sean and Tyler, are standing on the tarmac when I pull up on my bike. They introduce themselves politely and ask to take my duffel, which they will stow in the cabin, then point to where I can park my bike. I go inside the hangar to check in, which consists of me showing my Alice James passport to a sallow-faced guy behind a desk and promising that I am not carrying anything explosive or illegal in my luggage, which is mostly true. I climb up the airstairs, the day's events starting to catch up to me. It feels less like being hit by a wave and more like standing in the water while the tide is rushing out, threatening to pull me along with it.

When I step onto the plane, I see an enormous man sitting in one of two forward-facing seats. For an instant my defenses light up, and then I realize who the other passenger is. "Gus!"

"Hey, Miss Faulkner," he says. His eyes are blackened and there's a band-aid over the bridge of his nose, not to mention a line of stitches like a black centipede across the top of his bald head, but his crooked smile is warm and genuine. Then his smile falters. "You okay?"

"Yeah, why?"

"You're cryin'."

I touch my face and it's wet. I wipe my cheeks with back of my hand. "Sorry, just . . . I'm glad you're okay, is all. It's been kind of a shitty day, and seeing you is the best part."

"I don't know about that, but I hear you on the shitty day part. Don't ever let someone stick a knife in your chest, Miss Faulkner."

"Good advice." Part of me wants to hug him but it would be awkward, not just because he's still sitting. Then I see how stiffly he's holding himself in his seat and know he wouldn't welcome a hug right now, so I plop down in the seat next to his and give him a smile instead. "And you need to start calling me Suzie."

"Yeah, okay." His crooked smile is back. "Suzie." He considers the sound of my name in his mouth. "Feels a little weird."

"I'm a little weird, so that makes sense."

He starts to chuckle, then winces. "Don't make me laugh, Miss—Suzie. Hurts."

"What are you doing on the plane? I thought you were in the hospital."

Gus's face folds into a frown. "I hate hospitals. Give me the creeps. My sister lives in Detroit, and when I told Mr. Shaw I thought I'd go visit her, he and Mr. Gutierrez said I could catch a ride with you."

I look him straight in the eye. "You aren't here to babysit me?"

He looks straight back. "You don't look like you need no babysitter."

I lift an eyebrow. "Gus, are you flirting with me?"

His cheeks turn red. "I—I wouldn't—that—I wasn't—"

I lean across the aisle and put my hand on his forearm. "I'm just teasing, Gus. I'm sorry. That was mean. But I am happy to see you."

He nods, then keeps nodding like he's glad he's found something to do with his head. "Yeah, okay," he says, not looking at me. "Ditto."

We are saved from further awkwardness by Tyler and Sean stepping onboard. "Should be wheels up in less than ten minutes," Tyler says.

"Thanks," I say, taking my hand off Gus's forearm and sitting back.

While Sean and Tyler run through their preflight checklist, I use the plane's Wi-Fi to scan the local news on my new phone. The gas explosion is getting the most coverage, but there's a breaking news item about a midnight raid by local and federal agents on a house in Lawrenceville that is ongoing. Sources tell a local reporter that gang activity is suspected, and there seem to be multiple suspects being taken into custody. So Alisha Rondeau took care of business. I only hope that's the last of the Sureños.

I shut down my phone and look over at Gus, who's looking out his window. He notices me looking at him and gently shrugs. "Never been on a Learjet before," he says.

"Me either," I say.

He raises his eyebrows. "Hey, we're Learjet virgins." Then his face flushes the color of brick.

I suppress a smile and lean back in my seat, eyes closed. The plane starts rolling on the tarmac, but I keep my eyes closed. I'm exhausted and keyed up at the same time, and when we roar down the runway and lift off, I think there is no way I am going to get any sleep tonight.

The next thing I know someone is calling me Miss James and I open my eyes to see Tyler standing in the aisle at a respectful distance. "Just wanted to let you know we've landed," he says.

I look groggily out the window even as I sense that the plane is taxiing on the ground. I see some bright lights and the outline of what I guess is a terminal. "Already? Thanks," I say. Tyler nods and walks back to the cockpit.

In a stage whisper Gus asks, "Why'd he call you Miss James?"

I whisper back. "'Cause that's the name on my passport."

Gus nods solemnly at me. "What's your first name, Miss James?"

"Alice."

Gus brightens. "That's my sister's name. How about that?"

IT'S NEARLY ONE o'clock in the morning local time—two AM in Atlanta—when Gus and I walk out of the Detroit Metropolitan Wayne County Airport. Gus lumbers along like a wounded buffalo, hurt but undeterred. I head toward Ground Transportation to look for a taxi.

"Hold up, Alice," Gus says.

"You don't need to call me Alice."

"What? I'm just usin' your alias. Where you goin'?"

"Taxi."

"No need. My sister's comin'. Just waitin' for her shift to change. She's a nurse. Oughtta be here soon."

We wait outside baggage claim for half an hour. The night air is cool for June and I pull a hoodie from my duffel and put it on. Gus stands next to me, saying nothing, eyes considering the few cars that drive up or drive by at this late hour. Finally, Gus says, "There she is."

A wine-colored station wagon with wood paneling pulls up to the curb. The woman behind the wheel bears a distinct resemblance to Gus, although on a slightly smaller scale and with long brown hair. The passenger window lowers and she calls out, "Go on and get in the back, Gus. The young lady can ride up front with me."

Gus has a battered suitcase he puts in the back, then insists on doing the same with my duffel. He shuffles around to open the passenger door and lets me in like the chauffeur he is. Inside the car is vintage 1980s, complete with vinyl seats, boxy control panel, and cigarette trays in the door handles.

"You like it?" Gus's sister Alice says. "Got it for a steal from a family after their grandma died. It was her car, had fifty-eight thousand miles on it. Drove it to church and the grocery store and that was pretty much it. A steal. I'm Alice, by the way. I'm unfortunately related to that bag of stupid getting into the car."

Gus slowly eases himself into the back seat, the car listing as he sits. "Hiya, Alice," he says.

"Hiya nothing. What happened this time? You get shot or something?"

"Just beat up a little. You should see the other guys."

"Big tough guy. They probably tried to hit you over the head and broke whatever they were swinging at you. It'd be like trying to bust up a block of marble or something." Alice drops the gearshift and hauls away from the curb, pressing me back into the vinyl. "You hungry?" she asks me. "Need some food?"

"No, I'm good, thanks," I say. "I just need a hotel."

"Hotel?" Alice glances at me, then in the rearview mirror at her brother. "She thinks I'm taking her to a hotel." She laughs, a loud cackle that raises the hairs on the back of my neck. "I know you're from Atlanta, but we got hospitality up here in Detroit, too. You're staying with me tonight. Got two big empty bedrooms now that Dom graduated. Dom's my son, he's got a job with Amazon if you can believe that. My husband Murray died five years ago this August, so I'm happy to have company. Even if half of it is this ugly mook."

ALICE LIVES IN Taylor, a town outside of Detroit that's a couple of miles east of the airport. I'm yawning by the time we pull up to Alice's house, a narrow but deep ranch house on a leaf-lined street. It's pitch black and silent outside, not even a dog barking, and somehow I get into Alice's house with my duffel and mumble my thanks as I'm shown to the guest room. Alice says something about changing Gus's bandage and they start to argue like a pair of golden retrievers play-fighting, and I close the door and set an alarm for six AM. Then I lie down on the bed, only managing to kick off my shoes before I drop into a dark sleep, where I find myself in some sort of deep cavernous space, and there are other people there as well, carrying flashlights and calling out my name, but they are far across the cavern from me, and I'm not sure whether I want them to find me or not.

I WAKE UP at six AM to the smell of bacon and coffee. I take a quick shower, then pull my hair back into a severe ponytail and put on my one pantsuit, black with a white blouse. I look like a corporate bitch from hell. Perfect. I follow the sounds of pots and pans banging on a stovetop to the kitchen, where I find Alice in a housecoat peering into an oven. She waves me to a breakfast table in the corner and brings me a plate of thick bacon and biscuits with honey and a bowl of strawberries and a thick blue mug of coffee. I scarf down everything and Alice leaves me alone until I'm finished and sipping my coffee. She leans against a counter and sips at her own mug. "So you work with Gus?" she asks.

"He works for my uncle."

"You two dating?"

I nearly spit my coffee back into my mug. "No," I say. "Not at all. I mean, he's a nice man, and I like him. But not that way." I look around, hoping to God that Gus isn't hovering in a doorway listening in.

"Don't worry, he's down the hall sawing logs," Alice says. "I just wondered. He might be sweet on you. He's an idiot, but he's a good brother. I don't want to see him get hurt."

I shake my head. "Me either. Is he doing okay? He was in the hospital and checked out, I'm guessing against medical advice."

Alice shrugs. "Like I said, he's an idiot. Hates hospitals. I'm an ER nurse, so sometimes he uses me like his own personal doctor. I had to change his chest bandage. Some moron wrapped a mile of gauze and tape around him. You don't need that much." She sips her coffee again, looks out a window at the morning light. "He said a bunch of guys wanted to smash up your uncle's bar and he tried to stop them. He's lucky they didn't shoot him in the head. Course, a bullet would probably bounce off."

"They were gangbangers," I say. "He took out a bunch of them before they shoved a knife in his chest. Some of them left their teeth on the floor."

She nods, proudly. "Is that right," she says.

I drain my coffee and over Alice's protests rinse my dishes and put them in the dishwasher. "Thank you for breakfast," I say. "And the bed. But I have to get to Dearborn. Do you have a cab company out here, or I could get an Uber—"

"Take my car."

"Oh, that's really nice, but I can't."

"It's easy, you just go out here to Telegraph Road and head north, hit Michigan Avenue and you're there."

"No, I mean, I can't take your car."

"Why not? I've got the day off and I'll be stuck here with Gus. Just bring the car back in one piece. Fill up the tank if it'll make you feel better."

CHAPTER TWENTY-TWO

THE SKY IS BLUE WITH WHITE CIRRUS CLOUDS FEATHERING THE SKY, and I drive north in Alice's Town & Country like a suburban soccer mom circa 1985. I turn on the radio, the one relatively updated piece of technology in the car, and find an '80s station. You haven't truly lived until you've driven a woodie wagon in the Motor City while listening to "Home Sweet Home" by Mötley Crüe. Strip malls and car dealerships and fast-food restaurants line the six-lane road—Middle America writ large.

Michigan Avenue is more of the same, plus a healthy dose of Henry Ford, the patron saint of the American automotive industry—the Ford Engineering Laboratory, the Henry Ford Museum of American Innovation, the Ford Motor Company World Headquarters. But then I start to see signs for traditional Yemeni food, Haraz Coffee House, Lebanese take-out, and Ozoor Driving School. And then, across from a small park, I spot a RE/MAX sign on an Indian restaurant that has the name Yousef Hassan and a phone number. The restaurant has a general air of abandonment, the windows dark and dusty, the RE/MAX sign starting to show signs of wear.

According to Google Maps, the address Ellie Mangum gave me for Yousef is several blocks north of Michigan Avenue, within walking distance of a mosque. This neighborhood looks just like Alice's, tree-lined streets and skinny lots that run deep. Yousef's home is a white clapboard house with green trim and a porch that runs across the entire front of the house. A new dark-blue Cadillac sedan is in the drive-way. I drive around the block and park on the street three doors down from Yousef's house. It's seven thirty, time for good real estate agents to be getting up. I call the number that I saw on the RE/MAX sign on Michigan. It goes straight to voice mail and I leave a message using my Alice James alias, saying I've been on the lookout for a restaurant location and am very interested in the property he has listed on Michigan Avenue. I add that my business partners are very eager to close a deal soon, then leave my cell number and disconnect. I look up commercial real estate in the area, seeing how many other restaurants are up for sale. After twenty minutes, I call Yousef and leave a second message, saying there's another location in Claytown but I'm really interested in the Dearborn property, and I leave my number again. Five minutes later, my phone rings.

"Alice James," I say.

Yousef's voice is full of cheer, as if nothing could make his day happier than talking to me. "Miss James, this is Yousef Hassan from RE/MAX returning your call. How are you?"

"Well, Yousef, I'll be a whole lot happier once my partners and I find a property."

"Then we need to help make that happen," he says. "Are you here in Dearborn?"

"I am, but only for today."

"I'd be very happy to show you the property you called about. Would eleven o'clock work for you?"

"I'm terribly sorry, but I have to fly back to New York early this after-noon. Could we possibly meet any earlier this morning? I apologize for the rush. My partners and I work for a family with ties to the Detroit area, and late yesterday the old man—I'm sorry, I mean Mr. Henry—anyway, he called and said he was putting me on a plane and flying me to Detroit and that I needed to find locations today and then fly back to meet with him and the rest of the family." I pause as if considering my words. "Mr. Henry can be . . . *mercurial*, I suppose, but once he's made up his mind, he's made up his mind. But I know this location on Michigan Avenue would be perfect for what he wants to do."

"I see," Yousef says, which is total bullshit. *I* don't see it, and I'm the one making up the story. "I suppose I can see about shuffling a meeting around to open up something at nine o'clock . . ."

"Yousef, you are a gem," I say. "Mr. Henry will be very happy. Not to get ahead of ourselves, but if the property is everything I think it is, and Mr. Henry agrees, could I call you later this evening to get the ball rolling on paperwork?" I wait a beat, then before Yousef can say anything, I add, "There wouldn't be any financing involved. Cash only." As the property is listed at just over half a million, I'm hoping Yousef understands that the completely fictitious Henry family is wealthy enough to drop that kind of cash on a dime.

Apparently Yousef understands this quite well. "Not a problem at all, Miss James. Let's say nine o'clock?"

"Please," I say, smiling, "call me Alice."

AT 8:55 AM, the dark-blue Cadillac I saw parked in Yousef's driveway rolls up and parks on the side street next to the shuttered Indian restaurant. I'm waiting on the sidewalk by the front door, tapping on my phone like a very busy woman. I see Yousef get out of his car and approach, but I don't acknowledge this until he says "Alice?" and I look up, startled but not scared. "I'm Yousef," he says, smiling warmly and showing white teeth. He holds out a hand.

"A *pleasure* to meet you," I say, taking his hand and shaking it. He's a handsome guy, medium height with olive skin and black hair only beginning to salt-and-pepper on the sides. He's wearing a blue suit and an open-collar white shirt and tan Oxfords—classy and successful, but not overly expensive so as not to intimidate clients. I'm willing to bet Yousef is a good salesman.

"Let's take a look," Yousef says, unlocking the front door and opening it as if it's the door to a palace. I walk in, trying to look like someone who knows how to value a restaurant property.

Inside, the restaurant is dim and dusty, an empty space abandoned to spiders and probably mice. Yousef talks about how the seating area can take all kinds of configurations and how the open kitchen could use some updating but it's perfectly fine, excellent even, with a new walk-in cooler. As he leads me into the kitchen to show me the cooler, I think about my uncle's bar and how the Sureños destroyed the kitchen, leaving Frankie to try and pick up the pieces. The thought runs through me and makes me sad, and I don't want to play this game anymore. Plus we are far away enough from the front windows, even if someone bothered to try to look in.

"Yousef," I say as he reaches for the door to the walk-in cooler, "I need to talk to you about my father."

Yousef frowns slightly but still maintains his smile. "Your father?"

"Jimmy Faulkner," I say. "In Iraq."

The words wipe the smile from his face. "Who are you?"

"Susannah Faulkner. I need to know about the money you all took."

He stands in the dim, dusty restaurant, face pale, mouth open. "Please," he says, "don't kill me. Don't hurt my family."

"I'm not going to. I just want to talk."

"I'll give you the money." He raises a hand to brush his hair, a reflexive gesture. "It will take some time, but I—"

"You have the money?"

"In a bank account. We were going to give it back—"

"Give it back?" I ask. "Who's 'we'?"

"Your father and I," he says.

WE SIT ON a pair of bar stools to talk, our voices low but echoing in that empty restaurant. Yousef seems wary, but as he talks, he gradually gets more comfortable, or at least less panicky.

"Your father found a way to get the money out of Iraq," he says. "There are Gulf state banks who don't ask questions and are happy to accept large deposits of cash with little paperwork, for a healthy fee, of course. When Sergeant Finnegan was arrested, I helped your father negotiate with a Kuwaiti banker in Baghdad. The Kuwaiti was a parasite, someone who materialized after the American invasion, when the money planes started coming in—the kind of man who profits from war and misery. But he was a legitimate banker, and he wasn't interested in stealing a few million when he was planning to do business in Iraq worth billions. For a ridiculous amount of money, he took the duffel bags of cash and flew them out of Iraq to Kuwait. A week later, as planned, he returned with a receipt showing the money had been deposited."

"So my father did steal the money," I say, deflating. I don't know why I'm disappointed. Actually, I know exactly why. Because despite all the evidence, I was convinced my father wasn't a thief. I needed to believe that, needed to believe Finn was full of shit.

"That's not the whole story," Yousef says.

"What does that mean?"

"I got a special visa to emigrate to the U.S., along with my wife and my baby girl. Your father said that once we were in the States he would figure out how to send our shares of money—mine and Hector Cortez's. He said he could use his credentials to get the money transferred from the Kuwaiti bank to an American bank. But before he went home after finishing his tour of duty, he told me he was having second thoughts."

"Second thoughts? About giving you your share?"

"About taking the money at all."

"What are you saying?" And then, oh, dear sweet baby Jesus Christ, I get it. "He called the DoD because he wanted to tell them about the money."

Yousef nods. "That's what he said he was going to do. I argued with him, but I knew he was right. Nothing good had come of that money . . ." He trails off and looks at me, then glances away. After a moment he turns his head to look at me as if he's forcing himself to do it. "It took me longer to get out of Iraq than I thought it would, almost another year. After I moved to the States, I called your father. He was upset that I called. He told me the money was cursed, that nobody wanted it, nobody wanted to talk to him. Then he hung up." Yousef pauses. "Two weeks later, I tried calling him again to tell him it was okay, that I understood. And I did, honestly. I thought he would be calmer after some time. But when I tried to call, his number was disconnected. So I looked for him on the internet, and . . . that's when I learned he had died, just two days after I last talked to him."

He died. Everything comes back to that, my parents' deaths. The primal formative event in my life. I close my eyes and lower my head as if in prayer. It's like a stain I can never rub out, never erase. It would be easier to erase the sun.

"Are you all right?" Yousef asks.

"No," I say, my eyes still closed. "You mentioned money earlier. How'd you get it?"

"That was the strangest thing of all," he says. "Six months later, I open my front door one morning and find a duffel bag on the porch."

My mouth is dry. "Let me guess," I say. I open my eyes and look at Yousef. "It was two million in cash, and a typed note that said, 'From Jimmy.'"

Yousef's eyes widen. "How did you know?"

"Hector Cortez's widow got the same thing."

Yousef considers this. "Your father must have arranged it. Before he died."

"What did he mean by saying the money was cursed?" I ask. "That nobody wanted . . . what did you say, nobody wanted to talk to him?"

"That's right. He was very upset, almost shouting. I felt bad. Your father was good to me, and when he decided he was going to tell someone about the money, he told me first. He didn't have to do that." Yousef leans forward. "He sent me my share when he could easily have kept it. And I thought about returning the money, but . . ." Yousef brushes his hair with his hand again. "Now I have two daughters and a little boy. That money is for them. I haven't spent a penny of it. It's their future, something to protect them. Your father knew what I would do with the money. I told him more than once what I would do with it. I've worked hard here, built a career, a family. And that money is an extra insurance policy, for them." Yousef holds my gaze in his own. "Your father was a good man."

"My father was a thief." My voice is louder than I intended. I can hear the anger in it, see its effect on Yousef, who leans back, away from me. "He got in bed with a guy like Finn and stole millions of dollars. What do I even *do* with that?"

Quietly and with stiff dignity, Yousef says, "Did you not hear what I said?"

"I don't give a shit what you do with the money," I say. "Give it to your kids or buy a yacht or throw it in a fire, I don't care. I'm not mad at you. My father stole it. You helped him, okay, but you also had to leave your country, which we pretty much fucked up, and then start all over again here. You get a pass."

"I shouldn't get a pass," Yousef says. "I agonize over it. Your father did too. At least he tried to tell his government about it."

"Well, apparently they didn't want to hear it," I say. Which also bothers me, although that's a problem to solve another day. Right now I just need to leave, to fly back home.

"May I ask why you came here now?" Yousef says.

I consider lying to him, then decide to tell him the truth. As far as I know, he's been honest with me. "Because Finn is out of prison," I say. "And he didn't get a duffel bag with a note attached, and he wants to know why."

Yousef blanches. "Why didn't you tell me before?"

So you wouldn't freak out like you are right now. "He's in Atlanta," I say, thinking about Tane wired to explosives somewhere in the city, Finn holding his finger over the detonator. "Do you know anything about the rest of the money? Where it might be?"

Yousef shakes his head. "Just the money I found on my porch." He looks around the restaurant as if he has just woken up and is seeing it for the first time. "What happens now?"

"You go back to your life," I say. "And I go home and deal with Finn."

I THINK ABOUT driving straight to the airport and calling Gus to tell him his sister's car is in long-term parking, because I don't like goodbyes, but it's too much of a bitch move. And when I pull over to call Tyler the pilot on the number he gave me last night, he says the earliest we could leave today is two PM, and it's just after ten o'clock now. So I have no excuse not to return the car.

At a Sunoco I fill up the tank and then call Ethan to leave him a message. To my surprise, he answers the phone. "Everything okay?" he murmurs.

"Yeah, fine," I say. "Why are you muttering?"

"Because I'm in the hallway outside my classroom."

"I was just going to leave you a message."

"Your number came up on my phone so I ducked out in the hall. What's up?"

"I met Yousef. The translator. He said Dad did steal the money, but he also said Dad wanted to give the money back. That's why Dad called the DoD—he wanted to turn the money over to them." Saying the words aloud make me feel a bit better. It's absurd, but I can't deny the feeling of relief at my father's motives.

"So what happened?" Ethan asks.

"I'm not sure. Yousef said he called Dad a year later, after Yousef got to the States, and Dad was upset about the money, said nobody wanted it. Said it was cursed. Do you remember anything about this?"

"No. Why wouldn't they want the money?"

"Beats me."

"You could call and ask them," Ethan says.

"Well, shit, I shoulda thought about that already.'"

"You're welcome. Better get on it. You gotta call Finn at five o'clock."

"Don't rush me. I'm flying back this afternoon. Should land around four thirty. What are you teaching?"

Ethan says nothing for a moment. "You want to know what I'm teaching."

"I'm making light conversation."

"About my teaching?"

"I'd like to talk to my brother about something other than a psychotic asshole who's got me out looking for millions of dollars that said asshole stole with our dad. From Iraq. So yeah, what are you teaching?"

"*Paradise Lost.*"

"You're making your students read *Paradise Lost* in summer school?"

"Only parts of it. It's a great book. It's like fantasy and science fiction and religion all wrapped up together in an epic poem. It's bonkers."

"You're bonkers for teaching it. I remember God was kind of boring. Kept trying to explain to Jesus why He couldn't be blamed for anything."

"You read *Paradise Lost*?"

"I read books too. Satan was pretty cool. I like the part where he's at the gates of Hell and about to throw down with Death, and his daughter-lover Sin with all the hellhounds in her womb and snakes for legs is like, *No, Daddy, don't hurt your son, don't you remember me?*" I take a sip from a bottle of water I bought at the Sunoco when I paid for the gas. "That's some fucked-up shit."

"You're disturbing."

"Me? You're the one teaching this to children."

"They're seventeen, they're not—okay, I gotta go."

"Good talk, bro. See you tonight." I disconnect, then from memory I dial the DoD number that was on my parents' phone bill.

The same crisp voice from yesterday answers. "OIG, this is Manning."

"Hey," I say, leaning against the bumper of the station wagon. "I called yesterday looking for Steve Rogers."

"There's no Steve Rogers in—"

"Yeah, yeah, I know. It would be weird if there were, though, right? Captain America working for the Department of Defense? Or maybe that wouldn't be weird. Kinda hard to keep track of all the stuff going on in the MCU these days."

"Ma'am, is there something I can help you with?" Calm, all business, unruffled. He makes me want to ruffle some feathers.

"Yep," I say. "Sure is. James Faulkner. Captain Faulkner, actually."

Pause. "There's no James Faulkner—"

"I know there's no James Faulkner working there, Manning. Jimmy Faulkner was my dad. He's dead. But he called this number several times before he died, and seeing as he served his country and was calling y'all about ten million dollars that went missing in Iraq, I kinda figured someone in that office might be interested. You following me, Manning?"

Pause. "Hold, please."

"No," I say. "I won't hold. I'm going to call back in an hour, and I'd like some kind of answer. Otherwise I'm gonna call a lot of other people, including the press. James Faulkner, captain in the National Guard, deployed to Iraq in 2004. Talk to you soon."

I end the call and drive back to Alice's house, humming along to Pat Benatar's "Invincible" on the radio.

ALICE IS SAD that I have to leave so soon, but she appreciates me putting gas in her car and insists on driving me to the airport. Gus comes along as well, although this time I make him sit up front with his sister. On the way Alice talks about taking Gus to see a doctor, and Gus says he wants to go see the Motown Museum.

"Why you wanna go see some museum about music?" Alice says.

"Because it's culture," Gus says. "Somethin' you don't know about."

"I know I don't need to pay money to go look at some Motown star's shoes in a glass case," Alice says. "You wanna know about the Temptations or whoever, turn on a radio."

"I wanna go see where the Temptations recorded 'My Girl.' The Supremes. Stevie Wonder. Marvin Freakin' Gaye. I wanna stand in the place where they were, where they made those songs." Gus turns in his seat and tries to look over his shoulder at me, although he's so big—and his chest wound obviously hurts him—that he can only turn enough to see me out of the corner of his eye. "Suzie, you'd wanna see that, right?"

"Especially Marvin Freakin' Gaye."

He nods as if confirming something and settles back in his seat. Beside him, Alice shakes her head at our foolishness and peers at traffic.

At the airport, Gus painfully gets out of the car and gets my duffel, while Alice gives me a big hug. "You come back and visit, okay? And eat up some. Little girl like you needs some weight on her bones."

"I've got enough, trust me," I say, hugging her back. "Thanks, Alice."

Gus clears his throat and holds out my duffel. Alice decides she needs to get back in the car and leaves me alone with Gus. I take my duffel from his giant paw and sling it over my shoulder. "Thanks for everything, Gus," I say.

He shrugs. "Didn't do nothin'."

"You introduced me to your sister and kept me company on the flight up here. That's something."

Gus shifts from one foot to the other, which is rather like watching an elephant try to tiptoe. "I'm glad I got to keep an eye on you, too. Like, keep a lookout."

"So you *were* babysitting me."

Gus shakes his head. "No, it's just—there's some bad guys out there, Suzie. I know you can take care of yourself, but . . ." He stands there, tongue-tied and unable to unburden himself of whatever he wants to say.

I reach up on my tiptoes and kiss Gus on the cheek. "Thanks, Gus. You're a good guy. You go visit that museum."

He blushes a little, then gives his crooked smile, showing off a broken tooth. "Yeah, okay. You be good."

"I won't get caught. Get better soon. And come back to Atlanta." I walk through the glass doors of the terminal, then turn back to see Gus still standing there, watching me go.

I GRAB A highly overpriced plastic-wrapped turkey sandwich from a kiosk in the airport and head to the gate for private planes, where I learn Tyler and Sean are getting the Learjet refueled. I check the time and realize the boys at the DoD are due for their call, so I pull out my phone.

"OIG, this is Manning."

"We gotta stop meeting like this," I say.

There's a pause, maybe five seconds of dead air, and I'm about to ask Manning if he lost his voice or what, when another voice comes on the line, older, rougher, like the speaker smoked half a pack a day for a decade. "Miss Faulkner?" this older voice says.

"That's *Miz* Faulkner."

"You want to know about your father."

I watch a 737 make an ungainly landing, the wheels smoking, the jets shrieking in reverse as the pilot tries to slow the plane. "I want to know why he called and why you all ignored him."

"I believe you know why he called, Ms. Faulkner," the voice says.

The 737 shoots down the runway, its fin like a giant shark's, but it finally starts to slow. "I'm assuming you don't want to say because this is being recorded."

"Come to Washington," the voice says. "I can give you a copy of your father's file."

"Not a chance."

The voice sounds disappointed. "Ms. Faulkner, you reside at 412 Busbee Court in Denver, Colorado. We could have you picked up whenever we want."

The address he rattled off is a fake, an electronic smokescreen Caesar created for me a while ago. Still, the fact that they found that in an hour's time is a little unnerving. "Have me picked up for what?" I say. "Let me guess, national security issues?"

"We're not interested in you. Not in that way."

"There are other ways?"

"Come to Washington, Ms. Faulkner. We—"

"I am not coming to D.C. Just tell me what I want to know and I'll go away."

Pause. The 737 is taxiing to the terminal. I half expected the airport fire crew to rush out to the plane with sirens and fire-retardant foam. Watching the plane roll slowly to a gate is anticlimactic and oddly satisfying.

"Someone was thinking about career advancement," the voice finally says. "That someone was poised to be offered a high-level position in the government. Your father's story could have derailed that, so it got buried. And after your father died . . ."

"After he died, there wasn't a case anymore," I finish. Some lieutenant colonel at the Pentagon wanted to get a staff position at the White House or some fucking thing like that, and somehow that weasel calculated that Dad's story would hurt his career, so he shitcanned it. Politics.

"This is going to sound hollow and cliché," the voice says, "but I'm sorry for your loss."

I appreciate the gesture but I don't feel like acknowledging it. "What happened to the money?"

"What money?" the voice says. "Don't call this number again, Ms. Faulkner." He disconnects.

I sit there, watching the 737 roll up to a jet bridge at the terminal, until an outer door opens and Tyler sticks his head in to tell me the plane's ready.

ALONE IN THE back of the Learjet this time without Gus to talk to, I charge my phone and think. Not about Finn or the money so much, although I do think about both. I spend a bit more time thinking about Mom and Dad. They were in their thirties when they died, not even middle-aged yet. What would their lives have been like if they'd lived? In some sunshine-drenched corner of my mind, Dad would have gone to counseling to deal with his PTSD, and Mom would have continued as a teacher, loved by her students. We would have moved to a bigger house, maybe with a pool or a flat-screen TV. Then I could have told Fiona Gorchinsky to suck it because we were going to hang out at my house from now on. And Dad and I could have planted a huge garden, terraced and landscaped, with a fountain and a stream and all sorts of flowers.

It's a nice dream that lasts until Sean calls back from the cockpit that we're beginning our initial descent into Atlanta.

CHAPTER TWENTY-THREE

THERE IS SOMETHING ABOUT RIDING A MOTORCYCLE THAT JUST CLEARS my head, like a great wind rushing through my brain and emptying it of thought. That doesn't happen often. I've tried meditation, yoga, qigong, long-distance running, you name it. But I think the rush of forward movement, the sense of openness and exposure when I ride, all combine to center me, to help me escape my own head, at least for a moment.

By the time I turn onto Ethan's street, it's after four thirty and I could use another half hour on my bike, but I need to call Finn soon. Time is too short all around. I pull into Ethan's driveway and see the Frankenstein parked just behind Ethan's Corolla. The gang's all here. I walk in through the kitchen door, expecting Wilson to scamper across the room and leap on my legs.

What I don't expect is my uncle, sitting in Ethan's usual chair, looking like pale death with burning black eyes. His tweed flat cap sits on his head, a small paper bag on his lap. Ethan sits across from him, holding Wilson, while Caesar and Frankie sit on the couch.

"Uncle Gavin?" I take another step into the house, dropping my duffel to the floor.

"Susannah," he says. His voice sounds like someone took sandpaper to his vocal cords, but it's his voice, familiar, in control. "Come have a seat."

"How are you out of the hospital?"

"Signed myself out."

On the couch Frankie and Caesar are looking back over their shoulders at me. "You drove him here?" I ask them.

Frankie nods. "He asked to come."

"More like he told us to bring him here," Caesar says, and Frankie shrugs, conceding the point.

I roll my eyes at my uncle. "For fuck's sake, you just had open-heart surgery."

"Language," Uncle Gavin says.

I literally bite my tongue and walk around the couch to sit on the floor, facing everyone. Wilson leaps off Ethan's lap and runs over to me, licks my hand, then rolls on his back, the belly slut. I rub his belly. "So what's the emergency?" I ask Uncle Gavin.

"Needed to see you," he says. "All of you."

"What happened?"

My uncle tilts his head slightly as if to get a better view of me. "You did."

I take in the room. Ethan looks guilty. Frankie has closed his eyes, exhausted as usual. Caesar meets my gaze with something like pity. Wilson thumps his little tail on the floor, the only one in the room who is happy. "How did I happen this time?" I say evenly, but I feel my head beginning to buzz.

Uncle Gavin keeps his burning eyes fixed on me. "I wanted you to stop a gang war. Instead, you escalated one."

"It was escalating all on its own. I just got us to the end a little faster."

Uncle Gavin shifts in his chair, the paper bag on his lap crinkling. "With a shootout in a warehouse. And then a gas explosion in Doraville where two police officers died."

"Which I tried to stop," I say between clenched teeth. "And I sent the feds to the Sureños' safe house in Lawrenceville."

"I gave you Tane Kamaka," Uncle Gavin says with all the subtlety of a thrown grenade. "And you lost him."

"You *gave* me Tane?" I'm incredulous. I look around the room for support, but none of the others are looking at me. Even my own brother. Of all the men in the world, these four are the ones I hold in my dark, pitted heart, and three of them aren't saying a word while the fourth chastises me like a kid who just shit the bath. And now the howler monkeys in my head are starting their racket. I keep them shut in their cages and focus on my uncle's dark eyes.

"You had a heart attack," I tell him. "And while you were lying on the airport floor, your pulmonary valve squeezing shut, you managed to offload your problem onto me. And I took it, and I went into the Bluff, and I got Tane. That brought the FBI down on my back, and on Ethan too. And then I had to deal with Brad Cargill and the Sureños, who are now gunning for me. And maybe if you'd been a little clearer with your family or with Frankie about who Tane is and what he's worth to you, and what *you* were planning to do with him, we'd be in a much better place than we are now. Instead you were so busy trying to keep a lid on everything that when it all started to boil over, no one knew what the hell was going on. You set things in motion and then checked out right when you could have made a difference, and if you'd told Frankie or Caesar about any of this ahead of time, they could've handled it, and I would've helped them. Instead we were flying blind, so I figured it out and took care of it the best I could. And *then*, on top of that, I'm dealing with a psychotic ex-soldier who stole millions of dollars from Iraq with my father's help, and he's holding Tane hostage and has him wired up to a bomb, and he wants his money and I don't have a fucking clue where it is."

I stand, glaring at Uncle Gavin. "I don't want your pity, and I really don't need your fucking disappointment. I don't need you to come in and shake your head and let me know how put out you are that you have to save me. I don't need you to save me. I've been saving myself for a long time. I'm my own white knight. But the armor I have to put on to deal with this fucked-up world is so goddamn heavy that I don't need your condescension on top of it. I don't blame you for the world being a dark, fucked-up place. I blame you for dropping a big, sloppy bowl of chili in my lap, and then getting mad at me when some of it spills."

End scene. Cue dramatic silence. I'm breathing like I just ran up a long slope. Ethan, Frankie, and Caesar are all looking at me with wonder and fear. Even Wilson rolls onto his belly and puts his head down, ears and eyes alert. Uncle Gavin's eyes haven't shifted away from mine this entire time. Even half dead, he has a will of granite.

Then he blinks and looks away. "I'm sorry," he says. I'm so astonished that I can't say anything before he swings his eyes back to me, a pair of dark lamps. "I should have told Frankie about Tane and the Sureños. But now we've got more immediate things to deal with." He looks at his wristwatch. "Ethan tells me you have to call Finn at five o'clock. That's in two minutes, which doesn't give me much time."

I find my voice again. "Time for what?"

"Explanations," Uncle Gavin says. "So when you call Finn, tell him you've found the money. You can exchange the cash for Tane as soon as tomorrow."

"What money?" I say. "I haven't found any money."

"I have it," Uncle Gavin says.

I shake my head. "No, you aren't bailing this asshole out. Not with your own money."

"It's not my own money," Uncle Gavin says. "It's his."

Everyone turns to look at my uncle. My brain feels like it has a couple of wires crossed—I can't compute. "Say again?" I manage.

"I have his money. The money he stole from Iraq." He glances at his watch again. "Call him, Susannah. Or he'll do something worse to Tane."

I bring my palm to my head as if I'm going to smack it like a staticky radio. "You have the money," I say.

"Call him," Uncle Gavin says, and I take out my phone and dial Finn's number, putting the phone on speaker so everyone can hear.

"Susannah," Finn says upon answering.

I look at my uncle, pale and drawn and unyielding, and he nods at me. Eyes on my uncle, I say, "I found the money."

"Really," Finn says. "That was quick. Where was it?"

My uncle shakes his head. "Never mind where I found it," I say. "I have the cash and I'll exchange it for Tane, tomorrow."

There's a pause. "I'm not sure I believe you," Finn says.

My uncle reaches into the paper bag and pulls out something and holds it out to me. It's a brick of hundred-dollar bills. I stare at it. So does everyone else.

"Did I lose you?" Finn says on speaker.

I reach out and take the brick of cash from Uncle Gavin's hand. "One second," I say to Finn. I put the brick on the coffee table and with my phone take a picture. Then I send the picture to Finn. "Check your texts," I tell him.

Another pause, then a low whistle from Finn on speaker. "Nice work, Suzie Q. But like I said, that was quick."

"Haven't been doing much else for the past two days."

"I mean since this morning."

"What are you talking about?"

"I'm talking about what you told Yousef this morning. In Dearborn. About how you didn't know where the money was."

My spine turns to ice. "I don't understand," I say. I think I sound sufficiently puzzled, but it's hard to know as most of my mind is trying to figure out how Finn knows about Yousef.

"You aren't the only one who can fly to Detroit," he says. "I had to scramble a bit when you hopped on that private jet, but I managed to find another one. Cash is still king. And it was easy enough to find you and that giant you were with. Then it was just a matter of following you while you led me right to Yousef."

My pulse is thudding in my neck and I take a deep breath to try and calm myself. "He doesn't know anything about the rest of the money," I say. "He got the same duffel bag of cash as Hector Cortez's widow."

"He knew about your dad calling the DoD's whistleblower hotline to try to give the money back," Finn says. "Attacks of conscience are so cliché. Especially when the Pentagon told your father to fuck off."

My stomach shrinks into a cold, empty ball. "It doesn't matter what my father did. I've got the rest of the money. Just leave Yousef alone."

"First you're worried about Tane, now Yousef," Finn says. "You're a regular good Samaritan. Spreading joy like gunpowder all over the country."

"Finn—"

"Tomorrow morning," Finn says. "Eight o'clock, Stone Mountain Park. Be in the parking lot by the trailhead, near the South Woods Gate, alone. I'll call you then at this number with further instructions. You show with that money, and you come alone, or I'll do to Tane what I did to Yousef. But slower."

"Finn," I shout, but it's too late—Finn is gone. Fear and panic start spinning up in my chest like a pair of dynamos. I stand still, close my eyes, and let the feelings wash over me. For a terrifying moment I think they will drag me under with them, into the dark. My heart stops for a beat. And then it starts again, limping along at a rapid clip. It's passed. I still feel scared, but it's at a remove, and in the wake of my fear I can act. I take a breath and open my eyes. "Someone call the Dearborn police. And I need Gus Cimino's cell number. Now."

"I'll get the cops," Caesar says, tapping on his phone.

Frankie holds up his own phone, displaying his contact info for Gus. I dial the number on Frankie's screen, willing Gus to answer his phone. After the fourth ring, Gus answers. "Yeah?"

"Gus, it's Suzie. I need you to do me a favor. I'm going to text you an address for Yousef Hassan in Dearborn. He's a friend and he's in real trouble. We're trying to call the cops but I need someone I trust to go check on him. Can you do that for me?"

"Send me the address. I'll leave as soon as I get it."

"Thank you." I end the call and text him Yousef's address. A few seconds later he texts me a thumbs-up emoji. I glance up to see Caesar on his phone, speaking quietly.

"Suze?" Ethan says.

"I got Gus. He's going to check on Yousef."

Uncle Gavin speaks, his words like a severed head dropped onto the coffee table. "Yousef's dead. You heard him. Finn."

Ethan slowly shakes his head. "But . . . Finn's here, watching Tane."

"Unless he's got help," I say.

Caesar ends his call. "I got the Dearborn police. They're sending a squad car to Yousef's house."

"I've got Gus heading over there, too," I say. "Did you ever get a chance to look for those three soldiers? I found one, Stephen Chow. He was killed in a drunk driving accident. I need to know the other two."

Caesar pulls out his laptop from a case on the floor next to the couch.

"Why do you need to know about them right now?" Frankie says.

"Because I think at least one of them is alive, and whoever it is there's a good chance he's working with Finn. There's no way Finn would fly to Detroit and leave Tane alone."

Frankie shrugs. "Or he's already killed Tane."

"Finn needs Tane to help him launder the cash, maybe try to dip into one of the accounts Tane set up for the Sureños. He's got someone baby-sitting him. Finn's been in prison for years, disowned by his family. Who could he trust? Maybe someone he did time with, but a former soldier who served with him, who knows at least something about the money? That's my guess."

From his perch in the chair, Uncle Gavin says, "She's right."

"Thanks," I say. "Now you can explain what the fuck you meant when you said that you have his money."

Uncle Gavin thinks for a moment, and that's when I realize how old he looks, his face worn as an old hardcover. *He will die one day*, I think, and the realization is like being hit by a garbage truck.

"Your father came to me, a few months before he died," Uncle Gavin says. "He was desperate. He told me about the money, how it was sitting in a Kuwaiti bank. How he'd tried to contact the DoD but no one wanted anything to do with it. How he felt guilty about taking the money, and how by going to the DoD he felt he'd betrayed Yousef, Cortez, even Finn. He wanted to move the money stateside, but then he lost his job at the bank."

"And that meant he lost whatever inside access he had as a banker," I say. "It would be a lot harder to transfer that kind of money without leaving some sort of record or involving another banker."

"He wanted to get the money to the survivors of that day in Baghdad," Uncle Gavin says. "And for Alanna's sake, I said I'd help him. And then . . . and then they were killed, and I took you and your brother in, and I had to decide what to do with that money."

"It was you," I say at the same moment the thought strikes me. "You sent the duffel bags of cash to Cortez and Yousef."

"Only because your father said that's what he wanted to do with it," he says. "I knew someone who could transfer the money stateside without leaving an electronic footprint. And then I withdrew it all in cash."

"Why?" Ethan asks, and then answers his own question. "Less traceable."

"Virtually untraceable," Uncle Gavin says. "Cash can be more convenient than money in a bank account."

"Why did you never tell us any of this?" I ask.

"Because your father didn't want anyone to know." He pauses. "And I didn't want to damage your memory of him."

And there's nothing I can say to that.

Ethan clears his throat. "So where is it?" he asks. "The money?"

Uncle Gavin says nothing for a moment.

"Uncle Gavin?"

"There were eight million dollars," my uncle says. "Originally there was a little over ten million, but fees and hush money took a big bite. I sent two million each to Hector Cortez's family and Yousef Hassan."

I wait but Uncle Gavin seems to be done speaking. "What about the rest of it?" I ask. "That's, what, four or five million?"

"How's your locker at the Store-N-Go?" Uncle Gavin asks. "The gear in there? Your motorcycle? The other storage places around the country?" He leans forward slightly. "Where do you think all that came from?" He turns to Ethan. "The down payment on your house? Your college tuition? All from that."

I'm still trying to process all this, but all I can think to ask is, "What's left?"

"A little less than two million. I can raise it to an even two. But you need to decide how you want to play this handoff tomorrow."

I nod, trying to slow my brain down, analyze the problem. Stone Mountain is an enormous lump of granite bulging out of the flat plain just east of Atlanta. It's famous for an enormous carving of Confederate leaders on its north face, the largest such bas-relief artwork in the world. "Why Stone Mountain?" I ask.

"Maybe Finn's a little bit racist?" Frankie says.

"It's a big park," Uncle Gavin says. "Plenty of places to hide, even if you're just on the mountain itself."

"Isn't there a cable car or a skyride up to the top?" I ask.

Uncle Gavin nods. "Yes, but he's sending you to the trailhead on the west side of the mountain. The skyride goes up the north face, past the carvings."

"I've been on that trail," Ethan says. "Up the mountain. It's pretty steep in places. There's a lot of tree cover and outcroppings. And you can sneak into the park pretty easily. If you drive, you've got gates that require tickets. But you can walk in at some points without one."

"Then let's pull up a map of the park," I say, "and figure out how this is going to happen."

HALF AN HOUR later Gus calls back. Police have already cordoned off Yousef's house with crime scene tape, and an ambulance arrived just a few minutes ago, lights flashing but its siren off. That's when I know Yousef is dead, maybe his wife and kids, too. The ambulance isn't there to provide medical assistance—it's for body transport.

"I'm sorry, Suzie," Gus says at the other end. "If I'd gotten there sooner, maybe I coulda done somethin'."

"He'd already done whatever he did by the time I called you," I say. "I just wanted to make sure. Thank you, Gus."

"I'll stick around, see what I can find out. Alice might know the guys drivin' the ambulance. Was this guy a friend?"

"Friendly. Knew my dad. Seemed like a nice guy."

"You know who did this, yeah?"

"Yeah."

"Then I feel sorry for him. 'Cause I wouldn't want to piss you off."

Despite myself, I smile. "That's the nicest thing you've said to me. Say hi to Alice." I hang up. "Fuck!" I shout. I want to smash something. Preferably Finn. "Too late," I say to the room. "Cops are all over the place. Gus is going to see what else he can learn."

For a moment, we sit in silence. I think about Yousef, doing dangerous work in Iraq, escaping with his family to a new life in the U.S., only to be killed by one of the American soldiers he'd worked with. When I see Finn again, I'm going to shoot him between the eyes.

"Suzie," Uncle Gavin says.

I blow out a breath and nod. "Okay, where were we?"

"You need a car, not your motorcycle."

Frankie sits up straight. "Don't even think about asking me," he says.

"I need something less conspicuous than the Frankenstein. Plus I want something I don't mind getting banged up if necessary." I look at Ethan and raise an eyebrow.

Ethan shakes his head. "What would Uncle Gavin and I be in, then?"

Caesar interrupts by closing his laptop. "Found them," he says. "Mark O'Connor died in Iraq in 2005. Humvee hit an IUD outside of Ramadi. You found Stephen Chow, the one who died in a car accident. The third man's name is Julius Verne. He was a Spec4 in Iraq and served with Finn. Honorably discharged in '06, worked a series of odd jobs, got a record—assault, disturbing the peace, various traffic violations. One sexual assault charge, later dropped. And then, a year ago, he went off the grid. Deactivated his Twitter and Facebook accounts, broke his lease on an apartment in Oklahoma City."

"About the time Finn got out of prison," I say. "It's him. What was Verne's specialty in the military?"

"Explosive ordnance disposal. Got a citation for marksmanship too. Apparently wanted to try for Army Sniper School at Fort Benning but didn't get the required letter from his company commander."

So Finn has an explosives expert and a would-be sniper working with him. "Finn will have Julius Verne with him at Stone Mountain," I say. "Perfect place for a sniper to hide." I look at Caesar, Frankie, Ethan, Uncle Gavin. All are looking to me. "So, what am I driving?"

CHAPTER TWENTY-FOUR

I<small>T'S A FOG-SHROUDED MORNING, EVERYTHING SWATHED IN A WHITE</small> drizzle beneath a dark sky. Visibility is limited, the roads slick. I'm behind the wheel of a Suzuki Samurai that someone on Ethan's street has been trying to sell—I walked over last night and gave them eleven hundred dollars in cash. The Samurai rides high, and on the interstate it's as loud as a World War I biplane, but otherwise it's perfect for what I need.

I pull up to the main entrance to Stone Mountain Park and buy a ticket. Past the gate, Jefferson Davis Drive continues across the man-made lake that curves around much of Stone Mountain. The actual mountain is straight ahead, but the carving is hidden, the fog obscuring all but the most basic outline of the granite knob.

By the time I turn right onto Robert E. Lee Boulevard and then park in the lot by the trailhead, it's seven forty-five. The fog shows no sign of lifting, which is a double-edged sword—I'll have a hard time seeing Finn or Verne, but they'll have a hard time seeing me. Or anyone else.

"I'm in the parking lot," I say quietly. The microphone on the collar of my raincoat picks up anything above a whisper.

"We're already in the park," Caesar says through my earpiece.

"Ethan?" I say.

"On the scenic route," Ethan says. He and Uncle Gavin are slowly driving around the base of the mountain, Uncle Gavin armed with a camera in his role as a tourist.

The charcoal sky is beginning to pale. Somewhere beyond the fog, the sun is rising. I can make out the corner of a building at the edge of the lot—the Historical and Environmental Education Center, otherwise known as Confederate Hall, an antebellum-style mansion complete with white columns. Inside, every half hour you can see a short film about the Civil War in Georgia. Although Atlanta is a cosmopolitan city, much of the rest of Georgia seems determined to hold on to the nineteenth century.

As if reading my mind, Frankie speaks in my ear. "Did you know Stone Mountain Park opened a hundred years to the *day* after Lincoln was assassinated? *Qué chingados es eso?*"

Caesar replies drolly. "Are you suggesting the good founders of this park were trying to say something about the Civil War?"

In my best Southern drawl, I say, "I think you mean the War of Northern Aggression."

Uncle Gavin's voice cuts us off. "Quiet and pay attention, all of you."

"I'm getting out of the car," I say, and I open the door and step out onto the pavement. Even though it's June, the morning is unusually cool with the fog, although the sun will burn all this off. Whatever happens with Finn will be over long before that happens.

I open the back gate of the Samurai and lift a blanket that covers a large duffel bag and a small backpack. I unzip the duffel bag. Inside are stacks of hundred-dollar bills. I take a picture with my phone, zip the bag back up, and cover it with the blanket. I slip my arms through the straps of the backpack, close the gate and lock the Samurai, then pace around the parking lot, keeping my legs warmed up.

At eight o'clock, my phone rings. Finn. I answer. "I'm here."

"That's a small backpack to be holding millions of dollars," Finn says.

Although the fog obscures anything beyond the parking lot, the lot itself is clear enough. I can't see anyone, though. Maybe Finn is behind one of the parked cars—there are already a few dozen despite the early hour. "My pack holds five hundred grand," I say. "The rest is in a duffel bag in my car."

"Bring the duffel with you."

"I've got over two million in hundred-dollar bills. I'm not carrying fifty pounds of cash up a mountain."

"In Iraq we'd carry twice that weight in gear."

"We're not in Iraq. I'm texting you a picture of the cash in the duffel."

"And once I click on the attachment, it downloads malware onto my phone or some shit?"

"Yes, Finn, that's my plan, because I'm actually an NSA agent and have a satellite overhead tracking your every move. No, you dipshit, it's just a picture."

Silence. I can feel the others holding their breath. I text Finn the picture, then raise my phone back to my ear. "I just sent the picture. When you give me Tane, I'll give you the backpack and my car keys. You can take the car, too. The pink slip is in the glove compartment."

More silence. I start to wonder if Finn is in one of the cars in the lot, then decide against it. Wherever he is, he'll want to be able to move freely and quickly, which he couldn't do if he was inside a—

There's been a very faint noise in the background, almost like a tiny box fan, and now, just as my brain consciously registers the sound, my brain also identifies it. I look up and there it is, maybe a hundred feet overhead, black against the overcast sky—a quadcopter drone, hovering over the parking lot like a strange dragonfly. Drones are illegal in the park, but then again so is kidnapping.

I look directly at the drone and say into the phone, "What do you want me to do?"

"See the signs for the trail?" Finn says. "Start walking uphill." He ends the call.

I take a knee to tighten the laces on my shoes. My face down, I murmur, "He's got a drone over the parking lot. Keep your eyes peeled. He's sending me to the trail." I stand, cinching the straps of my backpack tighter, and start walking toward Confederate Hall. I resist the urge to look at the drone, but I hear the whirring sound fade as I walk.

Behind Confederate Hall is a concrete patio at the foot of the mountain, which rises like a giant fog-shrouded mound. A handful of people, many in workout gear, are either on the trail that runs around the mountain's base or are heading to the walk-up trail, which goes straight up the slope of granite. The path looks like the surface of the moon might look if it were free of dust and broken rock, with added clumps of pine and oak and scrub trees. A sign welcomes me to the park and informs me that various things including littering, painting, pets, fires, and wheelchairs are prohibited. I envision someone trying to push a grandma in a wheelchair up Stone Mountain, then accidentally letting go and sending the wheelchair careening down the path, mowing down the power walkers and the two neo-Confederates on the patio trying to hand out pamphlets saying White Lives Matter. I actually turn to look behind me, as if an old lady in a wheelchair has just bounced down the rocks, and that's when I see Caesar, in shorts and a skullcap, doing calf stretches down on the patio. He doesn't look up at me, but I know he's seen me. I take the opportunity to check the sky overhead but see no sign of the drone. I turn away and face the mountain, then start climbing.

The path at this point is a wide expanse of weather-worn stone with a few shallow crevices to navigate. A fine mist needles my face and hands, moisture beading on the outside of my windbreaker. There's a couple ahead of me, a Black man and a White woman, walking uphill hand in hand. I can see two others up ahead, each on his or her own, and then everything else vanishes behind an insubstantial wall of mist that seems to move with me. Sound is muffled—the couple ahead of me are speaking to each other, but I can't make out their words, and my own footsteps sound like I'm hearing them through a radio with the volume turned way down.

I pass a dais on my right with five flags on tall poles. Four are emblems of the Confederate States of America, including the famous Dixie flag or

Southern cross. The fifth is the American flag. A man stands at the base of the dais, staring up at the flags. I walk on and leave him behind me in the fog.

Soon another path cuts straight across mine. It's the safety road, partially paved in some places, gravel in most others, built to allow vehicles to ascend at least part of the slope. To my left the safety road runs back down the mountain; to the right it plunges into the trees where it will eventually turn uphill and run parallel to the walking path. As I look that way, someone in a red shirt slips behind a tree. I stop and try to peer into the fog.

My phone rings and I almost jump. "Hello?" I answer.

"Hanging in there?" Finn asks. "How's your heart rate?"

"I'm just fine. Let me talk to Tane."

"That's cute. And no. Keep walking." A click and he's gone.

I slip my phone back into my jacket pocket and bend to touch my toes. "Frankie," I murmur, "are you on the safety road?"

"The what?" Frankie says in my ear.

"It crosses the main path. What are you wearing?"

"A red T-shirt and jeans. Just went behind a tree to take a leak."

"Try to keep up." I stand, put my hands at the small of my back and stretch, then continue climbing.

Up ahead the walking path seems to peter out into a thin screen of trees. A few steps further and the fog recedes enough to show me the path is still there, but the trees are encroaching upon it, a few even growing right up in the middle of the rocks. The path is more uneven here, like rough-hewn steps carved into the hillside. A group of people all wearing identical blue T-shirts reading Christ Is King walk downhill through the trees, helping each other over the rocks. Visibility drops to maybe twenty feet, with few clear lines of sight unbroken by a tree trunk. Even if the drone is still flying, there's no way it can see me clearly. "Caesar, you on my six?" I say.

"Maybe a hundred yards behind you," he says.

"Frankie?"

"I'm on the safe road or whatever it's called. If Finn's up here, he might be using this like a back route."

"He's up here," I say. "Keep your eyes peeled for the drone. Ethan?"

"Still driving around the mountain. Uncle Gavin's getting loads of pictures. You see anything yet?"

"Just a lot of rocks and trees. I'll keep you posted."

I climb on.

The path widens again but becomes rockier, as if I'm walking in a long-dry creek bed. Then the trees fall away and I'm in a wide clearing of smoothed stone that looks like poured concrete. Power poles carrying electric cables march straight up the slope. I feel my shoulders hunch forward protectively. This is the most open area so far; if Verne is close enough to see through the fog with a scope, I'm an easy target. I still don't see the drone. Then I'm back in the trees and I release a breath I've been holding. Just as I'm thinking about calling Finn back, my phone rings. "Yes?" I say.

"Feels like you're exposed when you cross those open areas, doesn't it?" Finn says.

"You like trying to play mind games, don't you?"

"Oh, this is no game."

"Sure it is," I say, reaching out to grab a young pine tree trunk and pull myself up the trail. "You want to show you're in control, you have eyes on me, yada yada. Just remember I'm bringing you your money. You keep your end of the bargain, I'll keep mine."

Finn is silent for a moment, and when he speaks again his voice is flat. "In about a hundred feet you'll come to another clearing. Once you step out of the trees you'll see three flat rocks on the right-hand side of the trail. Directly across from them is a bush. I've left something for you in that bush." He ends the call.

I walk on, uneasy. When I step into the clearing, I see the flat stones he's talking about, the bush across from them. The couple holding hands is still ahead of me, but they're at the far end of the clearing. I see no one on the trail behind me. I take a knee and look in the bush. Maybe Finn left a rattlesnake for me. Then I see in the center of the bush a bright blue box, the kind you would open to find a ring inside. It's clean, so it hasn't been here long. I pluck it out and look around. Short pines stand vigil around the clearing. Through the fog I still don't see anyone below me on the trail.

I open the box. What lies inside could be an old, flattened apricot, except for the neatly sliced edge that has seeped blood onto the cotton below, blood that is now dried and almost black. It's a human ear. An ear missing its lower lobe.

There is a high, faint whir and I look up to see the drone hovering just above the tops of the pines at the bottom of the clearing.

I feel the scream boil up from my gut, and while I keep it throttled behind my teeth, my fingers close over a good chunk of rock. I stand and, with an explosive grunt, I hurl it. The drone slips to one side, dodging the rock.

My phone rings. I answer and shout, "What?"

"Do that again and I'll nail his other ear to a tree," Finn says.

"Fuck you, asshole."

"Any time, Suzie Q. Keep walking." And he's gone.

I stare at the drone that continues to hover above the treetops.

"Suzie?" Frankie says in my ear. "What happened?"

I turn away from the drone to hide my face. My voice is thick with emotion and I clench my fists, wishing my hands were around Finn's neck. "He cut off Tane's ear and left it for me in a box."

Frankie starts cursing in Spanish, too fast for me to understand. Then Uncle Gavin says, "Frankie, shut it. Susannah, where are you?"

I start walking uphill again. "Not quite halfway up."

"The cable car doesn't start running until later this morning," Uncle Gavin says. "If he has Tane with him, he had to walk him up the mountain earlier, which wouldn't be easy. So he probably didn't hike all the way to the top."

Or Tane's dead and Finn is just stringing me along. I don't say this out loud, though. But I know every one of us is thinking it. "Frankie, you still on the safety road?" I ask.

"Yeah." Frankie sounds a little winded.

"Caesar, you still with me?"

His deep voice is both comforting and ominous. "To the very end."

I walk on, climbing through the trees. My quads and calves are starting to ache. The mountain is beautiful, even with the fog, but I can't enjoy it. God, I hate Finn, even more than before if that's possible.

Almost two hundred yards later, my heart pumping and my breathing now heavier, I walk into the biggest clearing yet. I stop and get a bottle of water out of my backpack and drink, taking in the scenery. The trees continue in a green wall on the left, but to the right they drop away to reveal another expanse of bare rock, this one scattered with moss and grasses and sloping gently down from the trail. I return the water bottle to my backpack and walk on, scanning the clearing, then stop abruptly. Sitting on a patch of grass about twenty yards away off to the side of the trail, just visible through the fog, is Finn. Someone else sits next to him, slumped against a tree, a hoodie covering his head. I think it's Tane but the fog makes it hard to see. I walk down the slope toward them, hands open and spread wide.

When I'm maybe five yards out, Finn says, "That's enough." I stop and Finn rests a pistol on his knee. "Take off your backpack and bring it to me, slowly."

If Verne is tracking me with a scope, he's probably behind me, somewhere in that wall of trees on the other side of the trail. That would offer the best field of view. I take the backpack off my shoulders. "Tane," I say, "you okay?"

The hoodied figure shifts and lifts its head. It's Tane, his face pale, eyes blank.

"He's fine," Finn says, the pistol still resting on his knee. "Don't worry about him. Just bring me the backpack. Slowly."

I walk over, stepping carefully, and lower the backpack to the rock, a yard or so from his feet. From this angle I can see, sitting on the rock behind Finn, the drone. It's bigger than I thought, with four rotors and a camera built into the body. Next to the drone is a tablet Finn must use to control it.

Finn follows my gaze. "Wish we'd had some of these in Iraq."

"Oh my God," I say. "I'm so sick of you talking about Iraq."

Finn raises his eyebrows. "Did I hit a nerve, Suzie Q?"

"I'm just *over* it. The whiny rich kid steals a bunch of money and kills another soldier over it and then bitches *endlessly* about how life is unfair? Cry me a river, you pussy little silver spoon fuck."

Finn's face tightens like an angry facelift. I don't even see the pistol in Finn's hand move. One second it's resting on Finn's knee, the next it's pointed at my face. But the pistol doesn't scare me. What scares me is my own laughter. "So that's what it takes?" I say. "A couple of insults about you being a spoiled little brat? That's what makes you lose your shit?"

Finn sneers. "Says the damaged little psycho. Do you think the next time you're committed to a hospital you'll actually have the guts to slit your own wrists?"

I smile back at him, all teeth. "Not if they give me the good drugs."

"Hey!" someone shouts. It's Frankie, hurrying up the slope from the safety road. "Hey, Finn, you *pinche baboso!*"

Finn turns, the pistol in his hand tracking on Frankie. I crouch and lower my right arm, my baton sliding down out of my sleeve into my hand. Then I stand and swing the baton across and up, like drawing a sword. I strike Finn's hand just as he steadies his pistol. The pistol arcs out of Finn's hand and he stifles a scream. I ignore him and run for Tane, dropping my baton. "Get down!" I shout, and I leap at Tane. A rifle shot cracks as I tackle Tane and knock him flat to the rocks behind the tree he was slumping against earlier. Another rifle shot, this one splintering the tree a couple of feet above my head. There are faint screams from the trail, and the deeper *boom* of a large-caliber handgun. Caesar.

I lift my head and see Finn sprinting uphill along the trail. I reach for my CZ, but before I can even grip it Finn disappears into the fog.

Frankie runs up and drops to all fours by my side. "You okay, Suzie?"

I grab the front of Frankie's T-shirt and pull him down just as there's another high *crack*. Something ricochets off the rock a few yards behind us. Then there are three more *boom*s from Caesar's handgun, then silence.

I lean up against the tree, keeping the trunk between me and wherever Verne is. Frankie is lying face down on the ground. Next to him, Tane is curled in a fetal position, his eyes closed. There's gauze taped to the side of his head where his ear used to be. "Tane," I say.

In a faint but clear voice, Tane says, "Where the fuck have you been?"

I smile. "We're getting you off this mountain," I say. I pull off my windbreaker. "Give me your hat," I say to Frankie.

Frankie turns his head to look at me. "It's my Braves hat."

"I'll buy you a new one."

"This is my lucky hat," he says, but he takes it off and hands it to me, still lying face down. "What are you doing?"

I put the hat on my head, my hair already pulled back in a ponytail. Now if Verne sees me he might not recognize me immediately. "I'm going after Finn," I say to Frankie. "Take care of Tane. Get him down off the mountain."

"Suzie—"

I pull out my CZ, take a deep breath, then scramble around the tree and run up the path after Finn. It's only a few yards to the tree line, but every step I expect a bullet in the back. Then I'm in the trees.

Oak and pine trees loom out of the fog and I pass them, eyes sweeping the rocky trail and the undergrowth on either side. If I go too fast, I could miss him; if I go too slowly, he'll get far enough ahead of me to double back around, or set up an ambush. Soon my tank top is soaked. I grip the CZ in one hand, my quads burning, my lungs gulping oxygen.

A hundred feet or more of scrambling up the trail and I come to a small roofed pavilion with picnic tables. No sign of Finn. I press on.

The trees vanish and the granite face of the mountain spreads out on either side, the fog still close. Two figures like shadows appear ahead of me, coming down the trail. I keep my pistol by the side of my leg, ready to bring it to bear, but it's a young couple, the man wearing a hipster beard, the woman a blonde wearing a beanie. "Hey," the man says, raising a hand. "Did you hear gunshots?"

"Yes," I say. "Did you see a man run this way? Mid to late forties, black hair, silver at the temples?"

Both shake their heads. They are doing their best not to stare at the pistol I'm holding by my leg.

"Keep going downhill," I say, walking on.

The slope is steeper here, and soon a pair of metal railings materialize out of the fog, the posts inserted straight into the rock. People slowly descend the slope, shadows gripping the railings. I go up the outside of the right-hand railing, left hand grasping the metal, right hand holding the CZ. When I reach the end of the railing, the slope still continues up, the path twisting left around a stand of pines. The fog rolls past like tattered clouds, as if I'm standing on top of the world. To the left, through a break in the fog, I see far below a blanket of green trees dotted with roofs, stretching north and west to a gray horizon.

Finn explodes out from the stand of pine trees. I'm able to turn and raise the CZ before Finn collides with me and we both stagger across the rock. We struggle over the pistol, Finn grabbing my wrist while I punch and claw at him with my free hand. He reaches for my ponytail and I slam an elbow into his jaw. Then he twists my arm so it goes numb and the CZ springs from my grip, clattering on the stones and sliding off into the fog. I stomp on his instep and he grunts with pain, releasing my arm. I take three steps back to open space between us. Finn smiles and pulls a knife. I pull my own and we circle each other, feet searching for purchase on the slippery stone.

"I'm going to hurt you," Finn says. "I mean really hurt you. Leave you broken in ways you can't imagine."

"Uh-huh," I say, looking for an opening.

"I'll carve you up like a fucking turkey," he says. "And your brother, and your pathetic uncle. And your goddamned dog. I'll hurt everyone you love."

"You talk a lot," I say. "Especially for a guy who has nothing and nobody waiting for him."

Finn responds by attacking, a flurry of stabs and slashes I can barely keep up with. I block a stab at my neck and almost catch him with a thrust to his armpit, but he twists away, slashing my bicep and drawing blood. Then he's pressing me again, forcing me backward so I almost stumble. I slash, stab, kick, gouge. He blocks or avoids all my attacks. He cuts my forearm, then my shoulder, then nearly takes out an eye. I'm bleeding and starting to panic. He's too fast. I can't stop him.

"Broken," he says, his eyes shining. He sweeps my legs at the ankles and I fall, landing on my back, which knocks the wind out of my lungs. Then Finn is on me, trying to shove his knife into my neck. I cross my wrists to block his arm, but he has the weight and the leverage. The knife sinks another centimeter closer, the tip hovering above the hollow of my throat.

"I'm going to slip this into you," Finn says, his crazed smile inches from my face. "Hard and sharp and slow, and you are going to scream, it will hurt so much. And then I'll punch it into one of your lungs, and you'll feel it collapse and you'll start gasping for air like a goldfish on a floor. And then I'll skewer your fucking heart." The knife sinks lower, the tip almost touching me. "You'll taste your own blood as it wells up in your throat. I'll be the last thing you see before you die. And I'm going to enjoy—"

Opening.

I crane my neck and bite down hard on his hand, on the pad below his pinkie finger. It's like biting into a raw chicken thigh. Finn screams and instinctively pulls back, removing his knife from my throat. I stab my own knife upward, sticking it into Finn just above his collarbone, right in the trapezius muscle. I sit up, trying to shove the blade in further, and Finn rears back and rolls off me. I stand as he gets to his feet and backs away, blood already darkening the front of his shirt.

"I told you, you talk too much," I say, holding my knife, the blade wet with Finn's blood.

I hear the shot at the same time the bullet tunnels through me above my right hip, spinning me around so I drop to the rocks. The pain is like a white-hot rod of iron through my side. I gasp at the enormity of it. Dimly I'm aware that my knife is gone and Finn is nowhere to be seen. I'm lying on my back, hand pressed to the wound to stanch the bleeding, when I hear boots on stone. I turn my head to see a tall bearded man in camo approaching. He's carrying a rifle, looks like a Ruger with a short barrel.

"You must be Julius," I say. "You're uglier than I thought." The words sound far away. Cold sweat covers my face. It's the blood loss. I'll slip into shock soon enough if I don't get this hole in my side bandaged.

This is all rendered moot by Verne looking down at me from just feet away and raising the rifle to his shoulder, aiming at my face. I lift my bloody hand and manage to flip him off.

A whirring sound like a miniature buzzsaw causes Verne to turn just in time for the quadcopter drone to crash into his face. The rotors slice his cheeks and nose and forehead, then his fingers as he screams and raises his hands to protect his face. Blood sprays the air, dark against the fog. Verne stumbles backward and trips right over me, planting one foot on my thigh. He drops his rifle, which starts sliding down the slope, and I grab it by its sling. Verne falls and there's a heavy *thock* as his head hits the granite. Then he's sliding headfirst down the slope, gaining velocity even as he scrabbles for purchase, his eyes wide and desperate. I turn to see him slip over the lip of the rock and vanish.

I get to my knees and put both hands over the holes in my side. The holes are small but blood is still flowing from them slowly, dripping onto the rock. I look around to call for help, but all I see is the drone lying on the ground, rotors twisted and the body cracked.

There are running footsteps and a shape approaches out of the fog, and I pick up the rifle, but it's Caesar. I lay the rifle back down, exhausted. A nap sounds like a good idea right now. When Caesar reaches me he drops to his hands and knees. "I got you," he says. "I got you."

"Shock," I say to Caesar, my lips thick and rubbery.

Caesar slaps me, twice, not gently. Anger flares up, as does consciousness. "Thanks," I manage to say.

"You're welcome," Caesar says, leaning me back against an outcropping of stone. I hear zippers and Velcro tearing open, and then Caesar is lifting my tank top, peeling it away from the wound. I feel a slight stick in my side, and then Caesar is unwrapping something. "Clean through-and-through shot," he says. "Maybe a .22."

"He used that," I say, gesturing toward the rifle on the ground.

Caesar glances at it, then starts wrapping a compression bandage around my waist, gauze covering the two holes. "Where's Verne?"

"He went over the edge. What did you give me?"

"Ketamine," Caesar says, tightening the compression bandage and securing it. "A very small dose. You should be feeling it soon."

"Where's Finn?"

Caesar shakes his head. "Don't know. I was chasing Verne through the woods."

I grab the rifle and use it as a crutch to get to my feet. "We've got to find Finn."

"You need to go to a hospital. Are those knife wounds on your arms?"

"They're superficial."

"That gunshot isn't."

I walk carefully down the rock face in the direction Verne fell and peer over the edge of the slope where it starts becoming precipitous.

Below me I see Verne in a heap against a chain-link fence that stretches across the slope, a final safety barrier between hikers and the open cliff face that plunges hundreds of feet below. Even from here I can see the slashes in his hands and face from the drone rotors.

Caesar comes up beside me. "We're lucky there was fog this morning. Otherwise he could've picked us off easy."

"You did a pretty good number on him with the drone."

"That was Frankie. He got the drone airborne to try and find Finn."

I reach for my earpiece and realize it's gone. Must have fallen out at some point when I was fighting with Finn. I wondered why I hadn't heard anyone talking. "I told Frankie to get Tane off the mountain."

"He's doing that now," Caesar says. "Please, let's go to a hospital."

"Tell Ethan and Uncle Gavin to keep an eye out for Finn," I tell him. "Maybe he went down in the cable car."

"Suzie, there are gonna be cops all over this mountain in a few minutes. I guarantee there are cops down below with the cable car. Finn isn't going anywhere."

"I'm not taking that chance."

"You might have internal bleeding. You need a doctor. Let's sit down and keep an eye on Verne down there. I'll tell Ethan and your uncle to get the cops and a medic."

Whether it's endorphins kicking in or the ketamine, I don't feel so terrible all of a sudden. I lower myself to the stone and let Caesar take the rifle. I look up at the sky, squinting. The sun is bleary, like a light bulb held up behind a gauzy curtain, but it's there. And the fog is beginning to clear, like I knew it would, and the gray line that was at the horizon is now turning blue. It's going to be a beautiful day.

CHAPTER TWENTY-FIVE

It turns out Verne's little .22-caliber round perforated my large intestine, which leaked some of its contents into my abdominal cavity and led to a lovely case of peritonitis. To my everlasting regret, Ethan can now say that, for at least a short time, I really was full of shit.

Thankfully I'm in the hospital when the doctors catch it. The surgery to repair my bowel is relatively easy, although when I wake up in a recovery cubicle, a thin curtain drawn around my bed and bright lights shining down, all my fears of hospitals rush me at once. I panic and try to get out of bed, ripping off one of several wires attached to me, which causes a monitor to start beeping as if agitated. Two nurses get me back in bed as I gibber and weep, and finally someone knocks me out with a shot.

When I wake up again, I am in a proper hospital room, sunlight glazing the blinds. Ethan is sitting next to my bed, eyes closed, mouth open.

"Wakey-wakey," I croak.

Ethan starts, nearly knocking over a vase of flowers on the table next to him. "Hey," he says, wiping his face. "What. Huh?"

"You're hilarious," I say. My mouth and throat are dry and my tongue is coated in a sticky film. "Get me some ice chips or I'll stab someone."

Ethan stumbles out of the room and returns with a plastic cup of ice chips, which he places in my mouth one at a time.

"This is the most inefficient way to drink water ever," I say.

"That's why you have an IV. Open up."

I part my lips so Ethan can slip another ice chip into my mouth, where I let it melt on my tongue. "Where's Finn?"

"I need a shower," Ethan says, rubbing his face. He looks paler than usual, his red hair in unruly spikes.

"Where is he, Ethan?"

Ethan shakes his head. "Uncle Gavin and I waited at the trailhead, long after you got brought down the safety road by the fire rescue folks. We were watching for him. But he never came down that trail. Didn't come down the cable car, either. The cops searched every inch of that mountain and found nothing."

I want to throw something breakable across the room, but all I can manage is to shake my head on my hospital pillow in disgust. "We had him at the top of a fucking mountain. How could you lose him?"

"It's a mountain, Suzie, not an apartment building. He could have come down any of a dozen ways before we finally convinced the park police to shut it down. Julius Verne helped with that, actually. Started talking the second the cops showed up and convinced them there was another man. He called Finn a psycho and said he'd only helped Finn because he feared for his life."

"Please tell me the cops didn't give him a prize."

"They charged him with kidnapping and attempted murder. He's being held without bail in DeKalb County."

There's that, at least. "How's Tane?"

"He's down the hall. Twisted his ankle really bad coming down the trail. Plus he was dehydrated and, well . . ." Ethan gestures at his ear. "But he's okay. He asked to see you when you woke up, actually." He stands. "I'll go tell him you're up, and then I gotta get home, let Wilson out. Uncle Gavin sends his love."

I eye him skeptically. "He sends his love? This is the same Uncle Gavin, right?"

Ethan shrugs. "That's what the man said. I think he was really worried." He pauses for a beat. "We both were, actually." He leans over and kisses the top of my head. "Love you." And before I can form a response, he's gone.

I try to take a deep breath, then turn my head to look around the room. There's a small water closet in the corner, and another terrible hospital room painting, and a chair next to the bed, and a window with blinds. It's a nice enough room for a hospital. What I don't want to admit is that I'm relieved the door to the water closet is open to show that no one could be hiding in there, that the blinds to the window are drawn so no one can look in, that there are no bullets lined up on the windowsill.

TANE KAMAKA BANGS into my room in a wheelchair sometime later, one leg in a cast and extended in front of him like a lance. "Hey," he says brightly. "You're awake."

"I am now," I say, but I smile as I say it. "How are you?"

"I fucked up my ankle big time." Tane announces this like the world's proudest ten-year-old. "Gonna have to get a boot or something for it. And that bastard cut my ear off, but I talked to a plastic surgeon today, and he was so cool. They'd build a new ear out of my rib cartilage. Isn't that crazy?"

"Totally."

"I mean, they said they could create an artificial plastic frame and cover that with a skin graft, and part of me thinks that would be just as cool, but using my *own* cartilage is better in a whole lot of ways. I mean, my body wouldn't reject it, because, I mean, it *is* my body, or part of my body, and—"

"Tane."

"Yeah?"

I swallow, trying to lubricate my throat. What is it about hospitals and dry throat? "I'm sorry I didn't find you earlier."

Tane nods. "Me too. But thanks for coming. I mean, you were pretty badass."

I close my eyes. "I'm completely badass. But right now I need a nap."

"Oh, okay," Tane says. "Sure. You get some rest." I hear him start to roll away, his wheelchair squeaking.

"Tane?" I say, my eyes still closed.

"Uh-huh?"

I open my eyes a crack. "Come back and visit later, okay?"

Tane smiles. He's in a hospital gown, and there's a wad of gauze on one side of his head where his ear was sliced off, and he looks like he hasn't showered in a few days. But that smile is gorgeous. "Yeah, sure," he says.

BUT HE DOESN'T come back. Instead, the next day I'm visited by Alisha Rondeau. I hear her heels on the tile floor all the way down the hall. Then she's standing in the doorway. Today she's wearing a black pantsuit and an ivory blouse. Not for the first time, I wonder how many pantsuits she has in her closet. "Special Agent Rondeau," I say.

"Hi, Suzie," she says, and I'd be lying if I said my heart didn't flutter a bit. "Can I come in?"

"Mi hospital, su hospital."

Rondeau walks in and sits next to my bed. "How are you?" she asks.

"Fabulous," I say. "I've got wires and tubes coming out of me like I'm an experiment in a bad sci-fi movie."

Rondeau considers my monitor wires and IV tube. "You do sort of look like a low-rent Borg."

"If you tell me you're a *Star Trek* fan, I'll confess my undying love for you right here."

It's slight, but she smiles. "I wanted to tell you that Tane Kamaka has been discharged."

I blink in surprise. "Is he okay?"

"He's fine."

"Oh," I say. "Shit. You've got him in protective custody. Again."

She has the good grace to look mildly uncomfortable. "He's in the right hands this time. He's a material witness in an ongoing federal investigation."

"The Sureños will be looking for him."

She holds my gaze. "Which is why he is where he is. They'll be looking for you, too."

I give her a bleak smile. "Bring 'em on."

Neither of us says anything for a moment. My monitor makes its quiet *beep*.

"Actually," Rondeau says, "I wouldn't worry about the Sureños too much, at least any local affiliates."

Which is Feebie-speak for *they're all dead or locked up*. "Guess the Lawrenceville raid went well."

She looks at me impassively, all business. I really want to see her laughing, wearing something other than a pantsuit.

"How's Agent Scott?" I ask.

That gets a double blink, a crack in the wall of professionalism. "He's all right," she says. "He's on leave."

So the feds put Agent Scott in timeout. "How's Timmy?"

This time Rondeau smiles for real. "He's good. Hanging with his dad." She stands. "I'm glad you're okay, Suzie."

"Thanks. Can you give Tane a message for me? Tell him he's the badass."

Rondeau nods. "Will do." She pauses, then leans down and brushes a few strands of my hair off my face, tucking them behind my ear. I inhale her scent, eucalyptus and oranges and cedar. "Bye, Suzie," she says quietly, and then she's gone, her heels clicking down the hall.

I CHECK OUT of the hospital the next day with a bottle full of antibiotics that rattles in its paper bag. Frankie picks me up in the Frankenstein, which makes up a little bit for being rolled to the curb in a wheelchair like an invalid. Frankie drives carefully and talks about the bar. The insurance people are going to drag their feet, he says, but Johnny Shaw is already making noise about lawsuits. "Plus your uncle knows somebody who might be able to replace the ovens pretty quick," he adds.

"Of course he does. So the bar will be up and running soon?"

Frankie shrugs as he passes a minivan full of kids. "Might be another two weeks, but I think so, yeah." A smile slowly crosses his face.

"Look at you, all happy. Do you have a piece in the car?"

Frankie's smile freezes in place. "What for?"

"Need to make a stop before you take me home."

THE HOUSE IS a brick ranch that was brand new in 1960 but looks like nothing about it has been changed since except the light bulbs. The front lawn is mown down to within an inch of its life, and the bricks are a mottled pale red and dirty white. There's a single-car garage on one side of the house, and the garage door is down, but I'm pretty sure what's parked in there.

"Are you nuts?" Frankie says.

"You seriously still don't know the answer to that?" I take his .38 revolver from the glove compartment, check the cylinder, and stick it in my pocket. "Just stay here. Honk if there's a problem."

"A problem?"

"Cops. Godzilla. Whatever. Just don't leave." I get out and close the door behind me before Frankie can say anything else, and I walk up the driveway. There are times when stealth is required, and then there are times when you knock on the front door.

I pound my fist on the front door eight or nine times, then step back and put my hand in my pocket. When the door opens, I take the .38 out and point it at the man in the doorway.

"Jesus Christ," Brandon Cargill says.

"Nope," I say, stepping forward, .38 extended, and I force Cargill back into the house, like one magnet repelling another. I pull the front door shut, eyes and revolver both steady on Cargill.

"The fuck are you doing here?" He sounds more angry than scared.

"It's the Salvation Army." I cock the hammer back.

"Whoa, now, wait a minute—"

"And today," I say, putting the .38 in his face, "you get to save yourself. Stop moving your hand toward that drawer." Cargill's hand stops inching toward the drawer of the hall table behind him. I wave him toward the living room with the .38. "After you." As soon as he steps away from the hall table, I pull open the drawer and glance down. There's a Colt .380 Mustang in there. I slide the drawer shut and follow Cargill into the living room. It's got wood paneling and is full of crate furniture with dark navy cushions that look about as comfortable to sit on as life preservers. A stag head with eight points is mounted above a brick fireplace. Sliding glass doors to the right look out on a backyard almost as bald as the front. Beyond a thin line of pine trees at the back of the property is the parking lot of a McDonald's on Lawrenceville Highway.

"Anybody else at home?" I ask.

Cargill swallows and manages to turn it into a sneer. "Actually got a couple of buddies downstairs. You done stepped in a hornet's nest, girl."

"No cars out front. Your buddies walk over from Mickey D's?" I laugh when Cargill's face falls. "Hope your imaginary friends weren't coming over to play poker. You'd lose. Love your place, by the way. Kinda like a frat house and a midlife crisis had a baby."

Teeth gritted, Cargill says, "It was my deddy's.'"

That brings me up a little short. Not just because of my own daddy issues, but because it humanizes Cargill a little, and I don't want to think of him as a human being. "I'm sure he'd be right proud of his son. How's the garage downtown doing?"

"Least my deddy didn't go crazy from going to war," Cargill spits. "And he wasn't killed in his own house, neither."

I cross the living room so quickly Cargill can barely draw breath. When he opens his mouth to speak, I shove the cocked .38 between his lips, pushing his tongue back and making him gag. "My father was ten times the man your father ever was," I say. I'm furious, the howler monkeys going full tilt in my head. Cargill's eyes nearly cross as he tries to look at the gun in his mouth. He makes some sort of garbled plea. I want to pull the trigger and paint the wall with his brains, see his blood spatter across the wood paneling. *Do it*, a voice whispers.

I yank the .38 out of his mouth, nearly taking one of Cargill's teeth with it. Cargill moans and drops to his knees on the carpet. My hand holding the .38 is shaking, and with effort I still it. I lean down to whisper into Cargill's ear. "You weren't going to show me any mercy in that warehouse. I just did you a favor. Remember that. And don't ever cross my uncle again." With that, I turn my back on Cargill and walk away, leaving him blubbering on his living room carpet.

THE WEEKEND AFTER I get out of the hospital, Ethan has a barbecue. Initially it's just the five of us—me, Ethan, Frankie, Caesar, and Uncle Gavin. But Uncle Gavin shows up at Ethan's house with Johnny Shaw, and to my surprise they are both driven by Gus, who is standing outside by the car and gives me a big, ugly smile when he sees me. Turns out five days is about all of Alice that Gus can stand. "She's my sister, and I love her," he says. "But she's a lot, you know?"

"She's awesome," I say, "but I get it. I'm kind of a lot, too."

"Kind of?" Ethan says. He's standing at the front door wearing an apron that says WINE TIME.

I stick my tongue out at Ethan. "Come on in," I say to Gus. "Grab a plate."

"Absolutely," Ethan says.

Gus shrugs. "I'll eat anytime." He lumbers up the front walk and squeezes inside. I follow to find Ethan and Caesar in the kitchen, discussing dry rubs versus marinades, while Frankie is ignoring them and shaking something over a platter of steaks. "Seasoned salt and pepper," he announces. "My own private recipe I got from *Papá*."

"Ruben always knew how to grill a steak," Uncle Gavin says. He's sitting in Ethan's usual chair, hands planted on his knees as if he's on the verge of getting up and leaving.

"He was a good man," Johnny Shaw says from his chair opposite Uncle Gavin. Behind him stands Gus, who pretends to fade into the background. He's about an inconspicuous as a Great Dane in a wading pool.

"Gracias, Mr. Shaw," Frankie says. "Okay, steaks going on the grill. Suzie, how do you like yours?"

"Not mooing, but not burnt."

"Medium it is." Frankie sidesteps Caesar, who is checking something in the fridge, and carries the platter of steaks out the kitchen door into the backyard.

"Susannah." Uncle Gavin gestures at the couch next to him. "How are you?"

I lower myself onto the couch, wincing slightly at the pull on my stitches. "Good," I say. "Clean bill of health."

"Glad to hear it," he says. "I understand you made a little side trip on the way home from the hospital."

Damn it, Frankie. "Let's just say Brandon Cargill shouldn't be annoying you anytime soon," I say. "And if he does, just tell me."

Uncle Gavin fixes those black eyes on me. "So you're staying." It's a question wrapped in a statement.

"For now."

He nods appreciatively, and we say nothing for a moment. Then I ask, "Did you take care of that business for me?"

Before I got out of the hospital, I called Uncle Gavin and asked him to send whatever he could to Yousef Hassan's remaining family, a brother and sister-in-law in Dearborn. They adopted Yousef's children after the deaths of their parents. Uncle Gavin said he would get one last duffel bag of cash to them—two million dollars, all that was left of the Iraq money plus a bit extra, the same amount that would have been Finn's share. That plus the two million they already had won't replace their parents, but it's something.

Uncle Gavin nods again. "Delivered yesterday," he says. "Signed 'From Dad,' like you asked."

"Thank you. Being orphaned sucks. Hopefully this will help a little. Like it helped me, apparently."

Abruptly, Uncle Gavin says, "I'm sorry about Tane. You were right. I should have told Frankie and Caesar."

I open my eyes wide in surprise. "I'm sorry, did you just apologize out loud?"

"You should record it on your smartphone for posterity," he says. "And you did well, by the way. Not that you need my approval."

"I don't," I say. "But it's nice to have it."

He gives me a little smile then, more a twinkle in his eye than anything, but it's enough. "So what are you going to do next?"

I shrug. "Thought about waiting tables, maybe being a hostess. You know a place that needs either?"

"I might."

Frankie sticks his head back inside. "Ten minutes on the steaks. Caesar, what are you doing?"

Caesar is examining the contents of a large bowl. "Making sure nobody added anything unnecessary to the potato salad."

"Unnecessary?"

"My brother-in-law once brought potato salad to a family dinner," Caesar says. "It had raisins in it."

I grin. "No wonder you threw him out a window."

Caesar puts the bowl on the counter. "It was more of a shove."

Johnny Shaw turns on the TV to find the Braves game. Wilson, who Ethan had kept trapped in the bathroom, escapes and ends up running around happily and barking with excitement, getting underneath everyone's feet. In the middle of the mayhem, my cell phone vibrates in my back pocket. Caller ID says Unlisted. Could be Ellie Mangum following up about the Asturias family. I forgot to get a new burner phone. It's too loud in the house, so I step out onto the front porch, closing the door to keep Wilson from following me. "Hello?"

"Hi, Suzie Q."

An icy ball forms in the pit of my stomach. "What do you want?"

"So many things," Finn says. His voice is soft, almost a croon. "I'll settle for you."

I knew I should have dropped this phone for another one. "No chance in hell."

"I don't mean like that," Finn says. "Although you're attractive, that's not what I like about you."

"Must be my winning personality."

"It's your *drive*." He says the word the way an evangelical says *Jesus*. "You don't ever stop. You're like a shark, you have to keep moving or you die."

"Don't call me again. And if I see you, you'll wake up in whatever hell is waiting for you."

"Before I let you go," Finn says in that damn crooning voice, "take a look at the side of the front porch."

Cell to my ear, I turn to look at the front porch. It's a tiny square block of concrete with steps up the front, enough room for maybe two people to stand on the landing by the front door.

Something is blinking on the right side of the porch, behind a small dogwood bush.

When I get closer, I see a block of what looks like orange cheese duct-taped to the side of the porch, with a countdown timer attached to it. The timer reads *49, 48, 47 . . .*

"That timer hits zero, there's going to be a rather impressive *boom*," Finn says.

Is Finn watching me right now? No, focus, Suzie. Take care of the giant bomb he's taped to your brother's house. There's a detonator the size of a pen stuck into the plastic explosive, and the detonator is attached to the timer by two wires. When the detonator reaches zero, it will send an electric current down the wire to the detonator, which will explode in the Semtex and set off a much larger explosion. Everyone in or near the house would die.

"Two wires," Finn says, almost sing-songy. "Which one should Suzie try to cut? Assuming she has pliers, of course."

I pull out a Leatherman tool from one of my pockets and open the needle-nose pliers, then hesitate, looking at the wires. *40, 39, 38 . . .* One wire is black, one white. Cut the wrong one? Boom. Cut both? Boom.

"There's another option," Finn says.

"What?" *35, 34 . . .*

"Promise you'll come after me."

I look frantically around the front yard. Is he behind a tree? On the street? In the construction house again? "What are you talking about?"

"I lost my family," Finn says, as casually as if discussing a grocery list. "Or they lost me, depending on your perspective."

"Skip to the end." *29, 28 . . .*

"You leave your family here, and I won't do anything to them. You just have to chase me."

"Chase you?"

"I'm bored, Suzie Q. And you're the most interesting thing in my life."

"Lucky me." It's got to be the black one. That's always the one they cut in movies. My hand is shaking. I grab my wrist with my other hand to steady it. *23, 22 . . .*

"You're thinking the black wire," Finn says. "But maybe I switched them. Verne taught me a few things about explosives."

"How do I stop it?" I almost shout.

"You gonna chase me, Suzie?"

18, 17 . . .

"Fuck, okay, yes."

"Promise me. Swear on something you care about."

14, 13 . . .

"I swear to God, Finn, I'll—"

"Not *God*." Finn sounds almost disgusted. "You don't care about Him."

8, 7 . . .

"On my father!" I shout. "I swear on my father!"

6, 5 . . .

"Clip the white one," Finn says.

4, 3 . . .

I miss the white wire completely, snipping air. I move the pliers again and snip. The blades cut the wire in two. I look at the timer. It reads *1*. It's stopped.

"That was exciting," Finn says.

I'm bathed in sweat and I want to collapse to the ground in relief. Instead I stand and turn around, eyes darting everywhere. "Where are you?" I snarl.

"Not close enough for you to get to me," Finn says. "I hear Seattle is nice this time of year. Come play, Suzie, and I'll leave your family alone. But you have to leave right now. No confab with your uncle and your buddies. Leave your phone on the porch and drive off on your bike, right now. Or I'll kill every single person in that house."

"You want me to find you in Seattle?"

"You find people," Finn says. "I have faith in you. Tick-tock." A click, and he's gone.

I end the call and stand in my brother's front yard, head bowed, thinking. A squirrel chases another squirrel in the branches of an oak, sending a single green leaf floating to the ground in their wake. Then I fold up the Leatherman tool and put it back in my pocket. I look at my phone and memorize the number Finn called me from, although he's most likely ditched that phone for another one. Then I lay my phone on Ethan's porch. I look at the solid front door, hear the muted sounds of the ballgame on the TV, hear someone laugh. I close my eyes and put my palm on the door, only for a second. Then I'm down the steps and walking to my bike, the keys already in my pocket. I've got a few more things to get at the Store-N-Go unit, and then I'll head to the airport.

"Suzie?"

Startled, I turn quickly, hands up in a defensive position. But it's only Caesar, holding a bag of trash he's carrying to the garbage can by the side of the house. "What are you doing?"

"Finn called." I walk to the bike. "I have to go."

"What do you mean, you have to—"

"If I don't leave now, he'll kill all of you." I pull my helmet out of the storage compartment, then swing my leg over the seat, the stitches in my side tugging. That's going to be annoying. "I left my phone on the porch," I say. "Check the number. And the side of the porch." I start the bike, the engine firing up immediately.

"Suzie." Caesar looks almost lost, and that about breaks me. Caesar's made of iron. He can't be lost, because what would that make me?

"Tell everyone . . ." I say, then swallow. I grin, so widely it almost hurts my cheeks. "Tell everyone I love them."

I pull my helmet on and turn to face forward and head down the driveway, navigating the dips and bumps of the asphalt as the trees form a tunnel, one that's dark despite the lingering sunlight. And then I'm out of the driveway and on the street, and I turn toward Roswell Road and ride off without looking back.

I'm going to find Finn.

And I'm going to end him. Guaranteed.

Because until I am rid of him, I can never go home.

ACKNOWLEDGMENTS

THANKS TO MADELINE RATHLE, REBECCA NELSON, MELISSA Rechter, Dulce Botello, Rema Badwan, Matt Martz, and all the other folks at Crooked Lane Books. Special thanks to my editor Terri Bischoff for helping me bring Suzie to life.

Kudos to my agent Peter Steinberg as well as Yona Levin and everyone else at Fletcher & Company.

Many thanks to Talia Panowich for helping me to keep it real.

Special shout-out to the guys at the Moments of Truth podcast: Bill Coffin, Chris Crenshaw, Tom Hespos, Joe Pace, and Derrick Eisenhardt.

To my readers: none of this is possible without y'all. Thank you.

And to my first reader, my plot solver, my best friend, my wife, Kathy Ferrell-Swann. I love you.